STAR TEACHER

It's 1985, and as Jack returns for another year as headteacher at Ragley village school, some changes are in store. It's the year of Halley's Comet, Band Aid, Trivial Pursuit, *Dynasty* shoulder pads, Roland Rat and Microsoft Windows. And at Ragley-on-the-Forest, Heathcliffe Earnshaw decides to enter the village scarecrow competition, Ruby the caretaker finds romance, and retirement looms for Vera the secretary. Meanwhile, Jack has to battle with some rising stars of the teaching profession to save his job and his school...

STAR TEACHER

by

Jack Sheffield

Magna Large Print Books
Long Preston, North Yorkshire,
BD23 4ND, England.

British Library Cataloguing in Publication Data.

A catalogue record of this book is
available from the British Library

ISBN 978-0-7505-4396-5

First published in Great Britain in 2015 by Bantam Press
an imprint ofTransworld Publishers

Published in Large Print 2017 by arrangement with
Transworld Publishers

Magna Large Print is an imprint of Library Magna Books Ltd.

Printed and bound in Great Britain by
T.J. (International) Ltd., Cornwall, PL28 8RW

For my Band of Brothers, Roy, Nick and Rob,
with thanks for their support over the years

Contents

Acknowledgements

I am indeed fortunate to have the support of a wonderful editor, the superb Linda Evans, and the excellent team at Transworld, including Larry Finlay, Bill Scott-Kerr, Jo Williamson, Sarah Harwood, Vivien Thompson, Brenda Updegraff, Lynsey Dalladay and fellow 'Old Roundhegian' Martin Myers.

Special thanks as always go to my hardworking literary agent, Philip Patterson of Marjacq Scripts, for his encouragement, good humour, cycling proficiency and deep appreciation of Yorkshire cricket.

I am also grateful to all those who assisted in the research for this novel – in particular: Patrick Busby, Pricing Director, church organist and Harrogate Rugby Club supporter, Medstead, Hampshire; Linda Collard, education trainer and consultant, fruit grower and jam-maker, West Sussex; the Revd Ben Flenley, Rector of Bentworth, Lasham, Medstead and Shalden, Hampshire; Tony Greenan, Yorkshire's finest headteacher (now retired), Huddersfield, Yorkshire; Marilyn Glover, member of the Friends of Takapuna Library, Auckland, New Zealand; Ian Haffenden, ex-Royal Pioneer Corps and custodian of Sainsbury's, Alton, Hampshire; John Kirby, ex-policeman, expert calligrapher and Sunderland supporter, County Durham; Roy Linley, Lead Architect, Strategy & Technology, Unilever Global IT Innovation and Leeds United supporter, Port Sunlight, Wirral; Helen Maddison, primary school teacher and literary critic, Harrogate, Yorkshire; Phil Parker, ex-primary school teacher and Manchester United supporter; Helen Woodhouse, Chief Librarian, Takapuna Library, Auckland, New Zealand; and all the terrific staff at Waterstones, Alton, including Simon (now retired), Sam, Kirsty, Fiona, Daisy and Mandie; also, Kirstie and the dynamic team at Waterstones, York; and all the superb staff at Stratford-upon-Avon Library.

Finally, sincere thanks to my wife, Elisabeth, without whose help the Teacher series of novels would never have been written.

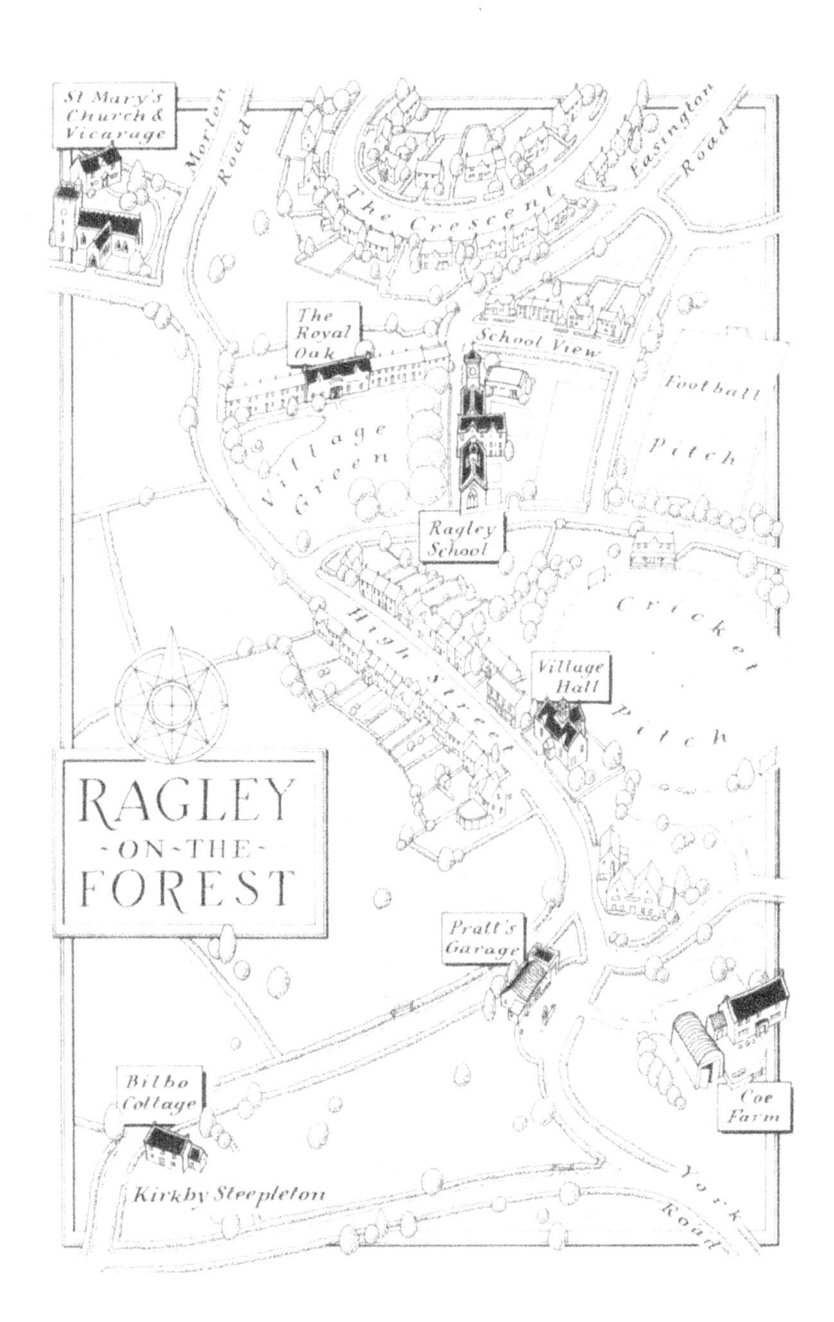
St Mary's Church & Vicarage
Morton Road
The Crescent
Easington Road
The Royal Oak
School View
Football Pitch
Village Green
Ragley School
Cricket Pitch
High Street
Village Hall
RAGLEY
-ON-THE-
FOREST
Pratt's Garage
Bilbo Cottage
Coe Farm
Kirkby Steepleton
York Road

Prologue

Decisions.

We are all faced with important choices in our lives. Some are based on necessity, others on ambition ... but some are based on love.

So it was during the summer of 1985.

My wife, Beth, had made such a decision.

Like me, Beth was a headteacher of a small North Yorkshire village school and the opportunity of a large school headship had arisen in Hampshire. At the end of a dramatic interview, Beth had turned it down.

I had expected her to be sad when she returned home, but it was not so. We put our two-year-old son, John William, in his cot and crept quietly downstairs. On that balmy evening, as the sun set over the distant Hambleton hills, we sat on our garden bench drinking coffee and breathing in the soft scent of the yellow 'Peace' roses.

'Why?' I asked simply.

Beth smiled. 'It didn't feel right,' she said quietly.

The final rays of golden light gilded the hedgerow and caressed her honey-blonde hair. We had reached a crossroads in our life.

'I thought this was what you wanted,' I said.

'Perhaps it was.' She sighed and rested her head on my shoulder. There was a silence that seemed to last for ever. 'But I wanted *you* more.'

I sat back, unsure in a sea of white noise. This

was not the response I had expected. Then she looked up at me and gave me that familiar mischievous smile. 'And then, of course ... there's my *mother.*'

Beth had stayed with her parents, John and Diane, in their Hampshire home during her interview. There was often tension between Diane and her equally determined daughter.

I knew when to keep quiet.

That had been six weeks ago and now the school summer holiday was almost over. During August, Age and Experience, those familiar companions, had taken me by the hand and I had moved seamlessly past my fortieth birthday. It was then that I considered my life, my achievements and, not least, my hopes for the future ... but they were intertwined with those of my wife. It was a shared destiny and, whatever the pathway, it was one we would walk together. But little did we know what lay ahead. The unknown was just around the corner, decisions would have to be made and there were secrets that would have to be kept.

The academic year 1985/86 had begun quietly on a perfect morning. It was Saturday, 31 August and I was sitting at my desk in the school office. Warm, late-summer sunshine slanted in through the windows. The beginning of the autumn term for the children of the village was a few days away and I was sifting through the post that had come from County Hall.

Meanwhile, on the office wall, the clock with its faded Roman numerals ticked on. In spite of the usual apprehension, I had always found the dawn of a new school year to be an exciting time, but little did I know that a battle was about to commence. The end of a world I had come to love was threatening like a far-off thunder cloud, and a year of secrets and surprises lay in store.

However, on that distant autumn day, all seemed calm as my ninth year as headmaster of Ragley-on-the-Forest Church of England Primary School in North Yorkshire was about to begin.

Up the Morton Road the church clock chimed midday. I took a deep breath as I unlocked the bottom drawer of my desk, removed the large, leather-bound school log-book and opened it to the next clean page. Then I filled my fountain pen with black Quink ink, wrote the date and stared at the empty page.

The record of another school year was about to begin. Eight years ago, the retiring headmaster, John Pruett, had told me how to fill in the official school logbook. 'Just keep it simple,' he said. 'Whatever you do, don't say what really happens, because no one will believe you!'

So the real stories were written in my 'Alternative School Logbook'.

And this is it!

Chapter One

New Beginnings

96 children were registered on roll on the first day of the school year. Ms Pat Brookside, our newly appointed teacher, took up her post in Class 2 with responsibility for computer studies and physical education. A meeting of headteachers to discuss the 'Rationalization of Small Schools in North Yorkshire' has been arranged for 1 October.

Extract from the Ragley School Logbook:
Wednesday, 4 September 1985

'Mornin', Mr Sheffield,' said a formidable lady with the build of a Russian discus-thrower.

'Good morning,' I replied with some trepidation. I was standing at the gate, welcoming the children as they arrived to begin another school year.

The lady took a final drag of her cigarette, crushed the glowing tip between a thumb and forefinger and flicked the stub into the hedgerow. Her bright floral dress sported cut-away sleeves to accommodate her huge biceps. At six feet tall she gave me a level stare. 'Ah'm Mrs Spittall,' she said cheerfully. 'Freda Spittall, that is ... an' my Gary starts t'day.'

'Pleased to meet you, Mrs Spittall.' I removed my black-framed Buddy Holly spectacles and polished them, wondering what was coming next.

Mrs Spittall's four-year-old son was dressed in what appeared to be an assortment of hand-me-down clothing. Gary was wearing an outsize *Star Wars* T-shirt, baggy grey shorts that hung way below his knees, York City football socks and scuffed sandals.

''E'll grow into his clothes soon enough, ah reckon,' said his mother. ''E's gonna be a big lad.'

I nodded in agreement. Already Gary was as tall as many of our six-year-olds.

'Well, welcome to Ragley School, Mrs Spittall,' I said. 'If you'll just go into the office and see our secretary, we can get Gary registered.'

'Thank you kindly,' she replied and glanced down at her son, who had begun to pick his nose with enthusiastic and well-practised dexterity. ''E's a good lad, is our Gary, but 'e's goin' through one o' them awkward *phrases.*'

'Is he?' I asked.

Gary was now sucking the finger that had been excavating his left nostril.

Mrs Spittall pondered for a moment. 'Per'aps ah ought t'mention to y'secretary about 'is *'abits.*'

'Habits?'

'Yes, 'e teks after 'is dad,' she said with a sigh.

'Does he?'

''E picks 'is nose.'

'Oh dear.'

'An' 'is ears.'

'Really?'

'An' any other horifice that teks 'is fancy.'

'Ah, I see.' I wondered what Vera in the school office would make of this. '*I'll* pass on your information, Mrs Spittall, so don't worry about discussing it with Mrs Forbes-Kitchener.' It seemed to me that some things were best left unsaid.

They set off up the school drive, Mrs Spittall striding purposefully towards the entrance hall while Gary began to scratch his bottom.

I glanced at my wristwatch. It was just after 8.30 a.m. on Wednesday, 4 September 1985, the first day of the autumn term, and my ninth year as headteacher of Ragley-on-the-Forest Church of England Primary School in North Yorkshire had begun.

It was a perfect morning of late-summer sunshine. I looked around me and relaxed in the welcome shade beneath the avenue of horse chestnut trees that bordered the front of our village school. As always on the first day of the school year, I felt a little apprehensive as I wondered what might be in store. Around me, excited children, suntanned after a long summer holiday, skipped by and waved a greeting as they hurried towards the schoolyard. Our tarmac playground was bordered by a low stone wall topped with high, wrought-iron railings decorated with fleur-de-lis. I watched the children as they gathered in groups. It was a time for old friendships to be rekindled and new ones to be forged.

A few girls were winding a long skipping rope and chanting out a rhyme as two nine-year-olds, Jemima Poole and Rosie Appleby, skipped in and out.

Little fat doctor
How's your wife?
Very well thank you
That's all right
Eat a bit o' fish
An' a stick o' liquorice
O-U-T spells OUT!

They appeared relaxed and full of good spirits as another school year in their young lives stretched out before them.

Ragley School looked fine on this special morning. It was a tall, red-brick Victorian building with high arched windows, a grey-slate roof and a distinctive bell tower. Generations of children had walked up the worn steps, under the archway of Yorkshire stone and through the old oak entrance door to begin their formal education. Back in 1977 the mantle of responsibility had passed to me and over time our school had become a centre of our community. The villagers were proud of its achievements and, in a small way, I felt content to be playing my part. It was a job I loved and I was happy in my world.

Suddenly a plump, red-faced lady approached me dragging a reluctant little boy with her. It was Mrs Dora Spraggon, mother of five-year-old Alfie, who was about to begin another year in Anne Grainger's infant class.

'Good morning, Mrs Spraggon,' I said cheerfully.

'Beggin' y'pardon, Mr Sheffield ... but ah don't think so,' she replied forcefully. Mrs Spraggon was always friendly but naturally curt and to the point. 'Ah tell it like it is, Mr Sheffield,' she had announced earlier in the week in the General Stores while I had been queuing for my morning paper. 'Ah always call a spade a shovel.'

I looked down at Alfie in his Wham! T-shirt, grubby shorts and grass-stained sandals. He looked decidedly fed up with life. 'Are you all right, Alfie?' I asked.

Mrs Spraggon shook her head. ''E's gorra conjunction, Mr Sheffield.'

'A *conjunction?*'

'Yes, in 'is eye.'

The penny dropped. 'Oh, I see,' I said.

On cue, Alfie rubbed the swelling beneath his left eye.

'Please mention it to Mrs Grainger,' I called after her as she hurried up the drive.

Meanwhile, the village was coming to life. Opposite the school on the village green a few mothers were sitting on the bench by the duck pond watching their small children making daisy chains. Next to the green, in the centre of a row of cottages with pantile roofs and tall, rickety chimneypots, stood the white-fronted public house, The Royal Oak. The barmaid, Sheila Bradshaw, in her see-through blouse, leather mini-skirt and high heels, was sweeping the porch and gave me a seductive wave.

To my left, Ragley's High Street was bordered by wide grassy verges and a row of village shops. Some of the shopkeepers looked busier than others. Amelia Duff was preparing to open her Post Office while, next door, Diane Wigglesworth was sitting on the step of her Hair Salon and smoking her first John Player King Size Extra Mild cigarette of the day. Nora Pratt was holding a bucket of soapy water outside her Coffee Shop, while Dorothy Robinson, her assistant, cleaned the window and swayed her hips to Tina Turner's 'We Don't Need Another Hero', blasting out from the old red-and-chrome juke-box. Next door, Nora's brother, Timothy Pratt, was polishing the brass door handle of his Hardware Emporium as if his life depended on it. Peggy Scrimshaw was receiving a delivery of Pond's Cream for the village Pharmacy, and Old Tommy Piercy was arranging a selection of pigs' trotters behind the window of his butcher's shop. Meanwhile, the General Stores & Newsagent had been open since eight o'clock and Prudence Golightly was selling four ounces of sherbet lemons to ten-year-old Damian Brown. The High Street was the heartbeat of the village and another day had begun.

'Good morning, Mr Sheffield,' announced a polite, well-modulated voice.

I looked around. It was Mrs Pippa Jackson with her identical twin daughters, Hermione and Honeysuckle. 'A beautiful day,' she added cheerily.

A year ago the family had moved into one of the most expensive properties in the village on the Morton Road. As always, the girls were immaculately turned out in matching gingham dresses, knee-length white socks and smart new leather shoes. Their blonde hair had been brushed and tied back with bright-coloured bows of different colours to assist Anne Grainger in telling one from the other in her reception class.

'Good morning, Mrs Jackson,' I replied, 'and hello, girls.'

'Good morning, Mr Sheffield,' chorused the twins in perfect harmony.

I followed them up the cobbled drive and overheard a snippet of conversation between Mrs Ricketts and Mrs Crapper. Brenda Ricketts was holding the hand of her five-year-old daughter, Suzi-Quatro, while Connie Crapper was spitting on her handkerchief prior to removing the last vestige of lipstick from the face of seven-year-old Patience.

'She's all posh curtains an' flock wallpaper is that one,' said Brenda Ricketts, nodding towards Mrs Jackson.

Connie Crapper nodded in agreement. 'Definitely stuck-up. All fur coat an' no knickers,' she added for good measure.

The ebb and flow of village gossip never changed.

Pretending I hadn't heard, I walked on towards the entrance steps, where I paused and took a deep breath. Then I glanced up at the scudding clouds sweeping past the bell tower and reflected that I was happy here in my village school in this peaceful corner of God's Own Country. However, beyond our little community, in the nation at large, times were changing fast.

For this was 1985. According to a recent survey, a remarkable 78 per cent of the population now had a telephone in their home, 61 per cent owned a car, 13 per cent went to church and 18 per cent of the country's 56.5 million people had reached retirement age. The miners' strike had ended and the wreck of the *Titanic* had been located, blood donors would soon be screened for AIDS and British Telecom had finally decided to phase out the classic red telephone box. The average UK house price had increased to £34,000, Cyndi Lauper had been voted best new artist and Dire Straits' *Brothers in Arms* was the bestselling album. Microsoft had recently released something called Windows and a remarkable thirteen-year-old, Ruth Lawrence, had achieved a starred first in mathematics at Oxford, becoming the youngest ever graduate. Meanwhile, we had already said a final goodbye to Sir Michael Redgrave and Yul Brynner, and were soon to lose Laura Ashley and Orson Welles.

However, in sleepy Ragley-on-the-Forest life trundled along and the school bell that had summoned the children of the village for over one hundred years was about to ring out once again to announce the beginning of another school year.

When I walked into the office our school secretary, Vera Forbes-Kitchener, a tall, slim, elegant sixty-three-year-old, was sitting at her immaculately tidy desk and labelling the new attendance and dinner registers, a pair for each of our four classes.

'Good morning, Mr Sheffield,' said Vera. Regardless of having worked together for eight years, Vera held on to the formality of calling me *Mr* Sheffield. In her world it was the proper thing to do. She smoothed the creases from the skirt of her new Marks & Spencer charcoal-grey, pinstriped suit and held up a letter.

'This came in, Mr Sheffield,' she said. 'It looks important ... and *ominous.*'

'Oh dear, what is it?' I asked, picking absent-mindedly at the frayed leather patches on my herringbone sports coat.

She passed over a document with the familiar North Yorkshire county crest above the heading 'Rationalization of Small Schools in North Yorkshire'.

'We've been through all this before,' I said. 'So I wonder what's new this time?' Back in 1981 we had been threatened with school closure but had survived and our numbers on roll had increased slightly.

It was a copious document, definitely bedtime reading. On the first page was an invitation to a meeting of North Yorkshire headteachers at High Sutton Hall on 1 October. I put it in my old leather satchel, completely unaware of the impact it would have on my life and that of our village school.

Anne Grainger popped her head round the door. 'Hello, Jack. Pat has settled in and Class 2 looks a picture,' she said with a reassuring smile. Anne, a slim brunette in her fifties, was our deputy headteacher and her reception class was always full of colour and creativity.

'Thanks, I'll call in to see her,' I said.

Pat Brookside had recently been appointed to teach the six- and seven-year-olds and today was her first day as a teacher at Ragley School. A tall, leggy, twenty-eight-year-old blonde, Pat had taught the infant age range at Thirkby Primary School in North Yorkshire and was a welcome addition to the staff.

Vera handed the new school registers for Class 1 to Anne. 'Here's to another school year,' she said.

Anne stared thoughtfully at the smart, pristine registers. 'Yes, another year,' she murmured. 'Let's hope it's a good one.'

Vera looked at her curiously. There was clearly something on Anne's mind and Vera determined she would pick the right moment to see if she could offer wise counsel.

I picked up my registers. 'And I'll deliver these to Pat.'

'Wish her good luck from me,' said Vera.

Sally Pringle, the Class 3 teacher, was in the school hall preparing the music for morning assembly. With her long, wavy red hair, baggy shirt with frilly sleeves, a bright mustard waistcoat and mint-green cord trousers, she cut a distinctive arty figure. She had propped her *Tinderbox* songbook on a music stand, opened it to number 31, 'Thank You for My Friends', and then rehearsed the opening chords on her guitar.

'Morning, Jack,' she said with a smile. 'Here we go again.'

'Hello, Sally,' I replied. 'All set for another year?'

'Yes, looking forward to it, and good to have a new experienced colleague next door. Pat has already volunteered to give me a few lessons on the computer. And I'm guessing we'll have a good netball team this year,' she added with a grin.

Pat Brookside was in her classroom putting a new HB pencil, a pack of wax crayons and a large sheet of white sugar paper on each desk.

'Morning, Pat,' I said, 'and hope all goes well.'
'Thanks, Jack, I'm sure I'll be fine.'

Her blonde hair had been brushed back into a flowing ponytail and she had dressed classically in a white blouse, grey pleated skirt and black leather shoes. I felt sure Vera would approve. Two years ago, when we had had a vacancy for a Class 2 teacher, Pat had been a strong candidate and had made the shortlist, but in the end we had appointed a young man named Tom Dalton. However, after a year and a half he had moved on and during the subsequent selection process it was clear that Pat, who applied again, appeared much more confident than when we had first interviewed her. She had been on a computer course and explained something called Windows version 1.0 in great detail. Her knowledge of the primary curriculum was outstanding and she had offered to support extra-curricular activities, including the netball team, if appointed. As a county-standard player herself, this seemed appropriate. At the end of the interview our chair of governors, the Revd Joseph Evans, asked why she wanted to move from Thirkby. 'I've just moved in with a new partner,' she explained, 'and he lives close by, in Easington.'

I recalled how Joseph had blinked at the directness of this positive and forthright young woman, and I smiled at the memory.

Pat had arrived early in her Mini Clubman Estate and proceeded to put the finishing touches to the displays in her classroom. They included a nature table; a collection of science experiments; posters of simple computer exercises; and a collection of model cars, boats, steam engines and aeroplanes for her 'Transport Through the Ages' project.

'This looks wonderful, Pat,' I said. 'Well done.'

She picked up a replica of the *Flying Scotsman*. 'My partner is still young at heart,' she said with a smile. 'David is proud of his train set.'

David Beckinsdale was a newly qualified general practitioner and worked in our nearby market town of Easington. Vera had mentioned that, as a handsome six-foot-three-inch thirty-year-old, he was considered quite a catch.

'If you need anything, just let me know,' I said. 'Here are your attendance and dinner registers.'

'Thanks Jack,' she said and a flicker of concern crossed her face. 'Anne mentioned that Vera is a bit of a stickler regarding record-keeping.'

'Well, if it helps, I'll do my registers quickly and send them in to you while you're introducing yourself to the class and setting them off on an activity. Then you can have a look at my registers and begin your own.'

She sighed with relief. 'I would appreciate that.'

'And, by the way, Vera asked me to say "Good luck".'

'She's a lovely lady,' said Pat as she placed a red and a black ballpoint pen alongside her registers.

'Between you and me, Pat,' I said quietly, 'we would be lost without her.'

Pat looked at her wristwatch. 'Almost time for the bell.'

'Yes,' I said with a smile and hurried out.

A few minutes after nine o'clock I walked into Class 4. The nine- and ten-year-olds were sitting quietly at their desks as I began to read out the register.

'Damian Brown,' I said.

There was no response.

A few of the children became animated.

'Ah've seen 'im, Mr Sheffield,' called out Ryan Halfpenny.

'So 'ave I,' added Sonia Tricklebank.

''E were buying sweets, Mr Sheffield,' volunteered Frankie Spraggon.

'Very well,' I said, 'let's carry on ... Stacey Bryant.'

'Yes, Mr Sheffield.'

'Ben Clouting.'

'Yes, Mr Sheffield.'

'Lucy Eckersley.'

'Yes, Mr Sheffield ... an' ah think 'e's 'ere, sir.'

There was a gentle tap on the door as Vera walked in with Damian Brown. He was red-faced and panting. 'Damian has *finally* arrived, Mr Sheffield,' said Vera pointedly.

'Good morning, Damian,' I said.

'G'mornin', Mr Sheffield,' replied an unconcerned Damian. He hurried to my desk and slapped down his dinner money. 'Here y'are, sir,' he said with confidence and a big smile.

Vera sighed and shook her head. 'You need to explain to Mr Sheffield why you are late.'

Damian pondered this for a moment. 'Well it's like this, Mr Sheffield,' he said, 'y'*started* before ah got t'school.'

Vera looked up at me, presumably reflecting on the logic of youth, and whispered, 'Well you can't say fairer than that,' then walked back to the office with a huge grin on her face.

After registration, the children were eager to know their monitor jobs. These carried significant status for the eldest pupils in school. Following a lively debate, Lucy Eckersley and Ben Clouting took charge of the Tuck Shop; Stacey Bryant and Harry Patch became Library monitors; Sonia Tricklebank with her spotlessly clean hands would look after the hymn books; Damian Brown and Frankie Spraggon nodded in satisfaction when given responsibility for paintbrushes; the tall netball captain Dawn Phillips was delighted to clean the blackboard; Ryan Halfpenny thought all his birthdays had come at once when he became the official ringer of the school bell; and, finally, the lightning-quick Barry Ollerenshaw smiled as he was selected to be the pupil who delivered messages to the other classrooms.

After distributing a Reading Record Card to each pupil along with a variety of exercise books, an HB pencil, a rubber, a Berol rollerball pen, an *Oxford First Dictionary*, a tin of Lakeland crayons and a wooden ruler, we began our lessons.

Soon the children were busy with their first piece of writing while I heard each child read to me and then selected an appropriate graded reading book.

'M'fingers 'ave f'gotten 'ow t'write, Mr Sheffield,' declared Damian.

'So 'ave mine,' agreed Ryan Halfpenny.

This was often the case after the summer holiday. However, those who had not picked up a pencil for six weeks battled on and soon rediscovered their individual writing style.

When it was time for morning assembly my children carried their chairs into the hall and arranged them in a line at the back. The little ones in Anne's class sat cross-legged on the floor while she sorted her sheet music on the piano.

I took the opportunity to call into Pat's classroom and was pleased to see that all the children seemed to be busy using their School Mathematics Project workcards. Pat was busy with a group of more able children doing some work on tessellation patterns. However, I noticed in the corner of the room six-year-old Sam Whittaker was sitting on the floor under his Formica-topped table. He was clutching a pencil tightly and counting to himself, then finally writing numbers in his mathematics exercise book. He was out of Pat's line of vision, so she had not noticed the little boy's strange behaviour. It was well known that Sam was one of our best-behaved pupils and I remembered Anne saying that he *always* did as he was told.

I crouched down next to him. 'Sam,' I asked quietly, 'why are you sitting on the floor?'

'Ah'm doin' m'sums, Mr Sheffield,' he answered, without looking up. He was clearly engrossed in his work.

'Yes, but why aren't you sitting at your desk?'

'Miss said we weren't to use our tables, sir.'

'Ah ... I see,' and I explained the different meanings of 'tables' while he settled once again in his seat.

Sally Pringle smiled as I popped my head through the open doorway of her classroom. She was busy winding up an English lesson concerning the structure of sentences and all the children were attentive. It was clearly going well.

'Give me a sentence beginning with "I",' she asked them.

Eight-year-old Ted Coggins was the first to put his hand in the air.

'Yes, Ted,' said Sally, clearly pleased with the boy's enthusiasm.

'I is...' he began.

'No,' interrupted Sally, 'it should be "I *am*".'

Ted frowned. 'Are y'sure, Miss?'

'Positive, Ted,' said Sally. 'Now, try again.'

'OK, Miss,' said Ted and he took a deep breath. 'I am ... t'ninth letter of t'alphabet.'

'Oh dear,' said Sally and I hurried away while she apologized and Ryan rang the bell for morning assembly.

The first assembly of the year was always a special time. The new starters waved to their older brothers and sisters. Some of them played with their wobbly teeth, while others stared in astonishment at the huge school hall and the crush of children. Gary Spittall had placed his index finger in the ear of the boy in front and I gave him a warning look.

All went well, the children sang with gusto, Sally advertised her choir and orchestra, and when I asked Pat to introduce herself the girls' netball team looked on in admiration. Finally, Sonia Tricklebank recited our school prayer:

Dear Lord,
This is our school, let peace dwell here,

Let the room be full of contentment, let love abide here,
Love of one another, love of life itself,
And love of God.
Amen.

I was on duty during morning break while the staff gathered in the staff-room and enjoyed a welcome cup of milky coffee. Vera was reading her *Daily Telegraph* and was pleased that her favourite politician, Margaret Thatcher, had reshuffled her Cabinet and demoted Home Secretary Leon Brittan to Trade and Industry. Meanwhile, Norman Tebbit, Douglas Hurd, Kenneth Baker and rising star Kenneth Clarke appeared to be moving to the fore.

Sally was keen to know more about Pat's handsome partner and Anne seemed preoccupied with her own thoughts. There had been harsh words with her husband, John, before school this morning and she wondered how it could be resolved.

At lunchtime I telephoned home to see how Mrs Roberts, our childminder, was getting on with young John William. Beth had persuaded the parent from Hartingdale, who had looked after John last year, to continue. All seemed well and I thought about how fortunate it was for Beth and me that we had such a loving and reliable lady to care for our son during the school week. Then I rang Beth's school and her secretary said she was busy in a meeting but would ring back. When she did so she was relieved that John was content with the familiar Mrs Roberts.

'Well, lots to do, Jack,' she said, 'must go.'

'See you later.'

There was a slight pause before she replied. 'We need to do well this year, Jack – it's important for both of us.'

When she rang off I pondered over the anomaly that was my dynamic and ambitious wife. In recent months she appeared to have dismantled her career and reassembled it. It was as if she was determined to seek a new destiny and, not for the first time, I felt a little lost as I wondered what went on in the mind of a woman. After all these years it remained a mystery.

I opened the office window and heard the familiar foghorn voice of our dinner lady, Mrs Doreen Critchley. Nine-year-old Hayley Spraggon had given her little brother, Alfie, a sharp push as he infiltrated her skipping game.

'Don't hit y'brother like that,' shouted Mrs Critchley across the playground.

'Ow 'bout if ah 'it 'im a bit softer, Miss?'

I smiled and returned to my paperwork.

Alfie Spraggon was a popular and honest little boy. During afternoon school he was typing on the new school computer, which was in Anne's classroom for the afternoon. I had called in while Sally was in the school hall talking to all the children in Class 3 and Class 4 about the use of musical instruments and the opportunity to join the choir.

'What are you doing, Alfie?'

'Ah'm writing a story,' he said. He didn't look up. He just continued hitting the keys.

'And what's it about?'
'Dunno, sir, ah can't read yet.'
Ask a daft question flickered through my mind and I hurried on to speak to Anne.

It was six o'clock when I drove the three miles to Kirkby Steepleton and pulled into the driveway of Bilbo Cottage. I thanked Mrs Roberts and she drove off back to Hartingdale. I had just finished singing 'The Wheels on the Bus' and 'Incy Wincy Spider' to a delighted John when Beth walked in. In her smart business suit and *Cagney & Lacey* coat with padded shoulders she looked her usual slim, attractive self, if a little tired. She picked up John and hugged him.
It was after we had put him to bed and enjoyed an evening meal that I remembered something. 'Oh, forgot to mention – there's some post for you on the hall table.'
Beth sifted through the letters and, spotting an envelope with the familiar North Yorkshire County Council crest, she opened it quickly.
'What is it?' I asked.
'It's from the office.'
I looked up. Official mail was usually delivered to school ... unless...
Beth smiled. 'Jack ... it's about that Group Four headship in York.'
'Yes?'
'The one I really want.'
'Well?'
'I've got an interview.'

Chapter Two

A Day to Remember

The Revd Joseph Evans called to say he would resume his weekly RE lessons on Friday of this week. The headteacher forwarded the school's response to County Hall's discussion document 'A New Curriculum for North Yorkshire Schools'.

Extract from the Ragley School Logbook:
Thursday, 19 September 1985

'It's my spectacles again, my dear,' said Rupert.

Rupert Forbes-Kitchener, in his mid-sixties, was one of the richest men in North Yorkshire and a prominent member of the Ragley School Board of Governors. A widower for many years, he had fallen in love with Vera, our school secretary, and they had married in December 1982. It had been a dramatic change for Vera, who for many years had been content living with her brother, the Revd Joseph Evans, in the beautifully furnished vicarage, a place of order and peace. However, Vera had adapted to her new life and established routines that included the Women's Institute, the twice-weekly cross-stitch club and coordinating the beautiful flower arrangements in St Mary's Church.

It was early morning on Thursday, 19 September and Rupert, smartly dressed as always in a white shirt, regimental tie, lovat-green waistcoat, cord trousers and highly polished brown shoes, was looking harassed.

Vera glanced up from her Women's Institute notice and sighed. 'They're on your forehead, Rupert.'

Rupert fumbled for them and stared in surprise. 'Oh dear,' he said, 'the last place I would have looked,' and hurried off into his study.

Vera looked after him thoughtfully and turned her attention back to the poster on the hall table. It read:

Ragley & Morton Women's Institute
'Our Memory Makes Us Who We Are'
A talk by Perkin Warbeck
7.30 p.m. on Thursday 19 September 1985
in the Village Hall

It occurred to her that Rupert was becoming very forgetful.

This was certainly not the case in Bilbo Cottage.

'Don't worry,' said Beth. 'I've checked everything twice and I'm sure I haven't forgotten a thing.'

It was the day of Beth's interview for King's Manor Primary School in York and we were standing in the hallway. Diane Henderson had driven up from Hampshire to take over childcare for a few days. She held her grandson by the hand. 'Good luck, Beth,' she said simply, kissing her daughter on the cheek. She lifted up two-year-old John William. 'Say bye-bye to Mummy.'

On cue, John stretched out his arms. 'Bye-bye, Mummy,' he said.

Beth kissed him on the forehead. 'Be good for Nana.'

'Nana,' repeated John.

Beth closed the metal catches of her slim, black executive briefcase and gave me a gentle smile. 'Well, here goes.'

We walked out to the driveway together and I opened her driver's door. 'Let me know when you can,' I said.

She put her case on the passenger seat and squeezed my hand. 'I should know something by lunchtime,' she said.

I walked back to the doorway and we watched her light-blue Volkswagen Beetle disappear into the distance. Diane looked up at me and shook her head. 'I'll never understand why she didn't take the headship in Hampshire,' she said as she stroked John's fair hair out of his eyes. 'I could have spent more time with my grandson.' Then she carried him back into the kitchen and put him in his high chair so he could finish his breakfast of toast soldiers and scrambled egg.

Finally, it was my turn to leave. Beyond the open door of Bilbo Cottage rays of autumnal sunshine lit up the border of chrysanthemums, bronze, amber and scarlet, and brightened the new day. In the distance the hazy purple line of the Hambleton hills changed to a golden thread. The drive on the back road to Ragley village was always very special on an autumn morning. The last field of ripe barley left to harvest rippled in the low sunlight with the rhythm of the seasons.

As the hedgerows rushed by, my thoughts returned to Beth and the challenge that faced her.

Vera was busy in the school office when I walked in. After preparing a harvest festival notice on a Gestetner master sheet, she had smoothed it carefully on the drum of the duplicating machine. Then she peeled off the backing sheet and began to wind the handle. The first inky copies were left to dry on the window sill. It was an operation Vera had completed so often that, with effortless ease, she managed to continue a lucid conversation with me at the same time. 'Good morning, Mr Sheffield,' she said. 'Mr Gomersall is in the staff-room.'

'Thank you Vera.' I recalled that our Senior Primary Adviser from County Hall had telephoned to say he would call in one day this week.

When I walked in, Richard Gomersall was sitting on a chair by the window, reading a copious, spiral-bound document. He closed it quickly and I noticed the distinctive County Hall crest on the cover. 'Hello, Jack,' he said with a rather forced smile.

A short, slight man in his late forties, with carefully coiffured, wavy, reddish-brown hair, Richard was well known for his outlandish fashion sense. Today he looked as if he had dressed for a part in *Miami Vice,* with a lagoon-blue linen jacket complete with huge shoulder pads. Matching baggy trousers, a figure-hugging pink pastel shirt and black leather Cuban-heeled boots completed the ensemble.

'Good to see you, Richard,' I said as we shook hands.

To my surprise, he stood up and closed the door. 'Jack, I can't stay long but I thought I ought to let you know the outcome of a meeting at County Hall.'

'Oh yes?'

'Miss Barrington-Huntley asked me to call in.'

'Did she?'

'As you know, she's chairing the interview panel today ... a big day for Beth of course.'

'Yes, I'm hopeful she'll do well.'

He paused as if he were searching for the right words. 'Jack ... there are *changes* ahead for small schools, and not just here in North Yorkshire.'

My heart sank. We had been through possible closure some years ago but somehow we had survived. I said nothing and simply waited for him to get to the point.

'The problem isn't so much for Ragley but rather *Morton* Primary School.'

'Morton? Really? I'd heard the new head is doing well.'

'Rufus Timmings – yes, he's certainly made an impact ... but it's a *numbers* problem, Jack. There are only twenty-eight children on roll at present and we at County Hall are committed to making savings wherever possible. Sadly, Morton School is no longer economically viable. There are simply not enough children living in the catchment area who would attend the school in the future.'

'So how does that affect Ragley?' I asked. 'We survived the last round of cuts and our numbers are increasing each year.'

He glanced at his watch. 'I've arranged to visit

Morton this morning, but Miss B-H insisted I alert you first.'

'I still don't understand,' I said.

'The thing is, Jack, we're arranging a series of meetings during this academic year with a view to the possibility of amalgamating the two schools.'

'Amalgamation – with Morton?'

'Yes, the children from Morton would come here.'

I began grappling with the implications. 'Richard … there would be huge opposition from the villagers of Morton. They're proud of their school, just as we are here in Ragley.'

He sighed as if I were stating the obvious. 'Yes, we've taken that into consideration and it is of course a very early stage in the proceedings.'

I looked out of the window at the children on the playground and shook my head. 'This is a small Victorian building. Our classrooms are tiny. Space is already an issue, as you well know.'

'Not a problem.' He gave a forced smile. 'We would provide a Portakabin. That's the norm in these cases.' He stood up and glanced nervously at his wristwatch. 'I'm afraid I'll have to move on. There's obviously a lot to discuss in the future, but for now please keep this under your hat.'

'Under my hat?' I said. 'This news will affect the whole staff.'

He sighed and glanced up at the staff-room clock. 'Jack, I've done you a personal favour by calling in this morning and this information is strictly on a need-to-know basis ... orders from on high. So for the time being keep this to yourself –

it's important. This discussion is *strictly* confidential and if the local press get in touch just say "No comment".'

I accepted the inevitable. 'Very well, Richard. I understand ... and thanks for letting me know.'

I stood by the window as he jumped into his bright-red Jaguar XJ6 and, with the smooth hum of its powerful six cylinders, accelerated swiftly down the cobbled drive. As I set off for my classroom it seemed to me he had left behind more questions than answers ... along with the burden of a secret.

Morning break came as something of a relief. I had found it difficult to concentrate on our English lesson, even though my class had responded well to the effective use of adjectives in their writing. I was on duty and relaxed a little as I walked outside to supervise the children at play.

Owing to a barrage of telephone calls just prior to the morning bell, Vera was later than usual preparing our morning coffee. It was a welcome sight when she brought out mine to the playground.

'Thank you, Vera,' I said.

Nearby two eight-year-olds, Stuart Ormroyd and Tom Burgess, were playing conkers and the Jackson twins were leading a circle of girls in a rendition of 'Ring a Ring o' Roses'.

'Good to see the children playing *traditional* games,' said Vera wistfully.

On a bare, flattened patch of earth next to the tarmac playground, Damian Brown was playing marbles with Ryan Halfpenny.

'My dad gave me these, Mr Sheffield,' said Ryan. ''E said 'e'd played with 'em when 'e were a lad.'

Damian shook his head forlornly. 'My dad's lost 'is marbles.'

'I'm sorry to hear that,' I replied with a smile.

However, I noticed Vera wasn't listening; she appeared preoccupied.

Later, after a school dinner of Spam fritters, chips and peas followed by jam roly-poly pudding and pink custard, I returned to the school office. I had just completed our response to County Hall's discussion document 'A New Curriculum for North Yorkshire Schools' when the telephone rang on Vera's desk. I looked up anxiously as she lifted the receiver.

'Hold on, Beth,' she said with a smile. 'He's here now.' She passed me the telephone, stood up to vacate her desk and crept out quietly to the staff-room.

'How did it go?' I asked.

'The best yet, Jack,' Beth said. 'Far better than Hampshire.' She sounded both excited and relieved. 'I've been recalled for the final interview tomorrow.'

'Well done,' I said. 'So ... this might be the one.'

There was a tired sigh. 'Yes, perhaps.'

'You don't sound too sure.'

'Well, this headship would be ideal, but we'll have to see. It's a lovely school but I've still got tough competition.'

'Who's that?'

'Two men. They're both heads of small schools, one from Stevenage and one from Bolton. They're nice guys, except...'

'Yes?'

'It's pretty clear they both think it's a straight contest between the two of them and I'm making up the numbers.'

'No change there then.'

'Let's hope Miss B-H puts them right,' said Beth. 'She chaired the morning interviews and she doesn't take kindly to male chauvinists.'

'Too true,' I agreed. Miss Barrington-Huntley, the chair of the Education Committee at County Hall, was renowned for her fierce support for equality of the sexes. 'Are you driving back to Hartingdale for afternoon school?'

'Yes, so I'll see you tonight. Mother is making tea.'

'Fine,' I said guardedly. When Vera left she had closed the door. I was in a private space. 'And I love you,' I whispered.

There was a pause. 'You too ... bye.'

Afternoon school went well and while the children in my class were getting changed for their Music and Movement lesson in the hall I called into Sally's classroom next door to borrow two tambourines and a drum. She was standing by the chalkboard, busy with a 'Counties of England' lesson. 'How do you spell "Yorkshire"?' she asked.

The enthusiastic Tom Burgess, from a farming family in the village, was the first to raise his hand. 'Y-O-R-K-S-U-R-E,' he recited confidently.

'No, sorry, Tom, that's wrong.'

Tom looked indignant. 'Well, that might be so, Miss, but you asked me 'ow *ah* spell it.'

Sally raised her eyes in my direction as I hurried out, clutching my musical instruments and trying not to laugh.

After an energetic dance lesson it was our turn to use the school computer and this always created great excitement among the children. We had purchased a BBC Micro for £299 and had been deeply impressed when the local adviser informed us it contained 'a massive 16 KB of RAM'. However, that had been two years ago and I was aware that many of the children in my class went home to a ZX Spectrum or a Commodore 64. I had also come across Ryan Halfpenny and Barry Ollerenshaw discussing how they would be hackers of the future after seeing the film *WarGames.* They were convinced they could one day infiltrate the top-secret networks of the USA and begin a thermonuclear war. The pace of technology was becoming frightening and many in the teaching profession were being left behind the level of competence of the children in their care.

Fortunately Pat was already proving invaluable and called in from time to time to offer advice. She had followed me into the school hall with her class. Her partner, David, had purchased a BIG TRAK, a mobile electronic vehicle, and Pat had brought it in to give the children experience in computing and control. With the opportunity to plot up to sixteen commands and use direction arrows, it was proving very popular. The added incentive to fire a so-called 'photon cannon', which was actually a small light bulb behind a piece of blue plastic, added to the sense of excitement.

During afternoon break I was busy with Pat discussing the purchase of new netball bibs while Vera served up mugs of tea. Meanwhile, Anne had picked up Vera's *Daily Telegraph* and had read with interest that Rock Hudson was reported to be unimpressed after being informed that he was the world's most famous AIDS victim. And Christopher Reeve had been offered $6 million to play Superman once again.

Sally was reading her *Art & Craft* magazine and was engrossed in an article about making papier-mâché puppet heads when Vera broke the silence. 'We've got an interesting speaker this evening at the Women's Institute,' she said.

'Who's that?' asked Sally.

'It's a gentleman from Harrogate,' said Vera. 'A Mr Perkin Warbeck speaking about "Memory".'

'Perkin Warbeck?' repeated Pat. 'That name rings a bell from my A-level history.'

As usual, Sally, our resident historian, knew more than the rest of us. 'He lived at the end of the fifteenth century,' she explained with conviction. 'He was a pretender to the English throne during the reign of King Henry VII.'

'What happened to him?' asked Pat.

'He didn't last very long,' said Sally. 'They took him from the Tower, then hanged him at Tyburn.'

She settled back down to her magazine and smiled reflectively. 'Good job I wasn't living then with my view of the monarchy,' she muttered to herself.

Vera frowned but said nothing. She had something else on her mind.

That evening, at Bilbo Cottage, Beth was recounting her day.

'The questions were pretty much what I expected,' she said, 'and I think I coped well. I answered all the queries about the curriculum, behaviour, religious education and so on.'

'So you're down to the final three,' I said.

'But the other two are men,' put in Diane guardedly.

'O ye of little faith, Mother!' exclaimed Beth. 'This is the 1980s and women like me are securing positions of responsibility.'

'Perhaps,' said Diane quietly.

So it went on, with Beth becoming increasingly frustrated with her mother.

Diane's childcare was greatly appreciated but came at a price.

It was seven o'clock and Vera was by the back door of her kitchen at Morton Manor. She was saying goodbye to her three cats, Treacle, Jess and her favourite, Maggie, named after Margaret Thatcher, her political heroine. After checking they had eaten their liver-flavoured Kitekat Supreme, she walked out to her shiny Austin Metro, placed her tin of freshly baked fruit scones on the passenger seat next to her handbag, checked her notes and drove off down the Morton Road towards Ragley High Street.

When she arrived, the village hall was almost full and soon the ladies of the Ragley & Morton Women's Institute were settling back in their chairs. Vera went to the front.

'It gives me great pleasure,' she said, 'to welcome

our speaker this evening, Mr Perkin Warbeck.'

An elderly man in a thick tweed three-piece suit peered myopically over his half-moon spectacles and smiled nervously.

'Mr Warbeck has travelled all the way from Harrogate to provide us with his informative talk entitled "Memories Are Made of This".' Vera glanced down at the diminutive, balding man and gave an encouraging smile. He appeared to be fidgeting unnecessarily, while the portly lady by his side, Miss Martha Clapp, prepared a series of 35mm slides on her carousel projector. It was soon clear to Vera's experienced eye that Martha worshipped the ground that Perkin walked on but, sadly, he was oblivious to her keen attention.

However, Perkin belied his appearance and spoke in a loud, confident voice. 'The more you know about your memory,' he said, 'the better you will be in later life.'

The ladies nodded in anticipation.

'Your memory is a sort of filing cabinet,' he continued, 'except instead of sheets of paper we have *neurons* ... probably a billion of them, so it's a big filing cabinet.'

Martha clicked the switch and the first photograph appeared on the screen. It was a bright-red metal filing cabinet.

Only three drawers, thought Vera ... *it wouldn't do for me.*

However, it wasn't long before she was leaning forward in her chair and hanging on to every word.

'Alzheimer's disease is the most common form of dementia,' explained Perkin. 'For example, you may become confused, have mood swings, become withdrawn and have difficulty doing simple tasks.'

Many of the ladies were nodding in agreement. 'Sounds like my Allan,' whispered Bronwyn Bickerstaff to Margery Ackroyd.

Thirty minutes and countless photographs later, Perkin was building up to the big finish. 'As a disciple of the esteemed American psychologist Cissie Snowball, I know that she advocates regular activity and socializing. This helps both short- and long-term memory.' He paused and surveyed his audience. 'And being a member of the Women's Institute clearly helps.'

This went down well and there were approving nods and smiles.

'So, in conclusion, ladies, our memory makes us who we are,' and Perkin bowed.

While Martha gave the cue for applause, Vera thought of Rupert.

Immediately there was a hubbub of well-rehearsed activity. The water in the Baby Burco boiler began to bubble and refreshments appeared as if by magic on a trestle table covered with a snow-white cloth.

Vera ushered Perkin towards the feast and noticed that Mary Hardisty had brought a plate of her prize-winning parkin.

'Would you like some parkin, Perkin?' asked Vera, without a flicker of amusement.

Martha was eager to help and lifted the plate of parkin. 'They look delicious, Perkin, don't you think?'

'I'm sure they are,' he agreed.

Martha was keen to press the point. 'Didn't your mother used to make parkin?'

'I can't recall,' he said guardedly.

Following his talk on 'Memory', it seemed an incongruous response and Vera presumed there was more to this than met the eye.

Later that evening at Morton Manor, Vera and Rupert were relaxing in the lounge.

'I've been thinking,' said Vera, putting down her cross-stitch.

'Have you, my dear?' replied Rupert, without looking up from his *Horse & Hound* magazine.

'Yes, I have.'

'Well that's jolly good,' he murmured, still engrossed in the article on fox hunting in North Yorkshire.

'Yes ... about our life together.'

'Well I would say it's all tickety-boo,' said her husband absent-mindedly.

'Tickety-boo?' repeated Vera with a frown.

'Yes, my dear.' He glanced up from his magazine, 'You know – all shipshape and Bristol fashion.'

'Really?' she said. 'But we see so little of each other these days.'

Rupert sighed. 'Why are we having this conversation, my dear?'

Vera gave him that enigmatic smile he had come to know so well. 'Because I'm thinking of *retirement.*'

'Retirement?' He put down his magazine and gave her his full attention.

It was Friday morning and the day dawned bright

as Beth prepared to leave for the final interview.

'Good luck,' I said.

'It will be fine,' she replied, 'and I'll give it my best shot.'

Then she handed me my leather school satchel. 'I cleaned it with some polish,' she said with a grin.

'How on earth did you find time for that?' I asked in surprise.

I barely recognized it. The brown leather now had a lustrous shine. I kissed her gently and smiled. Love wasn't simply never having to say you're sorry ... love was cleaning your partner's satchel!

On my journey into Ragley I prayed all would go well for Beth. I knew how important this was for her. I also remembered my conversation with Richard Gomersall. There were changes in store for Ragley School – changes that were confidential, at least for now.

I turned up the radio and hummed along to 'Money for Nothing' by Dire Straits.

Vera had stopped outside Prudence Golightly's General Stores to buy a packet of garibaldi biscuits to replenish the staff-room biscuit tin and a jar of Nescafé Gold Blend. Five-year-old Julie Tricklebank was standing on the pavement stroking her cat, Trixie, who was making a fearful racket.

Vera was familiar with most of the cats in the village. 'Why is your cat meowing all the time?' she asked.

'Ah don't know, Mrs F,' said Julie. 'Ah don't

speak cat-langwidge.'

After being a school secretary for more years than she cared to remember, Vera simply smiled, walked into the shop and joined the queue.

Mrs Spittlehouse was standing at the counter with her seven-year-old daughter, Rosie. She was looking a little flustered as she searched for her shopping list in her bag. 'Oh dear, I'm getting like my mother,' she said, 'always forgetting things.'

'Never mind,' said Prudence, 'I'm sure it will come back to you.'

'I know why my gran doesn't have babies,' announced Rosie suddenly.

Everyone went quiet in the shop and Mrs Spittlehouse wished the ground would open up.

Prudence tried to rescue the situation. 'And why is that, Rosie?' she asked gently.

'Well, she'd put 'em down somewhere an' forget where she'd put 'em.'

It was later that morning that Joseph Evans visited school for his weekly Bible stories lesson. The theme of 'Creation' with Sally's class seemed to have gone down well and Joseph was feeling pleased with himself. However, as usual, the children were full of questions.

Charlie Cartwright was insistent. 'If God didn't want Adam an' Eve t'eat them apples, Mr Evans, then why did 'E put 'em on trees in t'first place?'

Before Joseph could come up with a plausible response, Katie Icklethwaite spoke up. 'Mr Evans, was there a god before God?'

'How do you mean?' asked a perplexed Joseph.

‘Well ... ’ow did God mek ’imself?’

The bell rang for lunchtime and Joseph breathed a sigh of relief.

A few minutes later in the staff-room Vera was serving her brother with a much-needed camomile tea. She had been relieved to close her *Daily Telegraph,* which carried an article about an earthquake in Mexico City that concerned itself less with the loss of life than with the possible damage to the football stadia for next year’s World Cup.

It was a surprise when Rupert walked in with a beautiful bunch of roses.

‘For you, my dear,’ he said with a gentle smile.

Suddenly for Vera all thoughts of retirement faded as everyone gathered round to admire the flowers. She felt young again and, for a few brief moments, she was the girl she used to be.

It was then she noticed Rupert’s latest eccentricity.

He was wearing two wristwatches.

The telephone rang and I picked it up in haste. It was Beth.

‘What’s the news?’

‘I can hardly believe it,’ she said, her voice full of excitement.

‘Go on, tell me!’

There was an intake of breath.

‘Well?’

‘I got the job.’

Chapter Three

A Fine Romance

The headteacher attended a meeting at High Sutton Hall concerning the rationalization of small schools in North Yorkshire. Miss Valerie Flint provided supply cover in Class 4 during afternoon school.

Extract from the Ragley School Logbook:
Tuesday, 1 October 1985

It was the first day of October and the season was changing. Outside Bilbo Cottage robins and wrens were claiming their winter territory and chirping out shrill warnings. In the low sunlight the hedgerows sparkled with the intricate webs of spiders, while the red hips of dog roses gave notice of the dark days ahead.

However, when I arrived at the school gate a very irate Ruby Smith was not appreciating the wonders of the Yorkshire countryside. Our caretaker and her daughter, Natasha, were in conversation with our local bobby, PC Pike. I pulled up and wound down my window.

'Good morning, everybody,' I said. 'Is there a problem?'

'I've just been informed of a possible theft, Mr Sheffield,' said PC Pike. At five feet eight and a half inches tall, Julian Pike wasn't at first sight the most impressive policeman. However, everyone in the village knew that in his big black boots with double insoles, and with a pair of shiny Hiatt handcuffs in the pouch of his leather belt, you didn't mess with this particular lawman. The copy of his *Karate Monthly* magazine rolled up in his truncheon pocket confirmed this well-mannered young man as an all-action hero. He was polite and, as he had been trained by Sergeant Dan Hunter in York, everything was done *by the book.*

He opened his notebook, licked the tip of his HB pencil and looked admiringly at Ruby's curvaceous daughter. 'So, Natasha,' he said and his cheeks flushed, 'can you tell me what happened?'

'T'bird 'as bolted, Constable,' interjected Ruby.

'An' the 'orse 'as flown,' added Natasha for good measure, completely unaware that she had inherited from her mother a wonderful capacity for mixed metaphors.

'Pardon?' asked PC Pike, pencil poised.

Some clarity was called for. 'So what *exactly* has happened, Ruby?' I asked.

'It's 'eartbreakin', Mr Sheffield,' said Ruby. 'One of my Ronnie's racin' pigeons 'as gone missin'. Our Duggie told Natasha before 'e went t'work an' she came t'tell me an' PC Pike were jus' passin' on 'is bike.'

'Ah, so it's a missing *racing pigeon,*' said Julian Pike, trying to restore some semblance of control.

'Yes, Genghis Khan the third,' recited Natasha with a shy smile in the direction of the handsome bobby. 'That's 'is name – it's written on 'is leg.'

'Our Duggie wrote it wi' one o' them indelicate pens,' added Ruby. 'Y'know, one o' them y'can't rub out.'

PC Pike nodded and began to write neatly in his notebook.

Natasha looked appreciatively at Julian's attempt at a first moustache, modelled on Robert Redford's Sundance Kid. 'But ah don't know 'ow t'spell it,' she said.

Julian looked adoringly into Natasha's eyes. 'Don't worry, Natasha, I can spell it,' he said confidently. 'I did history at school.'

'Ooooh, ah do like clever men,' said Natasha.

Julian blushed furiously and for a moment he was tongue-tied. His love life was a distant memory and he had been bereft of female company for many lonely nights. His previous girlfriend, Monica, a waitress in the Tea Rooms in York, had told him she wanted a boyfriend who didn't spend his evenings polishing his handcuffs and had promptly left him at the first opportunity for a swarthy Italian carpet-fitter from Halifax.

I decided to leave this *crime with passion* and drive on. 'Good luck,' I said. 'I hope Genghis turns up.'

I parked my Morris Minor Traveller in my usual space, picked up my old leather satchel and looked back down the cobbled drive. Our caretaker, Ruby, had a heart of gold and was loved by children and staff alike in Ragley School. Natasha was one of her six children. Thirty-four-year-old Andy was a sergeant in the army; thirty-two-year-old Racquel was the proud mother of three-year-old Krystal Carrington Ruby Entwhistle; thirty-year-old Duggie was an undertaker's assistant with the nickname 'Deadly'; twenty-five-year-old Sharon was continuing her long-term engagement to Rodney Morgetroyd, the Morton village milkman with the Duran Duran looks; twenty-three-year-old Natasha worked part-time in Diane's Hair Salon; while twelve-year-old Hazel had just started her second year at Easington Comprehensive School. Ruby loved them all and had toiled to put food on the table and clothes on their backs. Throughout it all her beer-swilling, chain-smoking, unemployed husband, Ronnie, had offered little support. It seemed he spent more time with his beloved pigeons than with his hardworking wife. Finally, Ronnie had died on the last day of 1983 and Ruby's life had changed for ever.

Vera was busy in the office when I walked in. 'I've arranged for Miss Flint to do supply cover in your class this afternoon, Mr Sheffield,' she said.

'Thanks, Vera. I'll be leaving after lunch for High Sutton and I've read this at last.' I rummaged in my satchel and held up the rationalization document.

'Let's hope it doesn't affect us,' she said pointedly. 'Joseph said there were rumours circulating after church last Sunday concerning the future of Morton School.'

'Really?' I asked cautiously.

'Yes, there were a few tongues wagging.' She examined my reaction. Vera was a very perceptive lady.

'Oh well,' I said, 'I'm sure we'll know more after the meeting.'

It was a busy morning in my class and there were a few minutes to spare before the bell for assembly. I decided on a quickfire round of questions for my class, which didn't get the response I expected.

'What's the chemical formula for water?' I asked. Frankie Spraggon's hand shot up. 'H, I, J, K, L, M, N, O, Mr Sheffield,' he said confidently.

'Pardon? What do you mean?'

Frankie looked puzzled. 'Well, las' week, sir, you said it were H to O.' It occurred to me that perhaps my communication skills weren't all I wished them to be. 'An' Mrs Smith 'as lost 'er racing pigeon,' he added for good measure.

The question-and-answer session was replaced by a variety of possible sightings of the errant bird until, at 10.15 a.m. sharp, Ryan Halfpenny rang the assembly bell.

It was Pat Brookside's turn to lead the morning assembly and she had decided to focus on the theme of 'Honesty'. Soon she was telling the famous story of George Washington and all the children were captivated. Then came the denouement.

'But then,' said Pat, 'George Washington went out and chopped down his father's precious cherry tree.' The children gasped. This was clearly serious.

'Flippin' 'eck,' muttered Billy Ricketts and Patience Crapper in unison.

'And do you know what George Washington did?'

Hands shot up everywhere.

''E ran away, Miss,' said seven-year-old Scott Higginbottom.

'No,' said Pat with gravitas. 'He told his father

the *truth.*'

There was a stunned silence, finally broken by an exclamation from Sam Whittaker. 'Cor!' he said.

'What 'appened nex', Miss?' asked Rosie Spittlehouse, unable to contain herself.

'Well,' continued Pat, 'and this may surprise you but his father *didn't* punish him.'

There was a gasp of incredulity.

'So, everybody think hard,' said Pat as the moral of the story was finally revealed. 'Why didn't George's father punish him?'

'Ah know, Miss,' called out Ted Coggins.

'Well done, Ted.' Pat gave him an encouraging smile. 'So what do you think?'

'Mebbe,' said Ted thoughtfully, 'cos George were still 'oldin' that big axe that y'mentioned.'

Pat sighed deeply. 'Good try, Ted,' she said with feeling and then explained the true reason. Finally, it was time to cut her losses. 'Hands together, eyes closed,' she said.

Over morning coffee Pat was a little deflated as a result of her aborted attempt to develop the concept of honesty, and an article in Vera's *Daily Telegraph* rubbed salt into the wound. It appeared that Lambeth Borough Council was desperate to employ computer programmers and offer them a remarkable £1,500 on top of their basic £8,100 salary. She sighed and, for once, wondered if she was in the right profession. However, soon she was engaged in conversation with Sally about other events. Alex Higgins, the snooker player, had been arrested at his home in Cheshire following a 'breach of the peace' complaint, while

Robert Maxwell, the publisher, was determined to sue the International Thomson Organization after the collapse of the deal to buy the Withy Grove printing group.

I joined in when the discussion turned to Halley's Comet. Excitement had been building, as the famous comet was due to reappear next month. Its last visit had been in 1910 and, with this in mind, I had begun an astronomy topic with my class. This important event was often regarded as a once-in-a-lifetime experience, but I realized that many of the children would still be around when it appeared again in the twenty-first century.

Meanwhile, outside on the schoolyard, Anne was on playground duty when she heard Patience Crapper being unkind to the chubby, red-cheeked Julie Tricklebank. Julie was munching her way through a bag of crisps.

'You'll be fat when y'grow up,' shouted Patience, 'an' y'won't be able t'run.'

Julie considered this for a moment. 'Yes but ah'll be able t'*roll*,' she replied defiantly.

Good answer, thought Anne as she stepped in to deal with this first hint of bullying.

Ruby was in the General Stores and had shared the news about her missing racing pigeon with Prudence Golightly. Unfortunately, Deirdre Coe, the unpopular sister of Stan Coe the local pig farmer, was leaving the shop at that moment and, as always, spoke up in an unpleasant manner.

'They're vermin, them pigeons,' she declared, her double chin wobbling in indignation. 'An' my Stanley will shoot 'em if they fly over our land.'

The door crashed behind her and the little bell jingled madly.

'Take no notice, Ruby,' said Prudence. 'I'm sure it must be very distressing for you.'

'Ah'm sick o' that Deirdre Coe,' complained Ruby. 'In fact if looks could kill ah'd be dead as a doornail ten times over.'

'So, definitely deceased then,' said Prudence sympathetically but with a wry smile.

'Ah told 'er *pacifically* t'keep 'er nose out o' my business,' Ruby continued.

'Take no notice,' Prudence said again. 'Now then, Ruby, I've got that lovely crusty bread that you like...'

Ruby walked up the High Street to the village green, then decided to rest her legs for a short while and sit on the bench that had been dedicated to her late husband. She found solace sitting here and enjoyed recalling happier times, even though they were few and far between.

'Y'look deep in thought,' said a familiar voice. It was George Dainty, a short man in his early fifties with a ruddy face and a gentle smile. He removed his flat cap to reveal his balding head. 'Now then, Ruby, may ah sit down?'

'O' course, George.'

'Ah 'ope nowt's troubling you,' he said and moved a little closer.

Ruby sighed. 'Well, there's a lot goin' on.'

'Y'can tell me,' he said gently.

George had become a well-loved character in the village. As a young man he had shown entrepreneurial spirit when he left Ragley to open his own shop, The Codfather, a popular and lucrative fish-and-chip shop in Alicante in Spain. He had returned to his home village a couple of years ago and bought a luxury bungalow on the Morton Road. Rumour had it he was a millionaire, but George never spoke about his wealth. However, it was well known he had thought highly of Ruby ever since she had been the village May Queen as a young girl. It was on that day that the teenage George had fallen in love with the pretty girl with the wavy chestnut hair and the ready smile.

'You've been crying,' said George tenderly.

Ruby rubbed her cheeks with dumpy, work-red fingers. 'Ah cry a lot these days.'

George rummaged in his pocket, pulled out a large handkerchief and offered it to Ruby. She blew her nose vigorously and loudly.

'You keep it,' he said and Ruby put it in the pocket of her old raincoat.

'Our Duggie's racin' pigeon 'as gone astray,' explained Ruby. ''E promised 'is dad 'e would look after 'em.'

'Don't fret, Ruby. Ah'm sure t'bird'll turn up.'

'Mebbe so, George.'

George glanced over his shoulder. ''Ow about a nice cup o' coffee in Nora's?'

Ruby looked down the High Street towards the clock on the village hall. 'Ah'm not due back at school 'til jus' afore twelve t'put dining tables out,' she said.

'Then, come on,' said George, taking her hand, 'an' cheer up, it might never 'appen.'

'An' pigs might fly,' retorted Ruby with a smile.

Last month's number one, David Bowie and Mick Jagger's 'Dancing in the Street' was playing on the juke box when they walked into the Coffee Shop. Ruby sat down while George bought two frothy coffees. He seemed to spend an age adding sugar and stirring his coffee.

Finally Ruby broke the silence. 'C'mon, out wi' it. Or 'as t'cat got y'tongue?'

George sipped his coffee, looked up and took a deep breath. 'Ruby luv ... ah were seventeen an' you were sixteen,' he began. 'You were t'most beautiful girl in Ragley and ah were smitten. Then when ah plucked up t'courage to ask you out y'mother wouldn't 'ave none of it ... an' ah got m'marchin' orders.'

Ruby put down her cup and looked into the eyes of this quiet, gentle man while Bonnie Tyler's 'Holding Out for a Hero' started up on the juke-box.

'Ah believe you, George, but thousands wouldn't,' she said.

There was a long silence.

'Do y'miss 'im?' asked George.

''E were like blisters, were my Ronnie,' said Ruby with a mournful shake of her chestnut curls.

'Blisters?'

'Yes, y'know ... 'e never turned up 'til work were done.'

'Ah see,' said George.

'If ah said it once ah've said it a thousand times ... 'e were neither use nor ornament, were my Ronnie.' Then a smile crossed Ruby's flushed face. ''Cept ah were blessed wi' six lovely children.'

As Bonnie Tyler finally faded into the distance the Coffee Shop went quiet for a few moments.

Finally George spoke up. 'Ah were saddened when y'married Ronnie.'

'Ah didn't know that, George,' replied Ruby thoughtfully.

She had begun to wonder what might have been.

At lunchtime Vera was flicking through her newspaper. The Labour Party Conference was taking place in Bournemouth and she frowned. Nor was she interested in Frank Bruno, the Wandsworth heavyweight, who was due to fight at Wembley to take the European crown from Anders Eklund of Sweden. However, the ladies' tennis news caught her attention. In women's tennis her favourite player, forty-year-old Virginia Wade, had lost her latest match. *All good things come to an end,* thought Vera. Meanwhile, though she missed Sue Barker, she was confident that the teenager Annabel Croft showed promise.

Her friend, Miss Valerie Flint, had arrived to take my class during afternoon school. Now in her early sixties, she was an imposing teacher and renowned for her excellent classroom management and strict but fair discipline. We were fortunate to have such a 'safe pair of hands' as our supply teacher.

She was chatting with Pat and recalling that, at six feet tall, she had been an enthusiastic netball player in her younger days. Valerie was an elegant figure in a beautifully tailored trouser suit, her favoured style of dress. While the traditional Vera still frowned at female staff wearing trousers, Miss Flint had become a firm ally of mine on my first day at Ragley when I had ended this particular outdated restriction on female clothing implemented by my predecessor.

Finally it was time to leave for the headteachers' meeting.

'Good luck, Mr Sheffield,' said Vera and I wondered just how much she knew. Her husband, Rupert, mixed in higher circles and was familiar with local politics.

It had been difficult not to reveal the professional confidence shared by Richard Gomersall. The possible amalgamation of Ragley and Morton would have a huge impact on our school and community. However, soon I was driving along the Ripon Road in the hope that all could be resolved.

The wheels of my car crunched along the winding gravel driveway towards a magnificent Georgian mansion set in five hundred acres of the finest Yorkshire countryside. High Sutton Hall was a distinctive country house with a lake and a walled garden, and was a superb venue for meetings. It provided a welcome retreat for teachers to talk and share ideas, and the cuisine was always excellent.

The room was filling with men and women in grey suits and sombre expressions. I collected my package of booklets and leaflets and wondered how many trees had been sacrificed to facilitate this gathering. I found a seat and it wasn't long before Rufus Timmings, the head-teacher of Morton Primary School, sought me out.

Rufus was a short, squat, barrel-chested man, more a bulldog than a greyhound, although he moved at a surprisingly fast pace through the crowd when he spotted me. Although only in his early thirties, he was balding prematurely and reminded me of the irrepressible Gerald Campion, the actor who played the part of Billy Bunter of Greyfriars School.

He immediately engaged me in conversation. 'Hello, Jack, how are you?'

I noticed that his smart grey three-piece suit made me look a little shabby in comparison. 'Fine, thank you, Rufus,' I said. 'So, have you settled in?'

'Yes, of course,' he said with confidence. Then he lowered his voice and added in a conspiratorial whisper, 'But Miss Tripps had let things slide rather badly and I'm restoring order.'

I wasn't happy about him criticizing his predecessor, a dedicated lady who had always given her best for the children in her care. 'Miss Tripps was a wonderful servant to Morton village,' I said, 'but change is inevitable, I suppose.'

'Too true, Jack, and never more than now. My school will almost certainly be closed with such a small number on roll.'

'That's difficult news for the village,' I said.

'Yes, but it doesn't make *economic* sense to keep it open.' He tapped the cover of his spiral-bound booklet. 'That's why we're here today.'

His candour puzzled me. There was an obvious vibrancy and vigour about this young man. He spoke with an outgoing confidence, clearly comfortable in his own skin. I was surprised at his relaxed manner.

'You don't seem too concerned,' I observed.

He sniggered rather than laughed and tapped the side of his nose with a stubby forefinger. 'Well, the Morton headship is just a stepping stone for me ... simply the first rung on the ladder towards a bigger headship.'

'I see,' I said. The bell rang to signal the commencement of the conference. 'Well, good luck, I hope it works out for you.'

We shook hands and he hurried off to claim a seat in the front row.

Richard Gomersall introduced the agenda for the afternoon and began by emphasizing the finite resources at the disposal of the County Council. 'Maggie has tightened her purse strings,' he joked, but no one laughed. It was depressing to hear his view that we were becoming 'the poor neighbours of public service' while the salaries of Britain's senior company directors had risen by seventeen per cent this year.

There was a variety of speakers, mostly grey men in dark suits with degrees in economics, who ground down our spirits as the afternoon wore on. Finally Richard Gomersall reappeared to sum up. 'I've managed to visit the schools for whom the impact will be most felt,' he concluded. 'We must handle the coming events with particular sensitivity as the decisions we are making will affect many facets of local communities.' There were imperceptible nods of reluctant agreement from those around me.

Miss Barrington-Huntley sought me out as the meeting closed. 'I was delighted for Beth,' she said with enthusiasm. 'She will do well at King's Manor.'

'I know she's looking forward to it,' I said.

'Yes, Hartingdale's loss is King's Manor's gain,' she replied.

'In the meantime, I'm obviously wondering about the future of Ragley,' I said pointedly.

I could see her considering her response. 'I understand your concern, Jack, and I'm aware Richard has spoken to you.'

'Yes, he mentioned the possible amalgamation of Ragley and Morton, and I haven't discussed this with anyone else ... as he requested.'

'Yes, all very hush-hush at present,' she said. 'We must proceed with caution.'

She gave me a searching look as we shook hands and I wondered what else there was that I didn't know.

As I left I saw Rufus Timmings engaged in animated conversation with some of the senior figures who had spoken during the afternoon. There was a lot to ponder as I drove back to Ragley.

Fortunately there was some good news when I walked into the school entrance hall. Genghis the racing pigeon had been found.

'Ah'm thrilled t'bits, Mr Sheffield,' said Ruby, 'an' it's all thanks t'that young policeman. Genghis were in Deke Ramsbottom's pig trailer.'

'That's wonderful,' I said. 'You should celebrate.'

Ruby went quiet for a moment. ''Appen ah will, Mr Sheffield, an' 'appen ah won't,' but I guessed she had something else on her mind.

The bell rang out to mark the end of school and I returned to the cloakroom area outside my classroom. The children in my class filed out and it was clear they had enjoyed their afternoon. Sonia Tricklebank and Lucy Eckersley were hurrying off hand in hand.

'We've done loads wi' Miss,' said Sonia.

'Paintin' an' modelling' added Lucy.

'An' t'story about King Arthur was brilliant,' enthused Sonia.

'And where are you rushing off to?' I asked.

'We're off blackberryin', Mr Sheffield,' said Sonia. 'Lucy says there's loads in the 'edgerow up Chauntsinger Lane round t'back o' t'blacksmith's.'

The sensible Lucy anticipated my next question. 'An' don't worry, Mr Sheffield, my mam is coming with us.'

I smiled as they ran down the drive where Mrs Eckersley, complete with a variety of Tupperware tubs, was waiting for them.

Half an hour later the staff were completing end-of-the-day tasks. When Ruby called into the office to empty the wastepaper basket, Vera looked up from her desk and saw the concern etched on our caretaker's face. 'What's the matter, Ruby?' she asked.

'Ah'm frettin' summat rotten, Mrs F,' said Ruby. 'In fac', ah'm worried sick.'

'Oh dear,' said Vera.

'Don't you worry, Mrs F, we've all got crosses t'bear,' said Ruby with feeling, 'it's jus' that mine's a reight 'eavy one.'

'So what exactly is the problem?' asked Vera.

'Well ... it's m'*motions,* Mrs F.'

'Motions!' exclaimed Vera. Ruby was a dear

friend, but bowel movements were not an ideal topic for discussion.

'Yes, Mrs F. Ah don't know if ah'm comin' or goin'.'

'Really?' said Vera with forced sympathy.

'Yes, it's m'motions ... like ah used to 'ave when ah were courtin' my Ronnie. Y'know, all them 'ot flushes and feelin' giddy an' suchlike.'

The penny dropped. 'Ah, your emotions!' Vera looked at her friend with a new intensity. 'Come and sit down,' she said, smiling and nodding knowingly. She knew what it was that was causing concern for Ruby ... and it had nothing to do with bodily functions.

I was in the entrance hall after thanking Valerie Flint for her work when Vera stepped out of the office and gently closed the door behind her.

'I'll say goodnight now, Mr Sheffield,' she said. 'I'm having a chat with Ruby – she's got things on her mind.'

'Is there anything I can do to help?'

'Not really. It's more to do with, well ... affairs of the heart.'

'So, Ruby's not unwell?'

'No, she's fine.'

'I see,' I said ... though I didn't.

As she turned to go back into the office Vera paused and smiled. 'Let's just say, Mr Sheffield, that you can't beat *a fine romance*.'

I was none the wiser as I drove home.

Chapter Four

The Solitude of Secrets

A staff meeting was held following Mr Gomersall's visit to school to discuss the issues relating to the proposed closure of Morton School.

Extract from the Ragley School Logbook:
Friday, 25 October 1985

Vera was in her kitchen staring out of the window beyond the manicured lawns of Morton Manor. The cool fingers of autumn had touched the trees and the leaves shone bronze in the morning sun. Teardrop cobwebs were strung like pearls through the hedgerows while the gauze of mist caressed the soft earth like a soul stretched tight in sorrow.

Fantasie in F Minor was playing on her radio and its heartbreaking opening melody always brought tears to her eyes. For Vera, Schubert's piano duets were among his finest works, but on this particular morning it did not soothe her troubled mind. There were decisions to make ... important ones. However, for now they would have to remain a secret.

She glanced at her wristwatch, checked her appearance in the hall mirror, made a minute adjustment to the Victorian brooch above the top button of her silk blouse, smoothed the seat of her pin-striped business suit, picked up her royal-blue leather handbag, said goodbye to her three cats and then to Rupert, in that order, and strode out to her Austin Metro.

It was 8.15 a.m. on Friday, 25 October and Vera had something important on her mind.

On my way to school I called into Victor Pratt's garage to fill up with petrol. I parked next to the single pump and Victor, elder brother of Timothy and Nora, lumbered out.

'Fill her up, please, Victor,' I said and handed over a £10 note. 'And how are you?' I added, then wished I hadn't. As usual, he had an ailment.

'Not good, Mr Sheffield,' he said with a grimace. 'Ah've got shootin' pains in m'shoulder.'

'I'm sorry to hear that.'

'Ah'm in agony,' he went on. 'In fac' ah'm a martyr t'me misery.'

I considered this to be somewhat melodramatic, but pressed on regardless. 'Perhaps it's sciatica,' I suggested in an attempt to be both informative and sympathetic.

'No, it's definitely like ah said ... *shootin'* pains.'

'Shooting pains?'

'Yes – cos of t'recoil on m'shotgun when ah were shootin' rabbits on Twenty Acre Field.'

'Oh dear, I see,' I said with feeling. Having recently watched *Watership Down,* my sympathy diminished rapidly while Victor trundled away to get my change.

When I walked into the school office Vera looked up from her late-dinner-money register. She appeared concerned. 'Good morning, Mr Sheffield,' she said.

'Good morning, Vera,' I replied. 'A lovely day.' I gestured towards the window, from where we could see the children playing in the late-autumn sunshine.

'Yes,' said Vera without looking out of the window. 'I wonder if we can have a word at some time today?'

'Of course,' I said. 'Anne is preparing morning assembly so I've got a few minutes now if that helps.'

'Yes, thank you.' She got up and closed the door.

Suddenly the telephone rang and Vera hurried back to her desk. 'Yes, Mr Gomersall,' she said in her precise, clipped tone, 'he's here now,' and she passed the receiver to me and dashed out of the office.

Richard Gomersall sounded a little anxious. 'I need to pass on some news, Jack,' he said.

'Yes, go ahead, Richard.' There was a pause.

'I really need to call in ... perhaps at lunchtime?'

'Fine,' I said, 'I'll see you then.'

'Thanks. Say around twelve thirty.'

'By the way, what's it about?'

There was another long pause. 'Well, Jack ... I'm afraid it's *confidential.*' And he rang off.

As I walked out into the entrance hall Vera was in conversation with Anne.

'Mr Sheffield,' she said, 'before you go back to class could I have a word?'

'Yes, of course,' I said. 'I'm sorry we got interrupted. How can I help?'

It was strange, but for once Vera seemed lost for words. After a few hesitant moments she said quietly, 'I wondered if you could spare me a few minutes at the end of the day? There's a matter that has arisen recently that I should like to discuss with you ... in private if at all possible.'

'Of course, Vera,' I said. 'Let's meet in the office after school.'

She looked preoccupied as she nodded in acknowledgement and hurried back to her desk.

It was a busy morning and the immediacy of the needs of the children in my care meant that the concerns of Richard Gomersall and Vera were soon far from my mind.

I completed reading tests for all the children and was pleased to see that Damian Brown had finally achieved a reading age that matched his chronological age. The range of ability was remarkable and my best readers, the two ten-year-olds Stacey Bryant and Dawn Phillips, could read the final line of the Schonell Graded Word Reading Test: namely, *rescind, metamorphosis, somnambulist, bibliography and idiosyncrasy.*

Meanwhile, next door in Class 3, Sally was developing the concept of history in her 'Modern World' topic.

'Can you think of something really important that wasn't here ten years ago?' she asked expectantly. A host of hands shot in the air.

'Yes, Miss,' said Ted Coggins eagerly, '...me!' Sally reflected that it was moments like this that made the job worthwhile.

During morning break Pat was on playground duty and the rest of us gathered in the staff-room. Vera appeared to be in a world of her own and Anne, always quick to notice the concerns of others, asked, 'How is Rupert these days?'

Vera folded her Flowers of the Forest tea towel, sat down and picked up her *Daily Telegraph.* She smiled as if recalling a happy memory. 'He's taking me to see *Les Misérables* in London during half-term,' she said. The new musical by the Royal Shakespeare Company had opened at the Barbican Centre earlier in the month. 'Sadly, it's had poor reviews.' She pointed to the arts section in her newspaper. "A lurid Victorian melodrama", it says here.'

'Never mind,' said Anne, 'I'm sure you'll enjoy it.'

'I'm hoping it will cheer him up,' said Vera. 'He's been like a bear with a sore head since he read that foreign cars will be built here in the United Kingdom.' I looked up, remembering the news that Peugeot had begun to construct their new 309 in the plant that was famous for the Hillman, Humber, Singer, Sunbeam and Talbot. 'Rupert says it will be the death knell of the British car industry.'

Meanwhile, Sally picked up her *Daily Mirror* and smiled. 'At least there's some good news here,' she said.

'What's that?' asked Anne, looking up from her Yorkshire Purchasing Organisation catalogue and the price of powder paint.

Sally pointed to the article. 'It says here that five thousand pensioners have protested in Trafalgar

Square against the proposal by Norman Fowler, Secretary of State for Social Services, for the abolition of the state earnings-related pension.'

'Good for them,' said Anne.

The full basic rate of pension was £35.80 per week for a single person and £57.30 for a couple, so this had been a topical discussion in recent weeks.

'And it looks like the pensioners have won!' exclaimed Sally. 'What do you think of that, Vera?' It was a mischievous confrontation.

'Well, generally good news,' said Vera cautiously, 'but also something of a concern. I heard on the news this morning that the number of people over seventy-five will rise by over a third in the next ten years.'

'Who's going to look after them all?' wondered Anne.

Sally shook her head. 'The NHS is creaking as it is.'

'I presume people will have to use their savings for a retirement home,' said Vera.

'Savings!' exclaimed Sally. 'On a teacher's salary?'

'It will be difficult for many who just make ends meet,' said Anne, trying to establish a middle ground. She looked up at Vera, who had returned to the sink and had begun to wash the hot-milk pan a little earlier than usual. It was clear that she wasn't quite herself today.

It was just as the bell rang for school lunch that Ruby had finished setting out all the dining tables. She was later than usual.

‘What’s the matter, Ruby?’ I asked.

She shook her head. ‘It’s my Duggie, Mr Sheffield. ’E’s allus gallavantin’ about wi’ that mature woman.’

‘Well, so long as he’s happy,’ I said without conviction.

‘Ah’ll be pushin’ up daisies by t’time ’e finds a proper girlfriend,’ continued Ruby.

‘A *proper* girlfriend?’

‘Yes, y’know – someone ’is own age.’

‘I see,’ I said.

During school lunch the children in Pat’s class were lining up with their plastic trays. Shirley Mapplebeck always had a kind word for all the children, whereas Doreen Critchley, her formidable colleague, rarely smiled.

‘We ’ad strangled eggs f’breakfast, Mrs Mapplebeck,’ said six-year-old Madonna Fazackerly.

‘That’s lovely,’ said Shirley with a smile.

A few places further back in the queue, Billy Ricketts and Scott Higginbottom were exchanging secrets.

‘Ah know a swear word,’ said Billy, looking furtively around him.

‘What is it?’ asked Scott.

‘Friggin’,’ said Billy.

Scott looked puzzled. ‘Friggin’ ... what’s friggin’?’

‘Dunno,’ said Billy, ‘but my dad says it all the time.’

The queue shuffled closer to Shirley Mapplebeck, who was serving shepherd’s pie and carrots, alongside Doreen Critchley, who was offering a choice of ice cream or semolina and a

spoonful of jam.
'Ah dare you t'say it t'Mrs Critchley,' said Scott.
'Ah dunno,' said Billy, looking up at the fearsome sight of Doreen Critchley's bulging forearms.
'Y'scared!' said Scott triumphantly.
'Well ... d'you know any swear words?' asked Billy.
'Yes ...'ell,' said Scott.
'That's a good 'un,' said Billy.
'Ah know,' said Scott. 'Ah say it all t'time.'
Billy considered this for a moment. 'Well if you say *'ell*, ah'll say *friggin'*.'
'OK,' agreed Scott.
'You go first,' said Billy guardedly.
Mrs Mapplebeck served up shepherd's pie, carrots and a splash of gravy. Suddenly both boys were faced with Doreen Critchley.
'What's it t'be, Scott,' asked Doreen, 'ice cream or semolina?'
'Oh 'ell,' replied Scott, 'ah'll 'ave semolina.'
'GET TO T'BACK O' T'QUEUE!' shouted Mrs Critchley.
Scott ran off clutching his tray. He went to the end of the line and stared at his friend.
'Now then, Billy,' said Mrs Critchley, 'what do you want?'
Billy took a deep breath. 'Well, ah definitely don't want no friggin' semolina!'
Seconds later he joined Scott at the back of the queue.
'You'll 'ave t'ask y'dad,' whispered Scott.
'Ask 'im what?' said Billy.

'T'find out what *friggin'* means.'
'OK,' agreed Billy.
'So no more swearing,' said Scott.
Billy nodded and looked anxiously at the queue in front of him. 'Ah 'ope there's some ice cream left.'

I was just finishing my lunch when Anne tapped me on the shoulder. 'Richard Gomersall is here, Jack,' she said. 'I've asked him to wait in the office.'
'Thanks, Anne.'
'Be warned,' she said, 'he looked a little agitated.'
Our Senior Primary Adviser, in a smart purple cord suit, was sitting on the visitor's chair and I sat down behind my desk. He was studying his personal copy of the now familiar 'Rationalization' document and underlining a specific section.
'Good to see you, Jack, and thanks for your time,' he said. He glanced up at the clock on the wall. 'I'm aware of your teaching commitment, so I'll try to be brief.'
'Thank you, Richard. What can I do for you?'
'I have important news,' he said, 'and I'm afraid it affects you.'
'You mean the amalgamation with Morton School?'
'Yes, it's definite now.' He looked down at his notes. 'It will be announced officially next month that, subject to the usual red tape, Morton School will merge with Ragley commencing the beginning of the spring term 1987.'
'I see,' I said. 'So in just over a year we'll have almost another thirty children coming to Ragley?'
'That's correct.'

'You're aware of the problems of space in our small school, Richard, and I recall you mentioned a Portakabin.'

'Yes, that's been discussed and you'll have a temporary classroom added to the site.'

'Temporary?'

'Well, the usual Portakabin. We call them "temporary" but they finish up being permanent. The proposal is it will be sited on the grassy area next to the playground and will house up to thirty children.' He glanced down at his notes. 'Delivery is proposed for September next year, so everything will be in place for the spring term.'

'I've seen a few,' I said with a wry smile. 'Large green boxes that are cold in winter and with no running water. I taught in one at the outset of my career.'

'It will be the best we can afford at the time, Jack, but that apart, the implications are considerable.' He glanced down at the underlined script in his document. 'The school will be renamed as Ragley and Morton Church of England Primary School.'

'So you're dropping our "on-the-Forest" after Ragley?'

'Too many words and it doesn't sit neatly with the addition of "Morton".'

There appeared to be a finality to his prepared speech. 'I see,' I said.

'And there will be a new governing body,' he continued, 'with all the usual elections.'

'That will be news to Joseph Evans,' I said in surprise. Richard pressed on. 'Also, parents will need to be informed in the proper manner.'

'Of course,' I said. 'That's vital.'

'And there are transport issues,' he continued, ticking off his list.

'Transport?'

'Yes,' he said, 'a bus will be required to bring the children down the Morton Road... So, lots to prepare for.'

'What about staffing?' I asked.

'With over a hundred and thirty on roll, and with the anticipated increase in reception-age children in Ragley, the new school will be entitled to another member of staff.'

I was encouraged. An extra teacher would be more than welcome. 'What about the Morton staff?' I asked.

'Well, Miss Proud is in her sixties and she made it very clear she was keen to leave when Miss Tripps retired, so I don't see a problem there.'

'And the new headteacher, Rufus Timmings,' I said, 'what about him? He's only thirty-something. I presume you'll relocate him elsewhere?'

Richard looked surprised. 'I don't think you're quite following. Mr Timmings can of course apply for the new headship of Ragley and Morton Primary School.'

I stared in disbelief. 'You mean *my* job will be advertised?'

'Yes, Jack, and we would of course expect you to apply.' I sat back, aghast at the thought. 'So, it will be a choice between Rufus Timmings and myself?'

Richard sighed. 'Not exactly. We have to do this properly. You must appreciate that *anyone* can apply. Early in the summer term there will be an open advertisement in the *Times Educational*

Supplement, with interviews before the school closes in July. That provides all parties with plenty of time to prepare for the launch of the new school.' He stood up. 'I know this is a lot to take in, Jack, but you've been a good servant to Ragley and I'm sure that will be taken into account.'

For a moment I was lost for words. I walked with him to the door. He paused in the doorway and shook my hand.

'Well, thank you for letting me know,' I said.

'Remember, all this is strictly *confidential*.'

'What about my staff?' I asked. 'Surely I can pass on this news?'

He sighed. 'Just put their minds at rest. This is the beginning of a long process and it will be debated at length during the coming year in the two villages and up at County Hall. Give them the bare bones of what is likely to happen and we'll take it from there. Don't mention the headship implications at this stage. Let's take one thing at a time. It will begin with a letter to all parents, staff and governors and there will be a statement in the local papers.'

I stared out of the office window as Richard climbed into his Jaguar and roared off towards the Morton Road.

Vera came back in and caught sight of my ashen face. 'What is it, Mr Sheffield?' she asked. 'Not bad news, I hope?'

'We need to have a staff meeting, Vera,' I replied, 'as soon as possible.'

In the General Stores Ruby was stocking up on tinned peaches and Bird's custard. 'These are for my Aunty Alice – she's coming t'visit,' she said. 'She swears by 'er peaches. Them an' a bit o' custard an' she's in 'eaven.'

'That's lovely,' said Prudence. 'I heard she worked hard in the war looking after the refugee children.'

'Yes, she's full o' tales o' those days,' said Ruby wistfully. 'An' o' course, regular as clockwork she would roll up 'er most precious possession an' run into t'Anderson shelter.'

'And what was that?' asked Prudence, curious at the sudden turn in the conversation.

'It were 'er Spirella corset,' said Ruby. 'It were made t'measure an' she were a big girl, were my Aunty Alice.'

Ruby picked up her bag of shopping and trotted off, leaving Prudence to reflect on how the war had taken away the love of her life. As she tidied up the shelf of tinned fruit she wondered what life would have been like if the young pilot, Jeremy, had come home.

At 4.30 p.m. the last children had gone home and Ruby was cleaning the classrooms. I had decided to have a private word with her later. There was a sombre mood in the staff-room and I guessed my expression was sufficient to suggest I had significant news.

'Thanks, everybody, for staying behind,' I said, 'but something very important cropped up today and I need to share it with you.'

Everyone went quiet.

'Richard Gomersall called in with the results of a recent meeting at County Hall. As part of their rationalization process a few of the smaller village schools in North Yorkshire will be closed during the next couple of years.'

There was an intake of breath. 'Not us, surely?' asked Pat. 'I've only just arrived.'

'No, it's not Ragley,' I said quickly. 'It's Morton School.'

'Oh dear,' said Vera.

'And the children from Morton will be coming here.'

'Here?' said Anne in surprise.

'But we're bursting at the seams as it is,' said Sally.

'And with all the new building on the Easington Road there will be a lot of reception-age children in the pipeline,' added Anne.

'Yes, they've considered that,' I said. 'A Portakabin will be erected next year and our staffing will be increased by one teacher to accommodate the increased numbers.'

So it went on. The conversation ebbed and flowed as the implications for our professional lives sank in. As requested, I decided not to share the headship issue at this stage; it would wait until I had more information. An hour later we dispersed. 'And remember, it's *confidential* for the time being,' I added as a final thought.

Vera and I were the last to leave. 'By the way,' I said, 'I'm so sorry but you asked for a private word this morning and we never got round to it.'

Vera paused and nodded gently. 'Yes, Mr Sheffield,' she said quietly. 'Another time perhaps.'

'Very well, Vera, but I'm here when you need me.'

'Actually it was a personal matter – something close to my heart – but it will keep.' And she buttoned up her coat and walked out to her car.

I completed the logbook, checked the windows and locked up the school. It had been a day full of unexpected surprises, and my future in the job I loved was under threat.

Vera was quiet that evening as she sat in the kitchen listening to the evening news. A reporter was discussing the recent riots in Tottenham on the Broadwater Farm Estate where PC Keith Blakelock had been murdered in brutal fashion. It had been a terrible business that had shocked the nation and Vera thought there were more pressing problems than her decision on retirement.

On The Crescent, Anne was also listening to the news as she prepared an evening meal without any enthusiasm. She and her husband had barely communicated since she arrived home. Sadly, it was becoming the norm. John was reading *The Complete Encyclopaedia of DIY and Home Maintenance,* while Anne stared at her reflection in the kitchen window and considered her life.

In the vicarage Joseph was reading his well-thumbed Bible and preparing his next sermon. He had just returned from the Hartford Home for Retired Gentlefolk or, as it was known locally, 'God's Waiting Room'. One of the residents, a member of the Parish Church Council, was very ill and Joseph had provided solace and gentle words.

His heart lifted when Vera called in to speak to him and shared the news of the staff meeting. However, when she left he felt he was drowning in a sea of uncertainty. He missed his sister, his lifetime companion. Vera had moved on in her life and he had remained behind. There were times he felt like a shepherd in the wilderness. Once his life had been sure and strong, filled with the zeal of a young man. Now, with stiffening joints, he missed the clarity of his youth and the happy times shared with Vera. On this dark and lonely night only the ticking of the clock disturbed the silence of the vicarage.

Bilbo Cottage was also silent, and I went to bed unaware I was not the only one experiencing the solitude of secrets.

Chapter Five

It's All in the Stars

Mr Edward Clifton, amateur astronomer, visited school and gave a talk in assembly concerning Halley's Comet.

Extract from the Ragley School Logbook:
Friday, 8 November 1985

A frozen mist hung over the land like a cold blanket and the smell of wood smoke was in the air. The weather had changed and a long winter was in store. The villagers of Ragley found their warmest coats before setting off for Prudence Golightly's General Stores and the welcome smell of freshly baked bread. It was Friday morning, 8

November, and the first harsh frosts heralded the coming of winter.

On the back road from Kirkby Steepleton I stared through the windscreen at the leaden sky and the torn rags of cirrus clouds. It was a familiar sight – one I had witnessed many times. However, complacency is a relaxed companion. Recently we had enjoyed a variety of visiting speakers in morning assembly, including Lollipop Lil, our road-crossing patrol officer, and PC Pike with his 'Don't Speak to Strangers' slide-show. Today was destined to be different and I glanced up once again at the vast sky over the plain of York.

It seemed an unlikely day to consider a visitor from outer space.

Just before I reached Ragley I called into Victor Pratt's garage and pulled up by the single pump. Our local car mechanic shuffled out in his greasy overalls.

'Just a couple of gallons, please, Victor.'

'Comin' up, Mr Sheffield,' he said.

He didn't look well but I tried to be positive. 'So no more shooting pains, Victor?' I asked.

'No, them's all gone.' Suddenly he doubled up in a paroxysm of coughing.

'Oh dear, that sounds bad.'

'It's m'chest, Mr Sheffield,' he explained. 'Ah've got them pneumonics.'

I considered this turn of events. 'Perhaps you ought to see Doctor Davenport,' I suggested.

He shook his head as he removed the nozzle. 'No, ah'm goin' t'see Ruby's mother,' he said. 'What she don't know about pneumonics ain't worth knowin'.'

'Well, if you're sure,' I said.
'Bit of 'er mother's goose grease'll soon put me reight, Mr Sheffield, as true as true can be.'
It occurred to me that you couldn't argue with that level of conviction and I drove off to Ragley High Street. As I pulled up outside Prudence Golightly's General Stores to collect my morning newspaper I paused to admire the new shop sign. It was a recent gift from Timothy Pratt in celebration of a lifetime's service to the village community. In beautiful Roman letters painted in primrose yellow on an emerald-green background it read:

GENERAL STORES & NEWSAGENT
'A cornucopia of delights'
Proprietor – Prudence Anastasia Golightly

As I approached the door I was aware of a small crowd that had gathered outside Nora's Coffee Shop. They appeared to be staring at a poster in the window.
Meanwhile, in the General Stores Betty Buttle, a local farmer's wife and general gossip, was in animated conversation with the diminutive Miss Golightly. 'Ruby's mother says summat special is goin' to 'appen,' Betty was saying. 'She were 'ere when it came round las' time.'
'Yes, it's all in the papers,' said Prudence, pointing to one of the headlines:
'HALLEY'S COMET HEADING FOR EARTH'.
Betty nodded knowingly. 'Well, ah'm goin' to t'Coffee Shop tonight. There's one o' them star

gazers givin' a talk an' Margery says 'e knows all there is t'know about comets an' suchlike.' Betty picked up her loaf and paper and winked. 'An' Prudence – Margery says 'e's a *looker.*'

As Betty turned for the door she caught sight of me, blushed slightly and hurried out. 'Mornin' Mr Sheffield,' she said as the doorbell jingled.

Prudence held up a copy of our local paper, the *Easington Herald & Pioneer.* It was clear that the editor was less concerned with the night sky than with events here on Earth. The headline 'The End Is Nigh' was not referring to a possible collision of a distant comet with planet Earth but rather to the proposed closure of Morton village school. 'Surprising news, Mr Sheffield,' said Prudence. 'Morton children coming to Ragley is the talk of the two villages.'

'Yes – big changes,' I said guardedly.

She folded my copy of *The Times.* 'Anyway, I'm sure it will make sense in the long run.'

'And I'll take a *Herald* for the staff-room, please,' I added.

Fortunately there had been no mention of the future headship arrangements in the local paper, nor in any communications with parents, and I was hoping it would stay that way. However, when I had spoken to Ruby there was no doubt in her mind that she would continue as school caretaker. 'Possession is nine-tenths of t'law, Mr Sheffield,' she had declared defiantly.

'And, of course,' Miss Golightly added with a twinkling smile, 'it will mean more business for me with the Morton parents passing my shop.' She looked up at Jeremy Bear. 'More new friends for you, my dear.'

'Good morning, Jeremy,' I said with sincerity and reverence. It always pleased Miss Golightly when her customers treated Ragley's best-dressed teddy bear as something other than an inanimate object. He was sitting on his usual shelf next to a tin of loose-leaf Lyon's Tea and an old advertisement for Hudson's Soap and Carter's Little Liver Pills. Prudence took great pride in making sure he was always well turned out. Today he was dressed in his autumn ensemble – a checked lumberjack shirt, blue jeans, brown boots and a bobble hat with 'Canada' printed on the front. Jeremy was a well-travelled bear.

It was clear to me as I walked back to my car that after the amalgamation of the two schools there were going to be winners and losers ... and I wondered which of the two I would be.

As I drove past the village green Big Dave Robinson and Little Malcolm Robinson, our local bin men, had parked their refuse wagon and were collecting the spines of sparklers following the recent Bonfire Night celebrations. The two cousins loved their village and I had noticed they were always willing to tidy up the hedgerows, mow the grass in the churchyard and pick up any litter they spotted in the High Street. Big Dave, at six feet four inches, was a gentle giant while Little Malcolm, although a foot shorter, was one of the toughest Yorkshiremen you could possibly meet. They gave me a friendly wave as I drove by and, not for the first time, I was reminded that Ragley was a special place to live and work.

At school the season had turned. The hanging

baskets outside the front entrance had been stored away for another year and the leaves on the dahlias outside Sally's classroom were fading fast. A dusting of white frost covered the tips of the fleur-de-lis on the school railings and Ruby had salted the steps up to the entrance.

Vera was talking to Anne as I hung up my duffel coat and old college scarf in the little corridor that connected the office with the staff-room.

'Good morning, Mr Sheffield,' she said. 'I'm trying to persuade Anne to come along to the Coffee Shop this evening. The gentleman who is calling into morning assembly to tell us about Halley's Comet is giving a talk there.'

'Thanks anyway, Vera,' said Anne, 'but, believe it or not, I'm in for a treat tonight. John said he would take me out for a meal.' She pondered for a moment. 'That is, if he remembers.'

At 8.45 a.m. I was in the hall preparing for morning assembly and Anne had rehearsed the first bars on the piano of 'When a Knight Won His Spurs'.

Vera hurried through the double doors from the entrance hall and waved in my direction. 'Telephone call, Mr Sheffield,' she called. 'It's the local paper.'

The voice at the other end of the phone sounded high-pitched and unconvincingly cheerful. 'Good morning, Mr Sheffield. Merry here, Features Editor from the *Herald*.'

'Hello,' I said, 'and did you say *Mary?*'

'No, *Merry* as in Christmas.'

'Oh, sorry. What can I do for you?'

'I just need a quote for a piece about the

Morton children coming to Ragley. It's obviously causing a lot of interest and I'm sure you must be delighted.'

I took a deep breath, having learned long ago to be cautious with telephone calls from the press. 'Have you been in touch with the Press Officer in the Education Department at County Hall?' I asked.

'I shall be, Mr Sheffield, but for now we just needed a snappy one-liner from the horse's mouth, so to speak.'

'I'm afraid I've no comment, Mr Merry. You really need the official statement from County Hall.'

'Well, can I simply say that you're pleased your school numbers will rise significantly?'

'No, I'm afraid not.'

'Perhaps if I just say that you'll do your best to give them a good education.' Mr Merry was persistent if nothing else.

'But that could be misinterpreted as a suggestion that's not the case at present.'

'This isn't helping the article, Mr Sheffield, and I could show you in a good light to the general public.'

I glanced up at the clock. 'School will be starting very shortly, Mr Merry, and I need to go now to my classroom. So I'm afraid it's still no comment from me.'

'I have to say I'm disappointed. Goodbye.'

I trudged back to my classroom, hoping I had handled this appropriately and entirely convinced that Mr Merry was definitely not merry any more.

At ten o'clock in my classroom there was a quiet drone of murmured voices as the children read their reading books and, one by one, came out to me to read a few pages. Suddenly, Ryan Halfpenny called out, 'Ford Transit coming up t'drive, Mr Sheffield,' without appearing to look up from his copy of *The Lion, the Witch and the Wardrobe.* Ryan loved his cars.

The distinctive dark-blue van had been adopted by criminals in the 1960s as it had plenty of space and the speed for a quick getaway. However, this one looked the worse for wear. It rattled into the car park sporting the words 'Junk & Disorderly – E. Clifton of Thirkby' in gold letters on the side.

A few minutes later a tall, fair-haired, athletic man in his mid-fifties walked into the school hall accompanied by Vera. 'Mr Sheffield, this is our guest speaker, Mr Clifton from Thirkby ... here to talk about Halley's Comet.'

'Welcome to Ragley,' I said and we shook hands. He was comfortably two or three inches taller than me and wore a stylish, baggy linen suit, appropriately in sky blue.

'Pleased to meet you, Mr Sheffield,' he said. 'I'm Edward Clifton from Thirkby. I sell second-hand furniture and antiques in my shop, Junk & Disorderly ... and please, call me Edward.'

I had taken an immediate liking to this engaging man. 'I'm Jack,' I said.

He smiled. 'Thanks, Jack. I have a few posters to display, if I may.'

'Of course.'

'Don't worry, I'm used to this,' he said with confidence. 'I'll try to bring it to life for the children. It's a fascinating subject.'

I left him to arrange his display of bright pictures of planets and the approaching comet.

When Anne brought her children into the hall she didn't at first see our guest speaker. However, when she turned towards the piano she stopped in her tracks and stared in surprise.

He smiled at her and offered a handshake. 'Have we met before?'

Anne seemed dumbstruck. 'Er, no, perhaps not,' she mumbled and they shook hands while Edward's eyes lingered for a moment on our slim, attractive deputy headteacher.

The assembly was a memorable one and the children were fascinated by our visitor. 'This is our most famous comet,' he said, pointing to the first of his dramatic pictures, 'and it's named after our second Astronomer Royal, Edmond Halley. He was a scientific detective and worked out that the comet would return to Earth about every seventy-five years. It could be seen clearly in 1835 and in 1910, and is about to appear again now, but it will be much brighter next time around in 2061, so some of you will see it *twice* in your lifetime.'

Then he had a group of the younger children standing out at the front holding a selection of spheres to represent our solar system. 'This cosmic iceberg is roughly ten miles long and five miles wide,' he waved towards the older children, 'and here's a new word for you: it's *ellipsoidal* in shape.'

The talk finished all too quickly and I noticed that Anne rarely took her eyes off our handsome stranger.

Pat was on playground duty during morning break, so when I walked into the staff-room Edward Clifton was engaged in conversation with Sally. Anne was sitting quietly to one side, seemingly deep in her own thoughts and, on occasion, looking admiringly at Edward.

He was flicking through a copy of *The Day the Universe Changed* by James Burke and showing Sally some of the pictures.

'All I recall,' said Sally, 'is that the comet is traditionally associated with catastrophe.'

'That's right,' said Edward. 'It was seen in AD 66 just before the fall of Jerusalem, in AD 218 when Emperor Macrinus died and in 1066 when King Harold met his fate at the Battle of Hastings.'

'Well let's hope for a trouble-free experience this time around,' said Vera as she served coffee.

'Thanks for a wonderful assembly, Edward,' I said. 'When did this interest begin?'

'It's always been my hobby since I was a child,' he said, 'and now I'm a Friend of the Royal Astronomical Society.' He pulled out a well-thumbed magazine from his satchel. 'So I read their *Quarterly Journal.* It's fascinating.'

'I've not heard of it,' said Anne.

His blue eyes rested on her. 'It's for members of the public who have an interest in astronomy and geophysics.' There was a pause. 'In fact I could give you a copy if you come along to my talk in the village this evening.'

'Perhaps,' she said.

He looked at his wristwatch. 'Well, thank you, everybody, for the welcome,' he looked at Vera, 'and the excellent coffee ... but I have to go to

York to pick up some furniture.'

When he left I saw Anne walk out to the entrance hall. She was staring after him.

I caught up with Sally. 'What's wrong with Anne?' I asked. 'She seems quiet.'

Sally smiled. 'You've noticed then.'

'What do you mean?' I asked.

'Well, he's an absolute doppelgänger of her favourite man.'

'Favourite man?'

'Yes, David Soul.'

'Oh, you mean the actor from *Starsky & Hutch?*'

'That's the one.'

'Yes, I've seen it,' I said. 'They're American detectives. There's a tall blond-haired one and his little curly-haired friend and they drive around New York in a red Toledo.'

'Impressive, Jack,' said Sally with a grin, 'except it's not New York. It's Los Angeles and, for your information, they call it Bay City in the series, and they drive a Ford Gran Torino.'

'Really?' I said, and not for the first time I wondered how Sally knew all these strange facts.

Meanwhile Anne walked back to her classroom with much to think about.

Out on the playground two five-year-olds, Suzi-Quatro Ricketts and Alison Gawthorpe, wandered over to our new teacher and stared up at her.

'My name's Suzi-Quatro.'

'That's a lovely name,' said Pat with a convincing smile.

'An' mine's Alison.'

'That's a lovely name as well.'

Suzi-Quatro had already learned the direct

approach in her young life. 'What's your first name, Miss?'

'It's Pat.'

'Our dog's called Pat,' contributed Alison.

'Oh,' said Pat.

Suzi-Quatro considered this for a moment. 'Pat?... That's a great name for a dog.'

They wandered off to watch the older girls skipping while Pat pondered on the innocence of youth.

Across the village green on the other side of the High Street Nora Pratt was sitting behind the counter in her Coffee Shop and reading her *Woman's Own.* She was studying an advertisement for *Ambrose Wilson, Britain's No. 1 Corsetry Catalogue* that boasted 'all the benefits of the right foundation garments'. Then she glanced down at her plump figure, sighed and turned the page. Her horoscope caught her eye. It read, 'Distant places could play a big part in your love life. This could be the time to reorganize your affairs.'

It was then she thought about her boyfriend, Tyrone, who had just returned from 'a distant place'. He had been all the way to Hull to attend a training day entitled 'The Introduction of Bar Codes in the World of Packaging'. Tyrone Crabtree was a short, balding man with a Bobby Charlton comb-over. Now in his fifties, he had risen to become the manager in charge of cardboard boxes at the local chocolate factory. Nora was proud of his achievements and thought that perhaps it was time to go out with him every Saturday instead of once each month.

She wondered if Tyrone would be coming to the shop tonight and looked once again at the large poster in the window that read:

HALLEY'S COMET IS COMING!
A Talk by Local Astronomer, Edward Clifton
Friday, 8 November at 7.30 p.m.
in the Coffee Shop
Admission 50p including coffee and a jam doughnut
Reserve your seat to avoid disappointment

Nora's assistant, Dorothy, had taken delivery of some cheap doughnuts and was stacking them in what she considered to be an attractive pyramid.

'So who is 'e, Nora?' asked Dorothy.

''E studies astwology,' said Nora, who had never quite managed to pronounce the letter 'R'.

'Ah think ah'll tell 'im that ah'm an Aquarian,' said Dorothy, fiddling with her chunky signs-of-the-zodiac bracelet. 'An' it were lucky that ah married my Malcolm, cos 'e's a Gemini an' that makes us a perfect match.' Dorothy, the five-foot-eleven-inch would-be model with four-inch heels and peroxide-blonde hair, had married our five-foot-four-inch refuse collector just over a year ago and they were blissfully happy living above the Coffee Shop.

'That's a good idea, Dowothy,' said Nora, 'an' ah'll ask 'im about my Tywone as well.' In recent months Tyrone had become the man of Nora's dreams.

At the end of school Stacey Bryant and Lucy Eckersley were in excited conversation.

'Stacey's coming to our house for tea, Mr Sheffield,' said Lucy.

'And we're going to watch *Grange Hill* at ten past five,' added the precise Stacey.

'And we're a bit worried about Zammo,' confided Lucy.

'Yes, Mr Sheffield,' confirmed Stacey, 'he can't seem to do anything right.'

I didn't know who Zammo was ... but I sympathized with his predicament.

When their shift was over, Big Dave and Little Malcolm called into the Coffee Shop for a mug of tea before they returned their bin wagon to the depot.

'Ah've got dry 'air, Malcolm,' said Dorothy, lifting a handful of her back-combed, peroxide-blonde hair and pointing to an article in Nora's *Woman's Own*. 'It says 'ere ah'm short o' lanolin.'

Malcolm nodded sympathetically and carried two huge mugs of milky sweet tea back to the table.

'What's wrong wi' your Dorothy?' asked Big Dave. 'She's gorra face like a wet weekend.'

'Dunno, Dave,' said Malcolm, shaking his head and slurping the hot tea. 'Summat t'do wi' linoleum.'

'Tell 'er we've got some spare carpet offcuts that Mrs Dudley-Palmer chucked out. It's proper Axminster.'

'Thanks, Dave,' said Little Malcolm. It was another problem solved in a busy life.

After school I was sitting at my desk when the telephone rang. It was Beth.

'I'll probably be home first this evening,' she said. 'I've only got a brief meeting with the infants staff before I leave.'

'Fine, I'll be home by six,' I said, 'and there's a talk in the Coffee Shop tonight. It's about Halley's Comet.'

'That's interesting,' she said. 'My top juniors are doing a project on it.'

'Well, why don't you go?' I suggested. 'Vera said she's going with Anne and Sally.'

'It would be good to catch up,' she said. 'Yes, I think I will.'

At six o'clock John Grainger was busy with his workbench project in the garage. It was a huge construction that completely dominated the far wall and Anne stared at it in dismay. It seemed to sum up their life together. Standing on its eight four-inch-square sturdy legs it was a reflection of her husband – strong, functional but, ultimately, utterly boring.

'So when are we going out?' she asked.

'I need to finish this,' replied John without looking up. 'The glue hasn't set yet.'

Anne noticed he had become a man with a constant sprinkle of sawdust in his curly unkempt beard.

'I thought we were going for a meal,' she said, thinking that his fading suit in the wardrobe was for weddings and funerals only, but never for a surprise meal at the Dean Court Hotel in York.

'Sorry, not tonight,' he said. 'Too busy.'

At Bilbo Cottage, by the time I had put John to bed and washed up the plates after our sausage and mash evening meal, Beth had left for Ragley and I settled down with the *Radio Times.*

Blankety Blank with Les Dawson was about to start, followed by *Dynasty* at ten past eight. Apparently the relationship between Krystle and Blake, played by Linda Evans and John Forsythe, was destined to take a nosedive. Meanwhile, Joan Collins as the scheming Alexis was sure to encourage the rift.

Instead I selected a good book. *Far from the Madding Crowd* seemed an appropriate novel in the sanctuary of our home.

On The Crescent, meanwhile, life wasn't so relaxed.

'Halley's Comet?' queried John, a little uncertain of the pronunciation.

'Yes, *Halley*,' repeated Anne. 'Rhymes with *valley.* It's the famous comet about to come into view again after seventy-five years.'

'Oh, that one,' said John. 'It was mentioned on the news.'

'Well there's a talk in the Coffee Shop this evening,' said Anne.

John was writing in a dun-coloured notebook. 'Dome-headed screws,' he murmured to himself.

'I'm going now,' said Anne, buttoning up her coat.

John didn't look up. 'Fine,' he said absent-mindedly and continued with his list. 'Two feet of half-inch dowelling...'

Anne walked out, relieved to breathe in the cold night air.

The Coffee Shop was full, mainly with the ladies of Ragley village. Tea had been served along with somewhat dubious jam doughnuts and Edward Clifton had captivated his audience.

'Halley first observed the comet in 1680,' he told them, 'and predicted it would return in 1759 ... and it did.'

Anne was sitting alongside Vera, Beth and Sally and they nodded in appreciation.

'He was a remarkable man,' continued Edward, 'and his inventions in the seventeenth century also included the diving bell.'

At the end he was surrounded by adoring women.

Beth, Vera, Sally and Anne were chatting near the door when Edward was about to leave and they walked out together on to the frosty pavement. His car was parked across the road outside the village hall and, as he put his satchel in the boot he called out, 'Would you ladies like to join me for a nightcap?' and gestured up the High Street towards the welcoming orange lights outside The Royal Oak.

'I have to get back home,' said Vera, 'but thank you all the same.'

Beth looked at her wristwatch. 'Yes, I ought to go – early start tomorrow.'

Sally looked at Anne. 'I could stay a while,' she said quietly to her colleague.

'And what about you, Sally ... and Anne?' called Edward.

'Come on,' whispered Sally. 'He's an interesting man.'

Anne paused. It was just a thread, a strip of tarmac between them. She stepped off the kerb and walked confidently towards Edward. Under the glow of the street lamp he was smiling.

Sally was keen to know Edward's background and it proved to be an interesting story. He was born in 1929 in Napier, New Zealand, and as a small child had survived the terrible earthquake of 1931. It had measured 7.8 on the Richter scale and changed the landscape dramatically, with a huge area of sea bed becoming dry land and the land on which Napier stood being raised by an astonishing eight feet. When the earthquake struck, Edward's sister had lifted him from his cot seconds before it was crushed by falling masonry. There was sadness in his voice as he recounted that his mother, a nurse, had perished along with other hospital staff in the nurses' building. The steel reinforcement rods had been removed prior to construction to save costs. The city was rebuilt in the style of Santa Barbara to become the art deco centre of the world, but before then Edward's father had brought him and his sister to England to begin a new life.

'So that's my story,' he said.

Outside they paused under the black velvet sky. Anne shivered. 'I had better get home.'

'Shall I drop you off?' offered Sally.

'Please ... allow me,' said Edward.

'I live on The Crescent off the Easington Road,' said Anne.

'That's on my way,' he said.

'Well, thank you, that's very kind,' she replied.

Sally said goodnight and Anne and Edward walked back down the High Street as a bitter wind suddenly blew. 'Sorry, Anne, I wasn't thinking. You must be cold.' He slipped off his winter coat and draped it carefully over her shoulders. Anne held it close, feeling the rough fabric and the warmth of his body as it permeated through to her skin.

As they drove back to The Crescent, she looked at his large hands gripping the steering wheel. There was no wedding ring.

Her house was in darkness when they pulled up outside. Edward got out, opened the passenger door and for a brief moment they stood facing each other.

'So it's coming back again,' said Anne.

'Yes, and in Anglo Saxon chronicles it was referred to as "a source of tears".'

'That sounds sad,' she said.

Edward smiled and stared into the light of an ethereal sky. 'The mystery of the stars and planets is nothing when compared to life itself,' he said softly.

Anne said nothing. She merely drank in the words of this strange but appealing man.

Inside the house all was silent and she crept quietly into the bedroom where John lay asleep. She reflected that the two men were like the sun and the moon, like fire and ice. With Edward, for a brief time, she had bathed in his warmth, but here with John each night she lay cold and still. The young, clean-shaven and vigorous man she had married many years ago had gone now. There was no spark, no excitement.

As she undressed she recalled the gentle touch of Edward's fingertips on her collar and his cool appraisal of her slim figure. She opened her wardrobe and on impulse slipped on her favourite black nightdress. As she smoothed the silky fabric over her hips she thought of Edward.

The devil had come to call and, as the church bells of St Mary's chimed out the hour, she gave a whimsical smile at her sinful thoughts.

Chapter Six

Behind Closed Doors

Mrs Pringle began practice for the school Nativity play. A response was sent to County Hall following their request to fill the vacant role of local authority governor. Ms Brookside organized a staff night out at the Odeon Cinema in York.

Extract from the Ragley School Logbook:
Friday, 6 December 1985

It was Friday, 6 December and a severe frost crusted the rutted back road to Ragley village. Beyond the frozen hedgerows the bare forests on the distant hills had lost their colour and their skeletal leaves had fallen. In the harsh wind the first flakes of snow were drifting down from a gun-metal sky and they tapped gently against my windscreen, a reminder of the harsh winter weather that was about to descend on the high moors of North Yorkshire.

The bitter cold had frozen the surface of the pond on the village green but this did not seem to deter the early-morning brigade. They were in evidence as I drove slowly up the High Street. Deke Ramsbottom was perched on a noisy tractor heading up towards the Morton Road, while Heathcliffe Earnshaw was delivering the last of his morning papers before returning his canvas bag to Prudence Golightly. Ernie and Rodney Morgetroyd trundled past on their electric milk float and the postman, Ted 'Postie' Postlethwaite, gave me a wave as he drew close to completing his first round of the day. However, as he pushed each package and envelope through each letter-box, little did he know the impact today's correspondence would have on his customers.

Behind the closed doors of Ragley a few surprises were in store.

'Don't Break My Heart' by UB40 was playing on my car radio as I turned right at the top of the High Street and drove through the school gate. A group of children had been dropped off by their working mothers and, unperturbed by the biting wind, lined up like a guard of honour to greet my Morris Minor Traveller as it crunched over the cobbled drive.

When I walked from the car park Ruby was sweeping the steps in the entrance porch. 'Morning, Ruby,' I yelled above the wind.

'G'morning, Mr Sheffield,' she replied. 'A bit parky this mornin'.' Ruby's only concession to this freezing day was a headscarf double-knotted beneath her chin. She was made of strong stuff.

Vera was already busy behind her desk as I hung up my coat and scarf. She opened the last of the morning's post and gasped.

'What is it, Vera?' I asked.

'Oh no,' she said. All colour had left her cheeks as she scanned the official-looking letter with the crest of County Hall.

'It's from the School Governor Services Department at County Hall, Mr Sheffield. It says that they note from our records that, following the retirement of our local authority governor, Ragley-on-the-Forest Church of England Primary School does not have its full complement on its governing body.'

'That's correct,' I said. 'We have a vacancy following the retirement of Albert Jenkins.'

Vera shook her head. 'But you won't believe what follows. It goes on to say they would like to recommend the services of *Mr Stanley Coe* to fill this position, as they understand from his application that he is an active member of the local community and has significant previous experience in the role of a governor. It requests a reply by thirteenth December.'

'They can have it now,' I said. 'It's NO!'

Vera sighed. 'Thinking back, we didn't tell them the reason for him leaving in the first place.'

I recalled the unpleasant circumstances towards the end of my first year at Ragley when Stanley Coe had caused nothing but trouble. 'Yes, Vera, you're right. It was all very sudden as I remember.'

Stan Coe, local pig farmer and serial bully, had been *persuaded* to resign back in 1978 and we were all relieved when he had departed.

'It's just like the man to try to get back on a governing body,' said Vera. She scanned the letter again and looked thoughtful. 'I presume this letter will have gone to many schools in the area. As we know, governors come and go.'

I looked out of the window. A little white Austin A40 had pulled into the car park. Joseph had arrived to take his weekly Bible stories lesson.

'Let's see what Joseph says,' I said.

Vera held up another envelope with a Northallerton postmark. 'This is addressed to Joseph as chair of governors. It's probably the same letter.'

Joseph sensed the tension as soon as he walked into the office and we explained our concern. He opened his letter and sighed. 'Yes, it's the same as yours,' he said.

'And what is your response, Joseph?' asked Vera, sounding very much like the big sister.

'Well, I suppose there's not a great deal we can do about it,' said Joseph rather lamely. 'Maybe his absence from our governing body will have taught him a lesson and he will have realized that bullying at any level does not pay.'

'I very much doubt that,' replied Vera.

Joseph shook his saintly head. 'Well, I would hate to show hard feelings after all these years. Perhaps he deserves a second chance.'

'Absolutely not, Joseph,' said Vera firmly.

'Oh dear,' sighed Joseph and looked at me for help.

'Joseph,' I said quietly, 'this man causes trouble

wherever he goes. I don't mind a governor who challenges the work of the school but we need *support* as well. I can't see Stan Coe providing that. We need to stand firm on this. He was a notorious bully and that's why we dispensed with his services as a governor – although Governor Services were not made aware of this at the time.'

'I have to agree,' said Vera.

Joseph was clearly taken aback and looked at his sister in surprise. 'I see. Well, in that case I'll reply to say he is not an acceptable candidate for the post of governor given previous issues. Leave it with me.'

'Thank you,' I said.

Vera patted her brother's sleeve affectionately. 'Don't forget, you're leading assembly this morning, Joseph.' She gave him an encouraging smile.

Joseph was holding a few pages of crumpled notes and he looked down at them. 'Yes, I know,' he said cautiously.

'Well,' said Vera, 'now that we've decided what to do with that despicable man, what's your theme?'

'Love thy neighbour,' said Joseph with a sigh and walked out to the assembly hall.

Vera gave me a knowing stare. 'Oh dear,' she murmured as she returned to her dinner-money register.

At nine o'clock the bell rang to announce the start of the school day. Ruby packed away her mop and galvanized bucket and tapped on the door of the office.

'Come in,' called Vera.

Ruby walked in. 'It's me, Mrs F,' she said. 'Ah

need some advice.'

'Of course, Ruby,' replied Vera. 'How can I help?'

Ruby handed over a card. 'Ah got this in t'post this morning an' ah'm wond'ring what t'do.'

It was an invitation from George Dainty for Ruby to accompany him to the Yorkshire Fish Fryers' Christmas Lunch at the Queen's Hotel in Leeds.

'Mr Dainty is a true gentleman, Ruby, and this is a kind invitation.'

Ruby's cheeks were flushed. 'Y'don't think it's all a bit too soon after my Ronnie?'

'Not at all,' said Vera.

'Ah don't know what m'children would think.'

'Talk to them about it and let them know how you feel.'

Ruby considered this and nodded. 'Y'right, Mrs F, ah'll do jus' that.'

'You deserve some happiness,' said Vera, 'and here's a wonderful opportunity.'

'Thank you,' said Ruby. 'Ah'll look out a nice dress.'

'Good idea, and you'll enjoy going to Leeds.'

'An' there might be a chance t'look round some posh shops. There's something ah'd really like f'Christmas.'

'What's that?' asked Vera.

'A 'lectric deep-fat fryer,' said Ruby.

Vera smiled. 'An excellent choice,' she said and Ruby went out to hang up her overall.

Sally was using the morning assembly to practise a few carols in preparation for our fast-approaching Christmas Nativity. She propped her songbook, *Carol, Gaily Carol,* on her music stand, opened it to number 9 and the choir and recorders launched into 'Baby Jesus, Sleeping Softly'.

Nine-year-old Rosie Appleby, following her starring role last year on television, was due to reprise 'Silent Night', accompanied by an ex-pupil, thirteen-year-old Elisabeth Amelia Dudley-Palmer, on her violin. Since commencing her secondary education at the Time School for Girls in York, Elisabeth had excelled in her music lessons and, as her school was due to close for the Christmas holiday a day before Ragley School, she was free to support.

Expectations were always high in the village for this annual production and Anne, as ever, did her best to encourage the youngest children in our school to enjoy the experience.

Meanwhile, in Class 2, Joseph was keen to start his lesson, but he was surrounded by six- and seven-year-olds who wanted to share their news.

'I'm six now, Mr Evans,' announced Julie Tricklebank.

'That's good,' said Joseph.

Julie smiled and nodded, pleased this strange man with his collar the wrong way round was taking interest. 'It's the oldest I've ever been,' she added.

'Yes, I suppose it would be,' agreed Joseph. Julie was clutching her library book about dinosaurs.

'That's an interesting book,' said Joseph.

Julie looked thoughtfully at the bright cover with a picture of a smiling stegosaurus. 'Do dinosaurs have birthdays, Mr Evans?'

'I suppose they do,' replied a bewildered Joseph.

Julie smiled again, then paused and looked up curiously at our friendly vicar. 'Mr Evans,' she said.

'Yes?'

'Why has your hair slipped backwards?'

Joseph stroked his balding pate. 'I suppose it just happens to some people.'

'Well, never mind. Jesus will make it better.'

Sam Whittaker looked up with a puzzled frown. 'Did Jesus have a first name, Mr Evans?'

Joseph sighed and, once again, he marvelled about the secret garden that was the world of young children.

At morning break Pat Brookside was busy. She had a list of names attached to a clipboard.

'So is everyone all right for this evening,' she asked, 'before I make the block booking?' Pat had adopted the role of person in charge of staff social events and tonight staff and their partners had been invited to an evening at the Odeon Cinema in York.

'Well, John took some persuading,' said Anne, 'but I'm sure he will be there.'

Vera turned to Pat. 'Is your young man coming?'

'Yes, David has promised to meet us outside after his conference in York.'

Vera smiled. She was looking forward to meeting the young doctor.

Sally was on playground duty, so Pat slipped on her coat and walked out to confirm arrangements with her.

'Yes, Colin's coming,' Sally said, 'and my mother

is coming round to look after our daughter, Grace.' Pat ticked off their names.

Around them, children, impervious to the cold, were playing happily, although not quite everyone had entered the Christmas spirit.

Alison Gawthorpe was playing with Tracey Higginbottom when Madonna Fazackerly strode up to the infant with the blonde ringlets. 'What's your name?' she asked.

'Alison,' said the little girl.

'Alison ... y'mean like Wonderland?' said Madonna.

'Wonderland?'

'Yeah, y'know, Alice in Wonderland.'

'No, ah'm jus' Alison.'

Madonna tried another tack. 'Your big sister, Michelle, says you 'aven't got any stairs in your 'ouse.'

'No, we live in a bungalow,' said Alison. 'There's no upstairs.'

'Your mam and dad mus' be poor then,' said Madonna unkindly and walked off.

By the shelter of the school wall a group of small girls wanted to skip. Mary Scrimshaw was talking to Patience Crapper while she unravelled a skipping rope for her.

'We've been doing maths this morning,' said ten-year-old Mary proudly, 'and I'm on the blue box.'

Our School Mathematics Project workcards were graded into coloured boxes and the children gradually progressed through the course depending on their ability. By the time they reached my class the range of ability was already very wide, with the most able children already two years ahead of many in their age group.

Patience Crapper wasn't particularly interested in mathematics. She preferred talking about her collection of Barbie dolls. 'Ah don't like maths,' she said.

'I'm doing fractions,' said Mary as she untied the final knot.

Patience brightened up at this news. 'My mummy fell and she 'ad a fraction in 'er leg,' she said.

Mary decided to give up on this conversation and let Patience concentrate on winding the skipping rope.

Mandy Kerslake was talking to her friend Zoe Book in the shelter of the boiler-house doors when Ted Coggins approached. He looked at Mandy as if she had landed from another planet. 'Hayley Spraggon says you were *adopted,* Mandy,' he said. 'What does that mean?'

Mandy was a sensitive little girl and she thought for a moment. 'Well, I suppose it means I have two mummys and I live with one of them ... but my mummy says I grew in her heart and not in her tummy.'

Ted had no idea what she was talking about and wandered off to find a boy to talk to who made some sense.

After Ryan Halfpenny had rung the bell to announce the end of morning break, little Alfie Spraggon was panting hard as he returned to Anne's classroom and sat down.

'Are you all right, Alfie?' asked Anne. 'You sound out of breath.'

Alfie looked puzzled. 'No, Miss, ah've got a lot more.'

I should know better by now, thought Anne, and picked up her flashcards of simple words.

Meanwhile, on the High Street the post delivered by Ted Postlethwaite was beginning to have an effect. In the butcher's shop Old Tommy Piercy was looking glum. He had received a letter from his sister in Thirkby announcing she intended to visit her younger brother. He was discussing the problem with his grandson.

'What's she like?' asked Young Tommy.

'Well ... she's no oil painting.'

'No, ah meant 'er personality.'

'Personality?' repeated Old Tommy, looking puzzled. 'She 'asn't got one.'

Next door in the village Pharmacy, the morning post had been received with more enthusiasm. Eugene Scrimshaw was excited. His order for a new *Star Trek* uniform had been confirmed and payment received. He had converted his loft to resemble the flight deck of the Starship *Enterprise.* All that remained was to explain to his wife why it was important to look the part when acting out his fantasies as a Starship warrior.

He wasn't confident Peggy would understand.

Further up the High Street in the Hardware Emporium, Timothy Pratt was equally thrilled. In the post was a letter from his dear friend, Walter Crapper. Walter, a local accountant and, like Timothy, a single man, wanted to prepare a special Christmas dinner as described by Delia Smith. Timothy decided to reply saying he would be delighted to be Walter's guest and promised to bring his old Meccano set for an after-dinner entertainment.

By the end of the school day the winter sun was setting, flame red in the western sky, and the children trudged home excited by the thoughts of a fresh snowfall and a weekend of winter sports.

In the General Stores Prudence hadn't received a letter, but there was one she would read anyway. It was one she read each evening before she went to bed.

She was about to serve her last customer of the day and Ted Coggins had a difficult decision to make. He had been given some money for his birthday by a visiting aunt and had purchased a Curly Wurly, but he still had a few pence left over. On the bottom shelf of Miss Golightly's glass case there was a display of many of his favourites. Ted stared in wonder at the Rainbow Drops, Aniseed Balls, Love Hearts, Liquorice Torpedoes, Sherbet Dip Dabs, Gobstoppers, Candy Cigarettes and Black Jacks. He sighed and took a deep breath. 'Two ounces of Aniseed Balls, please, Miss Golightly.' *If you suck them slow they will last for ever,* he thought.

'And how old are you now, Ted?' asked Prudence as she passed over the bag of Aniseed Balls after adding a few extra for good luck.

'I'm nine, Miss Golightly,' said Ted.

'I can remember being nine,' said Prudence wistfully.

'My nana says when people get old they die,' volunteered Ted.

'That's right,' said Prudence, 'they do.'

'Are you old?' asked Ted.

'Yes, I'm old compared to you.'

Ted nodded. 'Yes, y'definitely look old.'

'Really?' asked Prudence.

Ted smiled, slipped an Aniseed Ball into his mouth and walked out, leaving Prudence to reflect on children's honesty.

Betty Buttle and Margery Ackroyd were standing outside the village hall when Petula Dudley-Palmer emerged from Diane's Hair Salon and walked to her car.

'She's a reight bossy boots is that one,' commented Betty.

'Look at 'er,' said Margery, 'done up like a dog's dinner.'

'Mark my words,' declared Betty with authority, 'she knows which side 'er bread's buttered does that one.'

'Well she married a man wi' plenty o' brass,' added Margery.

'An' jus' look at that 'ouse she lives in,' said Betty, 'all done out like a stately 'ome, wi' posh curtains an' fruit in bowls when there's no one poorly.'

'Mind you,' sighed Margery, 'mus' be nice t'be rich.'

'But bein' rich doesn't stop same problems as t'likes o' us, Margery,' said Betty. 'Y'know – 'usbands wi' wand'rin' eyes.'

Amelia Duff had closed up the Post Office and turned at last to her morning's post. She was pleased that the brochure from her Book of the Month Club had arrived. She thought Geoffrey Smith's *World of Flowers* would be an ideal gift for her lover, Ted 'Postie' Postlethwaite. However, it was *The Book of Love and Sex* and *The Complete Book of Sensual Massage* that caught her eye ... and she smiled.

On the Morton Road, in her state-of-the-art kitchen, Petula Dudley-Palmer was unwrapping a parcel. It was her catalogue order, a sapphire-blue paisley-print dress with long sleeves and white lacy collar, and she wondered when would be a good time to wear it.

She settled down to read her *Woman's Weekly* and an advertisement for Effico Tonic attracted her attention. Apparently it was a remedy for that 'tired, listless, run-down feeling' and Petula made a note to buy some. Then, after copying down a recipe for a 'Yorkshire Treacle Tart', she began to read a short story about love the 'second time around'. It was said to be 'lovelier than the first time' and Petula wondered if that might be true.

She heard a car pull up outside and the security lights lit up the driveway. Her husband, Geoffrey, had recently celebrated his executive status by spending almost £15,000 on yet another new car, a 1984 'A' Porsche 944 in black with a sun-roof and stereo. She guessed it was to impress his secretary.

Petula surveyed the material riches that surrounded her and remembered her life when she was a child in Manchester. 'Just to think,' she said out loud, 'I was the girl who queued for broken biscuits.'

Prudence Golightly had closed her General

Stores and was sitting in the back room. She held a letter in her hands, but not one that had been delivered that morning.

The faded envelope had a postmark dated forty-five years ago in 1940. Since then, Jeremy's last letter had held a special place in her heart. The brave young Spitfire pilot had not returned to Prudence and behind the closed door of the General Stores it was a time to remember spent promises and misty memories.

On my way home I collected Natasha Smith from Ruby's house. She had agreed to look after John while Beth and I went to the cinema. When we arrived at Bilbo Cottage Beth was preparing some home-made leek and potato soup while skimming through the Habitat brochure. There was a photograph of a large wooden train at £10.95 and Beth circled the order number.

At 6.30 p.m. we drove into York, parked near Micklegate and walked to the cinema. Pat had arranged for us all to gather in the foyer before the film and it was good to relax together. I met Pat's partner, David, and learned much about his busy life as a young general practitioner. Everyone had arrived apart from John Grainger. Anne explained that he was 'busy'.

The film, *A Room with a View* from the novel by E. M. Forster, was excellent and everyone appeared to enjoy their night out. For me the plot was fascinating. Lucy Honeychurch, played by Helena Bonham Carter, was on holiday in Italy with her cousin and chaperone Charlotte Bartlett. Charlotte, played by Maggie Smith, was manipulative, conventionally English and reminded me of my mother-in-law, Diane. Her younger cousin was carefree and free-spirited and reminiscent of Beth's sister, Laura. I kept these thoughts to myself while Beth rested her head on my shoulder.

At the end Vera announced to everyone that Judi Dench, Daniel Day-Lewis and Denholm Elliott were superb in their roles and English actors were the best in the world. The patriotic Rupert agreed wholeheartedly.

Vera was also impressed with Pat's partner, David the young doctor, who was polite, cheerful and engaging. 'You make a lovely couple, my dear,' she told Pat as we parted to make our way home.

Colin and Sally Pringle dropped off Anne on The Crescent and, once again, the house no longer felt like a home as she stepped inside and closed the door behind her.

John was sitting in the lounge. 'I'm home,' she said.

'Did you have a good time?' he called out.

'Yes, thanks,' said Anne. 'Would you like a hot drink?'

'Yes, please,' replied John.

While Anne took off her coat in the hallway she reflected on her life. Youth was now a mere memory. The brief passion she had experienced long ago with John Grainger, the handsome woodcarver, was long past. When they had first met the world had seemed a smaller, more intimate place.

As she stared into the mirror an attractive woman looked back at her. Her body was still firm and shapely and she wondered if there ought to be more to her life. Being a teacher at

Ragley School was her vocation and she loved the children in her care. Each day was different and brought fresh challenges. It was just that, when she arrived home and heard John enthuse about his latest DIY project, she felt tired of the *routine* of it all. *Excitement* was reserved for teaching a child to read or helping a five-year-old write his first sentence. Here in her home there was no joy and she realized that she wanted more ... before it was too late.

Anne shivered. Suddenly she felt cold. It was as if she had been standing in the shadows for too long.

As she walked into the kitchen she thought of Edward Clifton. He had called into school with some photographs of the famous comet. However, he had explained that owing to poor visibility the sightings were not spectacular. When Anne was alone in the entrance hall he asked if she might be able to visit his antique shop in Thirkby.

She blinked away a few tears as she stirred two mugs of Ovaltine for their usual night-time drink. Her heart was cool and there were times when her very soul felt shuttered and bare. She carried the mugs into the lounge. In an hour they would both be dreaming ... but she would be awake.

It was late by the time I had driven Natasha back to Ragley and returned home. She was looking forward to a weekend of part-time hairdressing, then a Saturday evening watching Cilla Black's new show, *Blind Date,* and wishing it was her selecting the man of her dreams.

Snow was falling, covering the villages of North

Yorkshire in a cloak of silence. Beth was in her dressing gown and had prepared hot milky bed-time drinks. We sat quietly for a while.

'What's on your mind?' she asked.

'It's late,' I said.

'Come on, I know there's something.'

'Well, there was a certain letter in today's post ... it got me thinking.'

'Go on.'

'County Hall requested we take Stan Coe on to our governing body.'

Beth put down her mug and looked aghast. 'I hope you said no.'

I nodded. 'Yes, Vera sent a letter straight back.'

'And?'

I smiled. Beth was so perceptive. She knew me so well.

'It made me reassess what I really want.'

'Yes?'

'Well, village politics can be wearing sometimes. Perhaps I should reconsider my professional future.'

Beth squeezed my hand. 'I understand ... but it's late,' she said. 'Let's discuss it over the week-end.'

She picked up the two mugs and carried them into the kitchen while I stared at the dying embers of the log fire. I sensed my private thoughts would soon become public knowledge. Ragley village was a small community and secrets did not remain hidden for long.

Chapter Seven

A Ragley Christmas

School closed today for the Christmas holiday, with 96 children on roll and will reopen for the spring term on Monday, 6 January 1986. Parents and friends of school attended the Christmas carol service and all children took part in the afternoon Christmas party. The school choir and children from Class 1 will perform at the Christmas Crib Service at St Mary's Church on Sunday afternoon, 22 December.

Extract from the Ragley School Logbook:
Friday, 20 December 1985

I awoke to a dawn of silence and light. Overnight snow had covered the vast plain of York and left behind a stark and desolate world. It was Friday, 20 December, the last day of the autumn term, and a Ragley Christmas beckoned.

At eight o'clock the sun was rising, gilding the distant hills and bringing light to Ragley High Street. On my way to school I called into the General Stores, where Prudence Golightly was putting the final touches to Jeremy Bear's Christmas outfit. His cardboard sleigh had been covered in kitchen foil.

'Good morning, Mr Sheffield,' said the tiny shopkeeper from the top step behind the counter, where she was on a level with me.

‘A dozen mince pies for the staff-room please, Miss Golightly.’

‘Freshly made,’ said Prudence as she filled a box with the festive pastries.

‘And a happy Christmas, Jeremy,’ I added.

‘He’s so excited,’ said Prudence, looking lovingly at the bear and adjusting the collar of his red shirt. ‘He has asked Santa for some new wellingtons and a warm cardigan.’

Twelve-year-old Jimmy Poole, an ex-pupil of mine, was behind me in the queue. His Yorkshire terrier, Scargill, was outside, tied up to the frame of his BMX bicycle. Jimmy still had his lisp. ‘Ah’ve asked for a Tharp Thientific Calculator for Chrithmath, Mr Theffield,’ he said.

‘Well I hope Santa visits your house, Jimmy.’

‘Tho do I,’ said Jimmy with a knowing smile.

I paid for the mince pies and collected my newspaper. The headlines confirmed that the spirit of Christmas did not extend to Defence Secretary Michael Heseltine. He was at loggerheads with Margaret Thatcher over the future of the Westland helicopter firm. Likewise, Environment Secretary Kenneth Baker was under fire following the new rates support group scheme to bring local government expenditure under control.

When I walked into the entrance lobby Ruby hurried from the hall carrying an empty cardboard box. She had clearly been busy.

‘Ah’ve ’ung up all m’presents on t’tree, Mr Sheffield,’ she said.

It was a tradition for Ruby to purchase a small gift for every child in the school, even though she could ill afford them. She had wrapped a packet of sweets in North Yorkshire County Council tissue paper and hung each gift on our Christmas tree, which dominated the corner of the school hall.

'Well done, Ruby,' I said. 'It's really kind of you.'

'It's a special time for all t'kiddies,' she said. 'They're only young once.' She looked back at the Christmas tree. 'An' y'can't beat a Ragley Christmas.'

By half past eight Pat was helping Anne in her classroom. A rehearsal for the forthcoming Nativity in church on Sunday had been arranged. Pat was repairing a plywood manger while Anne was attaching a large cardboard star to a bamboo cane. Sally was in the school hall setting up music stands for morning assembly, so I went into the office to check on the morning post.

Vera was busy with two new parents and their eight-year-old daughter, Katie Parrish. Like her mother, the young girl was tall and fair-haired. Her parents, both lecturers in York, had just moved into a large cottage on the Easington Road. Mrs Parrish had telephoned earlier in the week to ask if Katie could get to know Ragley school prior to starting full-time in January.

The meeting went smoothly, apart from the father making it clear he was in a hurry. He appeared to be dressed for a gunfight at the O.K. Corral, with a brown suede waistcoat over a collarless shirt and a long black coat that swirled around his Cuban-heeled boots. His long hair had a centre parting. However, Mrs Parrish was supportive and very grateful that Katie had the opportunity to settle in.

'We would like to thank you, Mr Sheffield,' she

said, with a stern look towards her husband, who was on his way out. She turned to Vera. 'We also appreciate your support, Mrs Forbes-Kitchener, especially on such a busy day for you.'

Vera smiled at Mrs Parrish, then studied her anxious husband for a brief moment. 'We're very proud of Ragley School,' she said, 'and we shall make Katie welcome in her new class.'

'We have an exciting day in store,' I said, 'with a carol service this morning and a party this afternoon.'

Mrs Parrish looked relieved and I followed her out. They had arrived in separate cars and her husband had already lit a cigarette and roared off towards York. We stood together for a moment and she gave me a tired smile. She was a beautiful woman with porcelain skin, but the lines around her eyes hinted at stressful times. We shook hands and then she was gone.

I decided to stand by the school gate and welcome the parents who were coming in to support the preparations for the Nativity. Traditionally the youngest children in Ragley School took part in Sunday's Crib Service at St Mary's Church and Anne was keen to have a brief rehearsal immediately after registration. Parents were coming in carrying rolled-up curtains, paper crowns, spare tea towels and sandals. The costumes for our Nativity were arriving in abundance and I smiled at their enthusiasm.

It was Christmas, the time of goodwill to all men, but in Ragley village there were exceptions. A car horn shattered the peace. Lollipop Lil was preventing Stan Coe's mud-splattered Land

Rover from continuing up the High Street by standing on her zebra crossing and making him wait a little longer.

''Urry up, y'useless woman,' yelled Stan.

'Stop y'grizzling, Stan Coe,' shouted Lil.

Some things didn't change.

As I walked back into school, blue tits were pecking at the foil tops of the milk bottles in the crate outside the front entrance and Anne's classroom was a hive of activity.

Morning assembly was earlier than usual, as the children in my class had to prepare the 'stage' for our eleven o'clock carol service. This comprised a few stage blocks on which the children in Sally's orchestra and choir would gather.

Joseph had called in to take the assembly and, after telling the wonderful story of the Nativity, he tried to recap. 'So, think back to the story. Why did Joseph and Mary take Jesus to Bethlehem?'

Several hands shot into the air. Unfortunately he chose Billy Ricketts.

'Because they couldn't get a babysitter,' said Billy.

Joseph sighed deeply as the bell rang for morning playtime.

In the staff-room Vera was standing by the window watching the children at play. 'The new girl looks happy,' she said.

In Class 3 Sally had given Katie Parrish a seat next to Mandy Sedgewick and they had struck up a friendship. The two girls took off suddenly to make first footprints on the snowy playing field. Katie ran with the confidence of youth and moved with the grace of a deer in the forest. On this day life stretched out before her and, like the other eight-year-olds in Sally's class, she thought she would live for ever ... but changes were coming. A Christmas she would remember always was just around the corner and, in the years to come, she would recall it with sadness. The safe cocoon of her world was about to change. However, on this winter morning all was well and a day of carols and party games awaited this gentle and innocent girl.

The carol service was a success, with parents and grandparents filling the hall. We sang traditional carols and Sally's choir and orchestra performed well. However, the highlight was undoubtedly the reprise of 'Silent Night' by nine-year-old Rosie Appleby, accompanied by Elisabeth Amelia Dudley-Palmer on her violin. It was an experience I shall always remember – the pure voice of the little girl and the haunting sound of the teenager's violin. It was a special moment in the service and I turned to look towards Mrs Dudley-Palmer and smiled in acknowledgement. She was sitting with tears in her eyes next to her younger daughter, Victoria Alice. Maggie Appleby sat on the front row, smiling at her precious daughter.

The final school lunch of the autumn term was always the highlight of the year for our school cook and her intrepid assistant. Shirley and Doreen had arrived early and worked hard with limited resources to ensure all the children had an excellent Christmas dinner. Ruby and her daughter Natasha had volunteered to help and between them they had worked wonders. Sally wheeled in our Music Centre – namely a record player on a trolley with two huge speakers on the bottom shelf – and played a compilation of Christmas carols.

Soon it was time to clear the hall for our Christmas party. While my class set out the chairs and games and decorated the windows with balloons and paper chains made from loops of multi-coloured gum strip, the younger children sat in their classrooms crayoning their Christmas cards. It was a party that was enjoyed by all. We played lots of games, including Statues, The Farmer's In His Den and Musical Chairs. Remarkably, mid-way through the afternoon, Shirley appeared from the kitchen with an additional surprise. Doreen was holding a huge tray of bright-green jelly, topped with a scattering of meringue.

'It's our special treat, Mr Sheffield,' said Shirley proudly.

'We call it Mushrooms in a Field,' announced Doreen.

The children soon devoured this extra treat, after which Sally took out her guitar and we finished with a rendition of 'Rudolph the Red-Nosed Reindeer'.

The sun was setting as parents came in to collect their children, and each child took home a balloon and a packet of sweets along with miscellaneous decorations and Christmas cards.

Mrs Jackson approached me with her twin daughters.

'Thank you for a wonderful party, Mr Sheffield,' she said. 'My daughters have had a marvellous time.'

The two girls were looking out of the window as stars began to twinkle in the vast black sky.

'Look at the stars, Mummy,' said Hermione.

'Jesus probably saw the same stars,' reflected Honeysuckle.

'I expect he did,' said Mrs Jackson. She gave me a smile. 'Special times, Mr Sheffield. Best wishes to you and Mrs Sheffield ... and I hope Santa visits your little boy.'

'I'm sure he will,' I said.

Frankie Spraggon and his sister Hayley came up to me to give me a home-made Christmas card.

'Thank you,' I said, 'and a happy Christmas.'

'Ah think ah'm gettin' a Cabbage Patch doll, Mr Sheffield,' confided Hayley.

Frankie gave her a stern look. ''Ave you been looking in t'cupboard under t'stairs?' he said. 'Mam won't be 'appy.'

'Well, ah only looked a little bit,' pleaded Hayley, 'because my eyes are small.'

Children's logic, I thought as they ran off.

Mrs Parrish was waiting in the entrance hall.

'Just wanted to say thank you, Mr Sheffield,' she said. 'Katie has already madc a good friend in Mandy Sedgewick and I've just met her mother at the school gate.' She sounded relieved. 'Today has proved to be a really helpful experience.'

'That's good to hear,' I said. 'Best wishes for Christmas.'

She smiled as she helped her daughter collect her coat and scarf.

After saying goodnight to all the staff I locked up

the school and eased my Morris Minor Traveller out of the car park. The sight outside the school gate was one to gladden the heart.

Each year Major Forbes-Kitchener donated a giant Christmas tree to the village and this was one of the best. It stood in the centre of the village green, festooned with bright coloured lights. Around the trunk a circle of straw bales marked its perimeter. Snow was falling and the pantile roof of The Royal Oak was covered in wavy patterns.

All the shops had been decorated and Timothy Pratt's Hardware Emporium stood out with a perfectly horizontal line of illuminated reindeer attached to the canopy above the shop window. Only Old Tommy hadn't excelled. In the butcher's shop a few desultory sprigs of holly on a tray of pigs' trotters was his token gesture towards the festive season.

As I drove home, beyond the frozen hedgerows the skeletal boughs of elm and sycamore hung heavy under their winter burden of newly fallen snow, and I began to feel the freedom that comes with a holiday.

Back at Bilbo Cottage, the kitchen table was covered in presents and cards. Beth looked tearful as she opened each one. 'The end of my first headship,' she said. 'I've made so many good friends ... but it's time to move on.' That steely determination I knew so well had reappeared.

We prepared our evening meal together, each of us deep in private thought and enjoying the solace of silence.

Silence was not on offer on Ragley High Street.

Heathcliffe Earnshaw and his brother Terry were trying to earn some Christmas pocket money by going from house to house singing carols. Sadly, neither of these intrepid Sons of Yorkshire had been blessed with anything resembling a singing voice.

Maurice Tupham hurried to his front door before they had finished the first verse of 'We Three Kings' and thrust a ten-pence piece into Heathcliffe's grubby hand. 'An' 'ere's another ten pence if y'promise not t'come back,' he said gruffly.

'Cross my 'eart an' 'ope t'die,' replied Heathcliffe as he pocketed the shining coins. Then, slightly puzzled by this reaction but nevertheless delighted with the reward, the two boys moved on to the Post Office and their next unsuspecting victim.

Unfortunately the postmistress, Amelia Duff, and Ragley's favourite postman, Ted Postlethwaite, were making passionate love on the hearthrug in the back room in front of a roaring log fire. In consequence they could not appreciate the brothers' off-key rendition of 'In the Bleak Midwinter', as Amelia was in a state of ecstasy while the heat from the flames was burning Ted's bare backside.

Meanwhile, up the Morton Road, a barn owl, like a ghost in the night, circled the tall elms in the grounds of the vicarage. Behind the closed curtains Joseph Evans was wrapping presents as he sipped a goblet of mulled wine. He was pleased with his choice of gifts for Vera. There was an LP of Kiri Te Kanawa singing ten arias by Verdi and Puccini, plus a cassette for her car, *Voices from the*

Holy Land. It featured a compilation of choral favourites by Aled Jones.

As he wrote the words 'For my dear sister' on the Christmas tag there were tears in his eyes. He missed Vera more than ever at this time of the year, but it was a secret he kept to himself.

On Saturday morning, as I looked through the frosted panes of Bilbo Cottage, bright winter sunshine lit up the distant land. The sharp clean air of the high moors had scoured the countryside and all was still after a new fall of snow.

Following a breakfast of hot porridge, Beth had dressed John in his warmest clothes and set off for some last-minute Christmas shopping in York, while I drove to Ragley to collect our turkey from Old Tommy Piercy's shop.

Ragley High Street was full of Christmas shoppers as I pulled up opposite the village hall and crossed the road. A breathless, red-cheeked Ruby was hurrying out of the butcher's.

'Hello, Ruby,' I said.

'Ah can't stop now, Mr Sheffield,' she said, 'ah'm off to t'Christmas market in Easington wi' our Duggie an' 'Azel. Y'can get some real bargains.'

'I might see you there later,' I said.

After collecting a turkey from Old Tommy and a bag of sprouts from the General Stores I decided to call into Nora's Coffee Shop for a welcome hot drink.

When I walked in Whitney Houston was singing 'Saving All My Love For You' on the juke-box and Dorothy was standing behind the counter fiddling with her plastic Christmas-tree earrings.

'What's it t'be, Mr Sheffield?'

'Just a coffee please, Dorothy.' I stared dubiously at the huge plateful of mince pies.

''Ow about one of Nora's mince pies?'

'What are they like?' I asked.

'Well my Malcolm's eaten two, but 'e's got teeth like Red Rum so it's 'ard t'judge.'

'Hard' was probably the operative word. 'I'll try one,' I said. At least the sprinkling of icing sugar gave them a festive look.

At a corner table Claire Bradshaw and Anita Cuthbertson, two nineteen-year-olds who had been in my class when I first arrived in Ragley, were sipping frothy coffee and studying the current pop scene.

'Hello, sir,' they said in unison. They gave me a cheery wave and returned to their reading. Claire had spent forty-three pence at the General Stores on the latest *Smash Hits* magazine, which featured Bob Geldof and John Taylor on the front cover. However, they had flicked past the pictures of the Pet Shop Boys, U2, Bronski Beat and Level 42 and were swooning over a picture of Bryan Ferry.

'Now, 'e's jus' perfect,' said Anita.

'Ah like 'em more rugged,' said Claire.

'So y'don't fancy 'im in Duran Duran?' asked Anita. 'Cos 'e's perfect as well.'

Duran Duran had edged out U2 and Wham! for yet another year as the top group and their record 'A View to a Kill' had been voted best single of the year.

'No,' said Claire, 'ah like *muscles.*'

Madonna's *Like a Virgin* had won the best LP category and Anita paused briefly to study the pop icon's latest outfit before moving on to the best films page. 'Y'mean like Rambo?'

'No, not *big* muscles. More like 'im in *Mad Max* – good lookin' wi' jus' a few muscles.'

Dorothy wandered over to their table with a damp dishcloth and wiped a few crumbs off the surface. 'Ah'm sick o' bloody Shakespeare,' she complained. 'Nora's practisin' in t'back room an' ah don't know why ah said ah'd 'elp out.'

'Why aren't we 'avin' a panto like we usually do?' asked Claire.

'Summat t'do wi' *culture,*' said Dorothy dismissively.

'So y'doin' a *Shakespeare* play on New Year's Eve?' asked Anita.

'Yes,' said Dorothy. 'It's s'pposed t'be a comedy.'

'So there'll be a few laughs then,' said Claire.

Dorothy lowered her voice. 'My Malcolm's in it an 'e's got a big part, but if y'don't laugh in t'right places 'e gets upset. Ah've been 'elpin' 'im wi' 'is lines.'

'Oh well, good luck,' said Claire.

'You've gorra customer,' said Anita, nodding towards the counter.

'By the way, Claire,' said Dorothy, 'a word in your ear. It's all round t'village about you bein' on t'pill and 'avin' "conjugals" wi' Kenny. If y'mother finds out she'll give you what for.'

'Oh 'eck,' said Claire.

The spacious cobbled square in Easington was the perfect place for a market and snow was falling again as I parked on one of the narrow side roads. The stalls around the perimeter of the square were ablaze with coloured lights and the Town Crier in his three-cornered hat and ceremonial frockcoat was ringing his bell and chanting 'O yea, O yea, O yea' – though no one seemed to notice because the Christmas number one, Shakin' Stevens' 'Merry Christmas Everyone', was booming out from huge speakers and the shoppers were singing along.

At Shady Stevo's stall I bought two cassette tapes for Beth – Fleetwood Mac's *Rumours* and Simon and Garfunkel's *Greatest Hits* – plus one for myself, *Heartbeats* by my personal favourite, Barbara Dickson.

'I've jus' seen Santa, Mr Sheffield,' shouted six-year-old Julie Tricklebank, 'an' 'is fairy gave me this.' She held up a stick of barley sugar.

Mrs Tricklebank smiled. 'Happy Christmas,' she said, nodding towards a little wooden hut covered in polystyrene snow. Outside was a big sign that read: *SANTA'S GROTTO – admission 10p – Ragley & District Rotary Club.*

Gabriel Book made an adjustment to his white beard, wriggled his toes in his warm socks and checked the time on his Mickey Mouse watch. In his mid-sixties, Gabriel was always the Rotary Club's first-choice Father Christmas.

This year he had two new sixteen-year-old assistants, Sharon and Tracy, who for £20 had agreed to give up a free afternoon. Their tacky outfits sported the labels 'Good Fairy' and 'Busy Elf'. Unfortunately for Gabriel, Good Fairy would have made a perfect Wicked Witch of the West and Busy Elf was anything but industrious.

'Just another few minutes,' he said, 'and then we can pack up.'

Good Fairy stubbed out a cigarette, cleared some of the spray-on snow from the window and stared forlornly at the last group of children. 'Ah'm sick o' these kids.'

Busy Elf was lounging on a folding picnic chair in the corner by the electric heater. 'Ah'm bloody freezin' in this outfit.'

Finally Good Fairy got up and opened the wooden door. 'Next one f'Santa,' she said through gritted teeth.

In walked Mrs Ricketts with Billy and Suzi-Quatro.

'Hello and a ho-ho-ho,' Gabriel greeted them cheerily.

''Ello, Santa,' said Billy.

'And have you been a good boy this year?'

'Yes, 'e 'as,' said Mrs Ricketts in a voice that brooked no argument.

Gabriel looked up at the fierce Yorkshire woman. 'Er, yes, of course you have.'

'Ah wanna Optimus Prime,' stated Billy bluntly.

'Pardon?' said Gabriel.

'It's a Transformer, Santa,' said Mrs Ricketts. 'It's all t'rage.'

'Is it?' asked Gabriel, none the wiser.

'It changes from a robot to a truck or mebbe an animal,' explained Billy.

'So it's versatile,' ventured Gabriel, trying to share in the enthusiasm.

'No, it's a Transformer,' said Mrs Ricketts.

'Well, I'll look in my toy cupboard at the North Pole and see if I've got one,' promised Gabriel.

'You'll definitely 'ave one,' said Mrs Ricketts with a knowing look.

'An' if you 'aven't, Santa, jus' look in m'mam's catalogue,' suggested Billy helpfully.

Perplexed at this turn of events, Gabriel simply nodded.

'An' ah wanna Godzilla,' added Billy confidently.

'Godzilla?'

'Yes, 'e's twelve inches tall an' made o' plastic.'

'An' there's definitely one up at t'North Pole,' said Mrs Ricketts with a firm stare.

'Oh, well, yes I suppose there would be.' He turned to Suzi-Quatro and said, 'Ho, ho, ho.' Gabriel was proud of his 'Ho, ho, ho' and had perfected it over the years.

Suzi-Quatro stepped forward.

'And what's your name, little girl?'

'Santa ... she's not *little,*' interjected Mrs Ricketts, 'she's a good size.'

'Of course she is,' agreed Gabriel nervously.

'Ah'm Suzi-Quatro.'

'Are you?' asked Gabriel in surprise.

'Yes, she is,' said Mrs Ricketts.

'Ah'd like a Princess Leia, please, Santa,' said Suzi-Quatro.

'Really? She sounds important,' said Gabriel.

'She's in *Star Wars* an' she 'as a posh 'air-do,' explained Suzi-Quatro.

Gabriel looked up at Mrs Ricketts, who nodded. 'Yes, I think I've got one of those,' he said.

Mrs Ricketts took them by the hand and marched them back to the door.

'We'll leave a biscuit f'Rudolph,' promised Suzi-Quatro.

'An' a glass o' sherry f'you, Santa,' added Billy.

'Well ... prob'ly milk,' said Mrs Ricketts, who

liked her sherry.

With a final 'Ho, ho, ho' Gabriel got up while both children were receiving a mystery gift – a packet of fruit pastilles wrapped in tissue paper – from Busy Elf, while Good Fairy rolled another cigarette.

On Sunday afternoon Beth and I drove out of Kirkby Steepleton while wood smoke drifted up towards a clear, powder-blue sky. When we reached Ragley High Street families were hurrying up the Morton Road towards St Mary's Church. The Crib Service marked the beginning of the sequence of Christmas services that attracted most of the villagers.

The church bells were ringing as we lifted John from the car and he walked up the pathway of Yorkshire stone while the snow settled in gentle curves against the church wall. On the notice-board something attracted Beth's attention and she smiled. It was another classic from the church secretary and organist, Elsie Crapper. The notice read: 'Don't let worry kill you – let the church help.'

We walked through the Norman doorway and found a space on one of the front pews so that John could have a good view of the Nativity. Vera was moving quietly through the sanctuary of this beautiful church, lighting tall candles. A kaleidoscope of flickering light illuminated the stained glass in the east window and gave a fiery glow to the altar rail of Victorian pine.

Vera walked over to us and smiled down at John. 'Welcome to our haven of peace in a busy world,' she said, then moved on to the two Norman arches on the north side of the nave to light the final candles. Sally was lining up her choir for the first of the carols, while Pat and Anne helped a group of mothers to dress the shepherds, kings and angels.

When Joseph approached the lectern the sound of children's voices subsided until only the ticking of the old church clock, installed in 1912 to commemorate the coronation of George V, could be heard.

Seated at the organ, Elsie Crapper felt composed. She had taken her Valium and all was calm. She played the introduction to 'Once in Royal David's City' and Sally's choir sang the first verse before the congregation joined in. As always, it was music blessed by angels, and the children acted out the timeless story dressed in tea-towel head-dresses and halos of bright tinsel.

Predictably, the gifts for baby Jesus created particular interest. 'Ah'd 'ave got 'im a Leeds United kit,' said Stuart Ormroyd.

'Or a nice tin o' biscuits,' added Patience Crapper for good measure.

'Who's t'baby, Mam?' asked a curious Dallas Sue-Ellen Earnshaw.

Mrs Earnshaw answered in a hushed whisper, 'That's baby Jesus.'

After a pause Dallas said, 'Who's that with 'im, Mam?'

'That's 'is mother, Mary.'

Another pause. 'Mam...'

'What?'

'Where's 'is dad?'

'Shurrup!'

Soon it was over and parents and children stepped out into the darkness of another winter's night. The staff stayed behind to help Vera clear up and finally the church was still with the silence of stone. When Beth and I walked out all was quiet apart from the ticking of the ancient clock. As we drove home I wondered how many more Christmases I would experience as the headteacher of our local school.

These were special times and, as Ruby had said, you couldn't beat a Ragley Christmas.

Chapter Eight

A Comedy of Errors

Mrs Grainger and Mrs Pringle with children from the reception class plus the school choir and orchestra will be supporting the Ragley annual village concert, A Comedy of Errors by William Shakespeare, in the village hall on 31 December.

Extract from the Ragley School Logbook:
Tuesday, 31 December 1985

Nora Pratt looked at her Alpine leather corset hanging in the wardrobe and sighed. She would have to let it out a little. After all, as president of the Ragley Amateur Dramatic Society, it was important to set a good example.

The annual New Year's Eve concert had arrived

and Nora wanted to look her best. She thought how, back in 1977, the corset had fitted perfectly for *Snow White and the Six Dwarfs*, but then the years went by and it had become rather snug by the time of *Jack and the Beanstalk*. During *The Wizard of Oz* it was decidedly tight and during last year's *Dick Whittington* she could barely breathe.

Nora stared at her reflection in the mirror and recalled the highs and lows of her acting career. It was a big day for this determined thespian, who always tried her best. A new era of drama had arrived in Ragley village and she wondered what the reaction would be. Turning to one of William Shakespeare's plays was a journey into the unknown and a far cry from the usual pantomime. However, undeterred by either her inability to pronounce the letter 'R' or her ever-expanding waistline, Nora was confident she knew her lines and that her moment of stardom would finally be within her grasp.

It was Tuesday morning, 31 December, and the production of Shakespeare's *A Comedy of Errors* was only hours away.

Outside Ragley School the tall horse chestnut trees were bare of leaves and stood like frozen sentinels. The air was clean and sharp, while bright winter sunshine lit up the playground and the frosted tips of the fleur-de-lis on the railings looked like candles on a cake.

Beth and I had driven into school so that I could collect the last post of the year before driving on to York to do some shopping. John was wrapped up warm in his pushchair and Beth pulled his woolly hat over his pink ears. 'How about a hot drink in Nora's Coffee Shop?' she suggested.

'Good idea,' I agreed, and I unbuckled John and let him totter over the village green. He loved making tiny footprints on the white frost. I noticed his speed was increasing as he grew older and stronger, and I put on a spurt to keep up with him. I picked him up to cross the High Street and we walked into the Coffee Shop. On the juke-box, Bruce Springsteen was telling everyone that 'Santa Claus Is Comin' to Town'. The fact that the man in the red suit had been and gone seemed to have passed unnoticed. Today there were much more important visitors, not least Felicity Miles-Humphreys, who was in animated conversation with Nora.

I walked to the counter while Beth found the old wooden communal highchair and set it up next to a corner table.

'It's a bit scawy,' said Nora. 'All this Shakes-peawian dialogue is a bit diffewent – it teks a lot o' concentwation t'get it wight.' Nora was playing the part of Adriana, wife of Antipholus of Ephesus.

'You will be wonderful, darling' said Felicity. 'In fact, I perceive a *triumph.*' As artistic director and production manager of the Ragley Amateur Dramatic Society, Felicity knew the importance of encouragement. 'We are introducing classical drama to the masses, my dear, and those with a little *savoir faire* will appreciate it.'

Nora nodded uncertainly. She could neither understand *savoir faire* nor, indeed, pronounce it, but Felicity had never let her down.

'So, what's it t'be, Felicity?' she asked.

'A filter coffee with hot milk and one of your simply scrumptious fruit scones,' said Felicity with dramatic emphasis but little belief. 'We shall need vital energy for our dress rehearsal this afternoon.'

Nora turned to Dorothy, who was rehearsing her lines next to the coffee machine. 'A fwothy coffee an' a fwuit scone, please, Dowothy,' and Dorothy reluctantly put down her crumpled script.

It was my turn.

'Two coffees, please, Nora, and a small glass of warm milk for John,' I said.

'Coming wight up, Mr Sheffield.'

After a couple of minutes the tall figure of Dorothy tottered over on her high heels and put a tray of welcome drinks on the table.

'Good luck tonight, Dorothy,' said Beth.

'We'll be there to support,' I added, trying to be encouraging.

'Ah'm reight excited,' said Dorothy. 'Me an' my Malcolm are in it an' we've been practisin' ev'ry night.'

'So what's your part?' I asked.

'Ah'm Nell, Nora's kitchen wench,' she said, 'an' ah wear this proper wench's outfit, which is reight short, wi' m'Wonder Woman boots an' m'chunky charm bracelet on a bit o' balin' twine round m'neck.'

'Sounds perfect,' I said.

'M'first *actin'* part, Mr Sheffield,' added Dorothy with gravitas.

'Well done,' I said. 'I'm sure both you and Malcolm will be terrific.'

'An' 'ere's a digestive biscuit f'John,' she said with a smile.

'Thank you,' said Beth, '...and hope it goes well.'

Beth and I always enjoyed our visits to York, the jewel in Yorkshire's crown, and soon the west towers of the Minster came into view.

We parked in Lord Mayor's Walk next to the ancient walls and walked up Gillygate and on into the city centre. After completing our shopping we stopped in St Helen's Square outside Bettys Café Tea Rooms, noticeably without the expected apostrophe in 'Bettys' on the large ornate sign, and stared in the window. John became excited when he saw the display of mouthwatering cakes, pastries and hand-made chocolates. We were ushered to a table next to the huge curved windows, elegant wood panelling and art deco mirrors.

The waitress who served us wore a starched white apron and neat little cap, and looked as if she had just stepped out of the pages of one of Agatha Christie's novels. I ordered toasted teacakes and a boiled egg and toast soldiers for John. As a special treat, this was followed by a plateful of Yorkshire Fat Rascals – fruity scones filled with citrus peel, almonds and cherries. Beth poured the tea, which was served in a silver teapot with a matching sugar bowl, silver tongs and a delicate tea strainer. Everything looked perfect. It was as if we had stepped back into a bygone era of white linen and silver service, which, sadly, was lost on John, who ate as if we had starved him for the past week.

'So, how do you feel?' I asked. Beth had been working hard since Christmas, learning all she could about her new headship. Many challenges lay ahead.

'I'm getting there,' she said with a tired smile. 'It's all new, but I'll be fine. The deputy and head of infants are coming round to the idea of me being their head and we're making progress.'

'Good to hear,' I said. 'You'll need their support.'

We walked up Stonegate past the Minster, along Goodramgate and returned to Lord Mayor's Walk. The imposing city wall, built of magnesian limestone, shimmered in the winter sunshine. Built in the thirteenth and fourteenth centuries, these walls formed almost a complete circuit of this medieval city and stood as a reminder of the days when defences were needed that would repel an invader.

Across the road was my old college, where I had trained as a teacher, and we paused to drink in the familiar view laced with many memories. Suddenly there was a call and an old friend waved in our direction. It was Jim Fairbank, my college tutor from the sixties. He hurried across the road to meet us, a slim, bespectacled figure in a thick three-piece tweed suit with a university scarf knotted round his neck.

'Jack and Beth – lovely to see you again,' he said, and then stared reflectively at young John. Jim had not married and parenthood was never to be part of his life. 'And this is your fine son ... he's growing fast.'

We shook hands. 'How are you, Jim?' I asked.

'Fine, thanks,' he replied, then added, 'and you've saved me a letter.'

I was curious. 'Why is that?'

He paused, searching for the right words. 'We

need your expertise, Jack, and I was hoping you might find time to help us out.'

'Of course,' I said. 'What have you in mind?'

'We're short of a tutor this term for one of the modules and you would be perfect. It's six sessions with a focus on classroom management.'

'I couldn't take time off school,' I said. 'As you know, I have a class full-time.'

'We could fit round your teaching commitments at Ragley,' said Jim, 'and the college would pay for a supply teacher to cover your class, providing your governors agree.'

'Well – it would have to be out of school hours.'

'You could start at four thirty,' suggested Beth quickly. She gave me that look I knew so well. 'It's an *opportunity*, Jack.'

I was captured by her enthusiasm. It also made sense in terms of a possible future employment opening.

Jim smiled. He had reeled in his catch. 'I'll call you at the start of term,' he said.

We shook hands, loaded up the car and put John in his baby seat. On our way back to Kirkby Steepleton Beth sounded animated. 'This could be a foothold in higher education,' she said. 'You never know where it might lead.'

'I agree,' I replied, 'and it might be a sign of things to come.'

Silence descended as the miles sped by and we were both immersed in our own thoughts. 1986 stretched out before us and uncertainties in our professional lives had to be met head on. I knew I had to develop a more determined streak. Beth had shown me the way and it was about time she saw my own ambition.

After dropping off Beth and John at home, I set off for Ragley. I had volunteered to help out once again with the scenery for the evening performance of *A Comedy of Errors.* Before that I called into The Royal Oak for some hot food and a drink.

When I walked in, Big Dave and Little Malcolm were enjoying a pint as they propped up the taproom bar with Ruby's son, Duggie, along with Deke Ramsbottom and two of his sons, Shane and Clint. In the background the television news was chattering away to no one in particular. The newsreader was talking about something called Comic Relief. It followed an outside broadcast from a refugee camp in Sudan that had featured on Noel Edmonds' *Late, Late Breakfast Show.* Founded by comedy scriptwriter Richard Curtis and comedian Lenny Henry in response to the famine in Ethiopia, it sounded a good idea and had caught the imagination of the country.

Meanwhile, Sheila Bradshaw was doing a roaring trade. Rabbit pie was on the menu along with boiled beef and carrots. This was followed by another of Sheila's specialities, spotted dick and custard, perfect on a freezing-cold day.

'It's goin' down a treat, Mr Sheffield,' said Sheila proudly.

'It's a proper feast is this,' confirmed an appreciative Deke Ramsbottom as he devoured his perfectly cooked rabbit.

With recollections of *Watership Down* still vivid in my imagination, eating the cast didn't seem appropriate ... so I chose the beef.

'So, big night t'night, Malcolm,' said Sheila.

'Y'reight there, Sheila,' said Little Malcolm, blushing profusely.

''E's a proper star, is our Malcolm,' said Big Dave proudly. ''E's doin' Shakespeare. It's one o' 'is comedies.'

The huge figure of Don, an ex-wrestler in his younger days, looked up from pulling a frothing pint. 'So what part y'playin', Malc'?'

'Well, it's a bit complicated,' said Little Malcolm. 'Ah'm this bloke, Antipholus of Ephesus.'

'Sounds foreign,' remarked Don as he placed the pint of Tetley's on a York City coaster.

'An' ah've gorra twin brother, but we were sep'rated at birth,' explained Little Malcolm.

'Bloody 'ell,' said Don, 'that's upsettin'.'

'An' t'poor little sod got lost in a storm at sea,' added Big Dave, who, after countless late-night weekly rehearsals after *Match of the Day*, knew the plot down to the last detail.

Don shook his head. 'Dunt sound much like a comedy t'me, Malc'.'

'Well, Felicity said 'e wrote comedies an' tragedies, did this Shakespeare bloke – an' this is definitely a comedy.'

'But there's a 'appy endin',' added Big Dave, eager to support his diminutive cousin.

'Well ah think it's wonderful,' said Sheila, 'an' a proper bit o' culture. Jus' what we need in t'village. So tek no notice o' my Don. 'E didn't read no Shakespeare, only comics an' then 'e only looked at t'pictures.' Ragley's favourite barmaid looked up at her great hulk of a husband. ''E's not int' *culture* – in fac', 'e wouldn't know culture from wet fish.'

Don thought he knew a lot about fish but decided to keep quiet.

Clint came to the bar to order the next round of drinks. He was sporting his new tattoo and Sheila and Don looked at it with interest.

'Ah went t'York t'Tattoos-While-U-Wait,' said Clint proudly, 'an' ah got this.' He bared his arm. The tattoo read: MAKE LOVE NOT.

'Make love not?' said Sheila. 'What's that s'pposed t'mean?'

Clint blushed profusely. 'My arm weren't wide enough so 'e 'ad t'keep goin' round.' The word WAR was hidden under his armpit.

'Never mind, Clint,' said Sheila, looking at Don's bulging biceps. 'Big muscles isn't ev'rythin'. A woman likes a bit o' *sensitivity.*' She saw Clint's reaction and added quickly, 'An' some *men* do too.'

Clint gave her a shy smile and glanced at his brother to make sure he was out of earshot. He leaned over the bar. 'Duggie's got a new girlfriend an' our Shane's spreading it round that she's a reight slapper,' he confided.

'So ah've 'eard,' said Sheila. 'It's that Tina ... an' if ah know 'er she won't tek that lyin' down.'

'She works in t'mattress factory,' said Clint.

'So mebbe she *will* tek it lying down,' said Don from the far end of the bar.

Clint smiled, picked up the tray of pints and walked back to his brother. Always a fashion icon, Clint had progressed to his Michael Jackson phase. He was wearing an oversized, slouch-shouldered, faded leather jacket with puffy sleeves, black leather trousers and sunglasses. In contrast, Shane was still part of punk subculture, with ripped jeans, a Sex Pistols T-shirt and a denim jacket decorated with safety pins. His Doc Marten boots with air-cushioned soles were his pride and joy. The letters H-A-R-D tattooed on the knuckles of his right hand caught the eye as he lifted his tankard.

Deke looked forlornly at his two sons and whispered to Don, ''E's allus in t'shit, is our Shane – it's only t'depth that varies.'

'Y'reight there, Deke,' agreed Don.

'All ah wanted were normal,' said Deke with a whimsical smile, 'an' I finished up wi' a psychopath an' a poofter.'

'Well your Wayne's a lovely lad, p'lite an' 'ard-workin',' Don consoled him.

Deke nodded thoughtfully. ''E's t'only one what teks after me.'

Sheila, with a knowing smile, kept her thoughts to herself.

'Anyway,' said Big Dave, 'our Malcolm will be a star t'night.'

Little Malcolm was having his doubts. 'But ah'm only a bin man,' he said.

Big Dave put down his pint. 'As ah see it, Malc',' he said, 'mebbe in t'scheme o' things an' lookin' at it objectively so t'speak ... y'reight at t'bottom o' t'pile.'

'Bloomin' 'eck,' sighed Little Malcolm.

'So t'only way is up,' said Big Dave with an encouraging slap on his back.

The afternoon dress rehearsal in the village hall

was not going well. I was putting the finishing touches to a sheet of plywood on which I had painted a stormy sea with the deck of a sinking ship in the foreground. I was quite proud of the result, considering I only had a four-inch brush, two tins of matt emulsion, blue and white, and some leftover brown Ronseal paint.

Around me it was the usual chaos, with few of the cast having a suitable costume, while Ted Postlethwaite as Dromio of Syracuse had not turned up because he was still busy delivering post.

In desperation, Felicity announced, 'Let's take five,' which turned out to be twenty minutes of drinking sweet tea and eating Elsie Crapper's dubious home-made flapjack with the consistency of damp cardboard.

Felicity's lanky son, Rupert, was playing the part of one of the twins, Antipholus of Syracuse. 'I'm not happy, Mother,' he declared, hitching up his baggy green tights. 'Do you think it was wise to select a *Shakespeare* play?' He had given this a lot of thought recently while deciding on which side to wear a pair of rolled-up socks in his string underpants.

'Of course, darling,' said Felicity with forced enthusiasm. 'We owe it to our calling to educate the proletariat.'

Elsie Crapper had vacated her prompter's chair behind the curtain and Rupert sat down. 'But what about Nora?' he asked. 'She can't say her Rs,' he said in disgust. 'It's just not professional.'

'I know, darling,' said Felicity, 'but we have to make allowances.'

'And that bin man who's supposed to be my twin brother is twenty years older than me,' protested Rupert.

'A little make-up has solved that, my dear.'

Rupert shook his head. 'But he's a foot shorter ... the audience will *notice*.'

Felicity looked at her gangling son, the supermarket shelf-stacker and would-be actor, and wondered where she had gone wrong. Then she adjusted her scarlet headband and desperately ran her fingers through her long, frizzy, jet-black hair. She stared at the protrusion in his tights and leaned forward. 'And please remove that unlikely bulge, Rupert,' she whispered. 'The shape is unnatural.' She didn't mention that a chipolata would have been more appropriate and hurried off to the kitchen, her tie-dyed kaftan flowing behind her. A camomile tea beckoned.

The curtains fluttered and Elsie Crapper returned to find Rupert rummaging in his tights. Her cheeks flushed and she went to find her handbag and her new supply of Valium.

By seven o'clock the village hall was full to bursting and a few extra folding picnic chairs had appeared, carried by the latecomers without tickets. A Shakespeare play was definitely something different and not to be missed. Beth and I had left Natasha Smith looking after John back at Bilbo Cottage and we joined Vera and her husband on the third row. The sense of anticipation was considerable.

'Isn't it wonderful?' said Vera. 'Shakespeare comes to Ragley.'

Having seen the dress rehearsal, I responded with a polite smile.

As usual, the well-lubricated Ragley football team had vacated the tap room of The Royal Oak and occupied the back row.

Timothy Pratt's big moment arrived as he turned up the brightness on his single spotlight, the curtains fluttered and Felicity Miles-Humphreys appeared, looking fraught. 'Welcome to the annual production of the Ragley Amateur Dramatic Society,' she announced.

This was greeted by guarded applause. As Old Tommy had reminded his customers, 'Shakespeare isn't everyone's cup of tea.' The only consolation was that the cost of tickets had remained at fifty pence.

'This evening we embark on a new pathway for the thespians of our village,' continued Felicity.

Ruby was on the front row with her daughter Hazel. 'What's a thespian, Mam?' whispered Hazel.

'Never you mind, luv,' said Ruby cautiously, misunderstanding the word 'thespians'. 'Everybody's different.'

Felicity pressed on. 'I thought it would help to set the scene, as this is *different* to past years.' Previous productions were done and dusted in an hour and a half, including an interval. Time was of the essence, so Felicity had decided to cut to the chase and act as narrator for the abbreviated version of the play.

'Aegeon, a merchant of Syracuse, has been condemned to death,' she announced.

'Bloody 'ell!' said Old Tommy. 'Ah thought it

were s'pposed t'be a comedy.'

Felicity was undeterred. 'But he has been granted one day to raise the thousand-mark ransom.'

This was greeted by cheers.

'There is also a confusion of identities with two sets of twins,' explained Felicity, 'and all this will become apparent... So, enjoy the show.'

The curtains opened and the prompter Elsie Crapper turned to her script at Act 1, Scene 1. It was at about this time that Felicity regretted selecting her husband, Peter, the stuttering bank clerk, to play the part of Aegeon. 'The p-pleasing p-p-punishment that w-women b-bear,' he said.

Members of the football team were quick to offer muttered opinions.

'Get on wi' it,' mumbled Kojak Wojciechowski, the Bald-Headed Ball Wizard.

'Give t'daft bugger a chance,' said Nutter Neilson. ''E's tryin' 'is best.'

'But ah've paid f'this rubbish,' complained Kojak. 'Ah'm entitled t'me money's worth.'

Big Dave's wife, Nellie, gave Kojak a withering look. 'Shurrup, Kojak, or ah'll tell everyone what ah over'eard las' time y'went t'Doctor Davenport.'

Kojak's bald pate flushed crimson and he settled back into his seat without another word.

As Rupert Miles-Humphreys had anticipated, it took some time for the audience to realize that he and Little Malcolm were meant to be twins.

'Clear as mud,' said Deke Ramsbottom. 'You'd have thought they'd 'ave been given different names at least.'

Little Malcolm was turning out to be the star of

the performance, with thunderous applause from the football team every time he appeared. In complete contrast, his so-called twin brother recited his lines in an affected pose that he thought was theatrical. 'I to the world am like a drop of water.'

'Ah allus said 'e were a big drip,' said Deke and Rupert glowered at Ragley's singing cowboy.

Meanwhile, Nora Pratt, playing the part of Adriana, was definitely taking the play seriously and knew her words to perfection. It was just a pity she had difficulty in pronouncing them. 'A wetched soul, bwuised with adve'sity. We bid be quiet when we hear it cwy.'

In Act 2, Scene 2, when Ted Postlethwaite as Dromio of Syracuse said, 'Ev'ry why 'as a wherefore,' the performance was halted when all the villagers who lived on School View continued their applause for longer than was expected. They hoped Ted would occasionally reverse his round to deliver post to them first instead of last, and Ted acknowledged this display of overt favouritism with a thumbs-up.

By Act 3, Scene 1, the audience was roaring in sympathy at the sight of Little Malcolm being excluded from his own home while his twin, Rupert, was inside dining with Nora, Malcolm's wife, who had mistaken him for her husband. As the plot unravelled everyone resorted to pantomime mode and cheered or hissed at appropriate moments. Likewise, Dorothy, as Nora's serving wench, enjoyed her moment of fame and strutted around the stage in her Wonder Woman boots, showing off the longest legs in Ragley to great effect.

Finally in Act 5, Scene 1, the confusions were

explained and everyone was destined to live happily ever after.

At the end Nora received her usual bouquet of flowers, Felicity thanked everyone for supporting this new venture and Little Malcolm was toasted as the new Richard Burton.

Beth and I joined the crowd in The Royal Oak for a post-performance celebration.

'Well, it were better than 1973,' said Old Tommy grudgingly. He still had vivid recollections of the time when the audience had demanded their fifty-pence admission be refunded following a disastrous performance of *Goldilocks and the Two Bears*.

Nora and Tyrone were sitting on the bench seat under the dartboard.

'You're a star,' said Tyrone.

'Thank you, y'big soft thing,' said Nora, loosening the laces on her Alpine corset.

Tyrone smiled. 'Y'right there, Nora, ah'm jus' like a meringue – 'ard on t'outside an' soft on t'inside.'

'Oooh, Tywone,' purred Nora, 'ah love mewingues.'

'Take on Me' by A-Ha was blasting out on the juke-box and Little Malcolm was standing at the bar with Dorothy. She was still in her serving-wench outfit.

'You're a star,' said Dorothy, 't'man o' my dreams.'

Little Malcolm felt ten feet tall. He raised himself up to his full height and pressed his face into Dorothy's cleavage. 'Thanks, Dorothy,' he mumbled.

It was late when Beth and I returned home.
The stars were shining like celestial fireflies, scattering the sky with stardust.
A new year had dawned.

Chapter Nine

Changing Times

School reopened today for the spring term with 98 children on roll.

Extract from the Ragley School Logbook:
Monday, 6 January 1986

A frozen world greeted the first school day of 1986. It was Monday, 6 January and Nature held the land in its iron fist. A bitter wind had scoured the countryside and the small creatures of the woodland were sheltering.

'Good luck,' I said, kissing Beth gently on the cheek.

She looked smart in her new charcoal-grey business suit. 'Will I do?' she asked as she checked her appearance in the hall mirror.

'Perfect,' I said and helped her with her winter coat.

It was seven o'clock as she stepped out into the darkness. On the driveway she stopped and glanced up at John William's bedroom window. 'I wonder how he is,' she said wistfully. 'I miss him already.'

At the weekend we had visited Beth's parents down in Hampshire for a few days and our son had remained with them. The intention was to give Beth the chance to settle into her new headship during her first busy week. It seemed strange to share an early breakfast together without him.

'Drive carefully,' I said as I scraped the frost from her windscreen.

'I'll be late home tonight,' she said, 'probably very late.' With that she drove off, determined to be first in school and, presumably, last out.

I watched her rear lights fade into the distance. It was the beginning of a new chapter for both of us.

In Morton Manor Vera was listening to the news while she cleared the breakfast dishes. She had been pleased to hear that Arthur Scargill's one-time left-wing allies appeared to be forming up against him.

How are the mighty fallen, mused Vera as she put on her coat to face the new term.

As I drove away from Bilbo Cottage a silent shroud of fresh snow covered the North Yorkshire countryside and all sound was muted. Overnight the back road out of Kirkby Steepleton had become a smooth white channel between the desolation of the brittle hedgerows and the sleeping trees. It was a hazardous journey to Ragley village along a silver ribbon of ice and I breathed a sigh of relief as I reached the High Street.

It was a gloomy sight, and a wolf-grey cloud of wood smoke hung heavy over the pantile roofs.

Inside their homes the villagers of Ragley were stoking their log fires. A bitter winter had greeted the new year.

I pulled up outside Prudence Golightly's General Stores and hurried inside. Mrs Tomkins was in front of me with five-year-old Karl. He was staring at Maurice Tupham, who had called in for a bag of sugar. Maurice had stubbed his eye on a stick of rhubarb and was wearing a large black eye-patch.

'Are you a pirate, Mr Tupham?' asked Karl.

'No, ah'm not,' said Maurice gruffly.

'C'mon, Karl,' said his mother. She picked up her tin of Pedigree Chum. It said on the tin it was 'recommended by Top Breeders' and nothing was too good for Flossie, her French poodle.

'But 'e looks like a pirate, Mam,' insisted Karl as they followed Ragley's famous rhubarb-grower out of the shop.

'Your paper, Mr Sheffield,' said Prudence, 'and a happy New Year.'

'And to you too, Miss Golightly,' I said, 'and, of course, to Jeremy.'

Ragley's favourite bear was well wrapped up in a bobble cap, an Arran sweater, cord trousers and green wellington boots.

Prudence looked up at her little friend and smiled. 'He says he's going sledging later and is so excited.'

I nodded in acknowledgement. It was well known that Jeremy enjoyed his winter sports.

The display of newspapers all featured the same surprising headline. Four test-tube babies had been born on New Year's Day and there were now around three hundred and fifty of these remarkable children in Britain. Science and technology were moving forward at a great pace. I needed to make sure I wouldn't be left behind in the race to create a brave new world.

It was 1986 and times were changing.

As I drove off, Deke Ramsbottom pulled in behind me. The villagers of Ragley preferred burning logs to smokeless fuel and Deke was dropping off another trailer-load at the General Stores.

In the school car park I collected my leather satchel and stared up at our village school. A short term lay ahead, only ten weeks owing to an early Easter. There was much to do: mid-year reports, reading tests and, not least, keeping the school warm enough for the children to work in comfort.

Our hardy school caretaker was sprinkling salt on the steps to the entrance porch.

'Happy New Year, Ruby.'

'An' t'you too, Mr Sheffield,' she replied. 'Let's 'ope it's a good un.'

'I'm sure it will be,' I said without conviction.

Ruby stared longingly at my Morris Minor Traveller. 'It mus' be lovely to be able t'drive,' she said. 'You'd be … well … free.'

'Yes, there is that,' I agreed, recognizing the eagerness in her voice, 'and it's never too late to learn.'

Ruby smiled. 'No … not for t'likes o' me, Mr Sheffield.'

She put her carton of Saxa salt against the school wall and picked up her broom. ''Ealth an' safety man called in early this morning, Mr Sheffield, checkin' doors an' winders an' that fire distinguisher in Shirley's kitchen.'

'Oh yes.'

'An' 'e signed a form an' left it wi' Mrs F.'

'Thanks,' I said. 'I'm sure all was well.'

''E looked 'appy enough when 'e left wi' one o' Shirley's 'ot scones.'

I smiled. The Health & Safety officer from County Hall was a frequent visitor and I guessed the fire extinguisher in our school kitchen received more attention than any other appliance in North Yorkshire. He always left with a slice of parkin or one of Shirley's famous fruit scones.

I shivered and looked back at the cleared path and the entrance steps now free of frost. 'Thanks for all your work,' I said.

'Allus a pleasure,' replied Ruby simply, but she looked preoccupied. Her yard broom was light in her work-red hands, but secrets were a heavy burden.

The office door was open and I hung up my coat and scarf. Vera was at her desk, talking to Mrs Freda Fazackerly, mother of six-year-old Madonna, and adding the name of her son to the admissions register.

Vera looked up and smiled. 'Good morning, Mr Sheffield.'

'Good morning, Vera,' I said, 'and hello, Mrs Fazackerly.'

''Ello, Mr Sheffield.'

Freda Fazackerly looked down at the little boy nervously clutching her threadbare coat. She rummaged in her pocket and pulled out a dusty wine gum. He accepted it gratefully, wiped the snot from his nose with the back of his sleeve and proceeded to masticate the sweet with enthusiasm.

'So, Mrs F, this is our Dylan,' said Mrs Fazackerly.

'Dylan?' queried Vera. 'As in Dylan Thomas?'

Mrs Fazackerly shook her head. 'No, it's jus' Dylan – there's no Thomas. Y'know, after Bob Dylan,' she added by way of explanation.

'Oh yes,' said Vera.

'Times they are a changin' an' all that,' continued Mrs Fazackerly in a sing-song voice.

'Are they?' asked Vera. It was our secretary's turn to look puzzled.

''E'll be five nex' Friday.'

Vera glanced at her calendar of the flowers of Yorkshire and wrote '10 January 1981' in the date-of-birth column of her admissions register.

'An' 'e's gorra lot o' talent, 'as our Dylan,' said Mrs Fazackerly proudly.

'That's encouraging,' said Vera politely.

''E 'as that.'

'Really?'

''E's a born musician, is my Dylan,' said Mrs Fazackerly with pride. She looked down at her son, who was picking his nose and then sucking his finger.

'That's wonderful,' said Vera without conviction.

'Yes, 'e plays wi' 'is ocarina in t'bath.'

It takes all sorts, thought Vera.

A few minutes later Mrs Blenkinsop was Vera's next customer. She had brought in her son. Like Dylan, he was approaching his fifth birthday. Judy Blenkinsop was also eight months pregnant.

'Do sit down, Mrs Blenkinsop,' said Vera.

'Thank you kindly, Mrs F,' she said. 'Ah think ah've got another rugby player in 'ere.' She patted her enormous tummy and sat down heavily in the visitor's chair.

'What's matter, Mam?' asked the little boy.

'Y'know what's matter – ah'm 'avin' a baby.'

'Mam ... can we 'ave a puppy instead?'

Vera considered it time to move on. She opened her admissions register once again. 'Now, your son's first name please, Mrs Blenkinsop.'

'Cheyenne,' said Mrs Blenkinsop.

Vera was still for a moment, pen poised. 'Cheyenne?'

'Yes,' confirmed Mrs Blenkinsop. 'We wanted 'im t'stand out.'

'I'm sure he will,' said Vera without any trace of emotion.

At nine o'clock Ryan Halfpenny rang the bell and the children hurried into their classrooms.

There was a tap on the office door and Vera glanced up to see Ruby polishing the handle. It was a sure sign she wanted to talk, so Vera put her register to one side.

'How are you, Ruby?'

Ruby stopped cleaning the shiniest piece of brass in North Yorkshire and shuffled into the room, closing the door behind her. 'Ah'm still worried 'bout our Duggie, Mrs F.'

'And why is that?' asked Vera. 'I saw him parking his hearse outside the Post Office and he appeared content with his life.'

'Yes, 'e's a good lad an' 'e's doin' well at t'fun'ral parlour, but 'e's still lost where women are concerned ... particularly that *mature* woman 'e's started seein'.'

'You mean a *different* mature woman?' asked Vera, recalling Duggie's previous liaison.

'Yes, 'er from t'shoe shop in Easington 'as gone off t'pastures new. She took up wi' 'im what owns t'dry cleaners in Helmsley. By all accounts she wanted summat more permanent an' she pressed 'im summat rotten.'

Vera decided not to comment on the owner of a dry cleaners being pressed. 'So he's moved on with his life,' she said.

''E 'as that,' said Ruby, stuffing her chamois leather into the copious pocket of her pinny. 'In fac', our Duggie's allus been that way inclined, Mrs F,' she added with feeling. 'Y'know, rollin' 'is own oats so t'speak. Prudence reckons it's a *phrase* they all go through.'

'I'm sure it is,' said Vera. 'So who is the new woman in his life?'

'It's Tina from Thirkby. She works in t'mattress factory an' at weekends in that tattoo parlour in Gillygate.' Ruby shook her head. 'It's beyond my apprehension.'

Vera recalled with amusement seeing the sign 'Tattoos-While-U-Wait' in the shop window the last time she had visited York. 'I know the shop but not the lady,' she said.

'She's no lady,' said Ruby. 'She's been round t'block too many times.'

'I see,' said Vera once she had interpreted the meaning.

'An' by all accounts she's givin' 'im a free tattoo.'

'Oh dear.'

'An' you'll never guess where,' whispered Ruby conspiratorially.

'In the tattoo parlour?' suggested Vera.

'No ... on 'is bum.'

Meanwhile, in Class 3 Sally had begun the day with mathematics and was busy doing some simple algebra with a group of children who required special help.

'Now write this down in your exercise books,' she said. 'X plus ten equals fifteen.' She paused while they scribbled in their books. 'So, boys and girls, what is X?'

Charlie Cartwright put up his hand. 'Miss, how do you spell X?'

Sally sighed deeply. 'Let's start this again,' she said.

At 10.30 a.m. Ryan Halfpenny rang the school bell to announce morning break. Anne was on playground duty and when I walked into the staff-room Vera was stirring hot milk in a pan. Pat was scanning the front page of Vera's *Daily Telegraph*.

'It says here we're living longer,' said Pat. 'Life expectancy for men has improved to sixty-eight and it's seventy-six for women.'

'Good news,' said Vera, hoping Rupert would exceed the average.

Pat continued to scan the newspaper. 'Yes, but during 1986 it says we'll have two million vehicles on the roads and smoking will account for a hundred thousand deaths at a cost of a hundred and seventy million pounds to the NHS.'

'Let's be optimistic,' said Vera. 'Our Prime Minister has said we should rejoice because of rising house prices and unemployment levelling out.'

Sally somehow remained silent. Unlike Vera, the venerable Margaret was not her favourite politician.

Eager to change the subject, Pat pressed on. 'I see Bob Geldof isn't included in the New Year's Honours List.'

After the successful Live Aid concert, Bob Geldof had been bitterly criticized by backbencher Nicholas Fairbairn, who had made his position clear. He had said, 'I am unimpressed by people who get glory out of misery. Why should this fool receive an award?'

Sally shook her head in dismay. She had spent twenty pence that morning on a *Daily Mirror* and Bob Geldof was front-page news. 'Well, according to my paper Mr Geldof was a citizen of the Irish Republic and his efforts were on behalf of people outside the Queen's influence.'

Pat read on. 'And David Steel the Liberal leader said he had ruffled too many feathers.'

Vera said nothing. She merely smiled as she served our milky coffee. *After all, when it comes to entertainers, what's Bob Geldof compared to the lovely, clean-cut Bruce Forsyth?* she thought.

She looked up. 'And how is John?' she asked. 'Still enjoying his DIY?'

Anne sighed deeply. 'Well, at Christmas he finally decided to embrace the eighties.' She rummaged in her shoulder bag and took out a newspaper cutting. It was a large advertisement that read: 'Amstrad VHS Video £299.90 – instant recording at the touch of a button'.

'That's wonderful,' I said.

'And you'll be able to watch *Starsky & Hutch* again and again,' said Sally with a mischievous grin.

Anne blushed. The thought of David Soul had that effect on her. 'Yes, perhaps,' she said cautiously. She was recalling the last telephone call from Edward Clifton. He had been very persuasive.

After morning break Pat Brookside was in the hall watching a BBC science programme with her class. I helped her wheel away the television at the end of the lesson. 'Isn't it exciting? What an opportunity for a teacher. I would love to be Christa McAuliffe,' she said.

The thirty-seven-year-old mother of two had been selected from over ten thousand entries in the NASA Teacher in Space Project and was set to become the first member of the public in space. Later in the month she was due to join six other astronauts in the Space Shuttle *Challenger.*

Back on *terra firma,* across the road in Diane's Hair Salon, Betty Buttle had decided she wanted a new hairstyle for 1986.

'Ah want t'look like Linda Evans,' she said.

Diane looked in the mirror at Betty's haystack of hair. It looked as though she had been dragged through a hedge backwards. 'Y'mean 'er in *Dynasty* wi' t'big shoulders?'

'No, not 'er,' said Betty. 'It's that Linda what sells second-'and books in Easington market. She said she came in 'ere before Christmas to 'ave 'er roots done. It looked like ’er what jumps out of a ’elicopter in a jumpsuit that shows off ’er bum.’

‘Anneka Rice?’

‘That’s ’er.’

Diane turned to check her shelf of hairspray. Hairdressing was evolving and it was becoming difficult to keep up.

After lunch I was in the office. The telephone rang and I picked up the receiver. ‘Ragley School,’ I said.

‘Jack, it’s Jim Fairbank here from the college.’

‘Jim ... a happy New Year,’ I replied. ‘And how are you?’

‘Fine, thanks, and best wishes to you for eighty-six.’

‘So, what can I do to help?’ I asked.

There was a riffle of papers. ‘I’m trying to complete the timetable for the temporary tutor we need for the coming term. The students are back this week.’

‘Well, you know I’ll help if I can,’ I said.

‘Could you do Tuesday afternoons commencing the twenty-first of this month?’

I looked in my diary. ‘Yes, that should be fine.’

‘Speaking of governors,’ Jim said, ‘I’m aware of the situation at Morton School.’

‘Are you?’ I wondered how much he knew. Jim had many influential friends.

‘Yes, I know the chair at Morton, Wilfred Bones. We sit on various committees.’ There was a pause as he seemed to be searching for the right words. ‘So ... beware. He is a tough negotiator. He told me the governors at Morton consider the school's closure to be the death of the village.'

'Rather extreme,' I said.

'Yes, Jack, but feelings are running high. In the meantime, do call in if you want to discuss the course further, but you've got the syllabus.'

'I'll be well prepared,' I assured him.

'I know you will ... and thank you once again.'

At 3.45 p.m. the bell rang for the end of school and, when I walked through the cloakroom area, Jemima Poole and Rosie Appleby smiled up at me as they put on their winter coats.

'Me an' Rosie are 'avin' tea at our 'ouse, Mr Sheffield, an' we're watchin' telly,' said Jemima.

'What will you be watching?' I asked.

'Roland Rat,' she said, 'an' 'e's moved.'

'Moved?' I didn't follow.

'Yes, Mr Sheffield,' confirmed Rosie. 'Roland's on BBC now.'

The fact that Britain's favourite rat had defected to the BBC had passed me by and, once again, I became privy to the secret world of childhood where puppets were more important than politicians.

Billy Ricketts had put on his coat and scarf and was clutching a tall plastic model that looked like a Tyrannosaurus Rex.

'It's Godzilla, Mr Sheffield, an' 'e can roar right loud,' said Billy.

He proceeded to make a passable imitation of a meat-eating dinosaur at the top of his voice and Pat, looking flustered, appeared. 'What's that noise?' she asked.

'Sorry,' I said, 'my fault. It's Godzilla.'

'I'll be glad when Godzilla becomes extinct,' whispered Pat.

'An' ah got Blaster, Inferno an' Skids, Mr Sheffield,' continued the enthusiastic Billy.

I had no idea what he was talking about and he ran off.

'They're Transformers, Jack,' explained Pat. 'I've heard nothing else from him all day.'

'Transformers?'

Pat grinned. 'You've obviously never met Optimus Prime,' and she hurried back to her classroom.

I realized that Pat and her infant children lived in a different world to me. In my class Barry Ollerenshaw and Ryan Halfpenny had received BMX bikes for Christmas and *these* I understood.

It was six o'clock and the school was quiet, so I decided to telephone Beth. She picked up on the first ring.

'How has it gone?' I asked.

'Hang on a moment.' There was a clunk as the receiver was placed on her desk and I heard her footsteps, followed by the closing of a door. 'That's better,' she said. 'I can talk now. I'm operating an open-door policy, so most of the staff have called in at the end of the day to share a concern or a proposal for developing the curriculum... Busy, but satisfying.'

'So no problems?'

There was a pause. 'Well ... I'll need to work on the head of the infants department. She's clearly resistant to change and keeps mentioning she's had ten years' more experience.'

'Will it become an issue?'

'Definitely not, Jack,' said Beth firmly. 'At the moment I'm just choosing my battles.'

'I see,' I said, recognizing the determination in her voice. Almost imperceptibly, a subtle shift had taken place.

'Anyway, why don't you treat yourself to a meal in The Oak on your way home and I'll pick up a takeaway? I'll be late. Also, I've spoken to my mother. John is fine and she sends her love. She knew late nights would be the order of the day for us.'

'Fine,' I said. 'Good to hear. See you later.'

I replaced the receiver and leaned back in my creaking, leather-covered wooden chair. Then I stared across the room at the neat rows of framed school photographs on the office wall and reflected on changing times.

'Love can move mountains,' Vera had once said to me. It appeared the foundation of our marriage was changing; the tectonic plates had moved.

Then I filled my fountain pen with Quink ink and shivered. Above my head, a mosaic of frost patterns etched the windows of the school office in their Victorian casements.

I took the school logbook from my bottom drawer, opened it to the next clean page and wrote the date, Monday, 6 January. The record for 1986 in the history of Ragley-on-the-Forest Church of England Primary School had begun.

It was after seven o'clock when I walked across the frozen village green towards The Royal Oak. The cold was intense. The grass beneath my feet crunched like brittle shards of glass and the water in the pond was iron.

The blast of hot air in the bar area was welcome. Aled Jones was on the juke-box singing 'Walking In The Air' but no one seemed to be listening.

In a haze of Old Holborn tobacco Old Tommy Piercy was sitting on his favourite stool by the bar below the signed photograph of Geoffrey Boycott.

'Good evening, Mr Piercy,' I said.

'Stop blowing smoke over Mr Sheffield,' ordered Sheila from the other side of the bar.

'Sorry,' said Old Tommy. 'Ah used t'smoke Player's Navy Cut, untipped – proper fags – but now ah'm a pipe man, y'can't beat it.' He took the pipe from his lips and rested it in the Tetley's ashtray.

'Would you like a drink, Mr Piercy?'

'Is t'Pope Catholic?' said Sheila. She was wearing a skintight crimson blouse with most of the top buttons undone. The finest cleavage in North Yorkshire was there for all to see.

'Two pints of Chestnut, please, Sheila,' I said, 'and something hot to eat.'

'Special tonight is steak an' kidney pie wi' mash,' said Sheila as she hand-pulled the pints.

'That sounds fine to me,' I said, taking out my wallet.

The television was flickering above the taproom bar. The newsreader seemed in good spirits as he announced that Britain was in third place in the World Happiness League. 'We are four times as happy as the West Germans,' he added.

'An' so we bloody should be,' said Old Tommy

as he supped on his ale.

''E's a reight Job's comforter, is Tommy,' said Sheila.

Deke Ramsbottom approached the bar. The newsreader had moved on to the sports news. 'Ah see Man U are top again,' said Deke. Manchester United had increased their lead at the top of the First Division by beating Burnley 1-0.

Old Tommy, a curmudgeonly Yorkshireman, scowled and changed the subject. He looked up at Deke. 'Ah 'eard young Duggie 'as tekken up wi' that Tina from Thirkby.' Following the death of Ronnie Smith, Deke had taken Duggie under his wing.

'Yes, 'e 'as,' said Deke.

It was well known in the village that Tina had a *reputation.* She could be found every Friday night in the summer leaning against the picket fence that surrounded the Ragley cricket pitch with the intention of meeting a different young man each week.

'She's flattened some grass in 'er time 'as that one,' said Old Tommy knowingly. As he mowed the square on the cricket field, Tina's summertime trysts with all the young bucks in the village had become a familiar sight. He had personally witnessed her enjoying very vocal sexual encounters with two opening batsmen, three fast bowlers and a wicket keeper, not to mention the occasional umpire.

'Ah 'eard she puts it abart a bit,' said Don from behind the bar.

'Y'reight there, Don,' said Old Tommy. 'She's insatiated.'

It was almost ten o'clock when I finally drove home. By coincidence, Bob Dylan was singing 'The Times They Are a-Changin'' on the car radio and I sang along.

It seemed apt.

Chapter Ten

Through a Glass Darkly

The headteacher will be visiting the college in York to deliver a series of lectures on curriculum development and classroom organization on Tuesday afternoons this term. Arrangements have been made for Miss Flint to provide supply cover in Class 4 and this has been confirmed with the school governors and County Hall.

Extract from the Ragley School Logbook:
Monday, 20 January 1986

It was Monday, 20 January and the stillness of winter lay heavy on the countryside. A cruel frost had arrived and the dormant trees shivered in the bitter wind. Vera was staring thoughtfully out of the office window and I stood beside her. We looked out on a world of frozen hedgerows and a spectral sky. On the high moors the temperature had dropped to minus twelve degrees and grey clouds that promised more snow rolled towards us over the Hambleton hills.

'A bleak day, Vera,' I said quietly.

Vera was clearly preoccupied and sighed deeply.

'Yes, Mr Sheffield,' she murmured.
'What is it?' I asked.
We looked out to where groups of children were playing in the snow. There were loud shouts, snowball fights, and Damian Brown and Frankie Spraggon had begun to build an igloo. Two rosy-cheeked seven-year-olds, Rosie Spittlehouse and Becky Shawcross, were rolling huge snowballs. However, watching them from a distance and standing alone was a tall eight-year-old girl with a patterned bobble hat, a fleece jacket, red mittens, blue jeans and bright-green wellington boots. She was well dressed for this bitterly cold day but, even so, she appeared to be shivering.
'It's the new girl, Katie Parrish,' said Vera. 'I'm worried about her.'
'Why is that?' I asked. 'She seemed happy enough when she arrived.'
Vera was always very perceptive where the children were concerned. She knew them all, including their family history. 'She's changed,' she said simply.
So it began ... a week in the life of Ragley School that had an impact on us all.

It was morning break when I saw Anne putting on her scarf and gloves in the entrance hall.
'Everything all right?' she asked. 'I know that look.'
'There's some concern about Katie Parrish,' I said, 'so I'll get an update from Sally.'
'I'll look out for her during break,' she said and walked out into the bitter cold, shivered, then smiled at the sight of children who appeared en-

tirely unaware that the temperature on the playground was minus five degrees.

Vera was serving coffee in the staff-room while the rest of us sat down in our usual chairs.

'I thought we could discuss Katie Parrish at lunch-time,' I suggested. 'Vera has picked up a few concerns.'

'Yes, she's a really bright girl, but she's been a bit down recently,' said Sally quietly, 'and she clams up when I enquire.'

'Why don't I sit with her during school dinner,' offered Pat, 'and see what I can find out? She might talk to a fresh face.'

'Thanks, Pat,' I said.

The conversation ebbed to and fro, but eventually we moved on. There were children to teach.

At twelve o'clock I called into Sally's classroom as Ryan Halfpenny unwound the rope from the metal cleat on the wall of the bell tower and rang the bell for our lunch-break.

'Sally, could you bring some examples of Katie Parrish's work to the staff-room after lunch so we can look at them while we talk?' I asked.

'Yes, that's fine,' said Sally, 'I'll see you there,' and she walked over to one of the eighteen-drawer mobile-storage units, removed Katie's grey plastic tray, collected her mathematics and English books and put them on her desk.

During lunch the children lined up while Shirley and Doreen served up a hot meal of cottage pie followed by rhubarb and custard. It was welcome on a cold day and while the children ate they kept peering out of the windows, full of excitement, as snow began to fall again.

After lunch Pat and I stood by the door as they all filed out. I looked at Katie Parrish. She appeared to be in a little world of her own as she collected her coat and wellingtons from the cloakroom area. There was no eagerness to follow the others as they hurried outside to play in the snow.

I headed for the staff-room. It was time to talk.

We settled down, Vera served tea and Sally took the lead. There was an unwritten procedure for this. We had done it many times before; however, it was relatively new to Pat and I saw her lean forward in her chair. It was important to exchange information and, on occasions, it could be vital for the welfare of our children.

'As you know, Katie arrived in my class at the beginning of term,' said Sally. 'I remember her first day so well. She was quiet and shy and her writing is wonderful. There's no doubt she's a bright, talented girl, but she's been reluctant to communicate recently.'

'Both her parents are lecturers,' said Vera. 'Her father works at York University and her mother is in the education department at the college. They live in rented accommodation on the Easington Road. My understanding is they want to settle in the area on a permanent basis.'

'Well, I'm at the college tomorrow afternoon,' I said. 'I begin my teaching sessions there, so there may be an opportunity to have a quiet word with Mrs Parrish. Did you learn anything over lunch, Pat?'

Pat reported back that during their lunchtime conversation Katie had said that her father appeared to have little time for her. Just as she was telling us this, Sally suddenly looked concerned.

'Oh dear,' she said. She was holding Katie's writing book. 'We were writing about things we like and dislike this morning and Katie went off on a tack of her own.'

'What does it say?' asked Pat.

Sally looked down at the small, neat lines of writing. 'She's written "My Daddy is always busy. He doesn't love me any more".'

Everyone was quiet for a moment.

'Do you want me to ring Mrs Parrish and ask her to call in?' asked Sally.

I pondered this for a moment. 'Thanks,' I said, 'but let's just monitor it for a while longer.'

Everyone nodded in agreement. It was too early for alarm bells.

Finally, as I walked back to my classroom, I thought how every school day is different and today was proving to be particularly challenging.

At the end of school we said a simple prayer and the children put their chairs on the table tops prior to Ruby coming round with her mop and large broom. I noticed she was humming to herself. At one time we had enjoyed listening to her wonderful singing every day as she cleaned the classrooms, but since Ronnie's death she had rarely sung and we missed it. At least this was a start.

Barry Ollerenshaw appeared in a hurry to change from his indoor shoes into his Wellington boots. He was tugging them on furiously as I walked into the cloakroom area.

'Are you OK, Barry?' I asked.

'It's *Thunderbirds* at half-past four, Mr Sheffield,'

he said breathlessly, 'an' ah never miss it.'

The international space-rescue team in the year 2086 was dedicated to the service of mankind but also, of course, to the imagination of the children in my class.

'Well, enjoy it, Barry,' I called after him, 'and tell me about it tomorrow.'

'OK, sir,' he shouted over his shoulder.

Shortly after the end of school I noticed Katie Parrish was sitting in the library area with Vera.

'We're waiting for Katie's father to arrive,' said Vera.

I looked at my wristwatch and crouched down next to Katie. 'He may have been held up, so don't worry.'

She gave me a shy smile and turned back to reading *Tom's Midnight Garden.*

'Something may have cropped up at the university,' added Vera.

Fifteen minutes later Vera popped her head round the office door. 'Still no sign,' she said. 'Do you want to sit with her while I make a couple of telephone calls?'

I sat down next to Katie and a few minutes later Sally appeared from the hall with some large sheets of sugar paper. She gave me a knowing look. People who were late in collecting their children were an irritation, but we knew it happened from time to time and we took it in our stride. Life wasn't easy for working parents.

Sally put down the paper on the old pine table. 'I'll wait here with Katie,' she said. 'You need to get on.'

I returned to the office, where Vera was replacing the receiver. 'Mr Parrish can't be contacted at the university. The secretary at the college says Mrs Parrish has been at a meeting in Ripon and may be driving back by now.'

I looked up at the office clock. It was a quarter to five. 'Let's give it until five,' I said.

'Then I could drive Katie home and see if someone is there,' offered Vera.

'Thanks,' I said, 'and I'll stay here by the telephone.'

At five o'clock Vera and Katie were about to walk out to the car park when bright headlights lit up the school drive. A large car slewed to a stop and Mr Parrish jumped out and ran up the entrance steps.

'I was delayed,' he said. He looked dishevelled and harassed. 'I'm so sorry, Katie,' he said as he scooped her up in his arms.

'You were supposed to come,' said Katie. 'Mummy said she had a meeting.'

'I know, darling ... but I was busy.'

They rushed out and drove home.

'Interesting,' said Vera and gave me that look I had come to know so well.

I was lighting a fire when Beth arrived home. Natasha Smith had become our occasional child-minder when Mrs Roberts had commitments in Hartingdale.

There was no doubt that Natasha took after Ruby. Her love of children was clear for all to see and John adored her. Fortunately it had little effect on her part-time work at Diane's Hair Salon and her increased income was welcomed by both Natasha and her mother. Also, George Dainty had volunteered to give her lifts to and from Kirkby Steepleton when required. It appeared to be a labour of love for George, while for our part it was a huge relief to have such reliable and caring support for our son.

Finally, when John was in bed, Bilbo Cottage became a haven of peace and we sat by a roaring log fire. Beth worked late into the evening planning curriculum changes for her school while I marked the children's books. This had become the pattern of our life during the winter months and it was good to be home.

On The Crescent, however, in Anne Grainger's home, the situation was different. The sound of loud banging shattered the peace. John was in the garage hammering nails into a rickety wooden construction that was intended to be a pair of saw horses. *Ideal for sawing large planks,* he thought.

In the lounge, Anne winced with each hammer blow and turned up the sound on the television. It was 7.40 p.m. and she had tuned in to BBC1 for *Starsky & Hutch,* who were about to launch headlong into another adventure. Unfortunately the plot involved David Soul as Hutch eating contaminated soup that resulted in a case of life or death. As the noise in the garage reached a crescendo Anne wished there was some of the soup left for her DIY husband.

On Tuesday I awoke very early and drove through the darkness into Ragley. It was a busy morning and it seemed strange when Miss Flint arrived and

I had to say farewell to my class for the afternoon. As I drove down the A19 towards York the weather changed and it became a day of fitful sleet and scudding clouds. I was a little apprehensive as I considered the beginning of my work with adults rather than the children usually in my care. I had prepared a lecture on curriculum development, followed by a workshop on classroom organization, and I hoped it would go well.

The first student had arrived at this college in 1841 and generations of teachers had passed through its doors and walked through the ancient halls. In the sixties, when I was a student, it was known as St John's College, but in the mid-seventies it had merged with the other Anglican teacher-training college based in nearby Ripon, so now it was the College of Ripon and York St John. As I drove in through the college gate on Lord Mayor's Walk, memories came flooding back.

I called in at Jim Fairbank's office and he glanced at his wristwatch. 'You're in good time, Jack, so perhaps you would like to join me in the refectory?'

'Actually, Jim, I've eaten,' I said, 'but I was hoping to have a brief word with Mrs Parrish. Her daughter attends Ragley School.'

A flicker of concern crossed his face. 'Well Rebecca should be in there now.'

The refectory was a huge room full of students, the crash of cutlery and loud chatter. It was busy and vibrant, and we joined Mrs Parrish at her table. In a brief conversation I explained that we had a few concerns regarding Katie and asked if she could meet with me in school. I avoided mentioning anything relating to what Katie had written about her father.

'Yes, I could call in tomorrow morning on my way into college,' she said. 'It will probably be just me, I'm afraid. Simon has various commitments on Wednesdays.'

In fact I thought it might be helpful to see her on her own. Katie's feelings about her father seemed to be problematic and we needed to dig deeper.

The lecture went better than I had hoped and the students were eager to learn. During the afternoon tea break, as I walked through the quadrangle, two of them approached me. One, a young man with a serious expression and an eager freckled face, called out, 'Excuse me, Mr Sheffield.'

'Thanks for the lecture,' said his long-haired friend. 'It was really helpful.'

'We have a problem and we wondered if you could help,' said Freckles, 'but it's a bit embarrassing.'

'Go on,' I said. 'What is it?'

'Well ... it's porridge.'

'Porridge?'

'Yes, it's all we've got left. We've had nothing else to eat this week and we've no money for food.'

'But haven't you got a grant?'

'Yes, but there's nothing in our accounts yet.'

'What about support from your families?'

So it went on. I hadn't expected to be dealing with pastoral issues on my first day, but this needed sorting out. I knew the location of the Bursar's office and left them in his capable hands.

Fifteen minutes later all seemed well as I began my classroom-management workshop with a slide-show of my classroom showing the pattern of the school day. I explained how to facilitate whole-class teaching, mixed-ability group work and the vital opportunities to hear individual children read. In the end I had surprised myself. This was a good experience and I felt comfortable in the new environment of higher education.

By Wednesday morning reality had set in once again as I drove to Ragley village. The rhythm of the windscreen wipers was hypnotic. They swept away the berms of snow, but not my racing thoughts.

Mrs Parrish was waiting for me in the entrance hall. 'Sorry, Mr Sheffield, early start,' she said and looked across to our library area. 'I've got Katie with me. I hope you don't mind, but I sat her in the library. Mrs Pringle said she would keep an eye on her.'

There was love in her eyes when she looked at her daughter, but also something else ... and I wasn't sure what it was. We left Katie reading quietly while we went into the office.

'We obviously want Katie to be happy here at Ragley,' I said. 'How has she been at home?'

Mrs Parrish studied me for a moment with guarded eyes. 'Generally fine,' she said. 'Why do you ask?'

Answer a question with a question, I thought.

She was concerned when I showed her what Katie had written. For a few moments she didn't speak and I could see her wrestling with her own thoughts, but then she said she would choose a moment to talk to Katie about how she was feeling and would keep a close eye on her at home. After that she relaxed and soon we were chatting easily as she opened up about their plans. 'Simon and I sold our home in Stamford Bridge,' she explained, 'and we're renting in Ragley. The intention is to buy one of the new Barratt homes on the development further up the Easington Road. It's right on the boundary line between here and Easington School, but we would prefer Katie to come here.'

She opened her leather shoulder bag and pulled out a cutting from the local paper. She had ringed the advertisement that read: *'Detached 3/4 bedroom houses, £64,250. Luxury and elegance in a village setting'*.

'Yes, these are lovely homes,' I said, 'and convenient for your drive into college.'

'Well, we certainly thought so ... but Simon occasionally has other ideas.'

There were unspoken words that echoed around the office.

'I spoke to my husband this morning,' she went on, 'and if convenient he said he'll call into school at twelve o'clock. He's going in late today. Many of his doctorate students can't come until later in the day.' As she left she shook my hand. 'Sincere thanks for sharing your thoughts, Mr Sheffield, and I'm pleased this was brought to my attention.'

As she turned towards the door I added, 'And we managed to resolve the problem on Monday evening when your husband didn't arrive to pick up Katie.'

'Really?'

'Yes, it was five o'clock when he arrived and we were unable to contact either of you. I know you have busy professional lives, but if you could let us know in future we'll always do our best to help.'

There was a hint of a frown, but she recovered quickly. 'Yes, of course.'

On her way out she spoke briefly with Vera and Joseph in the entrance hall. They both came into the office, intrigued and thoughtful.

'A perceptive lady,' said Vera.

'I agree,' I said.

'She was definitely *troubled,*' said Joseph.

Vera was thoughtful. 'It was,' she said, 'as if she sees life through a glass darkly.'

Joseph smiled and looked at me. 'Corinthians,' he said by way of explanation.

'Chapter thirteen, verse twelve,' retorted Vera in an instant.

He squeezed her arm affectionately. 'You always were better than me at our Bible studies.'

'It's familiar,' I said, 'but I can't recall the context.'

'"For now we see through a glass, darkly",' recited Joseph.

'"But then face to face: now I know",' said Vera, completing the next line.

Then I understood. Face-to-face meetings revealed so much, as I was to discover later in the day.

Simon Parrish arrived half an hour late for our appointment. He pulled into the car park in a 1985 'C' Saab 900i. With its distinctive cochineal-red metallic paintwork, it was certainly meant to stand out from the crowd.

He oozed confidence as he removed his flowing black coat and draped it over the visitor's chair. He was a tall, slim, handsome man with long, foppish brown hair, a baggy denim shirt, designer brown cords and highly polished brown leather brogues with the added affectation of steel toecaps.

He walked round my desk and stood by the window. 'Excellent wheels, don't you think?' he said. It seemed an incongruous opening and I wondered if he was being deliberately rude to mask his nervousness. 'Just bought it,' he continued. 'Four and a half thousand on the clock and not much change from ten grand.'

He turned back to the visitor's chair, sat down and stretched out his long legs. 'So, time's short – what's the problem?'

'Thank you for coming, Mr Parrish,' I said.

'Actually, *Professor* Parrish,' he interjected quickly with a laconic smile on his face. 'I'm the senior guy in the Humanities Department at the University of York ... but we needn't stand on ceremony.'

I remained impassive. 'As I was saying, Mr Parrish, I appreciate your coming in and, as we were due to meet at twelve, time is indeed short.' I looked up at the office clock. 'I'm teaching immediately after lunch.'

'So am I, but *we* work civilized hours,' he replied curtly.

I pressed on. 'We have a few concerns regarding Katie,' I said. I outlined some of the issues and finally I showed him Katie's writing book. He passed it back to me hastily. 'I'm sure it's nothing,' he said, 'and, of course, we could send her to Easington Primary School.'

'That's for you to decide,' I said. 'We simply want the best for Katie.'

He gave me a hard stare and stood up. 'Can I see her before I go?'

I asked Sally to bring Katie to the entrance hall and I watched father and daughter carefully. It was a meeting of tense silences and unspoken thoughts. There was distance between them.

As he left he crouched down next to his daughter. 'Mummy is collecting you straight from school ... so don't worry.'

As he drove away I walked out with Katie to the playground while a flint wind rattled the silent shutters of my mind.

At the end of school I was surprised to see Mrs Parrish waiting outside the office door. She looked a little tense, but her news was reassuring.

'Rosie Appleby's mother has invited Katie for tea,' she said, 'so I'm collecting both girls now and driving to Rosie's. Then I'll be picking her up later from there.'

I thanked her for letting me know.

Rebecca Parrish sat in her car outside Rosie Appleby's house and anger built up inside her. Simon hadn't mentioned he had been late in collecting Katie on Monday evening. In fact, recently, there was a lot he hadn't mentioned. She glanced down at her wristwatch. There were no departmental meetings, so she was free ... time that she hadn't expected to have. She made a decision. Home was up the Easington Road. Instead she drove down the High Street towards York.

The university car park was dark and she looked up at the Humanities Department building. Bars of light escaped from the closed blinds. She knew the way. It was a long corridor. Fluorescent lights blazed above her. The sign on the familiar door read 'Prof. S. Parrish' and she walked straight in.

A tall, lithesome woman about thirty years old was stretching up to kiss her husband. For a moment there was a frozen tableau of the professor and the student, and for Rebecca Parrish it was as if she had been struck.

It was only later that she realized why the impact was so great.

It wasn't that Simon was holding the woman's hand and looking into her eyes. Rather it was the fact that it was a *tender* kiss, a loving kiss, soft and gentle.

This was no fling, no casual relationship. She was staring at a pair of lovers.

'Now I know why you forgot to pick up our child on Monday evening.' Quiet words ... and cold. Briefly the atmosphere was suffused with acrimony. Then Rebecca Parrish retreated from the room and closed the door.

That evening, as snow pattered against the windows of the cottage, Beth and I settled down in the lounge for the evening. We were surrounded by white noise ... peaceful and calming as we sipped our mugs of steaming coffee.

Suddenly Beth broke the silence. 'I'm thinking of changing my car,' she announced.

I was surprised. 'I thought you liked your Beetle.'

She shook her head. 'It's no longer suitable for these winter drives into work and there's rust everywhere.'

It seemed the end of an era. 'What had you in mind?'

She had circled an advertisement in the *Easington Herald*. 'Have a look at this,' she said. It read: '1981 VW Golf CD Diesel, 5 door, blue trim, £2,995'.

'Three thousand pounds,' I said. 'A lot of money.'

'But I'm earning more now, Jack, and with part-exchange and easy terms it should be fine.'

I had to agree. It made sense.

After a meal of lasagne and a glass of wine we decided to put schoolwork to one side and unwind. We settled down shortly after eight o'clock to watch *Dynasty*, but my thoughts kept returning to my meeting with Simon Parrish.

On Thursday morning it was Mrs Parrish who called in before school. She looked pale but composed and requested a private word.

'I'm not intending to beat about the bush,' she said. 'I've asked my husband to move out.'

'I see,' I said.

'So ... we've separated and Katie and I are staying here in the village. Simon is moving on.'

'Moving on?'

'Yes, with his new partner. Katie doesn't know yet, but we will tell her this evening.'

'Do you mind me sharing this with the rest of the staff and Mrs Forbes-Kitchener?' I asked.

'They all have key pastoral roles in the school.'
'Of course,' she said. 'I understand.'
'I know you do,' I said quietly.
She smiled. 'After all, we're in the same profession. I deal with this frequently. I just didn't think it would happen to me.'
'So what's next?' I asked.
'Well, it's my intention to keep living in the area because I want Katie to continue at Ragley. Given the disruption she has faced she will need the security your school can offer.'
She stared out of the window. 'You have a lovely school, Mr Sheffield, and I'm grateful to you for all your help during this...' there was a strained smile, '...eventful week.'
At lunchtime I sat in the office looking out at the children playing in the snow on the school field. I saw Katie Parrish talking with Rosie Appleby and reflected that friendship was a simple thing when you were young. I marvelled at their innocence. It was a time of birthdays and bonfires, presents and parties; a time of freedom to climb trees and paddle in streams. In their cocoon of private space they enjoyed the scent of flowers and the breath of freedom.
Sally called in and we talked about Katie. 'We see a lot of this, Jack,' she mused. 'Sadly, Katie is an innocent in a guilty world.'
At the end of school Sally spoke to Katie and Rosie as they put on their coats and she was pleased that they seemed relaxed.
'We're going to watch *Blue Peter,* Miss,' said Katie with enthusiasm.
'It's about York Minster,' added Rosie.

Simon Groom, Janet Ellis and Peter Duncan were returning to York Minster after the great fire of 1984 to look at the restoration of the Rose Window.

Rosie and Katie walked out arm in arm, chattering excitedly.

On Friday morning rooks squawked their danger cries as the wind began to rattle the branches of their nests. When I arrived at school Mrs Parrish was talking to Vera in the entrance hall.

'We've talked about it, Mr Sheffield, and Katie understands what is happening. She thought it might be her fault, but I reassured her it wasn't.'

'We will keep an eye on her,' I said, 'and whenever you wish to talk, we're here.'

'Thank you,' she said. She looked at Vera. 'Both of you.' As she turned to leave she glanced back. 'You can learn a lot from a child's writing.'

We watched her drive away.

'At least she's no longer looking through a glass darkly,' said Vera quietly.

'It seems like the way ahead is clear,' I replied.

We both walked back into the office to begin our day's work.

Chapter Eleven

Driving Ambition

School reopened today following the half-term holiday.

Extract from the Ragley School Logbook:
Monday, 3 March 1986

The season was changing and, in spite of a bitterly cold wind, the first signs of a distant spring crept over the high moors. The raucous calls of curlews announced the end of winter as a pale sun touched the land with warmth and light. It was Monday, 3 March, the first day after the half-term holiday, and I felt a new optimism as I drove out of Kirkby Steepleton. Beneath the frozen earth new life stirred and lifted the spirits of the folk of North Yorkshire – with the exception of Victor Pratt.

He lumbered out of his untidy garage as I pulled up on the forecourt alongside the single pump. 'Fill her up please, Victor,' I said, '...and how are you?'

Victor's face was bright red and he wiped his brow with the back of his oil-smeared hand. 'Ah'm sweatin' cobs, Mr Sheffield,' he said. 'Ah think ah'm comin' down wi' summat.'

'Oh dear,' I said, 'I'm sorry to hear that.'

'Ah get 'ot when ah bend down an' dizzy when

ah get up,' he elaborated. 'Ah don't know if ah'm comin' or goin'.'

'Perhaps you need a pick-me-up from the chemist,' I suggested, more in hope than expectation.

'Mebbe so,' said Victor, brightening up, 'but first ah'm goin' t'Ruby's mother for a bottle of Uncle Billy's tonic. That'll put me right.'

'I could ask Ruby to collect it for you and then I'll drop it in when I'm passing,' I said, trying to be helpful.

'Thanks, Mr Sheffield, but ah've got young Kenny Kershaw comin' to 'old t'fort for me later this morning. 'E's a good lad and ah'm thinkin' o' trainin' 'im up t'be a mechanic. You've got t'give young uns a chance.'

'Very true,' I agreed.

'Ah'll sithee,' he said and took out a dirty handkerchief to wipe his brow.

'Get well soon, Victor,' I said as he gave me my change.

As I drove away I thought about Victor's words and the cycle of life in the village. A new generation was finding employment in a difficult world.

Meanwhile, in the High Street, Heathcliffe Earnshaw was finishing his paper round and he gave me a wave as I turned into school. I paused before driving through the school gate. The willow had come back to life on the village green and at the base of its trunk the spears of narcissi were forcing their bullet heads through the dense layer of leaf mould. It was a sight to refresh the soul and I felt encouraged as I drove up the cobbled drive.

Ruby was sweeping the entrance porch and leaned on her broom as I approached.

'Good morning, Ruby,' I said. 'How are you?'
'Fair t'middlin',' she replied.
'Better weather now,' I remarked.
'Mebbe so, Mr Sheffield,' said Ruby, 'but on t'news this morning it said we were in for adverb weather conditions ... so it dunt look promising.'
'Oh well, here's to a good day,' I said, trying to be cheerful, but Ruby was in one of her sombre moods again.
She propped her yard broom against the wall and pushed a few stray strands of her curly chestnut hair under her headscarf. 'To tell you t'truth, Mr Sheffield, ah'm beginning t'feel t'cold these days.' She looked down at her threadbare coat and gave a wan smile. 'It's been an 'ard winter an' ah could do wi' a warm coat wi' lots o' installation.'
'Come inside, Ruby, and warm yourself,' I said. 'I'm sure we can find time for a hot drink.'
'Thank you kindly, but ah said ah'd meet George Dainty in Nora's for a coffee,' and she took her broom inside to her caretaker's cupboard.
Vera was busy filing in the office when I sat down at my desk. She had stacked the morning's post neatly under my brass paperweight and I began to sort through it.
A few minutes later there was a tap on the door. It was Ruby. 'Ah'm getting off smartish, Mrs F,' she said, oblivious to my presence. 'Ah'm seeing Mr Dainty in t'Coffee Shop.'
'That's lovely, Ruby,' said Vera. 'He's a good friend.'
'Strange,' pondered Ruby. She was clearly thinking about her changing circumstances. 'Ah spent a life wi' my Ronnie, Mrs F, living on t'never-never

an' now ah've met a man wi' a load o' brass.'

'You certainly have,' said Vera.

'Yes, Mrs F,' said Ruby and, after glancing in my direction, she lowered her voice. 'So ... what do you think of 'im?'

I pretended to be immersed in the latest recommendation from County Hall for making sure our future half-term holidays coincided with the local secondary school.

'He's a very kind and generous man,' said Vera. 'He always helps towards our church funds.'

Ruby smiled. 'Yes, 'e's become a good friend. In fac' 'e's tekkin' me into York later t'day t'see our little Krystal.'

Vera nodded knowingly. 'That's lovely, Ruby. It's important to spend time with your granddaughter.'

'Our Duggie was s'pposed t'be givin' me a lift but 'e announced this mornin', large as life, 'e 'ad summat important t'do for t'funeral parlour. 'E never plans 'is life does Duggie, jus' like his dad wi' channel vision.'

'Never mind, Ruby, just go and enjoy your time with Mr Dainty.'

Ruby paused by the door on her way out. 'It's times like this ah wish ah could drive ... but it's too late for me.'

After the door had closed I saw Vera smile. 'We need to give Ruby a focus, Mr Sheffield,' she said, 'something to concentrate her mind ... and I think I may have the answer.' She proceeded to dial a local number.

George Dainty was surprised to receive a telephone call from the vicar's sister, but he listened intently and nodded thoughtfully when he finally replaced the receiver.

'There,' said Vera, 'that should do it.'

In the next village Rufus Timmings was standing outside Morton School and considering the school sign. His name was emblazoned in gold paint, followed by a string of letters that indicated he had a Bachelor of Education degree plus a number of obscure certificates and diplomas. He smiled in satisfaction. It made him appear to be North Yorkshire's best-qualified academic.

'Mornin', Mr Timmings,' growled a voice behind him.

Rufus turned round and looked up into the weathered jowls of a heavily built, fierce-looking man.

'Oh, good morning. Can I help?' asked Rufus, slightly perturbed at the sight of this sixteen-stone Yorkshireman who stank of last night's beer.

'Ah'm 'ere to introduce m'self ... ah'm Stanley Coe from Coe Farm in Ragley.'

Recognition dawned for Rufus. 'Ah, Mr Coe, I've been expecting you,' he said.

'Ah thought y'might,' said Stan. He pulled out an envelope from the inside pocket of his donkey jacket. 'Ah've just 'ad this letter confirmin' ah'm t'new local authority governor.'

'Yes,' said Rufus, 'our chair of governors, Mr Bones, was informed of your appointment by County Hall.' He paused to appraise this local farmer. 'So, welcome to Morton School. Would you like to come in?'

'No, ah'm off to t'abattoir, so ah can't stop.'

Rufus looked at him, slightly puzzled. 'If you don't mind me saying, Mr Coe, I'm surprised you want to be a governor here.'

Stan gave him a shifty look. 'An' why's that?'

'Well, with all the *upheaval*.'

'Up'eaval,' said Stan with a grin. 'That's why ah'm 'ere, lad.'

Rufus did not appreciate being called 'lad' but let it go. 'Well that's good to hear, but there are challenging times ahead.'

Stan weighed up this young man with his smart suit and soft features in the same way he assessed which of his animals would be slaughtered. 'Mr Bones mentioned about the 'eadteacher's job bein' advertised for t'new school.'

'That's correct,' said Rufus. 'That's the official procedure with it being an amalgamation of the two schools.'

Stan stroked the side of his bulbous nose with a nicotine-stained finger. 'An' tell me, Mr Timmings – will you be applying for t'job?'

Rufus puffed out his chest. 'But of course, Mr Coe, I certainly shall.'

Stan recognized raw ambition with a hint of cunning when he saw it and he looked up at the school sign. 'Then let's mek sure your name is painted over t'top o' present 'eadteacher's name.'

Rufus Timmings watched Stan Coe climb back into his Land Rover and roar off towards Easington.

Both men were smiling.

On the juke-box in the Coffee Shop, The Bangles were singing 'Manic Monday' and George Dainty was thinking they were probably right. His response to Vera's request had to be handled carefully. When Ruby came in he bought two frothy coffees and she sat warming her hands on the steaming mug.

George thought to himself that there was no time like the present.

'Ruby, ah was wond'ring if y'fancied learnin' t'drive?'

'Pard'n?'

'Yes, y'know ... you drivin' an' ah could learn you.'

Ruby shook her head in bewilderment. 'An' pigs might fly, George.'

'No, ah'm serious,' he said. 'It would give y'that *independence* y'need so y'could visit York an' suchlike an' see little Krystal when y'fancy.'

'It's a bit late in t'day f'me,' said Ruby. 'Ah'm not a spring chicken any more.'

'Mebbe not, Ruby,' said George firmly, 'but you could conquer anything if y'put y'mind to it.'

'D'you really think so?'

George stretched out his hand and laid it gently on top of Ruby's work-red, swollen fingers. 'Ah do,' he said simply.

'Well, ah can't say ah 'aven't given it some thought.'

'Go on, luv – nothin' ventured, nothin' gained.'

'Well ah might as well be 'anged for a sheep as a lamb.'

George smiled gently. He knew there was a sorrow to be healed.

During morning break Vera had other concerns

on her mind. 'I can't imagine how Margaret is feeling this morning.'

We all knew that when Vera mentioned *Margaret* in that tone of voice and with reverence, she meant her political heroine. In a television interview Ted Heath had snubbed the Prime Minister no fewer than three times while refusing to endorse her leadership in the next election. It dominated the news headlines and for once Sally and Vera were united.

'Sounds like sour grapes to me,' said Sally, 'particularly after Maggie booted him out.'

'She certainly had her reasons,' said Vera defensively and moved on to admiring a photograph of the Prince and Princess of Wales, who were due to open Terminal 4 at Heathrow Airport the following month.

Meanwhile, Sally took her copy of *The Healthy Heart Diet Book* from her shoulder bag and reflected that it was definitely a bargain at £3.95. However, Sally had selected to follow the Oxford Diet and appeared to be surviving on muesli, oatmeal biscuits and mixed vegetable soup. She looked longingly at the new packet of custard creams in the communal biscuit tin and sighed.

Pat Brookside was quiet as she read an article in the *Times Educational Supplement*. It confirmed that Ronald Reagan's Teacher in Space Project had been abandoned. Christa McAuliffe, with the other six astronauts on the *Challenger* Space Shuttle, had died as the rocket exploded just after take-off on 28 January. Teachers all over the world had mourned the death of this brave young woman. Pat pondered the fact that fate was occasionally a cruel mistress.

Our Reading Workshop had resumed after the half-term holiday, with parents and grandparents coming into school to hear children read. It had proved an excellent strategy to progress the children's reading at the same time as reinforcing links between home and school.

Six-year-old Julie Tricklebank was sitting next to her grandmother and pointing carefully to each word in her Ginn Reading 360 book. When she had reached the bottom of the page her grandmother smiled. 'Well done,' she said, 'you're a good reader, Julie. Your mother will be proud of you.' She looked around her at the old Victorian school hall and memories of times gone by flickered through her mind like an album of black-and-white reminiscences. 'I was taught to read in this hall,' she said, 'when I was a little girl just like you.'

'What was it like then, Grandma?' asked Julie.

'Well let me think,' she said. 'I recall we used to have a wonderful time in the village when I was young. We used to pick wild raspberries, skate on Manor Pond and we made swings in the wood.'

Julie considered this carefully. 'Ah wish ah'd got t'know you sooner, Grandma,' she said.

Her grandmother smiled and turned back to her reading book. 'Come on then, luv, one more page.'

When George and Ruby returned from York they pulled up at the village green in fitful sunshine.

'It's brightenin' up a bit,' he said. 'Let's sit a while on your Ronnie's bench.'

They walked on to the green, where the delicate branches of the weeping willow caressed the new grass and kissed the glassy surface of the pond. Ruby took off her headscarf before she sat down and gave the brass plaque a cursory wipe. It read:

In memory of
RONALD GLADSTONE SMITH
1931–1983
'Abide With Me'

She stared at the letters and suddenly her shoulders shook in distress with a paroxysm of sobs. 'Ah'm sorry, George,' she said. 'It comes over me from time t'time.'

'Don't fret,' said George softly. 'Grief is the price y'pay for love. An' what's a life wi'out love?'

''E used t'*drink* 'is pay packet, George, an' some Saturday mornings there was never a brass farthing.'

'Oh 'eck,' said George sadly. 'It must 'ave been 'ard f'you.'

'But my children never went 'ungry,' added Ruby defiantly.

'So, 'ave y'given some thought to me teachin' you t'drive?'

'Ah 'ad a feelin' you were goin' to ask me that, George.'

'Did you?'

'Mebbe ah've got that extra-century perception.'

George smiled. 'Mebbe you 'ave, Ruby.'

'Cos ah 'ave t'rely on t'bus to get me int'York t'see our Krystal,' said Ruby, 'so it would be wonderful t'drive m'self.' She had found comfort in her granddaughter and had begun to smile again. Their visits and the companionship of George Dainty had become the breath of life for Ragley's caretaker.

Ruby looked around her. Often when she was sitting on Ronnie's bench, waves of grief would descend.

'Don't fret, Ruby, worse things 'appen at sea,' said George.

Ruby burst into tears again. 'That's what my Ronnie used t'say an' 'e's pushing up daisies now.'

George looked fondly at his childhood sweetheart, but he kept his thoughts of Ronnie to himself.

In the General Stores Betty Buttle was at the counter. 'Ah've jus' called in for a few bits, Prudence,' she said. She heard a cat meowing in the back room. 'An' ah've 'eard 'bout y'cat.'

'Yes, Trio will make a good companion. I went to the cat sanctuary in York and she has such a lovely face.'

'Trio's a nice name,' said Betty.

'Yes, they gave her that name because she only has three legs.'

Betty considered this. 'Well, she won't climb over y'fence an' stray on to t'main road,' and Prudence smiled in acknowledgement.

Outside, Duggie Smith was polishing the chrome headlamps on his hearse. It was a magnificent and beautifully restored 1957 Austin FX3 and had recently been resprayed in lamp black.

His boss, Mr Septimus Bernard Flagstaff, took a

large brass watch from the pocket of his waistcoat. A grey-haired man in his mid-sixties, he was dressed in his familiar formal black three-piece suit. He always looked sad these days, fitting for his profession. While he was proud to be president of the Ragley and Morton Stag Beetle Society, it offered little solace in his otherwise lonely existence. He had never fully recovered from losing the love of his life, namely our school secretary, Vera, to the charms of Rupert Forbes-Kitchener.

'Ah'll be back in 'alf an 'our, Douglas,' said Septimus. 'So mek y'self useful while ah'm gone.'

Little Malcolm Robinson emerged from the Coffee Shop and stood next to Duggie as Septimus walked away up the High Street. An important client awaited.

'My Dorothy's servin' up some lovely pasties,' said Little Malcolm. 'You ought t'try one.'

'Mebbe ah will,' said Duggie. 'Boss won't be back for a while ... so will y'join me?'

Little Malcolm sighed. 'Ah wish ah could, Duggie, but ah'm into 'ealthy livin' now. My Dorothy's got me drinkin' that decapitated coffee an' eatin' broccoli an' suchlike. She sez ah'll be a new man.'

'Bloody 'ell, Malc',' exclaimed Duggie, 'that's no good t'me. Ah need proper food f'energy. That Tina's tirin' me out.'

'So ah've 'eard,' said Little Malcolm. He wandered off to his dustbin wagon and reflected on married life.

Betty Buttle had arrived in Diane's Hair Salon and once again Diane was about to attempt the impossible. Betty's hair resembled a bird's nest after a thunderstorm. The usual gossip flowed like a never-ending stream.

'That Petula is looking down in t'mouth these days,' began Betty.

'Oh dear,' said Diane, reaching for the curling tongs.

'Can't understand it,' Betty went on, 'livin' in a big house in comfort.'

'Yes, it's a lovely home,' said Diane as she lit up a cigarette.

'It's allus been a pigment o' my imagination,' said Betty.

'What's that?' asked Diane, blowing smoke towards the closed window.

'Livin' in luxury,' said Betty.

'Well, money's not everythin', Betty.'

'Mebbe not, but that Stan Coe's got plenty o' brass.'

'So ah've 'eard,' said Diane.

Betty nodded in agreement. 'Thing is, 'e's allus been a wolf in cheap clothin', 'as that one. 'E's up t'summat – buyin' land back o' t'playin' fields.'

Diane smiled. Running the village hair salon was better than *EastEnders* for intrigue and drama.

'An' that Duggie Smith is cleanin' 'is 'earse,' Betty informed her. ''E's a good worker.'

'Not like 'is father,' said Diane.

''E does a bit o' part-time work, does Duggie,' said Betty, 'an' ah'll tell y'summat f'nothing,' she added defiantly.

'What's that, Betty?'

''E painted my kitchen ceiling better than that Michelangelo did 'is sixteenth chapel.'

'Well, y'can't say fairer than that,' acknowledged Diane.

'Anyway, Ruby's picking up now that she's seein' that George Dainty,' Betty continued.

''E's a lovely man.'

'An' ah've jus' seen 'em sittin' on Ronnie's bench,' added Betty.

'Well, good for 'er,' said Diane. 'She deserves some 'appiness.'

'Yes, but she struggles wi' 'er legs, does Ruby,' confided Betty. 'Ah reckon she's got them very-close veins.'

'So what's it t'be?' asked Diane, staring into the mirror at Betty's mini-haystack of unruly hair.

'Like that Angie in t'Queen Vic in *EastEnders*, please, Diane.'

This was a popular choice for some of Ragley's more mature ladies and Diane smiled encouragingly into the mirror. 'OK, Betty,' she said, 'settle back for a perm.'

When I walked into the office Vera had just put down the telephone.

'Mr Gomersall rang from County Hall, Mr Sheffield.'

'What did he have to say?'

Vera glanced down at her shorthand notes on her spiral-bound pad. 'He said the meeting regarding the amalgamation of Morton and Ragley has been arranged for later this month, on Friday evening, twenty-first March.'

'And what's the venue?' I asked.

Vera gave me a sombre look. 'In the lion's den ... Morton village hall. He said he would represent

County Hall and there would be opportunities for questions from the floor. He expects you to be there, along with Mr Timmings and all the various school governors.'

'I see.'

'It's in the diary,' she said, 'and I'll tell Joseph and Rupert to be well prepared.'

'Thanks, Vera,' I said.

At the end of school Ruby hurried in to see Vera.

'Guess what, Mrs F?' she said. 'George Dainty said 'e'd give me drivin' lessons.'

'That's wonderful news,' said Vera with a self-satisfied smile. It was good when plans came together.

''E's given me a vote of continence, Mrs F,' continued Ruby.

Vera blinked but remained composed. 'I'm so glad he has *confidence* in you, Ruby.'

Ruby walked out to collect her mop and galvanized bucket, humming happily to herself.

Vera looked up again as there was another tap on the door. It was Joseph and he looked grey with anxiety.

'What is it, Joseph?' she asked.

'I thought I would come in to tell you in person,' said Joseph. 'Wilfred Bones has just telephoned me to say the vacant school governor post at Morton School has been filled.'

'Yes?'

'It's Stanley Coe, I'm afraid.'

'Oh no,' said Vera. 'Just what we didn't want. I can't imagine what Mr Sheffield will say.'

As I drove out of Ragley towards home, blue-grey spirals of wood smoke curled into the air and in the distance could be heard the forlorn hooting of an owl. The sombre sound seemed appropriate.

The news of Stan Coe's appointment had shocked us all. After his removal from our governing body all those years ago we had hoped he would never darken our door again. His return to a position of influence was a concern, and I had no doubt he would do his best to prevent my appointment as headteacher of the new school.

I turned on the radio. Diana Ross was singing 'Chain Reaction', but I wasn't hearing the words.

That evening Beth and I settled down after putting John to bed. For Beth the news of Stan Coe had been unwelcome and we had decided not to discuss it. However, Beth had a surprise of her own.

'Jack, I've been looking at our joint income and I think we can afford to take out a loan for an extension.'

'An extension!'

'Yes, the kitchen is too small and we need another bedroom for visitors, or maybe one day an addition to the family.'

Suddenly I was interested. 'Another child?'

Beth looked thoughtful. 'I'm not getting any younger and perhaps it would be good for John to have a little brother or sister.'

'I'm all for it,' I said enthusiastically, 'but what about the new headship?'

'That's the drawback. I really need at least a year or two to knock the school into shape and develop effective systems that will last and in which the staff have confidence.'

'I'm sure you can do it,' I said, 'and your governing body seem really supportive.'

'Yes. I'm not sure what their reaction to me taking maternity leave would be, but let's just keep it in mind for now. I'm thinking towards the future.'

'Yes ... the future.'

'I'm guessing you want to stay here at Bilbo Cottage,' said Beth.

I looked at the cramped kitchen with its battered units and ageing appliances. 'I love this place ... it's our home.'

'But what about your work, Jack? Do you anticipate being at Ragley for the rest of your career?'

'Well, I'm certainly going to fight for the new headship,' I said defiantly. 'I've worked hard there and I want to finish what I've started. Even so, I may not have the choice.'

'Exactly,' she said firmly.

'So if necessary I shall consider alternatives.'

Beth looked impressed. 'What about the college? You seem to enjoy teaching the students.'

'I do – but my heart is bound up with Ragley School.'

'What about ambition?'

'Ambition?'

'Yes, Jack. Where do you want to be in, say, five years' time?'

'With you,' I said simply.

'You know what I mean.'

'Well, I do have *ambition* ... perhaps it's different to yours, but it's just as determined.'

'So would you consider a bigger headship?'

'Yes, I would.'
'Or moving into higher education?'
'I'll give it some thought.'
'And the extension?'
'Gary Spittall in Anne's class – his dad is a builder,' I said. 'I'll ask him to call by.'
Beth smiled and went to prepare a nightcap.

It was very early on Saturday morning and Beth and I luxuriated in the warmth of our bed. John was still sleeping and the weekend stretched out before us.
'How shall we start the day?' I asked a little mischievously. I pushed a few locks of hair from her face and kissed her softly.
Beth gave a wry smile. 'Well I could rush downstairs to make your favourite porridge.'
I thought back to the impecunious students at the college. 'That's the problem with porridge,' I said.
'What do you mean?' asked Beth.
'You can have too much of a good thing.'
She looked up at me curiously. 'Are you sure? We might wake John.'
I nuzzled her neck and the scent of roses filled my senses.
'I'm sure,' I whispered.

Chapter Twelve

Eighties Man

School closed today for the Easter holiday and will reopen on Monday, 7 April. A meeting was held in Morton village hall to discuss the amalgamation of our local schools.

Extract from the Ragley School Logbook:
Friday, 21 March 1986

The view from our bedroom window in Bilbo Cottage heralded the changing season and a time of new life. It had been a slow, reluctant dawn, but as the mist lifted there was the promise of a fine day. It was Friday, 21 March, a long winter was over and spring had touched the land with soft fingertips.

The journey to school was uplifting at this time of year and I wound down the windows of my Morris Minor Traveller and drank in the heady scents. Beneath the sharp buds of the hawthorn hedgerows, the blunt arrowheads of daffodils were bursting through the woodland floor. The first cuckoo had announced itself, rooks cawed in the high elms and George Hardisty was preparing his vegetable patch for a crop of early potatoes.

Our world had come alive again. On Ragley High Street primroses brightened the grassy banks and above the school gate the sticky buds on the horse chestnut trees were bursting open. I was full of optimism as I drove into school. It was the last day of the spring term and all appeared to be well on this perfect morning.

However, hopes are sometimes quickly dashed – as I was about to discover. It was the day of the meeting in Morton village hall to discuss the amalgamation of our two village schools. The wonders of nature soon dissipated as I considered the challenges ahead.

On arrival at school I looked down at my shabby suit and scuffed shoes. According to Beth, my apparel was looking 'tired' and she was determined to bring me into the eighties. A shopping trip into York had been planned for Saturday morning. 'Clothes maketh the man,' she had said in that determined tone I knew so well. I had been too preoccupied to notice the splashes of poster paint on my baggy trousers and the chalk dust that impregnated my frayed cuffs. It was time to make a few changes and, hopefully, a new era awaited.

Vera was busy at her desk, completing the numbers-on-roll form for County Hall. It had been a short term owing to an early Easter and a two-week holiday stretched out before us.

'Good morning, Mr Sheffield,' said Vera. 'An eventful day is in store.'

'Yes,' I said, 'it should be an interesting meeting.'

'Rupert will be there to offer support,' she added with an encouraging smile.

'That's good to hear. It's certainly a journey into the unknown.'

She held up a smart spiral-bound booklet. 'And

the programme for the Stratford Conference has arrived.'

'Thanks, Vera.' I scanned the first couple of pages quickly. Beth and I had both applied to attend the National Headteachers' Conference in Stratford-upon-Avon during the Easter break. It was entitled 'The Eighties Curriculum' and the emphasis on new technology was significant. The world was changing fast and I needed to catch up.

I went to stand by the window and looked out at the children walking up the cobbled drive and on to the playground. The children of the eighties in my care appeared content and relaxed. Ragley School offered them a secure environment in which to grow and learn, and I was proud to be leading that journey.

For Vera, a busy day of administration lay ahead. She had also offered to assist Joseph with his forthcoming church services. Good Friday was only a week away and there were sermons to write.

Morning assembly was always special on the last day of term. The children were excited at the thought of the forthcoming holiday and the promise of Easter eggs. However, everyone listened intently to Joseph as he told the story of Jesus dying on the Cross followed by the Resurrection. The children were clearly impressed, and when Joseph walked into Class 2 for his follow-up lesson the questions came thick and fast.

'Do we all die, Mr Evans?' asked Julie Tricklebank.

Joseph sighed deeply. 'Yes, Julie, we do. It happens to us all. It's just the way of things.'

Zoe Book raised her hand. 'Then why is my

grandad frightened of dying?'

Joseph knew Gabriel Book well and decided he would pick a good moment to discuss this with him. 'Perhaps he's not really *frightened* ... more a little *curious,'* he suggested gently.

'Our Sammy died last week,' said Patience Crapper suddenly.

'I'm sorry to hear that, Patience,' said Joseph.

'An' it were *very* painful,' continued Patience with feeling. She gritted her teeth and pursed her lips as if she had just sucked a lemon.

'Oh dear,' said Joseph.

''E were all squashed,' shouted out Madonna Fazackerly. 'Ah found 'im on t'road outside our 'ouse.'

'Squashed?' repeated Joseph, struggling to comprehend.

'Yes,' confirmed Patience, ''e got out of 'is cage an' ran across the road.'

'Cage?'

'Yes, our gerbil, Sammy,' explained Patience. ''E can run real fast.'

'That's right, Mr Evans,' chipped in Dallas Sue-Ellen Earnshaw, 'an' my dad saw it 'appen. 'E said it were faster than shit off a shovel.'

Everyone laughed, except of course for Joseph. 'You shouldn't say that, Dallas. It's not a nice word.'

'Ah 'elped t'bury 'im in their garden,' said Billy Ricketts, moving the conversation on quickly.

'That's good, Billy,' said Joseph, 'and then he'll go to heaven.'

'Well, *ah* wouldn't 'ave buried 'im, Mr Evans,' shouted Sam Whittaker defiantly.

'Why not, Sam?' asked Joseph.
'Well, ah'd 'ave put 'im on top of a big 'ill.'
'A hill?'
'Yes, Mr Evans – then he'd be closer to 'eaven.'
Joseph smiled. 'That's a good thought, Sam.'
He looked at the eager face of the little boy and realized that no matter how long you taught small children, you never ceased to be surprised.

During morning break Anne had spent twenty pence on a *Daily Mail* and was sipping hot milky coffee while studying the gossip page. 'This is interesting,' she said. 'It says here that Sarah Ferguson's stepfather, the Argentinian polo player Hector Barrantes, is coming to the royal wedding.'

This was news that had featured in many of the gossip columns. The wedding would provide the first social meeting between Sarah's father, Major Ronald Ferguson, and Barrantes since the handsome Argentinian had gone off with the Major's wife, Susan.

Sally looked up in surprise. 'That won't go down well. I heard that her stepdad joined up with the Argentinian force in the Falklands.'

There was a photograph of Prince Andrew in his pilot's uniform. He was standing proudly next to his helicopter during the Falklands conflict.

'Looks like an eventful wedding is in store,' said Sally light-heartedly.

However, for Vera, our true-blue supporter of the monarchy, this was no laughing matter. She shook her head. 'Oh dear – whatever will Prince Andrew think?'

Meanwhile, on the playground, Pat Brookside's communication skills were about to be tested. Damian Brown was registering his disapproval of Hayley Spraggon and Michelle Gawthorpe. The two girls were playing cat's cradle with a loop of string.

'Girls is soppy, Miss,' he complained.

'Oh dear, Damian,' said Pat, determined to make him think again. 'Mr Sheffield wouldn't be pleased with your grammar. It should be girls *are* soppy.'

'So you think so as well,' said Damian with a grin.

Pat's tone changed abruptly and Damian realized quickly that you didn't mess with our new teacher.

As we were leaving the staff-room I spotted a rusty blue 1975 Reliant Robin coming up the drive and parking outside the boiler-house doors. It was the familiar shambolic figure of the local area art adviser, Norman Knight. With such a name it had occurred to me that he would have been better suited to be our history adviser, but Norman had followed a more esoteric career. Also, his ill-fitting lime-green corduroy suit made *me* look like the personification of sartorial elegance.

A corner of the entrance area had been transformed by Sally into a semi-permanent display of the best of our children's art under the bright label 'The Ragley Art Gallery'.

'Hello, Jack,' Norman said as we shook hands. He was a short man with long, unkempt fair hair, big expressive hands and a ready smile. He looked at his wristwatch. 'Just a flying visit I'm afraid. We're having a display of the best artwork in North Yorkshire up at County Hall.'

This was clearly an opportunity, for the school. 'Help yourself, Norman,' I said. 'Just let Sally know what you've taken. She's in her classroom and I'm teaching now.'

He stared up at eight-year-old Charlie Cartwright's painting. 'Wow! Look at this,' he said. 'Absolutely *perfect.* This is a magnificent example of vibrant colour and the innocence of youth. There's an immediacy about the brushstrokes ... a real talent.' He was genuinely enthused. 'This is definitely just what we're looking for.'

'That's good to hear, Norman, so, as I said, help yourself and see Vera if you want a coffee.'

He nodded in acknowledgement as he removed the painting from the wall and then smiled as he turned it over. In Anne's neat writing it read '*A Pig in a Field* by Charlie Cartwright'.

At lunchtime I joined the dinner queue. Shirley Mapplebeck and Doreen Critchley were turning out boiled eggs as fast as they could cook them. A huge delivery of fresh local free-range eggs had arrived that morning and Shirley thought it would make a welcome change. It also kept the older children busy helping the infants open up the shells to reveal the golden yolks.

Karl Tomkins had just enjoyed a runny boiled egg and approached the serving table for a second helping.

'Thanks, Mrs Mapplebeck,' he said, but he didn't return to his seat.

'What is it, Karl?' asked Shirley.
'Will you die, Mrs Mapplebeck?'
It wasn't the question Shirley had expected, but our cook took it in her stride. She had been serving food to small children long enough not to be disconcerted by their unlikely observations. 'Yes, luv,' she replied, 'we all do.' She picked up a sharp kitchen knife and sliced off the top of his egg.
Karl selected a couple of toast soldiers from the giant aluminium tray and stared in blissful satisfaction.
'Why do you ask?'
Karl looked up. 'Well, Mrs Mapplebeck, will y'teach me 'ow t'do runny eggs before y'go to 'eaven?'

Ruby was in the entrance hall talking to Sally. She was holding an advertisement from the *Easington Herald & Pioneer*. 'Ah've brought this t'show Mrs F,' she said. 'George 'as jus' bought it.'
It read: '1970 Austin 1100, harvest gold, good runner, over 30 m.p.g.'
Sally didn't mention it was the car to which Basil Fawlty gave 'a damn good thrashing' in the 'Gourmet Night' episode of Fawlty Towers way back in October 1975. It was her favourite episode and, at the time, she considered this model resembled the Mini's rather bookish big brother.
'Great news, Ruby,' she said. 'When is your first lesson?'
'This afternoon,' said Ruby, full of excitement. 'Ah've got m'predicatable licence an' some learner plates, an' George is tekkin' me round t'quiet roads on t'way t'Easington. Ah'm meeting

’im in t’Oak for a bit o’ lunch. ’E said ah need t’be relaxed afore we set off.’

A few minutes later Vera walked with Ruby out of school and across the village green to where an Austin 1100 was parked outside The Royal Oak.

‘It’s ideal, Ruby,’ said Vera, ignoring the sizeable patches of rust on the doors.

‘An’ it’s been well looked after. Jus’ one lady owner.’

‘That’s reassuring.’

‘An’ she were a reight posh lady, Mrs F,’ said Ruby. ‘George said she were one o’ them re-percussionists, ah think ’e said, y’know ... in one o’ them orchestras in Leeds.’

‘Well, good luck, Ruby, and do let me know how it goes.’

Back in school, the members of the lunchtime chess club were enjoying another half-hour of concentration and combat. Pat and Anne were taking turns to supervise and Anne was helping the Jackson twins with some of the basic moves.

As Hermione and Honeysuckle began their game, Anne stared out of the window of the library area. Daffodils were thrusting their blue-grey spears towards the sun and lambs were bleating in the fields. Her attention returned to the pieces on the chessboard and she smiled. She had been a pawn for too long, or perhaps, at best, a bishop that could move in straight lines, rather like the castle that was the embodiment of John. The love they once shared had died long ago and only embers of affection remained.

Whereas Edward Clifton was *different*. He was

a knight who could leap over anyone who stood in his way. Perhaps it was time to be a queen who could *choose* the direction she wishes to travel.

She was empowered by the thought. The choice was hers and hers alone.

Seeking similar empowerment was Petula Dudley-Palmer as she donned her jogging suit and headband and inserted her Olivia Newton-John music video, *Let's Get Physical,* into the video recorder. Petula was aware that her husband Geoffrey had sought companionship with his secretary. After a period of low self-esteem, Petula had decided to get fit and take a positive view of her life.

She was also an avid fan of the Green Goddess on BBC1's *Breakfast Time.* Most mornings she would stand in front of the television screen stretching, curling and generally leaping around. Each day she felt a little better about herself ... and Geoffrey had begun to take notice.

Ruby was in The Royal Oak, standing at the bar while George was outside fixing the learner plates to the front and back of Ruby's new car. Sheila and Don were serving drinks to the regular lunchtime crowd.

'Good luck wi' y'driving, Ruby,' said Sheila.

'Thanks, Sheila, ah'm looking forward to it,' said Ruby.

'Ah were jus' thinkin' that your Natasha's a good girl,' continued Sheila. 'Ah saw 'er in Diane's this morning. Ah was 'oping she might tek up wi' that nice young policeman.'

'So was I,' said Ruby, 'but there's a problem.

'Why, what's t'matter?' asked Sheila.

'Well, first of all she needs t'tell that window cleaner that she's not interested in 'im,' said Ruby. 'Y'know, 'im wi' a wooden leg.'

'That mus' be difficult,' said Don.

'Difficult? It's 'eartbreaking!' said Ruby.

'No, ah meant it mus' be difficult t'climb 'is ladder,' explained Don apologetically.

'Bugger 'is ladder,' said Sheila and slapped her giant of a husband with a tea towel. 'Tek no notice, Ruby, 'e 'asn't got t'brains 'e were born with.'

George arrived and looked at the menu. ''Ow about summat posh, Ruby?' he said. 'Like scampi an' chips?'

'Oooh, yes please, George,' said Ruby. 'Ah like erotic food now an' again.'

It was six thirty and I was on my way to Morton while Barbara Dickson sang 'Another Suitcase In Another Hall' on the car radio. I wondered what might lie in wait for me.

Morton village hall was a smaller version of the one in Ragley. There was a stage at one end and a kitchen with a serving hatch at the other. Rows of chairs had been arranged and most of them were filled by the time I arrived. A trestle table had been set up on the stage and Richard Gomersall was arranging his prepared text and making last-minute amendments. He was flanked by Joseph Evans, representing the governing body of Ragley School, and Wilfred Bones, the chair of governors at Morton. Mrs Joyce Davenport, the doctor's wife and minutes secretary for the Morton governing body, was a picture of composure as she sat at the end of the table with pen poised. She scanned the audience and gave the briefest of smiles towards her dear friend Vera before returning to her notebook.

At seven o'clock Richard Gomersall welcomed everybody and described the purpose of the meeting. He outlined the timetable for the closure of Morton School and the arrangements to accommodate the children at Ragley. This was followed by brief supportive statements from Joseph Evans and Wilfred Bones. The good news was that they seemed of one accord, so the meeting got off to a peaceful start. Even so, Wilfred was a slow and methodical man and, throughout his sixties, he had become acutely deaf with the result that now, at the age of seventy-two, he was regularly likened to a post.

Hands were raised and various views expressed by the villagers until the eager Rufus Timmings attracted the attention of Richard Gomersall. I was surprised, as I didn't think the headteachers would be expected to contribute. It appeared Richard thought the same and he frowned as Rufus stood up and addressed the audience from the front row. He looked immaculate in a tweed three-piece suit, a crisp white shirt and old school tie, black leather shoes with shiny toecaps and a silk handkerchief in his top pocket. He took out a sheet of carefully typed notes from his pocket.

'Distinguished guests,' he began with a nod towards those on the stage, 'ladies and gentlemen, good evening and thank you for the opportunity to say a few words on this momentous occasion. The end of an era is almost upon us.' He paused for effect and continued in a well-rehearsed manner. 'I know I speak for all those who have cherished Morton village school over the years.' He glanced down at his prompt. 'As you all are aware, I have been proud to be headteacher of our wonderful school and hope the children who move on to Ragley School will not suffer in any way. It is imperative that the excellent progress they have achieved is sustained.'

There were nods of approval from some of the Morton parents and some puzzlement on the faces of Ragley folk. Joseph looked down from the stage in my direction and his concern was clear to see.

Rufus continued with confidence. 'Whoever is appointed to be the headteacher of the new school must provide a full and meaningful education. This should combine the best of the past with the challenges of the future. We are now in the eighties, an age of computers and information technology ... and who knows what the nineties will bring? So let us embrace the challenge that awaits us and welcome this opportunity.' He surveyed the room in a statesmanlike manner. 'Thank you for listening,' he concluded and resumed his seat to loud applause from Stan and Deirdre Coe and a group of the Morton parents.

Richard Gomersall looked in my direction. 'Perhaps we should give an opportunity to Mr Sheffield to speak.' I took a deep breath and stood up. All faces turned towards me. Rufus was smiling. 'You all know me,' I began. 'This is my ninth year as headteacher in Ragley village.' I looked down at Rufus, then up towards the stage.

'I don't intend to use this forum to promote my educational philosophy – suffice to say, I love my work. Quite simply, it is my life. Whatever decisions are made for the future, the needs of the children must come first.' I sat down and, after a pause, there was applause that gradually spread around the room.

Stan Coe and Deirdre were sitting along with a few of his friends who frequented The Pig & Ferret in Easington. He raised his hand and, without waiting to be acknowledged, stood up and began to speak. The years had not been kind to Stan as he festered on his pig farm on the outskirts of Ragley. His greed had consumed him over the years and, while his sister Deirdre railed at his drunkenness, he continued to buy land and his estate had grown steadily. A web of veins formed purple tracks across his ruddy cheeks and gathered round his blackened nose.

'Ah'd jus' like t'say that we need t'be careful when t'new school opens. Ah went t'Ragley School an' we learned *right* from *wrong*.' There was an intake of breath from Vera. Stan pointed a finger towards me. 'An' ah'm sick an' tired of asking 'im t'keep t'children from trespassin' on my land an' damagin' t'fence nex' t'my pigs.' He turned to Rufus Timmings. ''Ere we 'ave a chance t'give t'new school a proper 'eadteacher wi' p'lite children an' up t'date wi' these compooters an' suchlike. We 'ave t'look towards t'future.' He sat down and his sister and a few of his cronies began to applaud.

Vera raised her hand and Richard Gomersall nodded in her direction. She stood up and surveyed the audience. 'I'm disappointed to hear Mr Coe's comments,' she said in a calm, controlled voice. 'Ragley School has the highest reputation for good behaviour and excellent leadership. I would simply ask you to consider facts rather than biased innuendo.' She sat down and, once again, there was a smattering of applause.

Stan Coe wouldn't know innuendo from a bacon sandwich and looked puzzled. His sister came to the rescue and jumped to her feet. She gave a murderous look towards Vera and her double chin wobbled with every syllable. 'We all know Mrs 'igh-an'-mighty wants t'keep 'er job an' that's why she's supportin' Mr Sheffield.'

The Major raised his hand and waited patiently for Richard to give him the floor. He stood up and in a strong, steady voice, as if he were addressing his troops, he said, 'Good evening, everybody, and thank you to Mr Gomersall and the education authority for providing the opportunity for this meeting.'

He stepped from behind his seat into the aisle and paused while he looked at Stan Coe with eyes of cold ice. 'This is not a forum for personal attacks and I have no intention of descending to that level.' Then he smiled and studied the faces around him. 'We are in fact of one accord – the best for the next generation of children from our two villages. Decisions on the leadership are for another day and will be taken by the proper authorities. What is important now is to ensure the children of Morton are safe and secure in their new school and that County Hall provide the necessary resources to give them an excellent education. I've every confidence that will happen.'

It was at this moment that Vera realized she had little to worry about regarding Rupert's state of mind. The meeting ended after a measured summing-up by Richard Gomersall and we all left the hall with plenty to think about.

On Saturday morning Beth and I drove into York, with John nodding his head in time to Cliff Richard and the Young Ones singing 'Living Doll' on the car radio. Beth looked in dismay at my old sports jacket. 'It'll have to go, Jack. It really has seen better days.'

It was like saying goodbye to an old friend.

'But there's still plenty of wear left in it.'

Beth looked up at me sympathetically. 'Perhaps in the garden,' she said.

'Well, I suppose it would keep me warm,' I acknowledged.

Beth smiled. 'Actually, I meant we could put it on a scarecrow.'

We parked in the centre of York and walked to a department store. 'You need a nice, lightweight, comfortable suit that you can wear for school and college,' decreed Beth once we were inside. 'It's time to move on.'

My colour blindness did not help the process of selection as we picked out a few of the suits.

Beth looked at me quizzically. 'Jack, what colour is this?'

'Grey,' I said.

'And what about this?'

'Light grey ... or possibly blue.'

In the end we selected a smart grey three-piece

suit and, unexpectedly, some casual clothing. I emerged from the changing room wearing a blue jacket, cotton trousers in pacific blue and a patterned sweater.

'Perfect!' said Beth. 'At long last, an *eighties* man.'

'Really?' I said. 'I thought I was fine.'

'To be perfectly honest, Jack, when we first met I thought you were a lovely man but a bit, well ... dull.'

'Dull?'

'Yes – but of course I mean your *clothing*, not you. It just wasn't all that exciting.'

'I see. So why did you say yes ... why me?'

She smiled. 'Because I fell in love with *you* and not what you wear.'

'And I love you ... always have, always will.'

She squeezed my hand. 'But it's not about what I want you to wear, because you need to feel comfortable in your own skin.'

'I really do want to get a bit more up to date,' I admitted. Above me on the wall by the changing room was a huge poster and I smiled. 'A bit like him.' It was Don Johnson in *Miami Vice*. 'Seriously, though ... last night's meeting convinced me of that. Rufus Timmings would be impressive in an interview.'

I looked at my reflection. It wasn't exactly a beautiful butterfly that had emerged from the cocoon of my life – it was just a new man!

Perhaps I had looked inward for too long.

I had finally stepped outside the boundaries of my life. I had been a shuttered lamp for too long ... it was time to move on.

Chapter Thirteen

The Stratford Conference

School reopened today for the summer term with 101 children on roll. During the Easter holiday Mr Sheffield attended the headteachers' conference in Stratford-upon-Avon on 5-6 April.

Extract from the Ragley School Logbook:
Monday, 7 April 1986

It was twilight on Friday, 4 April as Beth and I drove through the Warwickshire countryside. The National Headteachers' Conference in Stratford-upon-Avon was taking place the following day and, little though we knew it then, an eventful weekend was in store.

During the Easter holiday we had spent a few days with Beth's parents at Austen Cottage in Hampshire and had left our son in their safe-keeping. My father-in-law, John Henderson, had been his usual relaxed self, but Diane was still clearly irritated that her daughters appeared to prefer to be far from the family home. Beth had chosen to seek a larger headship in Yorkshire while her younger sister, Laura, was leading a helter-skelter life in Australia, where she was taking the Sydney fashion scene by storm and enjoying a string of wealthy boyfriends.

According to the programme, the conference

was due to begin at 9.00 a.m. on Saturday and conclude with a plenary session in the late afternoon. There was to be an opening address by a Birmingham headteacher, followed by a series of five-minute presentations by various educationalists. After coffee we were due to divide into working parties to discuss the conference theme, 'The Eighties Curriculum'. Beth, as a newly appointed headteacher, had been invited to lead one of these groups. Predictably it had been Miss Barrington-Huntley who had made the arrangements and an apprehensive Beth had agreed.

'Tired?' I asked quietly.

Beth was staring through the windscreen of my Morris Minor Traveller. 'A little ... but excited as well.'

Ahead was the busy market town of Stratford-upon-Avon, birthplace of William Shakespeare and home of the Royal Shakespeare Theatre. We passed a huge poster advertising the grand opening on 8 May of the new Swan Theatre and finally reached our destination. Situated between the Bridgeway and the River Avon was the impressive Moat House Hotel, previously the Stratford Hilton but now transformed into a thriving centre for business meetings. The reception area was busy when we checked in. There were over two hundred bedrooms and, at first impression, it appeared most of them were occupied by conference delegates and American tourists.

After our evening meal we were keen to settle into our room for a good night's sleep. We loved our son but, somewhat guiltily, we both agreed that a little precious time to ourselves was always welcome.

As we left the dining room we heard a familiar voice. 'Hello there, you two – so pleased you have made it.' It was Miss Barrington-Huntley, resplendent in a sparkling purple dress, and looking very much the lady of the manor. 'And how are you both and your little boy?'

Beth explained we had left John with her parents and they were due to drive up to the hotel on Sunday morning to return him to us and have a family lunch together.

'Delightful,' she said. 'It's important to have support in your busy lives.' She waved the programme in Beth's direction. 'I'm sure you will be fine leading your group, and do remember that you will be expected to provide a succinct feedback. All the flipchart summaries will be displayed in the conference room prior to the afternoon session so that delegates can evaluate the findings of each group.'

'Yes, I understand,' said Beth confidently.

Miss Barrington-Huntley smiled at her and nodded in acknowledgement to me before hurrying away.

'You're definitely her blue-eyed girl,' I said.

Beth grinned and blinked her green eyes. 'Incongruous, Jack ... but I know what you mean.' She held my hand. 'Now, Mr Sheffield,' she whispered in my ear, 'we're alone at last without John clambering into our bed at some ungodly hour.'

The message was clear.

We kissed when we reached our room. Our love had always been one of ice and fire and I had learned to understand this beautiful woman. It was time to relax together.

On Saturday morning I slipped quietly out of bed and padded barefoot across the bedroom. When I pulled back the curtain the first light of a pale sun gilded the rooftops of Stratford and the sights and sounds of this remarkable place filled my thoughts. Beth was still asleep and I stood there while the sibilant sounds of her breathing brought comfort to my soul. Under the feather duvet she was naked. We had made love long into the night, and I gave secret thanks to Beth's parents for looking after our son and also to Miss Barrington-Huntley for persuading Beth to take part in the conference. I crept back into bed and snuggled up to her once again.

'Oh, Jack!'

'What?'

'Your feet are freezing.'

'Sorry,' I said, passion rapidly subsiding. 'Would you like a cup of tea?'

'Yes please,' she murmured, but before the kettle had boiled she had fallen asleep again.

I made the tea anyway and sipped contentedly as I considered the day ahead. We had a treat in store after the conference. I had booked two seats at the Royal Shakespeare Theatre for a production of *Romeo and Juliet* and I settled back to read a synopsis of the familiar plot of the starstruck lovers.

Shortly after seven o'clock Beth slipped into the tiny shower and my attempts to join her proved fruitless, so I sat on the edge of the bed, switched on the television and watched the Open

University. Advanced calculus was interesting but not as stimulating as sharing a shower with a very desirable woman.

An hour later over breakfast Beth was busy making last-minute notes in preparation for her workshop. I picked up a copy of the *Stratford-upon-Avon Herald* that had been discarded on a coffee table outside the dining room. I soon discovered that you definitely got your eighteen pence worth from this local newspaper. 'Where Is Society Going?' blared the headline. The editor was concerned that Good Friday had not been observed appropriately. Supermarkets had opened their doors and it had been business as usual for the local factories. Environmental issues were also to the fore. The pupils of Stratford-upon-Avon Grammar School for Girls were making a case for a bottle bank to recycle glass following a recent survey they had carried out. Meanwhile, on the property page, I sighed when I saw the price of a beautiful semi-detached cottage. It'd have been perfect for Beth, John and myself, but I guessed the price of £37,950 was way beyond our means.

I flipped through the pages to the Arts section for a review of *Romeo and Juliet* and found it under a lively article about apartheid protestors wanting South Africa banned from the forthcoming Shakespeare birthday celebrations. It was a mixed review. The theatre critic had not pulled any punches in his article, 'Excess and Incongruity in *Romeo and Juliet*'. While Sean Bean and Niamh Cusack in the title roles received praise, he considered that theatregoers would be either appalled or merely intrigued by a production that drew telling parallels between contemporary society and Shakespeare's Verona.

Beth had closed her notebook. 'Come on, Jack,' she said, glancing at her wristwatch, 'time to go.'

There was a crescendo of voices as over two hundred delegates filled the huge lecture hall and Beth and I found seats near the back. On the stroke of nine the conference began with a powerful speech from the Birmingham headteacher. He described the current educational scene and seemed to think that the time in office for Sir Keith Joseph, Secretary of State for Education, was drawing to a close and that a minister such as Kenneth Baker, one of Thatcher's favourites, would eventually take over. I wondered about his source of information. The emphasis throughout was on headteachers being prepared for a changing world and the Prime Minister's recurring theme of 'value for money'. The world of education in the eighties was changing fast.

After less than enthusiastic applause, he introduced the next item: six short presentations by colleagues whom he described as the next generation of leaders. They included young deputy headteachers and a couple of recently appointed heads. He looked down at his list. 'Please welcome our first speaker, who is the headteacher of a small village school in North Yorkshire ... Mr Rufus Timmings.'

There was a gasp from Beth. 'Why didn't Miss B-H mention this?' she whispered.

'Perhaps she didn't know,' I said, though I found it hard to believe.

'This will be a feather in his cap,' said Beth ominously. She sat back and looked troubled. 'Jack ... you need to keep an eye on him.'

Rufus walked confidently to the lectern, immaculate as ever in his three-piece suit. He scanned the audience with his blunt, round face, bright-red cheeks and grey fathomless eyes, behind which brooded an alert intelligence.

'My paper is entitled "Meeting the Challenge" and copies are available,' he said clearly into the microphone. Like a well-rehearsed politician, the words flowed right through to his big finish. 'Change is unsettling,' he told us in a patronizing manner, 'and it is natural to resist it – but change can also be *enabling*. We need to recognize it as a tool for improvement.' He looked up at his audience. 'Do remember that our world of education is governed by a *limited* budget, necessarily so in times of austerity, but if we embrace the new opportunities we can make *more from less*.'

There was a muttering of discontent from those around me.

Then he turned to the senior advisers and education officers on the front row. 'Finally, colleagues ... we need to *rationalize* to survive.'

The polite applause was muted from the headteachers but distinctly enthusiastic from the senior figures at the front.

The speakers that followed ranged from a young woman who was proud to be teaching small children in a tough area of Newcastle to a deputy head from a large school in leafy Surrey where a city banker had joined the governing body and was transforming the school's finances. The contrast was considerable and made me appreciate my good fortune in teaching in Ragley village.

Over a welcome cup of coffee Beth and I were joined by two female headteachers from Nelson in Lancashire and we discussed the contributions so far.

'I rated the Newcastle head,' said one of them, 'but she's got her work cut out.'

'There were some terrific ideas for parental involvement,' said the other.

Suddenly Rufus Timmings was by our side and looking at Beth. 'I'm in your group after coffee,' he announced, 'and I'm happy to volunteer to compile our findings on the flipchart.' He pulled out a large felt pen from his pocket. 'I'm well prepared,' he added and strutted off to engage one of the senior advisers in conversation.

'Do you know him?' asked one of the ladies from Lancashire.

'He works in our area,' I said.

'Hard luck,' she said pointedly, as a bell rang and we hurried off to our seminar groups.

Beth didn't look particularly pleased when we met up again for a buffet lunch.

'He was insufferable, Jack,' she said. 'Way too full of his own importance.'

'He must walk around with a prepared presentation in his pocket,' I said.

'According to Miss B-H, he stepped in at the last moment,' she added, 'but don't worry – we've got his measure.'

I smiled. Beth was exhibiting that familiar combination of steely determination and silky tenderness that I knew so well.

The afternoon session went smoothly. We split into working parties and I learned much from colleagues employed in a wide variety of local authorities.

Then it was back to the lecture hall for the plenary session. A junior minister from the Department of Education delivered a carefully worded lecture on a curriculum appropriate for mixed-age classes. Once again, the emphasis was on making effective use of the new technology. 'Can a two-teacher school be justified on educational grounds?' he asked. He quoted examples of previous amalgamations with average savings estimated at £3,900. He was unconvincing and appeared removed from reality.

'Another twit from Eton,' grumbled a Lincolnshire headteacher in the row behind. 'He wants to spend a week in my school.'

However, the conference ended on a positive note when the Birmingham headteacher reappeared and gave a superb motivational speech that included a few pointed barbs aimed at the government minister.

As we left, Beth nudged me and nodded towards the stage. I saw Rufus chatting with the minister as if they were old friends.

Back at the hotel we telephoned Beth's parents and enjoyed a conversation with young John. He was beginning to form clear sentences now, even though past tenses were still to be acquired. 'I eated ice cream, Daddy, and feeded ducks,' he said. He seemed happy and content.

Later, while we changed to go out, the television flickered with the sound turned down – the usual Saturday early-evening entertainment of *The Muppet Show* and *The Dukes of Hazzard*. We wrapped up warm on this cold evening for the short walk to one of the pubs near the theatre. It was full of American tourists and, from the chatter around us, most of them appeared determined to enjoy a taste of Olde England.

The entrance to the Royal Shakespeare Theatre was thronged with people and we queued next to a large poster advertising the forthcoming production of *The Winter's Tale* with Jeremy Irons as Leontes. I marvelled at this wonderful place, and at the astonishing legacy of the world's greatest playwright who had been born and died in this little market town. I felt privileged to be here.

We had reserved seats in the dress circle for this opening production of the Royal Shakespeare Company's Stratford season and soon we settled down to one of Shakespeare's most famous plays. The set for *Romeo and Juliet* was not what I expected, consisting of severe vertical structures similar to the high-rise concrete of modern cities. It was a struggle to imagine there could be 'a grove of sycamores' nearby. Motorbikes and lively music were in evidence along with the substitution of flick knives for swords, and I wondered what the Bard would have made of it. The highlight for Beth was, predictably, Sean Bean's handsome Yorkshire Romeo, who seemed to capture the excesses of a young lover. However, for me it was Michael Kitchen's Mercutio that stole the show.

On Sunday morning over breakfast we caught sight of Rufus again, wearing the predictable three-piece suit but on this occasion sporting a bright bow tie. 'He just wants to be noticed,' said Beth.

Miss Barrington-Huntley came over to thank Beth for her contribution. 'Another successful conference, Beth, and I did appreciate your support.' She looked out of the window at the sight of Stratford on a bright sunny morning. 'We needed a cultural venue for such an important meeting.' She wished us a safe journey home and hurried off to join a group of her colleagues.

After breakfast we checked out and loaded up our luggage. We had a few hours to spare before Beth's parents joined us, so we decided to explore the town and call into Holy Trinity Church for their morning service.

We left the hotel, crossed Bridgefoot and walked along Waterside by the River Avon, which meanders gently through the town from east to west. Pleasure boats and anglers lined the banks, while early-morning barges, motor boats, canoes, punts and rowing boats gave the river a busy holiday feel. We paused to enjoy the views. In the distance, large farms and estates stretched out to the horizon, famous for their Hereford beef and their racehorses. Sadly, there were few swans left on the river and, according to the friendly concierge in the hotel, this was becoming a concern.

We found Holy Trinity Church in Old Town, in an idyllic setting on the banks of the river. It had a tall, elegant spire and we walked down an avenue of lime trees to the north porch. Here there were many ancient graves, including the burial place of William Shakespeare. I felt the sense of history as Beth and I walked hand in hand into the church and a shroud of silence muted our footsteps on the stone floor. The people of Stratford had worshipped here for over eight hundred years and, as we sat in one of the pews, the prayers of people past echoed throughout the centuries.

It was a simple communion service and the vicar announced various notices, including the forthcoming celebrations on 23 April, St George's Day, to commemorate Shakespeare's birthday. He expressed concern regarding the annual Ceremony of the Flags, when dignitaries from all over the world would unfurl their flags ... but not South Africa.

From there we called into the Shakespeare Centre with its library, lecture rooms and costume displays. The last time I had visited had been in 1965 when I was a student. After a pleasant walk to Anne Hathaway's Cottage, the childhood home of Shakespeare's wife which stands a mile outside Stratford, we made our way back towards the hotel. Children with padded knees and elbows plus safety helmets rode past on BMX bicycles to their local track on the Warwick Road. We enjoyed a final pot of tea in one of the riverside cafés before returning to the hotel reception area.

At one o'clock Diane and John arrived and John William was so excited to see us again, but even more pleased that he had seen boats on the river and a couple of swans.

'This could be a nice place to live,' mused Diane.

'What she means,' said John, 'is that it only took two and a half hours to get here – half the normal journey up to Yorkshire.'

Diane gave him a stern look but didn't pursue the point.

Finally we left the superb Warwickshire countryside behind us and headed north. On the radio Queen were singing 'A Kind of Magic' and we hummed along as the miles raced by.

We had John fed and in bed by the time BBC1's *Songs of Praise* came on, followed by *Hancock's Half Hour.* By coincidence, at 7.50 p.m. on BBC2 the Royal Ballet were performing *Romeo and Juliet,* so we settled down to watch an alternative version of the story while eating jacket potatoes in front of a log fire.

On Monday morning Bilbo Cottage was a hive of activity. It was the beginning of a new term and Beth and I intended to set off early for school. We were chatting over bowls of Weetabix.

'Well, Rufus Timmings certainly made his presence felt,' I said.

'The advertisement for the Ragley and Morton headship should be in the *Times Educational Supplement* any time now,' said Beth. 'We could work together on your application.'

'Fine,' I said. 'It needs to be impressive. The competition is certain to be tougher than last time.'

'And we need to keep the college in mind. Your course was well received and by all accounts the students thought your lectures were terrific.'

'Jim was very generous in his praise,' I said.

'That letter he sent was lovely.'

'There's no doubt he would have you in his Education Department in the blink of an eye. You could be a senior lecturer in Primary Education and have secure employment and an increase in salary. We could even share a car into York.'

'Perhaps,' I said, 'but I'm determined to give Ragley my best shot first of all.'

Beth was quiet as she looked down at John. He had moved on to munching a banana while a brief pang of nostalgia touched my thoughts. I knew that, in my professional career, my happiest days had been spent at Ragley.

We heard a car pull up outside and the patter of footsteps as Mrs Roberts arrived for another day of childminding. John's face lit up. He loved her, and a day of play and sleep and food stretched out before him.

Beth's look softened as she watched our son's reaction. Our childminder's contribution to our lives was worth its weight in gold, but I knew it pulled on Beth's heartstrings each time she kissed him goodbye.

'Let's talk about it tonight,' she said.

As she got into her car to drive to York there were unspoken words. Deep down I knew she was right, but at that moment I didn't want to think about losing my precious school and I regretted the silence between us.

In the school office Vera was sitting at her desk and studying her admissions register. 'We've passed one hundred on roll, Mr Sheffield,' she said with a smile. 'I would never have believed it.

The school has really grown.'

'And more to come in a year's time,' I reminded her.

Vera pondered my response as if there was some hidden meaning. 'Yes, our work gets busier year by year.' She lifted the pile of morning post with a wry smile. 'And may I say, Mr Sheffield, that you look very smart today.'

I glanced down at my new suit and black brogues. 'Well it's thanks to Beth,' I said, '...*her* choice.'

'Beth always did have good taste,' said Vera.

I smiled. 'We decided it was time for me to be an eighties man.'

'Really, Mr Sheffield ... well, I do think you have succeeded.'

So it was that, with a spring in my step, I set off to my classroom for the first day of the summer term.

Chapter Fourteen

The End of Days

The Revd Joseph Evans visited school to teach a Bible studies lesson in Class 2. We received the updated Health & Safety policy for North Yorkshire schools.

Extract from the Ragley School Logbook:
Friday, 18 April 1986

I opened the diamond-paned windows of our

bedroom. The heady scent of wallflowers wafted on the breeze and the distant hills were gilded with golden light. Soon a new dawn would race across the sleeping land. It was Friday, 18 April and Kirkby Steepleton looked refreshed on this perfect morning. However, my mind was unsettled. Ragley School was no longer the secure home it had always been. There were uncertainties in my professional life and decisions to be made about the future.

It was there on the breakfast table, the advertisement I never thought I should read. The *Times Educational Supplement* was open at the headteacher appointments page and circled in red pen was *'Headteacher required for Ragley and Morton Church of England Primary School, North Yorkshire, to commence January 1987. Application forms from County Hall, Northallerton.'*

I had completed the application form and supporting letter last night and I checked it once again before putting it into a large envelope. 'Well, let's hope for the best,' I said as I sealed it.

'You'll certainly get an interview,' said Beth, 'and there would have to be an exceptional candidate to deprive you of the post.'

I smiled at her level of conviction. 'Let's hope so.'

She leaned across the table and pressed her hand on top of mine. 'Jack, we all evolve and change in subtle ways. If you want to be a village schoolteacher so be it and I'll support you. It's obviously a job you love and you're good at it. Just don't stand still. There are new challenges out there.' She looked up at me thoughtfully. 'How about doing a Master's Degree at the university? It would be a new stimulus for you. You would meet like-minded people and the qualification could be a passport to a fresh opportunity in the future.'

'Yes, it makes sense,' I agreed.

Beth stood up and cleared away the cereal bowls. 'The world of education is changing and maybe this Timmings guy is a sign of things to come ... a new breed of managers who haven't got your skills as a teacher but can impress an interviewing panel. There's a revised curriculum on the horizon and it's rushing towards us like an avalanche. People like Timmings are going to be the ones jumping on the bandwagon. We musn't underestimate him.'

Beth was passionate and determined. I said nothing. It was a lot to take in.

The end of the world I loved seemed to have arrived.

Meanwhile, in the spacious kitchen of Morton Manor Vera was sipping Earl Grey tea and checking a letter she had written. It was addressed to 'Governor Services' at County Hall and in her neat copperplate writing she had chosen her words carefully. She had been troubled by the meeting at Morton village hall and it had rankled with her that such a dreadful man as Stanley Coe could cause problems. She had decided not to tell Jack that Stan was whipping up support for Rufus Timmings to be the new headteacher.

The envelope matched the writing paper to perfection, two subtle shades of lilac, and she slipped the letter inside, sealed it carefully and put it in her handbag. For now she would keep the contents of the letter to herself.

She stood up and looked with some satisfaction into the small mirror next to the window. Now there were threads of silver in her hair but she had disguised them well thanks to the regular visits of Diane the hairdresser. In the background Kiri Te Kanawa was singing 'Ave Maria' on the radio and Vera hummed along.

The door opened and Rupert walked in from his morning 'constitutional' as he called it; namely, a brisk walk to the nearby stables and some welcome fresh air. He slipped off his dark-green Burberry trenchcoat, draped it over the back of his carver chair at the head of the huge oak table and put his arm around Vera's shoulders.

Vera glanced up with appreciative eyes. Rupert looked every bit the part of a country squire in his brown cord trousers, a crisp white shirt, regimental tie and a bottle-green V-necked sweater. As always, his brown leather shoes were buffed to a military shine.

Old habits, thought Vera.

'So, my dear,' said Rupert, 'have a good day at school.' He kissed her gently on the cheek and then stood back as he recognized that her mind was elsewhere. 'Are you still going ahead with retirement? Whatever your choice, I'll support you.'

Vera paused and fingered the Victorian brooch at her throat. 'Thank you, Rupert,' she said quietly, 'but I've decided to put it on hold for the time being.'

'The school will have to do without you one day, Vera,' he said firmly, 'so why not now?'

'Because I believe that at this time I'm needed more than ever.'

'Really, how so?'

Vera picked up the silver tea strainer with her long delicate fingers and placed it with precision to rest on the rim of her husband's china cup. 'A cup of tea, Rupert?'

The Major recognized the tug of loyalty and the hidden message of unspoken words. 'Yes please, old girl,' he teased. He recognized a professional secret even in his own kitchen.

Vera glanced briefly at her husband and his knowing blue eyes and the love and devotion that lay beneath. He was honest and strong and trying hard to disguise his natural chauvinism as the years went by. An old wine with a new label.

Then she picked up the silver tongs and dropped a single cube of sugar into his cup. 'Perhaps just *one* sugar,' she said. 'We agreed you would cut down.'

In response, Rupert selected a thick slice of crusty bread, spread English butter with generous enthusiasm and applied a liberal layer of Yorkshire honey. For a moment he stared suspiciously at Vera's croissant with its merest hint of apricot jam. In Rupert's eyes this was vaguely continental and not entirely English, but he loved her in spite of her faults. *Love conquers all,* he thought ... *even an old warhorse.* 'Heard and understood, my dear,' he said.

Vera turned her attention to her croissant and the conversation was over.

No names, no pack drill, thought Rupert.

He knew intuitively that Vera was in possession

of a professional confidentiality and he respected the act of not sharing it ... not even with the one you loved.

On The Crescent there was also a reluctant silence in Anne Grainger's kitchen. Her husband John had left for another day of woodcarving, dovetail joints and sawdust. She stared at her reflection in the kitchen window and recalled the young teacher that used to look back at her. Then she touched the first hint of grey at her temples and sighed.

The passing of time was remorseless.

Outside, in the early-morning light, the last of the mist was slowly clearing from the fields beyond the Easington Road, but here, inside her brightly lit kitchen, her emotions were drowning in a sea of fog.

There were decisions to make and thoughts that were not for sharing.

I called in at the General Stores on my way into school and Betty Buttle was at the counter.

'No, ah'm goin' upmarket, Prudence,' she was saying. 'Ah'd like t'tek a prescription out for that *Cosmopolitan* magazine. Ah've jus' read one in Diane's an' it's my type o' readin' ... y'know, for t'modern woman.'

She walked out, pleased with her decision, and the bell over the door jingled.

'The world's changing, Mr Sheffield,' remarked Prudence. 'It's hard to keep up.'

'Yes, I agree,' I said as Prudence handed me my newspaper.

‘There used to be a *pattern* to the day, but that’s come to an end. I’m never sure what the next customer will want and I used to know, well ... everything.’

As I walked out of the shop she called after me, ‘At least *you* won’t change, Mr Sheffield.’

Then she looked up at Jeremy Bear in his new spring outfit. ‘And neither will you.’

At nine o’clock the bell rang to announce the start of another school day and the children hurried to their classrooms. Outside on the High Street Lollipop Lil had finished her stint as Road Crossing Patrol Officer and the children had crossed in safety for another day.

She was peering into the boot of her rusty Citroën 2CV, which she referred to as her ‘Tin Snail’. It was her metal pet, with headlamps like the eyes of a surprised owl. She was collecting for the church bring-and-buy sale and wondering what to do with a pre-National Health Service wooden leg and an electric candle that she presumed would be useless in a power cut. She smiled at the relics from the seventies, including a SodaStream with the slogan ‘Get Busy with the Fizzy’, a broken Teasmade and a fondue set. There was also a rusty egg slicer that she used to find so wonderfully satisfying with its mandolin strings. They created perfect rings that fitted exactly in her picnic sandwiches. An almost new copy of Geoffrey Smith’s *World of Flowers* caught her eye and she determined she would purchase this for herself. The last item she had collected, from Prudence Golightly, was a cast-iron nutcracker designed in the form of two shapely female legs. For the sake of modesty Prudence had knitted a pair of pink stockings and Lil smiled, impressed with both the endeavour and the perfect fit.

It was 9.30 a.m. when Ryan Halfpenny announced without appearing to look up from his drawing of an isosceles triangle, 'Austin Metro coming up t'drive, Mr Sheffield.'

'It's my mum, sir,' said Dawn Phillips.

'Oh 'eck,' said Ryan, scratching his head.

A few minutes later Staff Nurse Sue Phillips tapped on my door and gave me that 'Can I have a quick word?' look.

As always, Sue was immaculate in her light-blue uniform with a spotless white apron starched stiff as a board. She looked every inch our school nurse with her sensible, black lace-up shoes and a navy-blue belt that sported a precious buckle depicting, appropriately, the God of Wind.

I walked to the open doorway while Dawn gave her mother a shy smile. 'Hello, Sue,' I said. 'What is it today – nits, hearing, eyesight, height, weight?'

'Nits today, Jack,' she replied with a grimace. 'There's an outbreak locally so I thought I would call in to do a quick check.'

'You're always welcome,' I said, 'even with your metal nit comb.'

'I know,' she said with a grin.

'Would you like a hot drink before you begin?'

She glanced at her watch. 'No time ... and I'm afraid there are changes ahead. Cutbacks are in the pipeline, so you'll see less of me.'

'Oh dear,' I said, 'that's bad news.'

'I know, all good things have to end sometime.' She picked up her medical bag. 'Anyway, I'll nip round the classes now if you don't mind and I should get back from the hospital in time for this afternoon's netball match. Pat Brookside has certainly got them playing well.'

She hurried off to Anne's classroom while I reflected on how lucky we were to have such a high level of support and was saddened that it may be coming to an end.

In Joseph's weekly Bible studies lesson the six- and seven-year-olds in Class 2 were discussing prayers.

Dallas Sue-Ellen Earnshaw raised her hand. 'Mr Evans, my mam prays ev'ry night.'

'That's wonderful,' said Joseph.

'An' las' night she left my bedroom door open an' ah 'eard what she said.'

'Really?'

'Yes, she said, "Thank God she's in bed".'

Keen to return to the theme of the lesson, Joseph asked Zoe Book to read out her prayer.

Seven-year-old Zoe touched at his heartstrings when she read her neat printing in a loud clear voice:

Dear God
I went to church on Sunday with my Grandad.
We had a good time.
Wish you could have been there.
Love Zoe X.

'That was good of your granddad to bring you to church,' said Joseph.

'Yes, Mr Evans,' said Zoe, 'and he says when he dies he wants to go to heaven.'

'That's wonderful,' said Joseph. He looked around at the class. 'And what do you have to be to get there?'

Billy Ricketts was the first to put up his hand. 'Six feet under,' he said.

Joseph couldn't decide whether to laugh or cry.

By lunchtime the air was crisp and cold and the sky was primrose blue. It was a clear, still April day in North Yorkshire and we were drinking tea in the staff-room. Anne and I were busy ordering painting materials, Vera and Sally were reading newspapers and Pat was flicking through the pages of her most recent computer magazine.

Sally began chuckling to herself. She was reading an article in Anne's *Daily Mail* concerning the eighteen-year-old tennis star Boris Becker. The young German superstar had proclaimed his love for the American player Susan Mascarin. However, his trainer, Gunther Bosch, was not so thrilled ... particularly as Becker's last long-distance telephone call had cost £245.

Meanwhile, Vera, a fan of *The Archers,* had different concerns. Dan Archer was due to be killed off next week after thirty-five years in the radio soap opera. Actor Frank Middlemass, who played the part, had tried to soften the blow by explaining that Dan, at the grand age of eighty-nine, had enjoyed a good innings. It brought to mind her earlier thoughts of retirement and she stared out of the window.

'You look preoccupied, Vera,' observed Anne.

Vera returned her thoughts to the here and now. 'Anne, I always think pickled damsons go well with cold roast beef, don't you?'

It was incongruous, but we all nodded in implicit agreement.

Pat looked up from her computer magazine. 'Guess what,' she said, excitedly, 'I've got a new computer.'

'What is it?' I asked.

'It's a Commodore 128.'

'And are you pleased with it?' Anne tried to sound interested.

'Definitely,' said Pat. 'It can run 64K, 128K and CP/M software, so it's really versatile.'

For Anne and me this was even more unfathomable than the pickled damsons, but we nodded politely and returned to our Yorkshire Purchasing Organisation catalogue and the price of bristle brushes.

At lunchtime the school playground was filled with happy children playing in the sunshine. Mrs Doreen Critchley, the dinner lady, strode around her empire, keeping order where necessary but occasionally getting involved in unwanted conversations.

Dallas Sue-Ellen Earnshaw was pulling faces at Scott Higginbottom and Mrs Critchley pointed her finger. 'Now be'ave y'self, Dallas,' she shouted. 'When ah were a little girl my mother said if ah made funny faces it would freeze an' ah'd stay like that for ever.'

Dallas studied the grim, square-jawed, florid face of our dinner lady and came to a conclusion.

'Well, y'can't say y'weren't warned, Mrs Critchley.'

She'll go far that one, thought Mrs Critchley; then, as an afterthought, *Further the better.*

Meanwhile the children were playing in their own special ways. Small boys ran around the edge of the playground pretending to be lorries, Michelle Gawthorpe and Katie Icklethwaite were making friendship bracelets, Damian Brown was demonstrating how to 'Walk the Dog' and go 'Round the World' with his new yo-yo, while Ben Clouting had tapped 58008 on his calculator, turned it upside down and shown it to a puzzled Ryan Halfpenny.

During afternoon school Sally was busy with her 'Weather' project. She was talking about the Beaufort scale and the strength of wind. The children were writing words such as 'typhoon' and 'hurricane'.

'But these are *made-up* words, Miss,' said Charlie Cartwright.

Sitting next to him, Ted Coggins nodded in agreement. 'Charlie's right, Miss, an' if y'think about *words,* well, they're all made up.'

'I suppose they are, Ted,' said Sally.

'Miss, Miss,' called out Katie Icklethwaite, 'what does the wind do when it's not blowin'?'

Sally smiled. The unexpected always made the job fun.

I was on playground duty during afternoon break when little Ted Coggins came up to me and stared at the sky. The weather had changed and it was clear that Ted, after Sally's lesson, was observing it with a new appreciation.

'It's mizzling, Mr Sheffield,' he said.

I looked out at the damp sheen on the cobbled driveway and nodded. 'Yes, it is.'

The sons of local farmers had their own vocabulary for the weather. It was certainly a fine drizzle but I preferred Ted's interpretation. It was definitely mizzling.

Then I spotted two ten-year-olds from my class standing by the school gate and waving frantically.

'Come and look at this, Mr Sheffield,' called Dawn Phillips.

'It's PC Pike,' shouted Mary Scrimshaw.

An unlikely scene was unfolding on the other side of the village green and I hurried down to join them.

Our local bobby, PC Pike, armed with a dustbin lid and a rolled-up copy of *Karate Monthly*, was providing a convincing impression of a Roman gladiator. He was outside The Royal Oak doing battle with an angry dog.

'It's a black Labrador cross,' said the knowledgeable Dawn.

'It definitely looks cross,' agreed Mary.

'I recognize it,' said Dawn. 'It belongs to Mr Bones. He lives on Cut Throat Lane off the Morton Road.'

Julian Pike seemed to have the situation under control by the time the huge frame of Don the barman appeared and together they tied the dog to the cast-iron foot-scraper outside the pub entrance. He gave me a thumbs-up, returned his magazine to his truncheon pocket and came over just as Ruby arrived to check the school boilers.

'Our Natasha finishes work at six o'clock,' she said.

I noticed that the diminutive bobby blushed profusely at the mention of Natasha's name and I guessed a budding romance might one day be in the offing.

'Thanks for letting me know, Mrs Smith,' he replied politely.

'It looks like the dog belongs to Wilfred Bones,' I said.

'Yes, that's what Don thought. I'll let him know,' said our eager policeman. 'In fact, I've just seen Mr Bones going into Stan Coe's farmhouse. His dog must have escaped from his car.'

When I walked back into class I wondered what Stan Coe's business was with the chair of governors of Morton School.

At 3.15 p.m. the infants finished school for the day and parents arrived in the cloakroom area outside Anne's classroom to collect their offspring. Five-year-old Tracey Higginbottom was buttoning up her coat.

'You're growing up fast,' said Mrs Higginbottom. 'You're getting old,' she added proudly.

Tracey thought about this. 'Well, Mam,' she said, 'ah've been gettin' old since ah were born.' She looked at her mother's swollen tummy. 'Mam, why is your tummy getting fat?'

'Because there's a baby growing inside,' said Mrs Higginbottom.

Tracey looked at her mother with a new appraisal. 'So, what's growing in your bottom, Mummy?'

Half an hour later the bell rang to signal the end of the day for the older children. There was excitement among the girls as they prepared for their netball match, while two ten-year-olds in my class, Ben Clouting and Harry Patch, were deciding which house they should go to.

'Come to ours,' urged Ben. 'We've got Buckaroo an' Operation an' KerPlunk.'

'Yes,' said Harry, 'but I've got "Horace and the Spiders" on our ZX Spectrum computer and I'm up to the second level.'

It was no contest and the boys ran off to Harry's home.

In that moment I realized my world of Meccano and model trains was being usurped by virtual reality.

In the churchyard Madonna Fazackerly was standing next to her mother while she placed some flowers on her father's grave.

''E were a lovely man, were your granddad,' said Mrs Fazackerly quietly.

Madonna stared at the gravestone and then at the pebbles beneath. 'Mam, can we dig 'im up so ah can talk to 'im?'

'No, luv,' said Mrs Fazackerly, wondering what they taught them at school. 'Once y'buried you 'ave to stay in t'ground.'

'Mebbe 'e went to 'eaven,' suggested Madonna helpfully and stared up at the sky.

Mrs Fazackerly thought back to her father's three jail sentences, drinking and womanizing.

'Let's go to t'Coffee Shop,' she said.

The telephone rang in the office. It was Beth.

'Had a good day?' she asked.

'Fine, thanks.'

'And did you post the application?'

'Vera did it for me at lunchtime. She said she had to go to the Post Office.'

'Good news,' said Beth. 'So it's begun, and I know you'll do well.'

Her words were full of hope and love ... like a spring of fresh clear water.

'Thanks, Beth, and don't worry, I'm very determined.' For me ambition had never been a comfortable companion, but I knew it was time to change.

An hour later Vera and I were finishing off some paperwork for County Hall.

'You ought to be getting home,' I said, glancing up at the clock.

'Yes, that's finished now,' she said as she filed away the latest version of the county's Health & Safety policy. She collected her coat and put it on.

'By the way, Vera, I heard from PC Pike that Wilfred Bones was paying a visit to Stan Coe today.'

Vera pursed her lips. 'Up to no good, I should warrant.'

'Yes, it does make you think.'

'There's no doubt Stan Coe has clearly got it in for Ragley School, and you in particular,' said Vera. 'He's never recovered from being removed from our governing body.'

'He may have some influential friends,' I said.

'I've heard Wilfred Bones is in the same Rotary Club as some of the senior people up at County Hall.'

Vera looked thoughtful. 'Let's hope Wilfred sees him for what he really is. I'll speak to Rupert – Mr Bones is not the only one with influence.'

'Thank you, Vera.' I stood up and walked over to the window. 'I should be lost without you.' I stared out at the school grounds and fields beyond.

She turned back to me and smiled. 'Have faith and by God's grace, Jack, we shall find a way ... never fear.'

It was rare for Vera to call me by my first name and the significance wasn't lost on me.

She gestured with her hand around the office. 'Do you ever look beyond the here and now to a far horizon? Perhaps you should.' As she put on her scarf and buttoned her coat she paused by the door. 'This is not the end of days, Jack, merely the beginning of a new adventure.'

Chapter Fifteen

Heathcliffe's Scarecrow

School closed today for the May Day Bank Holiday and will reopen on Tuesday, 6 May. Reading tests were completed throughout the school. Children in Classes 3 and 4 are due to take part in an exhibition of maypole dancing on the village green on May Day.

The school staff agreed to contribute towards the village scarecrow competition.

Extract from the Ragley School Logbook:
Friday, 2 May 1986

It was Saturday, 3 May and the season was moving on. I opened the bedroom window and the soft balmy air brought with it the sweet scent of spring flowers. Under the kitchen window the bed of tulips with their bronze and yellow cups shone in the soft sunlight. I could hear the bleating of lambs while rooks wheeled lazily above the tall limes and a woodland carpet of bluebells.

It was a perfect morning to make a scarecrow.

The event had captured the imagination of the village. May Day was always a popular celebration in Ragley, but the idea of a scarecrow competition organized by the Ragley & Morton Women's Institute had added an extra dimension to the occasion and every organization was expected to make a contribution. So the teaching staff of Ragley School had agreed to meet for an hour or so on Saturday morning to make a scarecrow to be erected by the school gate. However, before I could set off Beth confronted me with unexpected news.

I was outside Bilbo Cottage preparing to leave for Ragley while Beth was strapping John into his child seat in her car. Suddenly she returned to the house and reappeared with two black plastic bags. She dumped them on the Yorkshire-stone paving by the 'Zéphirine Drouhin' climbing rose that was scrambling up the trellis next to the front door. Then she rummaged inside one of them and pulled out my favourite herringbone jacket. 'I'm finally taking it to the charity shop in Easington,' she said firmly.

It was a parting of the ways, the end of an era and there was nothing I could do about it. Beth was determined and I recognized the firm jaw and pursed lips.

'But there's a bit of life left in it,' I protested.

'It's going, Jack,' she said simply.

'Oh well,' I said. It was like saying farewell to an old friend.

'It's had its day,' she said, shaking her head in dismay. I looked in the bag. She had added my favourite grey baggy trousers, a thick checked winter shirt and an old flower-power tie to the collection. 'Don't forget,' she said, 'you're an *eighties* man now.'

It was faint praise and did little to raise my spirits.

Three miles away black bags were also in evidence in the Earnshaw household.

'What y'doin', Mam?' asked twelve-year-old Terry.

'Ah'm tidying up,' said a red-faced Julie Earnshaw.

There was a pause while Terry looked up at his big brother Heathcliffe. Both boys had puzzled expressions.

'Why ... who's comin'?' asked Heathcliffe.

Julie shook her head. 'That's t'problem livin' in this 'ouse,' she said.

'What is, Mam?' asked the boys in unison.

'Men,' she said gruffly. 'An' put y'dirty socks in

t'washin' basket.'

Terry grinned. 'No, Mam, ah tried that an' they keep coming back.'

The two boys collected their coats.

'There's some cake in t'kitchen y'can 'ave,' shouted Julie.

Heathcliffe and Terry stared at the Victoria sponge.

''Alf each,' said Terry.

'You cut ... an' then ah'll choose my 'alf,' said Heathcliffe with the wisdom of Solomon.

So the intrepid duo, each with a fistful of cake, headed for the front door.

'We're off out, Mam,' shouted Heathcliffe, but at that moment their mother neither heard nor cared.

Beth pulled up in Ragley High Street outside the General Stores, opened the boot and took out her shopping bags and the collapsible pushchair. Before she could erect it John began to yell for attention and food. Sighing, she was unstrapping him from his car seat when suddenly the cavalry arrived in the form of the Earnshaw brothers.

'Can ah 'elp, Mrs Sheffield?' asked Heathcliffe politely.

'We could put y'pushchair up,' offered Terry. 'We 'ad a lot o' practice wi' our Dallas.'

'Thanks, boys,' said Beth, 'that's very thoughtful of you.'

''Ow's Mr Sheffield?' asked Heathcliffe as he tightened the wheel nuts on the arms of the pushchair.

'Well, actually he's making a scarecrow with the

other teachers,' said Beth with a wry smile and nodded towards the school.

'We'd like t'mek a scarecrow,' said Heathcliffe with heartfelt pathos, 'but m'mam said there were no old clothes t'spare.'

'Ah bet we could've made a good 'un,' said Terry wistfully.

Beth had a thought and rummaged in the back of her car. 'Well, boys,' she said, 'perhaps these might help,' and she handed over the black bags.

Heathcliffe looked inside. 'Cor, thanks a lot, Mrs Sheffield. These are perfec'.'

Beth was in a good mood. Now she could do her shopping at leisure without the need to drive to the charity shop. 'And here's ten pence each for being so helpful,' she said.

As Beth walked away with John, Heathcliffe made an executive decision. 'You look after t'clothes an' spend your ten pence on some sweets. Ah'll keep t'other ten pence f'later. Ah'm off t'see Tidy Tim t'get some more stuff for t'scarecrow.'

'OK, 'Eath',' said Terry and the boys went their separate ways.

When I arrived outside the entrance of Ragley School Anne was stuffing wastepaper into an old pair of her husband's blue overalls and Pat was doing the same with a pair of her partner's discarded hiking socks. Sally was painting a cheerful face on a brown paper bag and had found an old sailor's hat to wedge on its head.

'Jack, you can tie him on to one of the broken chairs if you like,' said Pat, handing over a ball of baling twine. 'Then we can sit him outside the school gate.'

Ruby had stacked a pile of old wooden chairs next to the cycle shed for removal by Big Dave and Little Malcolm.

'And then we're going for a coffee,' said Anne.

'Vera is working with her Women's Institute friends outside the village hall,' said Sally. 'Apparently, they're the favourites.'

'They've got an actual mannequin,' said Pat, 'so they're taking it very seriously.'

It wasn't long before we had a figure that resembled a drunken sailor sprawled on a chair outside the school gate. It was a token effort, but at least we had tried, and we walked across the road to Nora's Coffee Shop with a sense of achievement.

Terry stared at the row of sweet jars. The choice was considerable. He scanned the familiar labels, including Rhubarb and Custard Pips, Midget Gems, Coconut Mushrooms, Liquorice Comfits, Pontefract Cakes, Pear Drops and Chocolate Bonbons.

'Perhaps you would like your favourite, Terry,' suggested Prudence.

Terry sighed and smiled in agreement. There was just something special about Sherbet Lemons. 'OK, Miss Golightly, ten pence worth o' Sherbet Lemons in two bags, please.'

Prudence measured them out with care on her ancient weighing scale and, as always, added one sweet in each bag for good luck and because Terry had remembered to say 'please'.

Terry passed over his precious coin and

Prudence bent down below the counter to the Penny Selection tray. 'Jeremy says here's a barley sugar stick for being such a polite boy.'

Terry accepted this with the reverence with which the folk of Ragley acknowledged this familiar teddy bear. 'Thanks, Jeremy,' he said, a little sheepishly.

Prudence glanced up at Jeremy Bear and tenderly made a small adjustment to his smart blue RAF uniform – a labour of love that'd taken many evenings of work. 'He says you're very welcome.'

Meanwhile, in Pratt's Hardware Emporium Timothy was unpacking a cardboard box with great satisfaction. His long-awaited order for various sizes of dome-headed screws had finally arrived and he knew his dear friend Walter, the model-plane enthusiast, would be thrilled, as would the members of the Ragley Shed Society.

The bell rang and he saw Heathcliffe Earnshaw hesitating by the door.

'Don't forget t'wipe your feet,' said Timothy. 'Remember, cleanliness is next to godliness.'

Heathcliffe Earnshaw thought if that was the case then Tidy Tim would already be halfway to heaven, because the Emporium was spotless.

Heathcliffe wiped his feet on the cork mat. ''Ello, Mr Pratt,' he said. 'Is there anything ah can do to 'elp?' He gave Timothy his famous fixed smile, the one that his Aunty Maureen told him if he did it too often his face would stay like that. 'Me an' m'brother can turn our 'ands t'most jobs,' he continued, with glassy-eyed humility.

'It's not Bob-a-Job week, is it?' asked Timothy.

'No, it's jus' that we need some bits o' timber an'

mebbe chicken wire for our scarecrow,' explained Heathcliffe, 'an' we thought if we did summat f'you then y'might be able t'give us some.'

The penny dropped and Timothy smiled. It was good to hear of young folk getting involved in the community.

At that moment the doorbell jingled and Mrs Tricklebank walked in with her daughter Julie.

'Ah need some batteries, please, Timothy,' said Mrs Tricklebank.

'Certainly,' said Timothy and he pulled out the drawer labelled 'Batteries'. As all the drawers were labelled in alphabetical order, this was achieved in seconds. While Mrs Tricklebank rummaged around in the drawer, much to Timothy's disquiet, he leaned over the counter. 'Ah were sorry to 'ear about your cat, Julie.'

Julie Tricklebank's cat had been knocked down by the milk float.

'Thank you, Mr Pratt,' she said.

'Don't worry,' continued Timothy quietly. 'Your cat is sleeping now.'

Heathcliffe had seen the unfortunate outcome. 'Sleepin'?' he said, looking surprised. 'Ah saw 'im this morning an' 'e looked stone dead t'me.'

Sensitivity isn't what it used to be, thought Timothy as Mrs Tricklebank gave Heathcliffe a cold stare, paid for her batteries and walked out.

A few minutes later Heathcliffe left with some offcuts of timber plus a roll of chicken wire and a borrowed pair of wire cutters. He joined his brother and they set up a base for scarecrow construction next to Ronnie's bench on the village green.

In Nora's Coffee Shop, Anne, Sally and Pat found a table while I collected a tray of four frothy coffees from Nora.

Teenagers Claire Bradshaw, Anita Cuthbertson and Kenny Kershaw were sitting at a corner table listening to the cast of *Grange Hill* singing 'Just Say No' on the old juke-box.

''Ello, sir, 'ave y'made a scarecrow?' asked Claire cheerfully. She was going through her Madonna phase in a tubular dress, bolero-style jacket and fingerless lace gloves.

'Yes, thank you, Claire,' I said. 'And how are you all?'

'Fine, thanks, sir,' said Anita, whose dress sense was slightly more relaxed. She had ripped a larger neckhole in her grey sweatshirt so it revealed a bare shoulder à la Jennifer Beals in *Flashdance*. A pair of Footloose leg warmers over her tight jeans completed the ensemble.

'We're 'elpin' Mr Piercy wi' 'is 'og roast, Mr Sheffield,' said Kenny, who thought he looked the most fashionable man in Ragley with his new hairstyle, short at the front and sides and long at the back. He was sporting a bright-pink T-shirt, cheap baggy jacket with the sleeves rolled up, jeans and espadrilles, plus a few days of beard growth.

Claire and Anita waved at Anne and Sally. 'We're lookin' forward to t'maypole dancing,' said Claire.

'Remember when we did it, Miss?' said Anita. 'We were brill'.'

Margery Ackroyd and Betty Buttle were standing

across the road from the village hall watching Vera and the ladies of the Women's Institute putting the finishing touches to their so-called scarecrow. It looked as though it should have been in Madame Tussauds in London. The elegant mannequin had been carefully dressed in the style of Emmeline Pankhurst, the famous suffragette.

'Perfect,' said Vera as the ladies secured their masterpiece with stout wire to the cherry tree outside the entrance to the village hall.

'Bit posh for a scarecrow,' opined Margery. 'Ah don't know what t'judge'll mek o' it.'

'That's nowt,' said Betty. 'Ah 'eard that Deirdre Coe got 'er Stanley to 'ire a proper costume for *'er* scarecrow.'

'Ah'm not surprised,' said Margery, 'an' y'know me, Betty, ah never speak ill of nobody ... but that Deirdre Coe is crooked as a corkscrew.'

'Y'reight there,' said Betty.

The choice of judge for the competition was remarkably obvious.

For the past thirty years 'One Eye' Clarence Drinkwater, an eccentric and bumbling local character, had erected a variety of scarecrows as a labour of love in Twenty Acre Field. He was proud of his creations, and the fact that they seemed to *attract* the local bird population rather than deter them did not dampen his enthusiasm. Stuffed with straw and with happy smiles on their varnished papier-mâché faces, along with colourful scarves and a variety of flat caps and sun hats, they had a distinctive style of their own.

The fact that Clarence dressed in a similar fashion to his scarecrows added a certain *joie de vivre* to his persona. Unfortunately, his habit of tucking his baggy shirts into his equally voluminous underpants, visible at the waistline, tended to take the edge off his appearance.

Back in 1956, on the day that Premium Bonds were introduced, a high wind blew down a scarecrow Clarence was in the process of erecting and it poked him in the eye with a birch-twig finger. However, this did not deter him from his weekday job of repairing shoes and ladies' handbags. As a self-employed, and now one-eyed, cobbler, it left his weekends free to indulge in the love of his life: namely, the pursuit of the perfect scarecrow. Consequently, when he was approached by Elsie Crapper in her role as the Women's Institute social secretary to be the judge of this novel competition, he was in scarecrow heaven.

Elsie chose to ignore the rest of the social committee when it was suggested that Clarence had been promoted beyond his final level of incompetence. After all, Elsie was a Christian soul and always thought kindly of her fellow man, even though Clarence had recently ruined her best pair of leather boots along with her favourite sandals. So when Sunday evening came around, Clarence laid out his brightest shirt and his cleanest pair of Y-fronts before going to bed.

On Monday, 5 May the overnight gentle rain had cleared to leave a new day of bright sunshine. A thrush on the roof of my garden shed trilled a song of spring, while the swallows had returned to their familiar nesting places in the eaves of

Bilbo Cottage. Almond trees were in blossom and the first flower stalks on the horse chestnut trees gave promise of the summer days ahead. Grape hyacinths bordered the path and the tight buds on the apple trees were about to burst from their winter cocoons.

It was May Day, and an eventful one was in store. When Beth and I drove into school we stopped by the gate in surprise.

'Oh Jack,' said Beth, 'it's terrific – just like you!'

A gangling scarecrow stuffed with paper and straw and wearing my old clothes had been tied to a chair and propped on the other side of the school gate from the one made by the staff. A cardboard sign pinned to a familiar sports jacket read: 'MR SHEFFIELD by HEATHCLIFFE & TERRY EARNSHAW'. A huge pair of black cardboard Buddy Holly spectacles added the finishing touch.

However, it was young John who confirmed the *fait accompli.* He peered out of the car window, pointed at the scarecrow and shouted, 'Daddy!'

Don and Sheila Bradshaw had made a big effort on the forecourt of The Royal Oak. A fat scarecrow wearing one of Don's old wrestling outfits was leaning against one of the picnic tables with an empty tankard attached to its hand.

Under the weeping willow on the village green, Madame Jacqueline Laporte, the French teacher from Easington Comprehensive School, along with her latest boyfriend, had made a superb scarecrow of Napoleon Bonaparte. The attractive Frenchwoman with the Brigitte Bardot looks and figure-hugging, pencil-slim black skirt turned a few heads as she had her photograph taken next to 'the little corporal' for the local paper.

The *Herald* photographer was busy walking up and down the High Street, snapping the various scarecrows. The ladies of the Women's Institute had gathered round Emmeline Pankhurst for a group photograph, while Stan and Deirdre Coe had arrived with their Henry VIII and had secured him firmly with baling twine to the post that supported the village noticeboard.

Deke Ramsbottom, with his sons, Shane, Clint and Wayne, had built a cowboy scarecrow, with a similarity to John Wayne, and it had been tied to the fall pipe outside the pub.

In all there were around twenty scarecrows, including one *inside* Oscar Woodcock's shed, which seemed not in accord with the fundamental purpose of a scarecrow. Word had it that Oscar merely wanted some company during the many lonely nights he spent in his shed. My two favourites were the Elvis scarecrow outside the Coffee Shop and the policeman scarecrow outside the red telephone box, a joint effort by Natasha Smith and her new boyfriend, PC Pike.

The May Day celebrations always attracted large crowds to the village green. The Scout troop had completed the erection of the marquees with their bright strands of bunting. The sun shone down and the rich aroma of Old Tommy Piercy's hog roast attracted a queue of ravenous villagers. The Ragley & Morton Brass Band played 'Jerusalem' and the Scout troop raised the flag of St George on the flagpole. The Morris dancers were waiting their turn to perform in their white linen shirts with coloured ribbon tied around their cord trousers. Meanwhile, Sheila Bradshaw in her sparkly flag-of-St-George boob tube, white leather mini-skirt and red high heels was serving them with drinks.

In the centre of the village green Rupert Forbes-Kitchener had supervised the preparations for the maypole. It was topped with eight bell garlands and Sally Pringle gathered together the group of children who were waiting to perform their first intricate dance.

First came the parade of the May Queen from the village hall up the main street to the village green. This year it was the turn of seventeen-year-old Cathy Cathcart, who had been in my class back at the start of the eighties. Her mother, Daphne, with her distinctive pink candy-floss hair and tombstone teeth that resembled Stonehenge, was the proudest woman in the village. It was a day when her regular habit of blushing went unnoticed. Her younger daughter, thirteen-year-old Michelle, clung on to her mother's arm and stared in wonderment at the sight of her big sister waving to the crowd.

The Jackson twins, Hermione and Honeysuckle, were the May Queen's attendants. With a band of flowers in their golden ringlets and matching white dresses with lacy collars, they looked like angels. Cathy sat on her 'throne' on a trailer towed by Deke on his tractor and the crowd cheered. It was a sight to gladden the heart. Meanwhile, Deke's sons had prepared a semicircle of straw bales to create instant seating and a natural theatre-in-the-round for the various performances. Children settled on the bales to watch

Captain Fantastic's Punch and Judy show while Vera and her colleagues began serving cream teas at one end of the Women's Institute marquee.

George Dainty was standing next to Ruby. 'Ah recall when you were May Queen in 1950,' he said. 'You looked a picture.'

Ruby's cheeks flushed at the memory. 'But best day were in 1980 when our Natasha were May Queen.'

'Ah bet she looked reight bonnie,' said George.

'She did that, an' my Ronnie were proud that day.'

George was thoughtful and said nothing.

Joseph Evans was in the queue for refreshments when a scuffle began among a group of the children, followed by some pushing and pulling.

'Now boys, remember what I said,' Joseph cautioned them.

'What's that, Mr Evans?' asked Damian Brown.

'Do unto others as you would have them do unto you.'

Damian considered this for a moment. 'Thing is, Barry did it unto me first so ah thought ah'd do it unto 'im.'

The logic left poor Joseph stranded.

Meanwhile, at the end of the queue, Scott Higginbottom on his eighth birthday had taken a liking to Patience Crapper.

He spat on his hands, rubbed them together and then attempted to smooth down his spiky hair.

'Patience,' he said.

'What?' asked Patience, not wishing to be interrupted.

'When is it OK for me t'give you a kiss?'

Patience gave him a withering look. 'When you're rich,' she said with feeling and turned away.

That were a waste o' spit, thought Scott as he trudged back to his friends.

'What 'appened?' asked Sam Whittaker. 'Did she give you a kiss?'

'No,' said Scott. 'Mebbe nex' year.'

'Ah don't like girls,' declared Sam.

'Problem is,' said Scott knowingly, 'you'll 'ave t'marry one one day.'

''Ave ah got to?'

'Yes,' confirmed Scott.

'Why?'

'Cos you'll need someone t'clear up.'

'Ah see,' said Sam and thought about it.

'Can you whistle?' asked Sam suddenly.

'Not like Ted Coggins.'

'Let's go an' ask 'im t'teach us,' said Sam and so, with girls forgotten until another day, they ran off.

George and Ruby were staring at the Coes' scarecrow. The Tudor monarch was certainly impressive.

Deirdre and Stan came over. 'Y'lookin' at t'winner,' said Deirdre. 'Rest don't stand a chance.'

Ruby and George turned to walk away.

'Don't look down y'nose at me,' Deirdre called after them. George pulled Ruby's sleeve, but Ruby glowered at Deirdre. 'Don't sit on yer 'igh 'orse,' continued Deirdre. 'There's changes comin' t'that school o' yours, Ruby Smith.'

'There'll be *big* changes come nex' year,' leered Stan.

'Well, there's plenty of us t'mek sure it dun't 'appen,' retorted Ruby.

'An' don't reckon on you an' Sheffield gettin' y'jobs back.'

'Who sez?' asked Ruby, her face flushed.

'You've no chance, caretaker skivvy,' jeered Deirdre.

'There's no need for unkind words, Deirdre,' said George.

'Get back t'yer fish-an'-chip shop,' growled Stan.

George flexed his burly shoulders and took a pace forward. He stared up into Stan's eyes. 'That's enough now, Stanley,' he said quietly, 'else it won't be just fish that gets a batterin'.'

Stan Coe blinked and took a step backwards. George was Dainty by name but certainly not by nature. He stood like a gladiator ready for battle.

'Tek no notice,' said Deirdre with an evil grimace. 'We've got better fish t'fry.'

'Y'reight there,' agreed Stan with a nervous smile.

'If y'can't say owt nice, then don't say nowt at all,' said Ruby.

'Judgement day is comin' f'you an' y'fancy man,' said Deirdre. 'My Stanley *knows* things.'

'You'll gerra clout if y'don't shurrup,' said Ruby.

Stan gave his sister a sharp look. 'Let's gerroff,' he said, taking her by the arm.

'Good riddance,' muttered George as they walked away.

'It's a worrying thought, George,' said Ruby. ''E's gorra lot o' effluence 'as that Stanley Coe.'

'Actually it's "influence", Ruby,' began George,

'...but, on reflection, ah think you were right first time.'

Beth had taken John to watch the Punch and Judy show while I bought soft drinks from Vera in the Women's Institute tent.

'A successful day, Mr Sheffield,' she said. 'The maypole dancing was excellent.'

'It certainly was.' I looked around me. 'Ragley really is a special place,' I said.

She looked up at me. 'And always will be.'

I noticed the familiar sight of Edward Clifton in animated conversation with Anne. They looked relaxed together and it was good to see Anne enjoying her day.

Suddenly a flustered Ruby appeared. 'That Stan Coe an' 'is sister 'ave been rude an' sayin' unkind things about what's goin' to 'appen to t'school.'

'Take no notice, Ruby, it's just hot air,' said Vera.

'Mebbe so, Mrs F, but like ah've allus said – there's no fire wi'out smoke.'

'No smoke without fire,' corrected Vera gently.

'That an' all, Mrs F,' said Ruby nodding in agreement. 'It's like a game o' chess wi' 'im an' we're one o' them prawns.'

'Can I buy you a drink, Ruby?' I asked, 'And perhaps one for Mr Dainty?'

George Dainty was chatting with Old Tommy next to his hog roast.

'Thank you, kindly, Mr Sheffield,' said Ruby and she hurried off with two large glasses of Vera's home-made elderflower lemonade.

Suddenly Major Rupert Forbes-Kitchener's voice could be heard over the microphone. 'Ladies and gentlemen, boys and girls, your attention please. Gather round ... it's time to hear the results of the scarecrow competition, to be announced by our esteemed judge, Mr Drinkwater.'

Clarence Drinkwater stood up and tucked his shirt into his underpants. His moment of fame had arrived.

'Thank you, everybody, an' it's wonderful t'see so many scarecrows 'ere t'day.' He stared into the distance. 'There's no sight more satisfying than a scarecrow flappin' in t'breeze in t'English countryside.' There was no doubt Clarence loved his scarecrows.

'So in third place are t'Girl Guides an' t'Scouts, who combined t'mek t'scarecrow from t'*Wizard of Oz*.'

Everybody clapped.

Clarence took a deep breath. 'Second an' first were difficult to sep'rate cos they were both so good. They were what ah would call *authentic*, in t'true spirit of scarecrow construction.' He surveyed the crowd. 'An' ah mus' say at this point ... ah don't alt'gether 'old wi' usin' *mannequins*.'

'Oh dear,' whispered Vera.

Deirdre Coe leered from a distance.

'Nor do ah 'old wi' 'irin' costumes like that King 'Enry.'

Deirdre looked as if she were about to explode.

'So, in second place is ... Mr Ramsbottom's cowboy scarecrow.'

Cheers echoed around the village green and Clarence knew he was guaranteed an evening of free drinks.

''Owever, after much deliberation an' wi' a lot

o' thought, the winner is ... Heathcliffe Earnshaw and his brother Terry with their excellent likeness of our local 'eadmaster, Mr Sheffield.'

Midst thunderous applause, Heathcliffe and Terry, wreathed in smiles, walked forward to receive the first prize of £5.

'Cor, we're rich, 'Eath',' said Terry.

We returned to our car with the Earnshaw brothers. Terry had taken charge of John in his pushchair.

'Well done, boys,' I said.

'Thanks, sir,' said Heathcliffe.

John stared once again at the scarecrow propped against the school gate. 'Daddy,' he said again. He clambered out of the pushchair, stretched up, grabbed the cardboard spectacles and put them on.

'Like father, like son,' said Beth and everyone laughed.

The *Herald* photographer captured the moment and it is a photograph I treasured in the years to come ... but not the headline by a certain Mr Merry that read 'Local Headteacher Looks Like a Scarecrow!'

Chapter Sixteen

A Pratt Called Bismarck

School closed today for the Spring Bank Holiday and will reopen on Monday, 9 June.

Extract from the Ragley School Logbook:
Friday, 23 May 1986

It was Friday, 23 May, the final day before school closed for the two-week Spring Bank Holiday, and I was in good spirits as I drove to Ragley. In Twenty Acre Field the sunlight on the green, unripe barley created sinuous shadows and the distant hills were streaked with purple heather. Above my head a flock of starlings wheeled in close formation over the vast tableland of the North Yorkshire moors. It was good to be alive on a morning such as this.

When I pulled up outside the General Stores Timothy Pratt was admiring the huge poster that dominated the window of his Hardware Emporium. It read:

GRAND DUCK RACE

In aid of the Village Pond Restoration Fund

Meet on Upper Foss Bridge at 1.00 p.m.
Spring Bank Holiday Monday, 26th May

Buy your official plastic duck from
Pratt's Hardware Emporium
Adults 20p Children 10p

'Fine morning, Mr Sheffield,' shouted Timothy. As always he was smart in his collar and tie, neatly pressed trousers, shiny black shoes and a brown overall with three pens in his top pocket.

'It certainly is,' I replied.

'Are you entering the duck race?'

'Yes, I need to buy one for John,' I said. 'He'll love to see all the ducks bobbing down the river.'

'I'll put one aside for you. They're all numbered.'

'Thanks, Timothy,' I said. 'It should be a good event.'

'Well, we 'ave t'keep t'village pond in good order an' safe for all t'children.'

'Quite right,' I agreed. I was always impressed by this conscientious, pernickety little man and his devotion to his village. 'And how are you?'

'Fine thanks, jus' gettin' everything shipshape for m'cousin visitin' from down south.'

'Oh yes, and who is that?'

'Our Bismarck.'

'Bismarck?'

'Yes, 'e's a sailor.'

I suppose he would be, I thought.

I walked into the General Stores, where Prudence was serving Old Tommy Piercy with his weekly supply of Old Holborn tobacco. He had also spent eighteen pence on today's *Daily Mirror* and was scanning the news while he passed the time of day with his next-door neighbour, Miss Golightly.

A photograph of Joan Collins at the Empire Theatre in London's West End had caught his eye. 'Now there's a fine woman,' he said. The *Dynasty* soap queen had tried to upstage Princess Di in a sexy, split-skirted green dress, complete with glittering jewels. Prudence had no doubt who had carried the day, but kept her opinion to herself.

'An' that Ian Botham's at it again,' went on Old Tommy, who admired the England cricketer in spite of him playing for a southern team. The larger-than-life sportsman had been smoking pot.

Old Tommy looked up at me. 'Tha' knaws secret o' long life, Mr Sheffield.'

'What's that, Mr Piercy?' I asked.

'Well, for m'dad it were wine, women 'n' whisky ... but f'me ah didn't bother wi' t'wine an' whisky,' he said with a twinkle in his eye and walked out to his butcher's shop.

Prudence handed me my newspaper with flushed cheeks. It was time to change the subject. 'And I need a card for our wedding anniversary, please.'

Prudence smiled. 'How many years now?'

'Four next week.'

'I remember it well, Mr Sheffield.' She pulled out a drawer of various cards, rummaged through them and selected one. 'How about this one?'

It featured two people sitting on a bench, looking out to a distant sun-kissed horizon. It seemed appropriate.

After driving up the High Street I paused by a familiar road sign next to the village green and smiled. Beneath a red warning triangle it carried a stark message: 'BEWARE OF THE DUCKS'.

The villagers of Ragley were proud of their duck population, even though they occasionally caused traffic hold-ups as they waddled in line and entirely unconcerned across the High Street. The exception was when Stan Coe hurtled by in his Land Rover, scattering ducks and feathers in every direction. The pond was one of the focal points of the village, but now it needed to be cleaned. There was also a proposal for a paved pathway around it if funds could be found. On this sunny morning Albert Jenkins, our retired school governor, was sitting on the bench feeding the ducks and he gave me a wave as I drove towards the school gate.

This week my class had completed a 'Pond Life' project and we had visited our village pond to study its teeming life. Environmental studies were always a popular aspect of the curriculum and the children loved to explore the outdoors. They were fortunate to live in such a beautiful part of North Yorkshire. Each day we had set out with nets, jam jars, notebooks, sketchpads and magnifying glasses. The resulting work was displayed in the school entrance hall and featured the children's writing and many wonderful illustrations and paintings.

After registration this morning we had an earlier assembly than usual as Anne had arranged for Mrs Tomkins to bring her baby, six-month-old Kylie, into Class 1 at 9.30 a.m. as part of their 'Growing-up' project. In the hall Anne played the opening bars of 'Morning Has Broken' and the children sang with gusto. As I surveyed their faces I was aware of how quickly the youngest children had settled into the routines of our school life. The twins, Hermione and Honeysuckle, held hands as they sang, word-perfect and in harmony.

I told the story of Noah's Ark, with regular contributions from the excited children.

'Elephants would 'ave tekken up a lot o' space, Mr Sheffield,' said the practical Scott Higginbottom, 'an' cleaning up after 'em,' he added as an afterthought.

'Ah know summat Noah wouldn't 'ave tekken on 'is wooden boat, sir,' exclaimed Tom Burgess at the end of the story.

'And what would that be, Tom?' I asked. 'Woodpeckers, Mr Sheffield.'

I looked across to Anne, who gave me a wide-eyed look as if to say *ask a daft question.*

Sally picked up her guitar, opened her *Tinderbox* songs for children, turned to number 50 and strummed the chords of 'Puff the Magic Dragon'. We finished with the Lord's Prayer and I was pleased to see that Gary Spittall could now recite all the words.

As we filed out to go back to our classrooms, a thoughtful Rosie Spittlehouse said, 'Ah wish ah could tell m'grandma 'ow much ah miss 'er, Mr Sheffield,' and I reflected on the power of prayer.

In Anne's class the children were so interested in their 'Growing-up' project that, when the bell rang at half past ten, they didn't want to go out to play. I called in on my way to the staff-room. A crowd had gathered round Mrs Tomkins and baby Kylie. The little girl had been fed, changed, weighed, measured, wiped clean until her face shone and was gurgling happily at all the attention. Her big brother, five-year-old Karl, had borrowed the cassette recorder from Sally's classroom and was displaying considerable expertise with the 'Record' button and a microphone as he taped the baby noises made by his sister.

'What are you doing, Karl?' I asked.

'Ah'm going to play it back when she grows up, Mr Sheffield, an' ask 'er what she meant.'

In the staff-room it wasn't often that Sally read Vera's *Daily Telegraph*, but this morning she was engrossed. 'Well, let's hope for the best – he can't be any worse than what's gone before.'

Kenneth Baker had become Secretary of State for Education and was promising reform. We all wondered what that might be.

The telephone rang and it was Norman Knight, the art adviser.

'Just completing the programme, Jack, for the art display, and I've got that lovely painting by Charlie Cartwright that I collected from your school.'

'Yes, Norman,' I said and looked towards Anne. 'It's about Charlie Cartwright.'

'And just checking the title is *A Pig in a Field*,' said Norman.

'A pig in a field!' I exclaimed.

Anne almost spilt her coffee as recognition dawned.

'No, it's not, Norman,' I said. 'It's his mother sunbathing in the back garden!'

'Really? It looks like a pig.'

'No, it's definitely his mother,' I insisted. 'I remember my conversation with him and I made the same mistake.'

'Thanks, Jack,' he said with a chuckle. 'I'll change it to *My Garden.*'

He rang off and Anne recalled scribbling the name and assumed title during the course of a busy day. We both breathed a sigh of relief. Mrs Cartwright would not have been pleased.

Meanwhile, on the High Street, Stan Coe was returning from The Pig & Ferret following lunch with his duck-shooting friends. After a large portion of fish, chips and mushy peas, washed down with four pints of Tetley's bitter, he pulled up outside Timothy Pratt's Hardware Emporium.

As a pupil at Ragley School back in 1933 Stan had been suspended for persistent bullying. After a lifetime of shady land deals and building contracts he was still causing trouble in his quest to become the most powerful man in the village. For Stan I had become public enemy number one and he was determined to get rid of me, using whatever tools were at his disposal.

'Ah need some four-inch nails,' he said gruffly.

'Coming up, Mr Coe,' said Timothy.

'An' 'urry up abart it.'

''Ow many?' asked Timothy.

'A bagful.'

Timothy was used to Stan's rudeness. He weighed out the nails and tipped them into a heavy-duty paper bag. 'That'll be–'

'Fifty pence should cover it,' announced Stan and slapped a coin on the counter. He turned to leave.

'Would you like a duck for the duck race, Mr Coe?' Stan turned back to the counter and took the plastic duck from Timothy's outstretched hand.

'Only twenty pence,' said Timothy.

Stan dropped the duck on to the wooden floor and crunched it beneath his large boot. 'Ah don't think so,' he sneered. 'Ah 'ate 'em.'

Timothy sighed and reached for his brush and shovel as Stan Coe walked out.

When the bell rang at 1.15 p.m. for afternoon school, Ted Coggins came in from the school field covered from head to toe in mud. I was standing on the playground checking that every child returned into school when he approached me.

'Who am I?' he asked with a mischievous grin.

I decided to go along with the charade. 'I don't know ... who are you?'

'Cor, Mrs Critchley were right, Mr Sheffield,' he said.

'What do you mean?' I asked.

'Well, she said ah were so dirty even t'teachers wouldn't recognize me.'

Afternoon school went well and ended with the last chapter of our class story, *Stig of the Dump* by Clive King.

'Great story, Mr Sheffield,' said Damian Brown. 'Ah'd like t'live in a cave.'

And there are times when your mother would agree, I thought.

In the cloakroom area Julie Tricklebank's grandmother was checking the lost-property box. Her granddaughter came up to me, excited about the holiday but, more particularly, about her wobbly tooth. One by one, she was saying goodbye to her milk teeth. To prove the point she opened her mouth wide and, with the tip of her tongue, flicked one of her front teeth. It responded like an obliging cat flap. 'There y'are, Mr Sheffield!' she said in triumph. 'What d'you think o' that?'

'Well I think the Tooth Fairy might be coming tonight,' said her grandma with a knowing wink in my direction.

'What's the going rate these days?' I asked.

'Five pence for every tooth,' she said.

Little Julie looked up at her expectantly. 'Grandma, please can ah borrow y'false teeth tonight?'

On Saturday morning Beth and I set off for Ragley. I had a few jobs to complete in school and Beth was going on to Easington to take John to the popular 'Story Time' session in the library, followed by some food shopping.

It was a fine morning and we drove in Beth's new car. It was a blue 1981 VW Golf CD Diesel and I felt a little strange being a passenger. John was excited and wanted to wind the handle for the sunroof. It looked really smart with its five doors and blue trim.

We had exchanged our views in a determined fashion last night about my Morris Minor Traveller, which, although showing signs of age, was ideal for me. Beth wanted me to change it but soon recognized there were some things in life that were too important to men like me.

She dropped me off on the High Street, where I was going to call into the Hardware Emporium to buy some hanging-basket containers for school. 'I'll collect you later,' she said and drove off up the Easington Road.

Timothy was arranging his new range of boot-scrapers on a trestle table outside his shop.

'Ah've got that duck f'your son, Mr Sheffield,' he said.

'Thanks, Timothy. I'll collect it now.'

We walked into the shop and I selected two metal hanging baskets. A large tin bath full of yellow plastic ducks was propped on a barrel next to the counter. Each duck had been neatly painted with a number.

'Here's yours,' said Timothy, 'number forty-eight.' He printed '48, John Sheffield' on the sheet attached to a clipboard and I passed over ten pence.

As I stood at the counter a man I didn't recognize appeared from the back room. 'Just going to Nora's for a coffee and a bite to eat, Timothy,' he said.

Timothy smiled. 'An' this is m'cousin, Bismarck.'

Bismarck was a slim, fit, athletic man with the tanned complexion of someone who loved the outdoor life. He was dressed casually in a bright-yellow waterproof coat with a fleece lining, blue roll-neck sweater, faded jeans and boat shoes.

'Mr Sheffield is our local 'eadteacher,' said Timothy.

'Pleased to meet you, Mr Sheffield,' he said with an engaging smile as he gripped my hand in a firm handshake.

'Welcome to Ragley,' I said.

'Lovely place,' replied Bismarck with a soft Hampshire accent. 'I've been meaning to come up here for a while now.'

As we were both going to the Coffee Shop it seemed natural for us to share a table. We bought a coffee and a sandwich while 'Lessons in Love' by Level 42 played on the juke-box and some of the local teenagers hummed along.

Bismarck slipped off his coat, sat down and pushed up his sleeves. On his right forearm he sported an interesting tattoo. Under a picture of an anchor were the Latin words *'Fortes fortuna adjuvat'*.

He glanced down and smiled. 'Fortune favours the brave,' he translated. 'A little immodest perhaps, but I studied Latin at university and it seemed appropriate at the time.'

This was clearly a well-educated man and during the next half-hour I learned a lot about his background.

Bismarck Pratt had been born in Southall, London, in 1947, the illegitimate son of a German prisoner-of-war and Timothy's aunt, Cortina Pratt. He had kept his mother's surname and, by the time he was a young man, he had reconciled himself to the fact that, with parents called Wolfgang and Cortina, being named after a German battleship was not so unlikely. He lived with his mother in Gosport during the sixties and worked for Camper & Nicholsons in their boatyard while studying at university. It was a healthy, active life for young Bismarck, building large yachts for rich people and establishing himself as a fine carpenter. In the seventies he progressed to fibreglass boats, including sleek thirty-six-foot cruisers. He was often asked to be a member of the crew during Cowes Week, when he would spend four or five hours racing on the Solent. He became a valuable crew member and relished the hard continuous work when the boat was tacking to and fro. He was skilled at operating a winch to pull up the halyard, could tie a sheet-bend knot with his eyes closed and developed into an expert navigator. His knowledge of the shifting tides and currents around the sandbanks of the Solent was second to none.

Now, still a bachelor, he lived in an attractive apartment overlooking the Solent and was never short of female companionship.

'I'm a huge fan of Latin,' said Bismarck. He looked to the heavens. 'It's the language of classical antiquity and, once upon a time, Latin was the *lingua franca* in Europe.'

Don't judge a book by its cover, I thought. 'I did a little at school,' I said, 'but I'm no expert.'

He sighed. 'You don't know what you're missing. You can't beat a bit of Cicero and Virgil.'

Deke Ramsbottom had arrived to look after the Hardware Emporium and Timothy had joined us in the Coffee Shop. 'We ought t'be goin',' he said. 'Ah need t'be back in t'shop in 'alf an 'our.' Timothy looked at me. 'Bismarck 'as agreed t'be t'judge for t'duck race an' ah'm tekkin' 'im up to t'bridge.'

'Good to share stories,' Bismarck said to me. He stood up. 'Well, come on then, Timothy, *tempus fugit* ... time flies.'

'Good luck,' I said.

Bismarck grinned. *'Carpe diem!'*

'Seize the day,' I translated with a smile, and I

followed them out to the High Street.

Outside school, Ruby was with George Dainty, standing next to her car.

'How are you, Ruby?' I asked.

'Ah'm 'avin' a drivin' lesson.'

'How's it going?'

'Ah'm 'appy as a pig in muck, Mr Sheffield,' she said cheerfully as George opened the driver's door for her. 'Ah'm doin' summat *positive.*'

'Well, you can't say fairer than that,' I said.

'Ah don't want t'sit at 'ome, Mr Sheffield, an' turn into a vegetarian,' she said.

'You'll always be young at heart, Ruby,' said George with a smile.

Timothy and Bismarck were on the Upper Foss bridge. 'This is t'start,' said Timothy, 'an' t'finish is that bend.' He pointed fifty metres downstream. 'T'local Scouts will be there wi' nets t'collect all t'ducks.'

'The current is very slow and steady, less than walking speed, and it narrows nicely at the finish,' observed Bismarck with a keen eye. 'It's perfect.'

'There's two prizes,' said Timothy, 'f'children an' adults.'

At that moment Petula Dudley-Palmer jogged into view in her new leisure suit and Chris Evert trainers. She had lost many pounds during her fitness programme and Bismarck admired her slim figure as she paused to take a breather and drink some water.

''Ello, Petula,' called out Timothy. 'Ah see y'still gettin' fit then.'

Petula smiled at the two men. 'Yes, thank you,' she said.

'This is m'cousin,' said Timothy. 'Ah'm jus' showing 'im where t'duck race is tekkin' place.'

Petula looked up at the handsome stranger.

'I'm Bismarck,' he said. 'A pleasure to meet you.'

Petula smiled. 'Hello,' she said. 'This really is a picturesque spot. I love this bridge and the river.'

'Yes, I can see why ... but, of course, all rivers are different,' said Bismarck. 'Look at this one, for instance. It looks as though it flows evenly, but there's a back-eddy over there about twenty metres away.'

'A back-eddy?' repeated Petula.

'Yes,' replied Bismarck, 'it's when the current flows in the opposite direction.'

Petula nodded in acknowledgement. 'So you would want to avoid that in a duck race.'

'Quite right,' said Bismarck.

Timothy was puzzled. ''Ow come?'

'You would need to float an object from the left-hand side of the bridge,' explained his cousin.

'But it's 'ardly movin' down there,' said Timothy, peering into the sluggish water near the left bank.

'Yes, but more haste, less speed,' said Bismarck with a wry smile in Petula's direction.

'Well, lovely to meet you,' she said, with a final searching glance at this interesting man.

'I hope we shall meet again.'

'So do I,' said Petula and she could hardly believe she had said the words. With a secret smile she jogged down to the path towards Ragley.

'A delightful lady,' said Bismarck almost to

himself. *'Suaviter in modo, fortiter in re* ... gentle in manner, resolute in deed.'

'Yes,' agreed Timothy, 'a shame 'er 'usband doesn't appreciate 'er.'

It was Bank Holiday Monday and as we drove past the village hall cascades of blossom lay heavy on the branches like fragrant snowflakes. Ragley High Street was stirring into life. Jimmy Poole's Yorkshire terrier, Scargill, was snuffling around Timothy Pratt's stock of plaster-cast garden gnomes. It was his new range, featuring Snow White and the Seven Dwarfs. Sadly, Happy had no reason to appear cheerful as Scargill cocked his leg and urinated on his bright-red hat.

We parked in the school car park and walked up the Morton Road. A huge crowd had gathered on the Upper Foss bridge and along the banks of the stream that meandered down towards York and the River Ouse. The entrepreneurial Earnshaw brothers were selling bottles of what looked like home-made Tizer from a wheelbarrow, while Timothy was preparing to blow a whistle to start the race. Bismarck was positioned on the finish line – namely, a length of baling twine held just above the surface of the water by members of the Ragley Scout troop. Other boys in wellington boots paddled in the sunshine, carrying nets to capture the plastic ducks as they trundled by.

Petula Dudley-Palmer was leaning against the parapet of the bridge with her younger daughter, twelve-year-old Victoria Alice. Her husband, Geoffrey, had taken Elisabeth Amelia into York for her violin lesson. Petula was looking at

Bismarck by the bend in the stream as he issued instructions to the boys around him and she thought about their conversation. 'Victoria,' she said, 'let's go to the far side of the bridge.'

I was holding John while Beth kept a firm grip on his plastic duck as Timothy called out, 'One, two, three,' then blew the whistle. With a loud cheer parents and children tossed their ducks into the water below. John repeated, 'One, two, three,' then added 'four' for good luck and shouted, 'Bye-bye, duck,' as he released it into the water.

Then everyone hurried down to the bank sides to cheer on the bobbing multitude of plastic ducks. Some bounced off stones, others caught up in tussocks of grass and many ended their adventure in Bismarck's 'back-eddy', where they swirled around in ever-decreasing circles.

It was impossible to identify the numbers of the few that reached the finish line, but the clear winner was one that had enjoyed a steady, trouble-free journey down the left-hand side of the stream.

A happy and relaxed group of villagers gathered near the finish while Timothy collated the results on his clipboard. Bismarck presented a certificate to the winners: 'The winner of the adult duck race is Mr Maurice Tupham and the winner of the under-sixteens is Victoria Alice Dudley-Palmer.'

A shy Victoria Alice stepped forward for her prize with her mother.

'*Veni, vidi, vici* – I came, I saw, I conquered,' said Bismarck with a smile, and Petula returned his gaze.

Fifteen minutes later Beth and I were sitting with John at a picnic table outside The Royal Oak enjoying a soft drink in the sunshine.

'Petula Dudley-Palmer looks animated,' said Beth perceptively.

At another table Petula and Victoria Alice were enjoying Bismarck's company. 'I remembered your comments about the flow of the stream,' said Petula.

Bismarck stirred his coffee thoughtfully, then looked into her eyes. 'There's a Latin saying,' he said, '*exitus acta probat* ... the end justifies the means.'

That evening Geoffrey Dudley-Palmer glanced across the lounge at his wife. She had changed in recent months and once more resembled the young woman with whom he had fallen in love long ago. His secretary was history now, gone if not forgotten. He considered his wife once again and realized what he was missing.

'I was thinking of booking a holiday,' he said, 'for the four of us ... perhaps New York.'

There was a long pause.

'Or maybe Newquay.'

Newquay had been their first holiday together when they were young lovers.

'In fact, wherever you wish,' offered Geoffrey.

'I'll think about it,' replied Petula. She was holding the prize-winning plastic duck and smiling.

Chapter Seventeen

Jack to the Future

The Revd Joseph Evans took morning assembly. The school agreed to loan plates, cutlery and beakers to the village hall committee to support the afternoon tea event on the day of the forthcoming royal wedding.

Extract from the Ragley School Logbook:
Friday, 4 July 1986

A pink dawn crested the horizon and caressed the fields around the village of Kirkby Steepleton. After a night when mist lay heavy on the sleeping earth, a humid summer day had dawned and Bilbo Cottage was bathed in the sunshine. It was Friday morning, 4 July, and John's cereal included freshly picked raspberries. Yesterday we had been in the garden and the sweet air of summer had refreshed the soul as we collected the ripe fruit. Beth was busy at the kitchen table while I fed John with his breakfast. She had cut out an advertisement and was completing a reply slip.

'Jack, if we save fifty pounds each month with this Sun Alliance scheme we'll have twenty thousand by the millennium.'

'Really?' The year 2000 was fourteen years away and at that moment it seemed like an eternity. 'Fifty pounds sounds a lot of money,' I said.

Beth was concentrating on the small print. 'I

know ... but by then it could be worthwhile to have such a huge lump sum available to us. John may need support and it would be a nest egg for us at a time when retirement might be on a not-too-distant horizon. I'm thinking of our *future.*'

'Why now?' I asked. 'Life seems a little uncertain at the moment. I've not had a reply yet to my application for the headship.'

'That could come any time soon,' she replied. 'Interviews will need to be completed by the end of term.'

'That's only three weeks away.' I was becoming concerned.

'So what do you think?' urged Beth, pointing with her pen at the form. 'We would, of course, have to consult a financial adviser first.'

'Do you have to complete it now?' I asked.

She smiled. 'Not exactly, Jack, but if I send it off now, we'll get a free carriage clock.'

When I walked out to my car it was a beautiful morning but the heat was building and a summer storm was forecast. I wound down my windows and turned on the radio. Thankfully, last month Doctor and the Medics had pushed 'The Chicken Song', from *Spitting Image,* from the top spot and I hummed along to their version of 'Spirit in the Sky'. Beyond the honeysuckle in the hedgerows, the sibilant whispers of the branches of the high elms provided an accompaniment to the swaying dance of the bright golden barley in the fields. Cattle looked up as I drove by, swishing their tails to deter the persistent flies. It was high summer in North Yorkshire and ladies in summer frocks were shopping in the General Stores.

When I pulled up on the High Street I was surprised to see Edna Trott, who had been school caretaker before Ruby and was now closing in on her eightieth birthday, parking her brand-new mobility scooter.

'Good morning, Mrs Trott,' I said. 'That looks impressive.' The label on the side read: Rascal Electric Super-trike.

Edna saw my surprise. 'Electric mobility, Mr Sheffield,' she said. 'You wait an' see ... it's t'future for folks like me.'

I guessed she was right. It was another giant stride for new technology.

In the General Stores Prudence was serving Mrs Ricketts, who had the vociferous and forthright Suzi-Quatro by her side.

'Miss Golightly, why doesn't your skin fit your face?' asked Suzi-Quatro. Mrs Ricketts bought a large sliced loaf and hurried out as fast as she could drag little Suzi-Quatro after her.

Prudence held up my newspaper and pointed to the headlines. 'Here you are, Mr Sheffield – more silly ideas, I'm afraid.'

The Peacock Committee had reported that, by the end of the century, pay-as-you-view television would be the norm and the licence fee would be put out to tender. 'And I knew that young man had a problem,' she added. There was a photograph of Boy George, who was reported to have admitted to being a heroin addict. 'Where is it all going to finish up?' wondered Prudence.

'Who knows?' I said and hurried out.

Meanwhile, thinking back to Suzi-Quatro's observation, Prudence looked at her reflection in the mirror on the stockroom door. She decided to call into the Pharmacy at her earliest opportunity and buy a large jar of face cream. The passage of time was remorseless.

As I drove past the village hall, the cast-iron arrow on the weather vane on the roof creaked as the first hint of a breeze sprang up. With the grinding of metal it turned slowly towards the distant hills and the gathering clouds. A storm was coming.

In the school entrance hall Ruby was excited. She had told Vera that another driving lesson was in store and she was enjoying the experience. As Ruby hurried back to her caretaker's cupboard with her mop and galvanized bucket, Vera smiled at her enthusiasm. We walked into the office. 'If anyone can take away the sadness in Ruby's heart, then it's George,' said Vera. 'He's such a loving soul.'

An Austin A40 pulled into the car park. 'And speaking of loving souls, here's another one,' I said mischievously.

Joseph Evans had arrived to take morning assembly.

I went to my classroom while Vera typed a letter to the village hall committee to say we should be happy to loan our plates, cutlery and beakers from the kitchen. An afternoon tea was to be organized to celebrate the forthcoming royal wedding.

The school hall was stifling hot, so we opened the windows and made sure all the children had a drink of cold water before our morning assembly began with Sally's recorder group. They presented a well-rehearsed round of 'Frère Jacques', followed by a solo on her clarinet by Dawn Phillips. Finally, Joseph told the tale of Cain and Abel. When he had finished, he invited questions but really should have known better by now. Damian Brown was the first to raise his hand.

'What is it, Damian?' asked Joseph.

'Well, ah were jus' thinkin', Mr Evans, that their mam could 'ave sorted it out, no bother.'

'Really?' said Joseph, a little surprised.

'Yes,' said Damian, 'she should 'ave given them their own rooms, like me an' my brother.'

I was on duty at morning break and I watched the children play in the sunshine. Katie Parrish and Mandy Sedgewick had become firm friends and they were practising three-legged racing prior to next week's sports day. It was their private world of here and now, and I smiled as I reflected that they had one thing in common. They believed they would be friends for ever.

Meanwhile, a tearful Cheyenne Blenkinsop had fallen while playing leapfrog with four-year-old Joe Burgess, the younger brother of Tom. He had scraped his knees on the playground and Anne was in the entrance hall administering first aid with cotton wool and clean water. The life of a reception class teacher was never dull.

Vera, Sally and Pat were in the staff-room and Vera was getting excited about the forthcoming wedding of Prince Andrew to Sarah Ferguson on Wednesday, 23 July. 'It's a normal school day,' said Vera, 'as it's not a public holiday, but I'm sure many will miss work.'

'I guess people will record it and watch it when

they get home,' said Pat.

'The village hall committee will be doing exactly that,' said Vera. 'Joyce Davenport is organizing it and they're serving tea from five o'clock onwards for villagers and children to call in and watch it on the large television.'

'That's a wonderful idea,' said Pat. 'I'll certainly be there.'

'Did you know Sarah is descended from Charles II?' announced Vera proudly.

Sally looked up from her *Cosmopolitan* magazine. 'Didn't he have a dozen illegitimate children?' she asked pointedly.

Vera said nothing and chose to return to her *Daily Telegraph.* Hana Mandlíková had defeated second seed Chris Evert on the Centre Court at Wimbledon to set up a final with Martina Navratilova. Vera sighed deeply and hoped that in the not too distant future another Virginia Wade would emerge. Then she smiled; there was a photograph of Richard Branson giving Margaret Thatcher, her joint-favourite lady along with the Queen, a speedy 60 m.p.h. ride up the Thames in his *Virgin Atlantic Challenger II.* However, when Vera saw that the next article was advertising a 'chat-up line' for frustrated men, she closed the newspaper quickly and washed the coffee cups.

When the children had returned to their classrooms at the end of morning break, Mrs Snodgrass had called in to inform Anne that young Emily was absent because of chicken pox.

'Has anyone else had chicken pox?' asked Anne.

Karl Tomkins put up his hand. 'No, Miss, but ah've 'ad Coco Pops.'

There's always one, thought Anne.

Across the road in the Hair Salon, Diane was offering Claire Bradshaw the benefit of her wisdom.

'Y'need t'be careful an' think about y'future,' she said knowingly. 'Remember that men only want you for one thing. Then if y'let 'em 'ave their wicked way y'don't see 'em f'dust an' they'll be gone faster than Seb bloody Coe.'

Claire thought that Diane was talking from bitter experience and wondered what had happened in her early life. 'But Kenny's not like that,' she pleaded. ''E's carin' an' kind an' 'e'll 'ave a proper job one day an' mebbe even a car.'

Diane sighed and lit a cigarette. 'Fair enough, luv, but don't say ah didn't give you fair warnin'.'

Claire nodded and they both stared in the mirror. Diane took a puff of her cigarette and put it in the ashtray next to the closed window. 'So, what's it t'be this week – Bonnie Tyler or Kate Bush?'

Next door in the Coffee Shop, Nora was also considering the future. She was reading her *Woman's Own* and thinking about the royal wedding.

'In this 'owoscope it says Pwince Andwew an' Sawah will make a lovely match.'

''Ow come?' said Dorothy.

'It's cos 'e's a Pisces an' she's a Libwan,' explained Nora.

Dorothy stared down at her chunky signs-of-the-zodiac charm bracelet. 'That's jus' perfec', Nora,' she said. 'If it's written in t'stars then it mus' be right.'

Nora nodded knowingly and looked down again

at the text. 'This astwologer says they'll 'ave two kids, the odd wow, a few tears, but they'll be weally 'appy.'

'Jus' like me an' Malcolm,' said Dorothy, '...'cept wi'out the rows and the kids.'

At the end of school lunch Vera came to find me in the school hall. 'Telephone call, Mr Sheffield. It's Mr Fairbank from the college in York.'

I closed the office door and settled behind my desk.

'Hello, Jack. Have you got a few minutes to spare?'

'Of course.'

'I'll come straight to the point. We have a staffing vacancy in the Education Department for next term. I was hoping you might be interested. Your course in the spring term was well received and, with your background of primary-school headship, it could be an ideal move for you.'

'Thanks, Jim,' I said. 'I'm obviously flattered that you have thought of me.'

'I ought to mention that I'm aware of the forthcoming headship interviews for Ragley and Morton.'

'Yes, although I've not heard yet if I've been short-listed.'

There was a pause. I suspected Jim knew more than he was saying. 'I'm sure you will have a good chance, but it was, after all, an *open* advertisement and the school will be a popular one. The shortlist will no doubt include some strong candidates.'

'Perhaps it will, Jim, but I couldn't comment.'

'Of course, I understand.'

'What exactly is the college post?'

There was a shuffle of papers. 'The official title is Senior Lecturer in Primary Education and it will include all the usual duties, including lectures, pastoral duties and teaching-practice supervision, where you will obviously have considerable credibility. The salary is higher than your current pay scale and in time, at your age, there would be a significant opportunity for promotion to Principal Lecturer.'

'It sounds attractive,' I said.

'Yes, give it some thought, but I need to know as soon as possible and certainly before we close for the summer break.'

'Thank you, I'll do that.'

'Well, good luck, Jack. I hope it goes well for you and, if it doesn't, at least there is the possibility of an alternative professional future.'

I put down the receiver and stared out of the window.

It was encouraging news, but not what I really wanted. Deep down I knew I needed to keep the job I loved.

It was lunchtime in The Royal Oak and Chris de Burgh was singing 'The Lady in Red' on the juke-box when Deke Ramsbottom arrived. He had arranged to meet his sons for a lunchtime pint. The television was on above the tap-room bar and they were discussing the recent World Cup.

'Turn down that warblin', please, Don,' said Deke. 'It's 'ard t'concentrate.'

'What's t'matter?' asked Don and he turned down the volume control on the juke-box.

Deke pointed up at the television set. 'It's that bloody Maradona.'

'Should be banned,' said Don shaking his head.

Diego Maradona's 'Hand of God' goal, which had helped Argentina to beat England 2-1 in the World Cup, was being replayed. Even though Gary Lineker had followed up his hat-trick against Poland in Monterrey with a goal for England, it had been in vain. The little curly-haired Argentinian had scored both goals and Argentina had gone on to beat West Germany in the final, much to the disgust of the Ragley Rovers football team.

'In fac', turn it off, Don,' said Deke. 'Ah'd rather 'ear that warblin'.'

Clint Ramsbottom arrived at The Royal Oak in a state of blissful harmony. He was listening to a Boy George compilation on his Sony Walkman. New technology had changed the life of this fashion-conscious farmhand ever since he had witnessed the sight of the Ragley ladies' jogging group trundling down the High Street a few years ago. On that memorable day he had stared in amazement at Petula Dudley-Palmer in her fashionable Olivia Newton-John headband, but not because of her skintight Lycra jogging bottoms. Instead he was captivated by the pair of thin wires that culminated in tiny earpieces. Petula had been jogging in time to Abba's 'Mamma Mia' while Clint had been carrying his ghetto blaster over his shoulder. It was the size of a small chest of drawers and he had put it down on the pavement. In that moment his life had changed and he had joined the music revolution of the eighties.

There was a familiar swishing sound as Clint

entered the bar in his nylon fluorescent lime-green shellsuit. It had a round collar, a zip down the front, puffy sleeves and elasticated wrists. Down the front were pink arrows. His Nike trainers were worn with the tongues sticking out. Clint was inspired by David Bowie and Duran Duran, with a bit of Michael Jackson thrown in for good measure. Most evenings he practised his moonwalk on the linoleum kitchen floor, grabbing his crotch in a suggestive manner. Although he looked like a prisoner from a futuristic science-fiction film, Clint thought he was the coolest man in Ragley.

Deke looked at his son in despair. 'Where's y'brother?' he asked.

'Jus' pulled up outside on 'is tractor, Dad,' replied Clint.

When his eldest son walked in Deke looked at him with equal puzzlement. Shane had splashed his stone-washed jeans with bleach to make them look even more distressed. His baseball cap, worn back to front, sported the word 'BAD'. Shane had also taken to shoving a shuttlecock down the front of his jeans to impress the girls who frequented the bars outside York station. Sadly, it didn't seem to have the desired effect ... in fact, his private parts had suffered a severe chafing.

Deke wondered again why he had been blessed with such dysfunctional sons. Don came up to serve them. 'Right, lads,' said Deke, 'what you 'avin'?'

'Pint,' said Shane.

'Lager an' lime,' said Clint, and Don gave Deke a knowing glance.

On the High Street Margery Ackroyd was passing the time of day with Betty Buttle when Deirdre Coe stopped to look in the window of Old Tommy Piercy's butcher's shop.

'Ah wouldn't trust 'er as far as ah could throw 'er,' said Betty.

'She's too knowin' by 'alf, is that Deirdre,' said Margery. Betty nodded. In the pecking order of gossipmongers, this was damnation indeed.

Ruby and George had pulled up by the Post Office and Ruby got out of the driver's side. George took her place and, as he drove up the Morton Road, Betty and Margery watched Ruby as she waved goodbye.

''E's not 'xactly what you'd call a 'eart-throb, is 'e?' remarked Betty.

'Accordin' to Ruby's mother, 'e med a fortune in Spain,' said Margery.

'Old Tommy said t'batter on 'is fish were t'nectar of t'gods,' said Betty.

Margery nodded. 'Well 'e should know.'

'She's allus 'ad t'count 'er pennies, 'as Ruby,' continued Betty.

'An' 'er mother could stretch a shillin',' added Margery for good measure.

On the other side of the road, the new, slimline Petula jogged by in her latest leisure suit and matching headband.

'An' 'ere comes Miss Moneybags,' said Betty.

'She's all parquet floors an' shag-pile rugs,' contributed Margery.

'Very true,' agreed Betty, 'but word 'as it 'er 'usband is beggin' for forgiveness.'

They watched as Petula disappeared up the

Morton Road.

'Well ... good for 'er,' said Margery.

'Mebbe she's not so bad after all,' acknowledged Betty.

In the centre of York Geoffrey Dudley-Palmer was looking for an expensive gift for his wife in Dixons camera shop. He had left his executive office at the Rowntree's factory and for once he hadn't sent out his secretary to buy the present for him. He was approached by a young male assistant with a ponytail and a nose that rivalled both Barry Manilow and Concorde. 'Can I help you, sir?'

'I'm interested in this,' said Geoffrey, pointing to the display case.

'Yes, it's our top-of-the-range Auto-Focus Camcorder,' said Ponytail, 'a bargain at one thousand one hundred and ninety-nine pounds.'

It was rather more than Geoffrey had anticipated, but he had to do something extravagant to regain Petula's attention.

'Why is it so expensive?' he asked.

Ponytail had rehearsed his sales pitch. 'It's got three hours of playback, a batt'ry an' a carry case, sir.'

'I see,' said Geoffrey, unconvinced.

Ponytail moved effortlessly into another gear. 'Sir, wi' point-an'-shoot technology an' eight-millimetre video, plus a six-times power lens, y'looking at t'*future*.' It was time for the ace in the pack. 'An' sale ends t'morrow, sir.'

Geoffrey nodded. 'I'll take it,' he said.

Ponytail was delighted. 'Good choice, sir.' He began to wrap up the gift. 'And don't f'get, we 'ave forty years of experience in photography at Dixons.'

'And how long have you worked here?' asked Geoffrey. Ponytail smiled. 'Since Tuesday, sir.'

It was two o'clock and Ruby had enjoyed a successful driving lesson with George. They had practised reversing and she was enjoying a new confidence.

She was sitting on Ronnie's bench and the tranquil peace on the village green had become a cloak of comfort for her. It was good to pause and reflect on the few happy times in her life. Around her, butterflies landed on clumps of nettles in the hedgerow and spread their delicate wings. Tall lupins swayed in the gentle breeze and trailing pelargoniums and lobelia brightened the colourful tubs outside The Royal Oak. As her thoughts drifted she began to hum 'Edelweiss' from *The Sound of Music* softly to herself.

It was then that Ruby noticed the glowering sky in the distance. Dark clouds were gathering over the Hambleton hills and suddenly the air seemed full of menace. She stood up and hurried back towards her home on School View.

In school, Ryan Halfpenny rang the bell for afternoon break while all the staff closed their classroom windows and made preparations for an indoor playtime.

When the storm arrived, forked lightning split the sky and thunder shook the earth. It was a hailstorm from hell, a malevolent torrent. Rain battered the school roof like steel shards. The bright white lightning was followed almost immediately by the boom of heaven's fury. We were at the centre of the storm and the school drive had become a channel of rushing water. Lightning flashed again.

'Mr Sheffield, is that God takin' a picture?' asked little Alison Gawthorpe.

It passed over as soon as it had begun. Finally, sharp orange sunlight gilded the distant hillside like molten gold and our world was silent once again.

'Thank goodness we didn't have to drive through that,' said Pat. She had organized another staff night out at the cinema and a relaxing start to the weekend was in store.

It was six thirty, Natasha was babysitting and we had set off for York. Beth was driving and Rod Stewart was singing 'Every Beat of My Heart' on her car radio. During the ten-mile journey we discussed Jim Fairbank's proposal for the lectureship at the college and Beth was encouraged. 'This is positive news, Jack,' she said. 'Things are looking up.'

We parked outside a launderette with a big sign in the window, 'Drop Your Pants Here', smiled and walked on hand in hand. All the staff had assembled, but their partners were otherwise engaged. Rupert was attending a Rotary Club meeting, Pat's partner was on call at the surgery, Colin Pringle was looking after daughter Grace, and John Grainger was varnishing his new tool rack. The film was *Back to the Future* and proved to be light-hearted escapism. Michael J. Fox played the main character, Marty McFly, who travelled back in time to 1955 in 'Doc' Emmett Brown's DeLorean car. There he met his parents as teenagers in Hill Valley. The car had something called a 'flux capacitor' and the speed of 88 m.p.h. was critical for its success in travelling through time.

It was an enjoyable evening and good to catch up with news on this balmy summer evening. When we returned to the car and drove north on the A19 I found myself thinking about my own past. Arriving in Ragley village and taking on my first headship had provided both challenge and purpose.

'You're quiet,' observed Beth.

'Just thinking,' I said.

'About time travel?' she quipped.

'Not exactly,' I said. 'Although hindsight is useful.'

Meeting Beth back in 1977 had been life-changing. In that moment it seemed as though a future had been determined for us both. However, during this academic year external forces over which I had little control had been at work.

It was a different world and the rules had changed.

On Saturday morning I rose early and made a decision that would go towards determining my own future. I filled my pen with black Quink ink and began to complete an application form for the Master of Education degree at York University beginning in the autumn term.

It was a part-time Educational Management course over three years, including two years of evening tutorials and a final year during which a dissertation had to be undertaken under the supervision of a personal tutor. I was busy with it when Beth appeared with John. She peered over my shoulder.

'That's good,' she said quietly and kissed me on the cheek. Then she took John outside into the garden to pick strawberries, but mainly to leave me in peace.

I had just finished it and read it through carefully when the morning post arrived. Beth came back into the kitchen, sifted through the letters, paused and passed over a large cream envelope with the crest of North Yorkshire County Council. I opened it quickly, scanned the letter and smiled.

'Well?' she asked.

'Good news ... I've got an interview for the Ragley and Morton headship. It's on Thursday, twenty-fourth July in Northallerton,' I glanced up at the calendar on the wall, 'the day before the end of term.'

Beth stretched over the table and squeezed my hand. 'Well done,' she said. 'And so it begins...'

Chapter Eighteen

For Whom the Bell Tolls

The school supported the royal wedding celebrations in the village hall. The pupils' report books were completed prior to being sent home at the end of term.

Extract from the Ragley School Logbook:
Wednesday, 23 July 1986

It was Wednesday, 23 July and, as I drove up the High Street, colourful bunting was displayed outside the village hall and the parade of shops. The royal wedding had captured the imagination and, even though it was officially a normal working day, much was being done for the folk of Ragley to join in the celebrations. The owners of each of the village shops had made their own unique contribution to this special day.

Prudence Golightly was giving away small cardboard Union Jacks with every newspaper and Jeremy Bear was sporting his new sailor suit. Old Tommy Piercy had displayed a large tray of 'Royal Wedding Sausages' in his window that looked very much like the usual tray of pork sausages that were there every day of the week. In the Pharmacy, Peggy Scrimshaw had draped a string of flags of St George over her new range of cod liver oil capsules and Neutrogena hand cream. Timothy Pratt was displaying a royal family of garden gnomes on a trestle table outside his Hardware Emporium, including one of Prince Charles with particularly large ears. Nora Pratt had advertised 'Prince Andrew Cream Horns' in her Coffee Shop, while Dorothy was standing in the doorway, swaying her hips and singing along to Robert Palmer's 'Addicted to Love'. Diane Wigglesworth had put a photograph of Sarah Ferguson on the door of her Hair Salon under the words 'Would you like Titian locks?' Diane wasn't entirely clear who Titian was, but she had read that particular description of Sarah Ferguson's flowing red hair in an old *Cosmopolitan* magazine. Finally, outside the Post Office, Ted Postlethwaite and Amelia Duff had draped a huge Union Jack around the postbox prior to returning to the back room and their well-thumbed copy of *The Joy of Sex*.

On the village green, Shane and Clint Ramsbottom were unloading the Ragley Scouts' marquee from the back of a trailer, while Rupert Forbes-Kitchener supervised the raising of the flag of St George on the flagpole in the centre of the village green. Meanwhile, Sheila Bradshaw, in a bright red boob tube, blue skintight hot pants and white high heels, was putting up a parasol above each of the picnic tables outside The Royal Oak and she blew me an extravagant kiss as I drove by.

There was no doubt that Ragley village loved a wedding.

Ruby was emptying the playground litter bin when I walked in from the car park.

'Good morning, Ruby. How are you?' I asked. It was noticeable that she was looking a lot happier these days.

'Fair t'middlin',' she replied cheerfully. 'Ah've gorra drivin' lesson wi' George this mornin'.'

'How's it going?'

'George says ah'm doin' well an' we're gonna do 'mergency stops soon.'

'He's a good friend to you, Ruby.'

'Thing is, Mr Sheffield, 'e's too gen'rous to a fault ... allus *givin'* me stuff.'

'I'm sure he just wants to help.'

'Mebbe so an' ah'm grateful, but ah've told 'im till ah'm blue in t'face not t'be allus puttin' 'is 'and in 'is pocket f'me,' she said forcefully, 'but would 'e listen? Would 'e 'eck!'

'Well, he's a kind man and obviously thinks a lot of you.'

Ruby pondered this for a moment and smiled. ''Appen 'e does. Like m'mother allus says, there's nowt so queer as folk,' and with that she carried her black bag of rubbish to the boiler house.

It was good to see Ruby returning to her old self and I walked into the entrance hall. Vera, in a beautiful summer dress of delicate lilac, stood facing Miss Valerie Flint, attaching a rose to the buttonhole of her linen safari trouser suit. 'An exciting day, Mr Sheffield,' said Vera.

'Yes, indeed,' I agreed.

'There now, Valerie, straight from my garden,' went on Vera, 'a beautiful *Rosa mundi* with a splash of crimson to match your zest for life.'

'Thank you,' replied Valerie. 'A fitting gesture on a special occasion.'

'Yes, the royal wedding.' Vera smiled up at me.

'Well, actually, Vera,' said Valerie with a slightly strained look in my direction, 'I was thinking more of me taking over your secretarial duties. This is outside my comfort zone – I feel like a probationer again.'

'We're all grateful to you, Valerie, for coming in to help out,' I assured her.

'Well, I couldn't let my dear friend miss a royal wedding,' said Miss Flint with a slight frown. She loved teaching, but taking over in Vera's office was intimidating to say the least.

A week ago I had realized that such a staunch royalist as Vera would be heartbroken to miss the wedding of Prince Andrew and Sarah Ferguson. It was a relief when I heard that her friend, Miss Flint, had offered to take over in the office while Vera was out of school. Vera proposed to leave at 10.30 to go to the village hall to watch it live on the large television. She would also help to prepare the tea party for the villagers and children arriving there after school. She had assured Miss Flint she would be back by afternoon break, much to our supply teacher's relief.

Also, as Vera was officially a part-time clerical assistant – although no one would have dreamed of referring to her in that way – she was entitled to the time off.

'Beautiful roses,' I said.

Vera had a pale-pink rose in her buttonhole. 'A "Blush Noisette", Mr Sheffield, the first rose ever presented to me by Rupert eight summers ago.' She glanced down and smiled at the memory. There was a clatter of crockery from the kitchen. 'In the meantime I had better check with Shirley that all is in hand,' she added.

We had agreed to loan our crockery and

cutlery, plus our Baby Burco boiler, to the village hall committee and Shirley and Doreen were busy in the kitchen counting out plates and beakers prior to them being washed after school dinner and delivered to the village hall.

'Never fear, Valerie, I shall be back to go through your duties once again,' said Vera over her shoulder as she hurried off.

'Oh dear,' murmured Valerie.

It was a busy morning, with the end of term in sight and the children's report books to complete. Also the children were excited at the thought of a party in the village hall after school.

For my part, with my interview only twenty-four hours away, I had other concerns. It was a relief that Sally had offered to lead morning assembly and I was able to gather my thoughts at the back of the hall. Her theme was an appropriate one, the 'Kings and Queens of England', and this promoted much discussion, particularly concerning Henry VIII, Queen Victoria and Queen Elizabeth II.

'Will our Queen retire when she gets t'sixty or sixty-five, Miss?' asked Lucy Eckersley.

I recalled having the same conversation with Vera, who was adamant that Queen Elizabeth II was in the job for the duration ... and that meant *life*.

'I don't think so, Lucy,' said Sally.

'If I was king, ah'd banish cabbage,' said Rufus Snodgrass defiantly.

'An' boys,' added Jemima Poole with feeling.

Meanwhile, outside Pratt's garage, Ruby had just experienced her first setback as a learner driver. During her mid-morning lesson with George she had driven on to the forecourt of Victor Pratt's garage, where our local mechanic was filling up Deadly Duggie's hearse with petrol. Duggie had just polished his pride and joy and it stood there gleaming in the morning sunshine. However, Ruby had been a little slow pressing the brake pedal and George's last-minute attempt to pull on the handbrake had been in vain. The little Austin had bumped gently into the back of the hearse.

Deadly Duggie ran round the back of his vehicle to check the damage. Fortunately there was only the merest scratch.

Ruby wound down her window. 'Sorry, ah didn't see y'luv.'

Duggie looked at his mother in astonishment. 'But Mam, m'flippin' 'earse is big an' black an' eighteen foot long!' he exclaimed.

George changed places with Ruby and reversed the car a few feet, then he got out and approached Duggie. 'Ah'll see y'right, Duggie, if there's any damage,' he said.

Duggie knew that George was a man of his word and respected him for the offer and, not least, for the care he showed his mother. 'Nowt t'speak of, George,' he said. 'No damage done. Bit o' spit an' polish an' it'll be good as new.'

'Thanks, Duggie,' said George and then whispered in his ear, 'Ah wouldn't want to upset y'mother,' and he climbed back into the car. Ruby was still looking concerned. 'Don't worry, Ruby,' George reassured her, 'we'll practise emergency stops next time we go out.'

'Thanks, George,' said Ruby reflectively. 'Ah don't want t'pack in cos of a setback.'

'Ah don't want to *ever* pack in,' said George quietly and Ruby stared out of the windscreen at Duggie's hearse. The road to healing was a long one, but she felt that she was close to journey's end. Perhaps it was time to sing again.

It was during afternoon break that Vera reappeared looking like the cat that got the cream. Sally was on duty and I was helping Valerie with the late-dinner-money register while Anne and Pat were checking each other's report books.

'So what was it like, Vera?' asked Anne.

'Simply wonderful,' said an elated Vera. 'We really do this so well in England, don't we?'

'Did it all go to plan?' asked Valerie.

'Of course,' said Vera. 'Sarah arrived in a glass coach with her father, Sir Ronald, only a couple of minutes late.'

'What was the dress like?' asked Pat.

'Quite spectacular,' enthused Vera. 'Ivory silk, stitched with crystals and beads to depict her coat of arms of thistles and honeybees, plus a train over seventeen feet long.'

'Sounds magnificent,' said Valerie.

'Yes,' Vera went on, 'and it was fitted beautifully and showed off her slender waist to perfection.'

'I heard it cost eight thousand pounds,' remarked Sally with a shake of her head. Sally was not a fan of royalty.

'Worth every penny,' retorted Vera.

The bell rang and Vera resumed her work as

secretary, much to the relief of Miss Flint, who left for the village hall. Meanwhile, we returned to our classrooms. Anne and Pat were discussing the possibility of a marriage in the offing for Pat, while I brought up the rear with Sally, who was grumbling about paying taxes to keep a privileged family in luxury.

At the end of school the children ran out into the sunshine, where a posse of mothers greeted them and marched down the High Street to the village hall for the royal wedding tea party.

I was in my classroom completing record books at my desk when Pat and Sally called in.

'We just wanted to wish you well for tomorrow, Jack,' said Sally.

Pat nodded and smiled. 'It goes without saying that I want to continue working with you,' she said. 'I owe you a lot and I feel I'm just settling in. Next academic year should be exciting. So I'm looking forward to working alongside you and Sally and Anne.'

'You've made a wonderful start in the school and I appreciate your support,' I said. 'And thanks to you, Sally.'

'I'm sure it will be fine, Jack,' said Sally, 'and you know we'll be here wishing you all the best.'

'Thanks. I promised to ring Anne when I know the decision and she will get in touch with you all.'

When they left and closed the door I looked around at my familiar classroom, the books and paintings and the chalk dust at my feet. Ragley School was my life and to lose it would be like the passing of an old friend.

Half an hour later I had completed all the record books. At the end of term, each pupil would receive a sealed manila envelope containing a written report in an A5-size booklet that had to be signed by the parent and returned to school. It was an arduous but important task, and particularly helpful for those parents who worked long hours and rarely had the opportunity to visit school and communicate as much as they would have liked. Like most village teachers, I knew all my pupils well and it was the brief after-school conversations, usually at the school gate, that were often far more valuable than any written reports.

Finally, I left everything prepared for Miss Flint to take over my lessons tomorrow and, on impulse, walked into Anne's classroom.

She had just finished tidying the Home Corner and had begun to prepare large individual folders of artwork and writing for each child to take home at the end of term.

'Hello, Anne. I thought I would confirm that all is well for tomorrow.' Anne would be acting headteacher for the day.

She sat down on one of the low, plastic-topped tables and looked at me patiently. 'It will be fine, Jack. Val Flint knows what she's doing and you'll be back on Friday for the final Leavers' Assembly. I'll make sure everything is prepared for that. The PTA have delivered the books for each school leaver and Joseph is leading assembly.'

There was a pause and she walked over to the window. 'I hope tomorrow goes well, Jack.' She appeared tense and almost tearful. I guessed she was simply tired.

'Thanks,' I said, 'and I'll ring you when I have news.'

She nodded and stared out at the empty playground. 'It's a strange feeling,' she said quietly. 'I can't imagine Ragley without you. You really *must* get the job for the sake of everyone. It really does affect us all.'

I felt there was a hidden message. Anne had never sought a headship and was happy in her role as deputy. We had forged an effective partnership over the years and I wanted it to continue.

'We've made a good team,' I said, 'and you know how much I have appreciated your work over the years.'

'I'm not altogether sure what I shall do if you don't get the job.' She forced a smile. 'Good luck,' she said quietly.

When I walked into the office Vera was giving the framed photograph of her three cats a final polish before leaving her desk in its usual immaculate state. She looked up at the clock. 'I'm going now, Mr Sheffield,' she said. 'Are you calling into the village hall before you go home?'

'Yes, no doubt I'll see you there.' She looked up at me with a steady gaze. 'And best wishes for tomorrow.'

'Thank you, Vera. I'll ring Anne with any news and she will contact you.'

Suddenly, outside, there was the familiar rattle of a galvanized mop bucket.

'Well, at last,' said Vera. 'Just listen to that.'

Ruby was singing 'Edelweiss'.

It felt as though we had witnessed her life come

full circle.

We stood there in silence listening to her clear voice. Then there was a long pause and, in the distance, the bells of St Mary's rang out. Vera smiled and squeezed my arm. 'For whom the bell tolls, Jack,' she said quietly.

The village hall was almost full when I walked in. The television had been set up on the stage and a semicircle of chairs had been arranged for the grown-ups to watch the broadcast in comfort while children sat cross-legged on the floor.

The ladies of the village hall committee, many of them also members of the Women's Institute, had provided an impressive afternoon tea in the marquee. Cold meats, pork pies, pickles, hard Wensleydale cheese and freshly baked bread had been laid out on a snow-white cloth. There were dainty cucumber sandwiches and a host of butterfly buns and pastries that would attract the children. Jugs of home-made elderflower cordial, orange juice and lemonade stood alongside. It was a veritable feast and it included a huge plateful of Vera's raspberry-jam tarts.

Vera, Joyce Davenport and a few ladies from the village hall committee were serving tea and cake at the back of the hall and bright bunting decorated the trestle tables. Elsie Crapper was handing out little flags for the children to wave and Clint Ramsbottom, in his imitation Sylvester Stallone aviator sunglasses, had taken charge of the television set and had tuned it in to perfection. He had videotaped the ceremony and was replaying what he described as 'the best bits'.

Two large speakers on either side of the stage ensured everyone could hear.

I collected a cup of tea and stood to one side as David Dimbleby explained there was a worldwide television audience of five hundred million watching the events unfold in Westminster Abbey and that the US First Lady, Nancy Reagan, and the Prime Minister, Margaret Thatcher, were among the guests. I saw Elton John sitting with his wife, Renate, on the front row, along with Michael and Shakira Caine and David Frost and Lady Carina. Billy Connolly and Pamela Stephenson appeared happy to be on the fourth row.

Sarah Ferguson spent four minutes walking slowly down the aisle to Edward Elgar's *Imperial March* while two thousand guests looked on. It was interesting to note that, unlike Diana, Sarah agreed to *obey* her husband when reciting her wedding vows.

We were told that ninety minutes before the ceremony the Queen had conferred the title of Duke of York on Prince Andrew, last held by King George VI and traditionally reserved for the sovereign's second son. Prince Edward was the best man for his twenty-six-year-old brother and Prince Charles read the lesson. The service was conducted by the Archbishop of Canterbury, Dr Robert Runcie, and everything appeared to be perfectly rehearsed, even though Sarah stumbled by repeating one of her husband's middle names. Finally, the bride marched Andrew down the aisle and winked at two of her former boyfriends.

At the back of the hall, Petula Dudley-Palmer

was about to walk up the High Street to meet her husband when she spotted her neighbour, Pippa Jackson, queuing for a cup of tea.

'It's the interview tomorrow for the headship of the school,' said Petula.

'I heard he might be going back into academia,' said Pippa.

Next to the picture of the Queen on the Scouts' noticeboard was a map of the world. Behind them, Betty Buttle studied it thoughtfully. 'Where's that then?' she murmured. Academia sounded like a far-off place.

As I left the village hall, the bells of Westminster were ringing and the young couple were no doubt thinking not so much of the wedding party at Claridge's hotel but rather their honeymoon in the Azores and a long life together.

The marquee on the village green outside The Royal Oak was full of villagers who preferred to buy an alcoholic drink and then sit at one of the picnic tables and enjoy the late-afternoon sunshine. Much of the conversation concerned the royal couple, but teenagers Claire and Anita had pop royalty on their minds. At the end of June they had attended the Wham! Final Concert at Wembley Stadium, where the duo had performed for the last time in front of seventy-three thousand adoring fans. Nearly a month later, Claire and Anita were discussing all the details of their special day out for the thousandth time.

As I walked across the village green I saw the astronomer Edward Clifton carrying a tray of drinks to a table where Anne, Pat and Sally were sitting.

Behind the trestle table where Don had set up a barrel of Chestnut Mild, he was talking to Big Dave and Little Malcolm. It was clear the tall David Soul lookalike had created some interest.

'Who's 'e then?' asked Little Malcolm.

'Ah 'eard Mrs Pringle saying t'my Sheila summat abart 'e'd gorra doppelgänger,' said Don.

'That'll upset Old Tommy,' said Big Dave, 'what wi' all 'is war medals.'

''Ow come?' asked Don.

Big Dave shook his head in dismay. 'Well, when 'e finds out 'e's gorra German car.'

'Y'reight there, Dave,' said Little Malcolm.

I decided not to intervene, bought a half of Chestnut Mild and stood for a while surveying the summer scene.

Petula Dudley-Palmer had been joined by her husband, Geoffrey, at one of the tables. Their daughters were attending private music lessons in York at St William's College and Petula was about to leave to collect them.

'Why don't we go out for an expensive meal tonight?' suggested Geoffrey.

'Let's see how the girls feel,' said Petula.

'Or you could use your new video recorder around the house and gardens,' said Geoffrey eagerly.

Petula sighed and got up to leave. 'I've passed it on to Elisabeth to use for one of her history projects at school.'

Geoffrey was perplexed. 'But it was a special anniversary gift.'

'Anniversary?' said Petula. 'Of what exactly, Geoffrey – your indiscretions?'

‘Please...’ said Geoffrey. ‘I was wrong ... so wrong.’

Petula gave him a level stare. ‘Yes, you were.’

‘And I’m sorry,’ he added, but Petula had walked away.

A different kind of conflict was occurring at the next table. Peggy Scrimshaw was not happy. Eugene had worn his new *Star Trek* uniform under his white coat. When Peggy told him it wasn’t appropriate to serve in a chemist’s shop dressed in such a way he had sworn at her in Klingon.

‘And don’t think that I haven’t worked out that when you call me “Worf” you’re referring to a Klingon-human hybrid,’ snapped Peggy in disgust. ‘Why can’t you find a normal hobby, like Timothy with his Meccano set or Old Tommy with his dominoes?’

‘Sorry, luv,’ said Eugene. He had obviously gone too far this time, but life was always tough when you had to run a shop as well as an inter-galactic spaceship.

Meanwhile, Sally and Pat had got up to leave. As Anne Grainger and Edward Clifton both reached to pick up the empty glasses, Edward’s fingers brushed against hers. It was just a touch.

In their private cocoon, Anne looked at Edward and his blue eyes did not waver. For a moment it was a meeting of minds and Anne wondered if, one day, it might be a meeting of souls.

Finally, I walked to my car as the clock tower of St Mary’s chimed out the hour, followed by another peal of bells to celebrate the events of the day. I stopped and looked up at the school with its familiar tower. This was my school. By this time tomorrow I hoped it would still be so.

It was much later that Vera ventured out into her kitchen garden. She had created it within sight of her kitchen window and it was bordered on three sides by an ancient hawthorn hedge. There was a comfortable bench under a gnarled old apple tree that caught the late-afternoon sun and Vera had taken to sitting there while compiling shopping lists, drawing up the rota for church flowers and, when the light was sufficient, completing a cross-stitch pattern.

'So here you are, my dear,' said Rupert. He sat down beside her. 'What a beautiful evening.' He looked around at the bountiful garden with its abundance of climbing roses, vegetables and ripe fruit ready for harvesting. 'You really have worked wonders here in such a short time.'

'Your gardeners do much of the heavy work,' said Vera graciously, 'but I do enjoy this little corner. It's a haven of peace for me.' She held Rupert's hand. 'It's a good place to *think*.'

'And what's on your mind, as if I couldn't guess?'

Vera smiled. It was often the words Rupert didn't express that had the greatest gravitas. 'School, of course,' she said quietly, 'and what might happen to Mr Sheffield tomorrow.'

Rupert settled back and put his arm around her shoulders. 'Yes, let's hope it goes well ... but I sense you have something else on your mind.'

There was silence between them while butterflies circled the purple blooms on the buddleia bushes in the nearby border.

Finally, Vera turned to face her husband. 'If Mr Sheffield does not continue as headteacher ... I shall hand in my resignation.'

They sat together for a long time, hand in hand, as the sun slowly descended towards the far-off hills and the shadows lengthened.

Chapter Nineteen

Star Teacher

The headteacher attended for interview at County Hall, Northallerton, prior to the amalgamation of Ragley and Morton schools. A. Grainger (acting headteacher).

Extract from the Ragley School Logbook:
Thursday, 24 July 1986

It was a new dawn and I had barely slept. A disc of golden light had risen in the eastern sky and the Hambleton hills shimmered in the morning heat haze. I showered quickly and dressed in my best suit. The countryside was waking and a breathless promise hung over the land. An eventful day was in store.

It was Thursday, 24 July, and the interview for the post of headteacher of Ragley and Morton Primary School had arrived. The letter inviting me to attend for interview had stated registration was at 8.30 a.m. at County Hall in Northallerton. I was eager to make an early start and I couldn't leave anything to chance.

Beth was in the hallway while John built a Lego tower at her feet. She looked cool and elegant in a beige linen suit and a green blouse that exactly matched her eyes. 'Good luck,' she said with a reassuring smile.

I kissed her on the forehead and stroked her honey-blonde hair. 'Thanks, I'll do my best,' I said. 'Let's hope it works out.'

'You'll be fine,' she said, glancing up at the clock, 'and you've got time for breakfast.'

At that moment I couldn't eat. 'I may stop in Thirsk. I'll see how I feel.'

Beth recognized the anxiety; she knew me so well. 'Do that, Jack. You'll feel better for it.'

I put a copy of the supplementary letter I had attached to my application form in my jacket pocket and bent down to pick up John. 'Happy birthday, John,' I said. 'I'll try to get back for your party.' I gave him a hug and he said, 'Bye-bye, Daddy,' and kissed me on the cheek. Beth smiled and wiped the residue of porridge from my face.

It was John's third birthday and Beth had arranged to get home in good time from her school for his party. The timings for me were unknown. I walked out to my car, tapped the chrome-and-yellow AA badge on the grille for good luck, and prayed today would go well.

I drove north on the A19 towards Sowerby and Thirsk, en route to Northallerton and skirting the North Yorkshire moors. As the miles sped by I looked back on the academic year that had passed. It had begun with spoken messages that had to remain confidential, followed by a series of secrets and surprises. Finally the denouement was approaching and the endgame was in sight.

I glanced at my watch. The early-morning traffic was sparse and I realized I had time to spare. A short break in Thirsk seemed a good idea and I pulled into the cobbled square outside a quaint tea shop. I found a table by the window and settled down with a pot of tea and a toasted teacake. A lady had discarded her *Daily Express* as she left and I picked it up. The headline read, 'FABULOUS FERGIE – a loving kiss for the radiant royal bride'. The reporter noted that tears of happiness ran down her freckled face under her sequinned pure-silk veil. However, it was William, the four-year-old future king, who stole the show by sticking out his tongue at the bridesmaids and playing with the elastic band on his saucy sailor hat. There was a detailed description of the bridal dress, but I had other things on my mind and I closed the newspaper and replaced it on the table whence it came.

I stared out at the line of rooftops and tall chimney pots. They formed a sharp division beneath the long ridge of the Hambleton hills that towered like a guardian over this quaint market town. The deep-purple bell heather was blooming, laced with the dark-green invasive bracken. I stared out at the sleeping land ... and I wished it could last for ever.

Refreshed by the break and the clean air of the high moors, it was time to move on and I turned on to the A168 towards Northallerton. Beyond the ditches and hawthorn hedgerows, black-faced sheep wandered freely, looking curiously in my direction. Soon I was on the outskirts of the sprawling town of Northallerton, and County Hall was in my sights.

I pulled into the familiar car park of the imposing building. After checking in at reception I was directed up a huge marble staircase to the first floor. There, behind a large desk, was a severe-looking lady in a grey suit who bore a distinct resemblance to Rosa Klebb, the fearsome Russian agent in the James Bond film *From Russia with Love*. Sadly, she shared a similar demeanour.

'Your name?' she asked in a sharp, clipped tone. Wasted words or pleasantries were not part of the diminutive lady's vocabulary.

'Jack Sheffield,' I said, 'here for interview for the Ragley and Morton headship.'

The formidable administrator jabbed her pen over her right shoulder towards the door behind her. 'Wait through there and you will be called for interview in due course.'

The reception room was furnished like a stately home with a large dark mahogany table in its centre and a collection of hard, uncomfortable chairs lined against the walls. A circular, oak-framed clock with Roman numerals ticked off the minutes and added to the funereal atmosphere.

Two women I didn't recognize were already there, sitting on opposite sides of the room. They looked up briefly as I took a seat. There was a murmured 'Good morning', but nothing more. By 8.45 a.m. there were six of us waiting in silence, three men and three women. Rather like in a doctor's waiting room, we had all spaced ourselves around the perimeter of the room as far as possible from one of the other candidates.

Gradually, one or two of them opened up and offered an introduction. There was a plump, voluble, grey-haired man who explained he was a village-school headteacher from Doncaster in South Yorkshire and a mature lady whose school was being closed down and this was her fourth interview. The other two women were a young and clearly dynamic deputy headteacher in her early thirties and a tall, slim lady of about my age who was a headteacher of a small village school. She was also from South Yorkshire and clearly knew the Doncaster headteacher. He had expressed surprise to see her and his cheeks flushed as they exchanged greetings. Then they settled back with their own thoughts.

Finally, there was Rufus Timmings, who sat in eerie silence listening to the occasional snippets of conversation but offering nothing in return. He appeared calm and supremely confident.

At the far end of the room was a heavy oak door with a brass plate that read: Room 109. As it opened, we all looked up, each torn from our private reverie. Rosa Klebb was standing there with the look of an executioner who enjoyed her work.

She glanced down at her grey clipboard. 'Miss Arnold,' she said, 'this way,' and the mature lady got up and followed the Russian secret agent into the unknown.

Rufus spoke up for the first time. 'Alphabetical order,' he said knowingly.

The tall lady from South Yorkshire looked at him and nodded. I thought she said, 'Obviously,' but I couldn't be sure.

Thirty minutes later the interviewee reappeared and, if anything, looked more stressed than when she went in.

'Mr Hardisty,' said Rosa Klebb. The plump man heaved himself to his feet and walked with head held high to meet his fate. He returned twenty-five minutes later and was quickly followed by the young female deputy, who clipped across the marble floor in astonishingly high heels.

Then it was my turn. I walked into a vast room, where an isolated wooden carver chair looked lonely in the centre of the floor, facing a big, curved desk. Five faces were staring at me intently, and I knew them all. From left to right, they were Bernard Pickard, the Assistant Chief Education Officer; Richard Gomersall, Senior Primary Adviser; Miss Barrington-Huntley, chair of the Education Committee; Joseph Evans, chair of governors at Ragley School; and, to my complete astonishment and dismay ... Stanley Coe, presumably representing the governing body of Morton School. I wondered what had happened to Wilfred Bones. It occurred to me in that moment that I had already lost twenty per cent of the votes.

I waited politely behind my chair. Miss Barrington-Huntley looked her usual imposing self. 'Do take a seat, Mr Sheffield,' she said, and so it began.

The interview flew by. Each member of the panel was invited to ask an opening question, followed by a battery of more demanding queries offered up by Miss Barrington-Huntley.

Bernard Pickard asked, surprisingly, why I had

applied, as he had assumed I would be ready to move on. I explained I loved my school and had unfinished work there. Richard Gomersall wanted to know how I would accommodate the demands of the wider curriculum, particularly information technology. As he had led much of the in-service training, he nodded when I repeated the main substance of his courses.

All seemed to go well until Stan Coe made a broad hint that discipline was a current problem at Ragley and wanted to know what I would do about it. I countered his accusation with facts about the high standards of honesty and good behaviour that underpinned our school ethos. He didn't look happy and glowered in my direction.

Joseph Evans interjected with a less demanding question. He asked what amendments, if any, would occur when the title 'on-the-Forest' was dropped from the name of the new school and, once again, I responded cautiously, relying on local knowledge and the recent directive from County Hall. 'Also, Mr Sheffield,' added Joseph, 'I note you are proposing to undertake a higher degree course at York University.'

'That's correct,' I said. 'It's a Masters in Educational Management, part-time and spread over three years.'

Miss Barrington-Huntley looked at me intently. 'That's quite a commitment, Mr Sheffield,' she said.

'Yes, it is.'

She leaned forward in her chair. 'So could you tell us why you intend to take on this extra workload?'

I was on familiar ground here. 'I wish to improve myself as a professional and, in doing so, strive to ensure that all our children achieve their potential. Realistically, I don't expect it will provide me with all the answers ... but it will enable me to ask the right questions.'

Miss Barrington-Huntley sat back in her chair and smiled. Then there was an imperceptible nod of acknowledgement but no more. The chair of the Education Committee was a formidable lady and didn't take prisoners. She then went on to make it clear that I was faced with strong competition and that their task was to find the best candidate, regardless of me being the 'sitting tenant'.

She glanced left and right, paused, shuffled the papers in front of her and asked if I had any questions. I turned it round with a statement saying that if appointed I would do everything I could to ensure that County Hall kept their promise regarding the additional classroom and extra staffing. I sensed this might have been a mistake, as Bernard Pickard, who had been making copious notes throughout, looked up sharply in surprise and with no attempt to hide his displeasure.

I walked out with mixed feelings, but felt I had done myself justice.

Back in the waiting room, Rufus Timmings was trying to judge my demeanour. 'Mr Bones was unwell,' he said with a broad smile, 'so Mr Coe stood in at the last minute.' He strutted into his interview as if the job were already his. Sadly, he returned the same way, with a self-satisfied look on his face.

Rosa Klebb read out the last name on her list.

'Miss Wainwright,' she said and the tall lady walked serenely into Room 109.

The plump gentleman from Doncaster smiled as the door closed behind her. 'Jenny Wainwright,' he said by way of explanation. 'I appointed her straight from college. She was my star teacher and I knew then she would go far.' He sat back in his chair. 'I just never imagined that one day I would be applying for the same job as her.'

Miss Wainwright's interview lasted significantly longer than anyone else's and she emerged looking entirely cool and collected.

The clock was ticking round to one o'clock when Rosa Klebb appeared and asked for the man from Doncaster, the mature lady and the young deputy headteacher to join her outside. She reappeared alone and looked at the three of us. 'You are requested to attend a final interview this afternoon, commencing two o'clock. In the meantime a trolley of refreshments will be provided for you.'

It was a subdued trio that drank tea and coffee and nibbled at sandwiches with an indeterminate filling. I was irritated that Rufus had known his ally, Stan Coe, would be on the panel and intrigued by Jenny Wainwright, who seemed to take everything in her stride. Promptly at two o'clock the humourless Rosa Klebb reappeared and didn't require reference to her clipboard. 'Mr Sheffield,' she said.

I was first in and pleased it would soon be over. The second interview included a new face on the panel. She was introduced as Ms Cleverley, a recent senior appointment as deputy to Miss

Barrington-Huntley, and she dominated the following thirty minutes. She had short cropped hair and angular features, with high, prominent cheekbones. Her stare was both intense and searching, and her questioning was demanding and incisive. In part it related to how I would respond to some of the initial proposals made by the new Secretary of State for Education, Kenneth Baker.

'Why do you want this headship, Mr Sheffield?' asked Ms Cleverley.

'I love Ragley School – it's been my life.'

Ms Cleverley scribbled a note. 'That would appear to be an *emotional* response,' she said curtly, 'and there are other headships ... larger ones than Ragley village.'

'I have unfinished business,' I said.

'Really? What might that be?'

'County Hall has regularly praised Ragley School as a good example of work of a high standard in all subjects, particularly in English, mathematics, information technology and the creative arts. So I wish to complete the curriculum reform I have begun with the children in my care.'

'And when will that be?'

I returned her level gaze. 'I'll know,' I said simply.

Miss Barrington-Huntley could sense the impasse and interjected. 'Time is up, Mr Sheffield, and thank you for your responses. The question we ask all candidates is, of course, may we presume that if offered the post you intend to accept?'

'Yes,' I said.

When I walked out I hoped Ms Cleverley

would question the other candidates with equal rigour.

Then all I could do was wait. Rufus Timmings went in and thirty minutes later reappeared not looking quite as confident as before, unlike Miss Wainwright, who was in there for almost forty minutes. I wondered why she was taking so long. When she returned, once again she relaxed into her seat with a calm, assured confidence.

We sat there in silence while the clock ticked on. From Room 109 there came a faint murmur of voices but no discernible words. A shaft of sharp sunlight streamed through one of the high, circular windows and motes of dust hovered like tiny fireflies, floating without purpose or direction. Time went by. It felt like an eternity.

The norm was for the successful candidate to be summoned first and formally offered the post. So we waited for Rosa Klebb to return with her clipboard and invite one of us to follow her back into Room 109. Finally, the door creaked open and to my surprise it wasn't Miss Clipboard but rather Miss Barrington-Huntley with a stern expression on her face.

There was a pause as she measured the import of her words. 'I'm sorry,' she said, 'but there's a lengthy debate going on and we still have much to discuss.' She saw the reaction from the three of us. 'So, with this in mind, I shall contact you all by telephone this evening with our decision. Thank you, and I wish you a safe journey home.' With that she closed the door firmly. It was unusual to say the least and simply served to draw out the uncertainty and tension.

Jenny Wainwright walked down the staircase with me. 'I hear you're the present headteacher of Ragley,' she said.

'That's right, for the past nine years.'

'Well, I wish you luck.'

'And you,' I replied.

She walked briskly and with a natural confidence towards her car, apparently unconcerned, and I remembered the words of the Doncaster headteacher, who had described her as one of the rising stars of education in South Yorkshire.

Rufus caught me up in the car park. 'That was strange,' he said. 'I wonder what caused the delay.'

'No idea,' I said. I had no wish to talk.

He pointed towards Jenny Wainwright, who was starting up her Vauxhall Nova. 'She was in there a long time.'

I nodded, but said nothing.

He pressed on regardless, eager to impart more information. 'While you were being interviewed I discovered that she and I had both been short-listed next week for the headship of a large primary school in Bridlington.'

'You have another interview?'

'Two more,' he said with a smug smile. 'The second is in Cumbria two days later.'

'Well, I hope it works out for you,' I said.

He set off across the car park, then paused and called over his shoulder, 'But of course I may get the Ragley and Morton headship.'

Beth had arrived home early and John's birthday party was in full swing. He had started to attend the local nursery class, two mornings each week, and four of his friends had arrived to share his special day. Two of the mothers had stayed to help, along with Mrs Roberts and Natasha Smith, who were in the kitchen clearing away the party food.

Beth had kept John's birthday cake on top of the fridge, waiting for me to share the moment. She looked up at me expectantly as I walked in and I kissed her on her cheek and whispered, 'They're ringing the candidates tonight with the decision.'

There was momentary surprise, but her composure was excellent. She recognized my concern and squeezed my hand. 'Time for John's cake,' she said.

We sang 'Happy Birthday to You' and John blew out his candles. 'Again, Mummy,' he cried. Blowing out candles was fun. Natasha lit them again and his friends joined in.

By 6.30 everyone had gone home and the house was quiet. I got John ready for bed while Beth prepared an evening meal. The minutes ticked by and I kept looking up at the clock on the kitchen wall.

Eventually Beth said, 'Jack, why don't you take John into the garden?'

The early-evening sunshine was welcome and I sat on the bench with John on my knee in his pyjamas. Next to me the 'Peace' roses were in full bloom and their fragrance filled the air. I was reading a colourful book, *The Gingerbread Man*, and John was repeating the words. He loved to turn the thick cardboard pages with his strong little fingers. It was one of his favourite stories and he regularly repeated, 'Run, run, said the gingerbread man.' Our hero, the Seb Coe of the biscuit world, escaped the clutches of everyone until finally he met his nemesis – namely, the wily fox who swallowed him up on the last page. It always struck me as a particularly unfortunate and violent end to the tale, but John was entirely unconcerned and merely said, 'Again, please, Daddy.'

The salivating fox had just devoured the distinctly naive gingerbread man for the second time when I heard the telephone ring. I picked up John, hurried inside and sat him in the hallway next to his pile of Lego bricks.

Beth held out the receiver. 'It's Miss Barrington-Huntley,' she said simply.

I knew the next conversation would determine my future career.

Over the years my happiest days had been at Ragley School and I prayed they would continue.

I took a deep breath and listened to her words. They were calm and precise. She spoke at length.

Finally I knew.

And in a heartbeat ... I began a new journey.

The publishers hope that this book has given you enjoyable reading. Large Print Books are especially designed to be as easy to see and hold as possible. If you wish a complete list of our books please ask at your local library or write directly to:

Magna Large Print Books
Magna House, Long Preston,
Skipton, North Yorkshire.
BD23 4ND

This Large Print Book for the partially sighted, who cannot read normal print, is published under the auspices of

THE ULVERSCROFT FOUNDATION

THE ULVERSCROFT FOUNDATION

... we hope that you have enjoyed this Large Print Book. Please think for a moment about those people who have worse eyesight problems than you ... and are unable to even read or enjoy Large Print, without great difficulty.

You can help them by sending a donation, large or small to:

The Ulverscroft Foundation,
1, The Green, Bradgate Road,
Anstey, Leicestershire, LE7 7FU,
England.
or request a copy of our brochure for more details.

The Foundation will use all your help to assist those people who are handicapped by various sight problems and need special attention.

Thank you very much for your help.